PILLARS OF SALT

Pillars of Salt

JOANNA BELL

WILLIAM HEINEMANN : LONDON

Published by William Heinemann in 2001

1 3 5 7 9 10 8 6 4 2

Frist published in the United Kingdom in 2001 by William Heinemann

The Random House Group Limited
20 Vauxhall Bridge Road, London, SW1V 2SA

Random House Australia (Pty) Limited
20 Alfred Street, Milsons Point, Sydney, New South Wales 2061, Australia

Random House New Zealand Limited
18 Poland Road, Glenfield
Auckland 10, New Zealand

Random House (Pty) Limited
Endulini, 5a Jubilee Raod, Parktown, 2193, South Africa

The Random House Group Limited Reg. No. 954009

www.randomhouse.co.uk

A CIP catalogue record for this book is available from the British Library

Papers used by Random House are natural, recyclable products made
from wood grown in sustainable forests. The manufacturing processes
conform to the environmental regulations of the country of origin.

Typeset in Palatino by SX Composing DTP, Rayleigh, Essex
Printed and bound in the United Kingdom by Biddles Ltd,
Guildford and King's Lynn

ISBN   0 434 00807 9

To laughing out loud at least once every day,
And all doctors who still manage it.

Acknowledgements

To the Swan Surgery, Bury St Edmunds, for inspiration (but absolutely no arguments).

To Crispin for a barmy sense of humour.

To the West Suffolk paediatrics team for laughter, chaos, exhaustion, support and too much coffee.

To St Nicholas hospice for welcome, friendship and baked potatoes and to my family, for all of the above.

Prologue

It was an ordinary day when Robert Vane died, when his heart gave way, simply and unexpectedly, rather as knees sometimes do when carrying shopping upstairs. One moment he was there, breathing, dreaming, laughing, *living* – and the next moment Alice Vane and her children were alone, Alice's life fractured in so many places that, like Humpty Dumpty, it seemed impossible that she could ever put what she had always recognised as herself together again. And the next moment is always so close to the last one, so very close that at first, at very first, the past is only a breath away, close enough to reach out to touch it, to change it . . .

But Rob was dead. Actually, more than dead. Dead was far too simple a word for it – because Rob hadn't just died, he had actually been amputated from Alice. If, as she had told the hospital chaplain at the time from behind the huge owlish spectacles that Rob had always found so endearing, if you were to *scrape* someone's arm off with a piece of rusty scrap metal, and not bother to sew up the oozing, jagged hole afterwards – the huge, ragged, gaping, filthy *cesspool* of a wound – then that would be nearly what it was like. Nearly.

The chaplain had sighed as shards of her pain bounced into him, pierced deep by glittering daggers of broken hope. He had cleared his throat softly. 'You have to go on without him, Alice. You have to keep him in your heart, and you have to live. Just a step at a time at first. Just one step, just one, at a time . . . and then one day you'll find it easier to look up, to see the way ahead.'

1

But Alice couldn't for the life of her imagine how she could do that. Not now. Not after sixteen years of marriage. No one could do that, surely?

Alice and Robert had been together for ever. Love at first sight – Rob had always said it was like something out of a film, when choirs of angels roar into song and strange lights glow in the sky. Sweethearts from the moment they met at medical school, married as soon as they qualified, Annie, Daisy and Fergus born in swift but well-planned succession – then GPs in practice together . . . they had been made for each other.

Their lives, people had often said, were charmed. Rob, with that slightly cynical streak he sometimes displayed, had liked to say that such comments were meaningless. Life, he had occasionally mused, was like frozen cheesecake – what's inside may superficially resemble the picture on the box, but it's never quite as perfect and always has far fewer cherries. But Alice, laughing at the joke, had known that in their case life *had* been perfect, as if someone had scripted them in order to give others something to aspire to – with three children, a floppy but pleasant dog, beautiful thatched cottage in Fox Colne, a village full of kind, well-coordinated people with regularly trimmed hedges. The cottage had been perfect too, with all its rooms painted in imaginative and exciting shades of Dulux.

Alice had even had the ideal part-time job at Rob's practice because they needed a woman doctor to see any patients who were adolescent, small, violent or snotty (all of which scare male doctors to bits) . . .

It had been the sort of life doctors are generally widely believed to have – respectable, clean and bright, like a kitchen after the full crew of an advertising agency have been to work on it with power sanders and bleach before making an advert pretending that it got that way because of two squirts of lime-scented foam and a brief flick of a cloth. The only imperfections had been the acceptable, middle-class ones – like the garden being a complete jungle because Alice was very good at planting things but absolutely no good at pruning them, and Alice not being able to make a decent meringue. And even they didn't matter – for Rob had not really cared about the garden and professed much to prefer meringues the way Alice made them – with the middles too gooey so that they spread across the plate. Things, he had liked to say, were better not too perfect.

But then Rob, her perfect Rob, had died, as absolute and selfish an act as a husband can possibly come up with. And that hadn't been in the script at all. He had died and he had left Alice behind, with three fatherless children, a house painted all sorts of silly grandiose colours and a garden she couldn't even get the mower round, a garden that would need a thorough hosing with Agent Orange before you could ever hope to see the pond in the corner.

And he hadn't even died properly. Why couldn't he have been run over by a bus outside Marks and Spencer, or struck by lightning on the golf course? For when someone dies scandalously and without dignity their death becomes coated in farce – and there had been no ignoring the fact that Rob had been somewhere he shouldn't at all have been when he died. In Marcie Crombie's bed, to be precise. Marcie Crombie, who campaigned for fair rates for prostitutes and solicited in Bayswater on Sundays.

The press had been full of the story for days, turning tragedy into printed sleaze, adding a dreadful embarrassment to the sense of astounded, bewildered outrage that had clung around Alice like a cloud of angry bees. Reams of tacky copy about the kind of rates the average GP might think fair. Pompous reviews in the broadsheets by other doctors who clearly had never been warned about glass houses and, in any case, had dismissed Rob as disgraced the day the story broke . . . A time of confusion, distress, anger, and of a violent sense of unfairness, all balling up together into a giant lump of indigestible rage, which seemed to make any sort of grieving completely impossible.

Maybe that was why Alice accepted full-time partnership at Rob's practice, with dear fatherly James, whom they had known since medical student days when he'd been Rob's tutor, and eccentric but trustworthy Ian, whose sense of adventure had now taken him off to Papua New Guinea for a sabbatical. It had seemed something to do, something that made the ordinary things like washing hair and buying shoes and *breathing* not completely pointless. It had seemed a sort of refuge – and it had seemed a way to fill in the time until she could actually swallow the brick in her throat, do the proper thing and cry . . .

The newspapers moved on, in time, to other disasters, and Rob's death passed into the realms of those things that people vaguely remember without really remembering whom they happened to. Rob's three children grew three years older and remembered him with a wistful but mainly adoring distance. Alice, unable to tolerate life in Rob's dream house, with Rob's dream thatch and Rob's dream paint (loganberry red in the dining room, sage green for the study), moved into Cambridge lock, stock and barrel, bought contact lenses and painted her new home entirely white.

Otherwise the world seemed surprisingly unaffected by the loss of Robert Vane. People still smiled in the street and went to church on Sundays. Rob's patients became Alice's patients. Of course, every now again someone who hardly ever visited the surgery turned up to see Alice and uttered the dreaded words, 'Oh, I thought Dr Vane was a man,' but Alice never rose to the implied question. Even the dog failed to spend his days pining miserably on the stone in Fox Colne churchyard on which Alice had finally had engraved 'Beloved Husband and Father' because he had been that once, and for such a long time, even if he wasn't any more.

Everyone told Alice that she had coped amazingly. And

4

she had, of course – in that absolute, grim and determined manner that is seen in those with no alternative. Everything in Alice's life had been put neatly back where it should be again, and she ran on a completely even keel. She was absolutely fine. She was a doctor – she knew about dealing with grief, and she had dealt with it. She had cast aside her spectacles and moved on to contact lenses. She had become a neat gardener and an independent woman. She had embraced white emulsion and minimalism. She had moved on and survived, intact. Apart, that is, from still feeling so bloody angry.

Chapter One

The idle drone of a wandering biplane from Duxford was the only thing cutting into the clean summer air. It shouldn't have been so, because it was a Wednesday morning and Alice Vane's alarm clock should not have been sitting fat, smug and silent on her bedside table, pretending it was a lazy Sunday in peaceful alarm-clock nirvana.

'Bloody hell!' Alice was awake in that still-asleep-but-panicky way that feels so desperately uncomfortable, pushing her hair out of her face. Why wasn't the bell screaming in her ear like Daisy when she wanted pocket money or one of the many things she felt it was unfair to expect her to spend it on (shoes/clothes/sanitary towels/pens/anything available from Sainsbury's)? Why was the clock so obviously wrong? Why had she got a jolly, don't-be-cross-with-me Wallace and Gromit alarm clock anyway? Why did she feel hung over when she hadn't drunk a thing last night? Well, just one small gin and tonic, perhaps. Just one, to help face the fact that today was the twentieth of May. Was she actually awake, or was this going to turn out to be one of those awful dreams where you wake up late and go to work naked? Better get some clothes on, though, just in case it isn't, she thought.

You could, Alice had found, if you tried very hard, be dressed, made up, get your contact lenses in, and be out of the house in under five minutes – although only if you were prepared to risk the inadvertent application of air freshener where you meant to put deodorant. It was also very important not to attempt to think during the process as

7

thinking slowed you down that extra, critical little bit, making smudged mascara almost inevitable. It was particularly important to ignore that niggling ache in the head that spoke of a poor night's sleep, for there certainly wasn't going to be enough time to find paracetamol. She could always use one of the free samples in her medical bag later. Mind you, they were certain either to be out of date, ineffective or to cause an allergic reaction so severe that her face would resemble a giant Victoria plum and no one would recognise her for a week. As a GP Alice had a healthy respect for medicines when contemplating putting them into her own body rather than someone else's.

Bursting into the kitchen with only one leg in her tights – and that backwards – Alice found her children fully dressed and finishing breakfast in a leisurely fashion, apparently oblivious to the need for the dishwasher to be loaded. In front of the cooker the dog, Paddy, lay whining musically, and eyeing the space into which he hoped a few scraps of bacon might fall, were someone to see fit to cook some. By the window Mordecai, once Rob's parrot (and hideously loyal, judging by the way he treated everyone else) eyed Paddy with relentlessly unblinking malevolence. The kitchen clock, mercifully, said quarter-past seven.

'Thank God for that – I thought I must be dreadfully late. Why didn't any of you wake me?'

Daisy shrugged. Pleasantness wasn't her strongest point before eight in the morning. She was holding her face as still as possible, to give her foundation a chance to set properly, so she didn't smile when she spoke. 'You're the mother – waking everyone up is your job. We're the kids – we're supposed to be sullen and disagreeable.'

Alice grinned and tousled Daisy's hair, unwittingly undoing fifteen minutes of careful arranging. 'And you do that so remarkably well.' She helped herself to a bowl from the cupboard, found the paracetamol, took two dry and gagged. 'Clearing up is your job today but that seems to

8

have passed you by. Where's the paper?' She reached for a glass, filled it with water, gave Fergus a quick morning hug, which he shrugged out of rapidly. That was one thing about Fergus – he might look like Rob but he was totally transparent, nothing about Fergus was ever disguised.

'Paddy ate it,' Daisy informed her and took the hairband out. She would have to start again. She had an audition coming up and it was important for her hair to have the right look, so she was trying out appropriate styles. She frowned at her mother disapprovingly. 'You're going to choke doing that one day.'

'I could save you,' said Fergus cheerfully. 'I've learned the Heimlich manoeuvre at life saving.'

'I'm surprised you learned anything.' Daisy was unimpressed. 'You only went so you could learn to snog on the plastic Annie.'

'Plastic Annie. Plastic Annie,' repeated Mordecai relentlessly.

'I never should have agreed to let that dog sleep in the house,' said Alice darkly, pouring Rice Krispies into her bowl, acquiring in the process a plastic model of Fu Manchu from, as the box explained, the 'Heroes and Villains of History' plastic figure collection. Fu Manchu looked, she thought, unaccountably like Rob. Although perhaps everyone looked like Rob this week . . . 'He may look like a dog, but underneath he's a Clanger. Annie, will you put the milk away?'

Anemone pushed back one of a million beaded plaits hanging down her back and across her shoulders. 'I wish you'd call me Anemone, Mother. Everyone else does now and it's a much better name for an artist.'

Alice sighed, wondering if other people's lives were equally complicated by name-changing teenagers. Most of the time, she thought, as I hurtle from one task to the next, it's all I can do to remember my own name. 'I'm sorry – but if I'd wanted to call you Anemone I'd have done it seventeen years ago when I had the chance.'

9

Anemone sniffed. 'No one ever asked me what I wanted to be called.'

'If I could have chosen my own name I'd have been James,' said Fergus cheerfully, 'as in Bond.'

'It's a good job you were never asked,' said Alice. 'A few years ago you'd have wanted to be called Noddy, as in Noddy, so be grateful you're just Fergus. It was your father's idea to call you Fergus . . .'

'Mr Bond, Mr Bond,' said Mordecai, like a Hollywood baddy. 'Pieces of eight.'

Alice glared. 'A parrot may be for life and not for Christmas,' she told him, 'but you may well be for elevenses if you don't put a sock in it.'

'Sock in it,' said Mordecai mournfully, 'sock in it.'

Fergus frowned. 'Dad always said Mordecai would live to be a hundred.'

A bit longer than Rob himself managed, then, thought Alice bitterly, feeling a sudden rush of sparklers behind her eyes. Oh God, she thought, I'm going to cry again and Fergus will think it's his fault . . .'I think I'll just brush my hair . . .'

'That's the third time she's rushed off to the loo at breakfast this week,' said Daisy, affecting supreme unconcern because she was fifteen, but saying it anyway. Daisy's theory was that Fergus was starting to remind Alice of Rob. She had suggested to Anemone that they dye his hair to minimise the resemblance but Anemone had poured scorn on the idea, and, in any case, Fergus had made it very clear that he wouldn't co-operate. Red hair, though. She and Anemone were blonde, like Alice – but Fergus had that hair. Just like Dad's.

'Weetabix does that,' said Fergus in gruesome tones, having not noticed her strained face, 'especially to Paddy. Look, it's Fu Manchu. D'you think Mum's got PMT?'

'Don't be silly. It's your week for walking Paddy,' said Anemone, not wanting to speculate with Fergus. 'Go on, be quick.'

Fergus glowered at her and dragged himself unwillingly out of the kitchen. 'It's rotten being the only . . . being surrounded by women.'

'Don't, Fergus,' said Anemone, 'please.' And Fergus, who from long habit had already censored himself in any case, disappeared without retort.

Daisy gave up on the hairband and tucked her hair behind her ears, then checked to see that her skirt, which was rolled up around her waist in the currently preferred fifth-form style, hadn't committed the unacceptably naff fashion disaster of unrolling to the point of being visible beneath her jumper line. 'What?'

'I didn't say anything.'

'No, but you *looked* it. What?'

'It was their wedding anniversary today,' said Anemone. 'She's upset. So don't push it.'

Daisy glared. 'How was I to know? No one told *me* it was their wedding anniversary.' She used the petulant tones of a teenager who feels hard done by in so many ways that she has ceased to expect any consideration at all. 'Anyway, it's not my fault. If Dad hadn't been so bloody stupid and just – just *died* . . .' A tear rolled down her face, surprising her.

'I'm sorry I didn't mean –'

'I'm not upset,' said Daisy fiercely. 'For God's sake, why should I be? It was *ages* ago. And every day's an anniversary of something, anyway. Every day. The day they met, the day they went out for a meal, the day they first had sex . . . I can't be expected to remember all of them!'

Anemone said nothing and Daisy was suddenly angry – angry that her sister had had a father until she was fourteen, whilst she, Daisy, had been forced to make do with twelve, angry that Anemone was assuming this patronising, understanding personality, leaving Daisy with only the grumpy, teenage one to choose. Anemone was supposed to be the rebel. She *was* the one with the tattoo, after all, even if it was only of a dolphin on the back of her leg. If I had a tattoo,

11

thought Daisy, I'd have a cello on my bottom. And the bow on the other cheek. Even then some stupid bloke would wink and say, 'That's a big cello you've got there,' though, wouldn't he? That was just life, that was.

Upstairs Alice stared briefly at the photograph of Rob which stood beside her bed now, after a year in her sock drawer and another year at the back of the dressing table behind the one of her mother, then turned it face down angrily, blaming it for the ambush by memory.

'Why did you have to leave me like that?' she demanded of it. 'I thought I knew you.' The back of the photograph frame looked up at her, dead, disinterested, and Alice righted it hastily, feeling that she had somehow buried him again.

Ten minutes later she was back on track, gathering children, cello music, clarinet music, sports kit and all the luggage of her children's complex daily calendar. But the ten minutes made all the difference, as the hands of the kitchen clock spin faster in the morning. There was never time to stop and mope for long.

As she hurried outside the beeping of the refuse collection lorry reminded her that she was running late and would now be blocked into the drive until they decided to move. It was very important not to look as though you were in a hurry, either, or the refuse men became extremely slow at emptying the refuse.

She sat in the car, trying not to mind that they had just spilled a dog food tin onto her garden, trying not to look even slightly, discernibly, minusculely rushed, and trying not to look at the garden itself at all. That would mean seeing the poor hebes planted woefully together around the edge and admitting that the reason they were so utterly failing to thrive was that she, Alice, simply couldn't nurture a garden any more.

The Cambridge traffic was, Alice had learned, entirely

predictable. At eight fifteen the roads in the heart of town would have been smoothly free-flowing. Dark-suited and sober-faced men in air-conditioned BMWs with hands-free phones drove towards calm offices in which secretaries waited with coffee, the diary or possibly a blow job (well, that's what men are like, Alice told herself, knowing she didn't really believe it but endlessly feeling that perhaps a little more acquired cynicism might help ward off the pain). By eight thirty, though, the roads had become a sudden Armageddon, crowded with mothers in power-steered MPVs who seemed to think wing mirrors were purely for unseating cyclists and indicators were pointless devices which made an annoying clicking noise whilst the children were trying to go through their French vocab. Now it was eight forty, so to this scene of almost biblical chaos were added the bicycled scrum of potential prime ministers and would-be MI5 agents who make up Cambridge's under-graduate population.

A party of tourists regurgitating from a coach into the fresh morning air on Silver Street watched them pass and waved. Fergus waved back, accustomed to the Morris Minor Traveller attracting the odd wistful glance or interested greeting from people who once owned one, wanted one or lost their virginity in one. It didn't mean they gave two hoots about who was inside, thought Alice. It didn't mean they remembered a salacious newspaper article from three years ago, and a snatched bit on *News East*, which had shown her getting into the very same car on the day of the inquest and not having any comment.

There seemed little chance of starting surgery on time. Alice felt like leaning on her horn and screaming at them all to get out of the bloody way, or ramming them off the road, if only that were possible when you are driving a Morris Minor and they a Sherman tank. For a moment the image of a dozen metallic-painted people carriers being shunted unceremoniously into the Cam whilst their air-conditioned occupants continued to finger their pearls and try to persuade Olivia and Horatio to say their six times table just once more almost made her smile.

It was her own fault for leaving late. Why had she been so disorganised today? It wasn't as if today meant anything now. You can't have an anniversary when there's only one of you.

A tangle of cyclists surging into the university library left her sitting for some time on West Road outside the Fir Trees, the rest home for the elderly she would doubtlessly be visiting later. A lone peacock, property of one of the residents, strutted snootily along the pavement. Alice wound down her car window and was blasted by the alarming sound of a Chinese pop-singing tape being played over a loudspeaker system of no pedigree at all.

'God,' said Daisy, beside her in the front seat now that Anemone preferred to make her own way to sixth form college, 'that's horrendous. What is it?'

'It's the Fir Trees. It's not like other rest homes, it can be a little eccentric.' Alice could see the residents pirouetting stiffly on the grass at the back like geriatric ballerinas, peacocks wandering amongst them giving the scene a faintly Oriental air. It looked a little like t'ai chi, as it might be performed by people who had never been shown how to perform t'ai chi but who had read about it once, years ago, and taken a guess.

'It must be brilliant to be old,' said Fergus, in the back because he'd left his bike at school with a puncture. 'Just imagine – having nothing at all to do all day. And it must be fun to be able to take your teeth out. You could just suck trout off its bones.'

'That's revolting,' said Daisy. 'I hope I'm never old.'

Fergus shrugged. 'Fred says it's better than the alternative. He says living at the Fir Trees is a riot. Those are his peacocks, you know.'

'I don't know why you spend so much of your time there,'

Daisy frowned at him.

'Because Fred's really interesting. No one knows how old he is, and he made his fortune turning dung into gold.'

'His surname wouldn't be Rumpelstiltskin, would it?' asked Daisy drily, but Fergus was not that easily riled.

'Fred's my friend,' he said. 'And old people are much more interesting than young ones. Fred always says that the only trouble is that the older you get and the more you learn, the less notice anyone takes of you.'

Alice, concentrating on the traffic, swallowed. Rob was never old. Her Fir Trees population, on the other hand, were mostly elderly spinsters, deprived of marriage by war or family duty. What irony that they should live to be eighty, doing nothing for all those years, sexually unused whilst Rob – Rob, who was a doctor, a father, a husband . . .

Beside and behind her, Fergus and Daisy continued to gibe in that slightly calculating way that children do when hoping for adult intervention, each self-righteous moan followed by an expectant glance and a brief silence. Alice ignored them. She felt as though her personal cloud of mourning had enveloped her again, the one she had struggled so hard to throw off this morning. It felt as dense as the night – yet it was invisible to the world outside.

'I have an idea,' said Fergus, in the measured tones of one who is sure that for a boy of twelve he has just been very, very clever.

'I should notify the press,' said Daisy, who was finding sarcasm an attitude worth honing in the shark-infested boyfriend-hunting waters of teenagedom.

Fergus ignored her. 'Mum? You know this traffic?'

'Ye-es?'

'Well, why don't they just fasten all the cars together, then the front one could pull them all along? We'd go much faster that way, and you wouldn't have to drive. Think how much petrol it would save.'

'God,' said Daisy, 'imagine all those fighting kids and

cross mothers all joined together, all trying to get to school and to work. It would be like a giant column of misery.'

'Sounds exactly like a train to me,' said Alice. 'Maybe you should suggest it to Richard Branson.' She glanced in the rear-view mirror at Fergus' mop of red hair and smiled. I'm so lucky to have him – to have them all. I should count my blessings. I must have dreamed of Rob, she thought, as the traffic lurched forwards another few yards. That's why I woke up feeling so bereft. Maybe some merciful quirk of nature prevents the remembering of dreams, which might otherwise be too painful to leave.

By the time she had dropped off Daisy and Fergus at St Alupent's School, the school where they had been ever since the age of four, the traffic was building to gridlock. Alice, struggling with the lack of synchromesh on first gear, and slightly worried about her fuel level, wondered if she ought really to get another car. She could afford it, after all. She had no mortgage these days, and money in the bank – but that was because Rob was dead. When Rob was alive there was never much spare, not after the mortgage repayments on Pipe Tree Cottage and its thatch. But it had been their dream home. 'We'll pay it off, one day,' Rob used to say when she wished they didn't owe quite so much – but it had been paid off rather sooner than either of them had dreamed. And sold. It just went to show you should be careful what you wished for. Anyhow, just because you were now debt free you didn't immediately rush beaming into the BMW salesroom saying, 'My husband's dead, so I'll have one of your nice air-conditioned saloons, please,' did you? Not when you still couldn't quite admit to yourself that life was always going to be without him.

She reached the surgery at ten past nine – and there was nowhere to park.

There were four doctors practising at Lammas Surgery – the three partners, James, Ian, Alice – and Roland. Practising

16

was the right word, since none of them, as the receptionists enjoyed saying when it wasn't day twenty-six, seemed to have got it right yet. It was Rob who had always joked that the receptionists were fully synchronised in the hormonal stakes, like isolated communities of Finlanders. He had always maintained that there was a week during every month when none of them said very much at all, just squabbled over the chocolate biscuits and turned the front-of-house area into a pit of doom. 'Remind me,' he had once said, 'when we next employ someone, that we specify they have to be post-menopausal.' Alice, though, had always felt that the atmosphere in the surgery had far more to do with Roland. Roland, who made Attila the Hun look like a small harmless bloke with, if anything, a rather excessive empathy for the minority peoples of Central Asia. Roland who, Alice was beginning to believe, was out to ruin them all.

She wondered suddenly and horribly if her own cycle had been synchronised with Marcie Crombie's. Marcie Crombie's number had been in Rob's address book. Perhaps her menstrual cycle had been in his diary. Maybe that explained why he was always so obsessed with the receptionists' PMT.

Roland's Mercedes was using up more than its fair share of parking spaces, as always, and next to it a new BMW occupied her own named space. There was a rather trendy sports car parked in Ian's space, but that was because Ian was away on a six-month sabbatical doing research into CJD – the car belonged to the locum whom he'd employed to cover his absence. If only Roland had retired, Alice thought, then I'd have had somewhere to park, as well as all the other advantages of not having to spend any part of my day within a hundred yards of him.

Everyone had thought Roland might retire gracefully after that worrying brush with the GMC (nothing proved in the end, so he hadn't been struck off, despite two patients claiming sexual harassment). Unfortunately, though, he had simply left the NHS partnership and become a private GP, and continued to occupy the same consulting room – and the same array of parking spaces. It had been impossible for the rest of them to stop him, as he owned the building. Not long before he died, Rob had told Alice he sometimes feared that Roland Liversill would one day evict his former partners from the surgery, lock, stock and stethoscope, but Alice had thought that ridiculous. So had James and Ian, who were both far too fair and open to imagine that their now former partner might not be.

How wrong they had been. Roland had bided his time for nearly three years after Rob's first suspicions, but Alice had realised soon after Ian left the country that Rob had been right about Roland after all. The hints about the many difficulties he faced due to having an NHS practice operating in his building were becoming more than just hints. It seemed to Alice that Roland had deliberately waited for Ian to depart, picking the practice at its most vulnerable moment to begin a campaign to evict his former partners. It had been subtle at first, and James still refused to believe it, but Alice could see it now. Roland was working towards getting them out.

Would Roland be doing this if Ian were around? Definitely not – Roland was rather in awe of Ian, who was a rugby prop forward in his spare time. Ian would never have gone abroad if he'd had an inkling of what Roland was planning. Mind you, Rob would never have let him get away with it either. Rob would have thumped him.

Alice shook herself mentally. Rob had always disliked Roland, because he had made no secret of fancying Alice. But then Roland made no secret of fancying most women – and had Rob been any better? Roland's treachery was nothing compared to Rob's. In any case, there seemed very little she could do about it other than worry.

She parked across the back of the thief who had stolen her

parking space. That would show them she was not a woman to be trifled with.

Inside the building the atmosphere was quiet, barely lifted by the faint sound of Norma's Richard Clayderman tape playing a selection of tunes almost too unbearably easy on the ear. Norma was the senior receptionist, and she chose the front-of-house music. The others had once slipped some heavy metal into the CD player for a joke, but Norma had been so upset that she had gone home early and someone else had had to file the temporary residents' forms, so they hadn't touched it again. So Richard Clayderman continued to impart a laid-back, casual, unrushed air to the reception area.

Sometimes Alice wished life at the surgery could feel more like those American emergency room soaps, the ones in which heroic doctors run from patient to patient, making life-saving decisions, pursued by Quentin Tarantino with a low-slung camera and a bevy of make-up women to eliminate all traces of sweat. The ones in which everyone gets to do something extremely clever and rewarding at least once in an evening. Sometimes she longed for just a bit more excitement in her life. But then, as her friend Martha liked to say with that irritating American logic of hers, if you want excitement you have to take the odd risk.

'Good morning, Dr Vane.'

'Morning, Norma. Am I fully booked?'

'Course you are, and five urgent extras at the end. Can I give you some emergencies?'

I never wanted to be a full-time GP, thought Alice, collecting her notes for the morning. Ten lots of thin notes, half a dozen lots of medium notes and two so thick that you wondered how the people they referred to were walking at all.

She felt you could judge a lot about someone's health from the weight of their notes. Those with weighty notes are either having a terrible time with an awful chronic condition

19

or are perfectly well but are still having a terrible time due to an unshakeable disbelief that that could be the case. But then perhaps the definition of illness should be that you think you're ill, rather than that your doctor thinks you are. Likewise, perhaps you get over your husband's death when you believe you have . . .

Mind you, if Rob hadn't gone and died I might have been able to carry on doing my couple of sessions a week to keep my hand in until I retired, instead of trying to do his job. I'm only here because his partners felt sorry for me – well, Ian and James felt sorry for me and Roland fancied me – and because I didn't know what else to do.

'What are the urgent extras I've already got booked if they're not emergencies?'

Norma looked embarrassed. 'We're very short of appointments.'

Alice was exasperated. 'What about Dr Lovejoy?'

'Oh, Dr Lovejoy has to get off early this morn –'

'Ah, the beautiful Alice. Good morning,' and Dr Lovejoy swept into the reception area looking like an advert for men's jeans. 'How are you this fine day?'

Alice smiled tightly. The locum, Tom Lovejoy, who had been standing in for Ian for the last four weeks, was almost as handsome as Rob, but he left her cold. Probably, she admitted to herself privately, that was why he left her cold. However, absolutely every other woman who crossed his path seemed to gasp and flush, which annoyed her terrifically. The receptionists had the vapours whenever he wafted into the coffee room with that faint scent of sandalwood that followed him like a fan club. Patients adored him; old ladies had been known to whisper in reception that it was nice to have another dashing young man to check their blood pressure and send it soaring, as they had so missed Dr Rob. Everyone on the medical grapevine thought him one of the best doctors they'd ever met. His CV was astounding, his references perfect. He would, in fact, have been the perfect person to work with if he hadn't been so untrustworthily handsome. Since Rob's death Alice had noticed that all handsome men had the same untrustworthy look.

'Fine, thank you,' she told him now without warmth. 'How much longer are you going to be here with us?'

She picked up her post. On top was another memo from Roland about the practice premises. These notes were increasing in number in a rather sinister fashion, even though individually they ranged from the petty to the ridiculous. The last one had been particularly absurd, suggesting that the NHS practice should pay a higher proportion of the air-conditioner repair bill on the basis that NHS patients cumulatively necessitate more air freshening.

'Well, actually . . .' Tom flashed his teeth, glitteringly.

God, thought Alice –, disliking him intensely whilst aware it was for no other reason than that it seemed the safest option, all things considered – it's enough to give you retinal burns.

Behind her the youngest receptionist, Lisa, who was plump and pretty, sighed audibly and earned herself a poke in the ribs from Norma. Mind you, even Norma felt a little spark. It was the HRT, of course. She hadn't felt sparks in that department for decades before she started on the HRT. He was a wonderful man, that Dr Lovejoy. He had prescribed that first little packet and Norma's Ron had completely stopped going out to the darts club as a result . . .

'Ah, Alice? I need a word.' Her senior partner, James Ferguson, appeared, a man so old-fashioned he made morris dancing look dangerously trendy. 'Would you mind?'

I hope Roland hasn't been getting at James, thought Alice. She had tried to keep the worst of Roland's unpleasantness concealed from his former partner, even though it meant her only ally was Ian, now in Papua New Guinea which

21

might as well be a million miles away as he took seven days to reach by post and was not phoneable at all. But James would be retiring soon and he hadn't been himself. She felt he needed protecting.

Alice raised an eyebrow at Norma, and followed James into his room with a nod at Tom Lovejoy.

Tom watched her go, a thoughtful look etched lightly but flatteringly upon his handsome brow. 'Norma – if there are any more extras just put them in with me.'

'Oh, but Dr Alice never minds—'

'Alice seems to be her own worst enemy,' said Tom. 'She looks as though she needs a break. Just don't tell her, will you? I don't want her feeling guilty.'

Norma could feel her Mills and Boon alarm sounding, like the emergency siren on the *Titanic*: 'Romance! Romance! Romance!' She beamed at Tom. Could he be The One for dear Dr Vane? It was about time . . .

'That's so good of you – dear Alice gets a little stressed around this time of the year . . .' but Tom was gone with a shrug and a wave, avoiding the thanks. He was habitually chivalrous and disliked being thanked for it. Actually, he was also habitually heroic and disliked being thanked for that too. Tom's past was a TV scriptwriter's dream. Seeing a few extra patients when a colleague is having a bad day – that was nothing. Delivering twin babies in the dark in broken-down cars stuck in country lanes; making chest drains out of coat hangers and tubing on jumbo jets at 30,000 feet; being lowered down a flooded potholing system to rescue a diabetic child; climbing into the London Zoo gorilla pen to rescue an injured tourist – those were the sort of things he was accustomed to being thanked for, and even then he hated the fuss. Appearing on Richard and Judy, interviews on Radio Four – those were all awkward and an effort – but not so the heroism. Heroism came naturally to Tom.

*

James Ferguson's room was a little like him – cosy, untidy, and full of a mixture of ancient bits of things which somehow blended smoothly to form a pleasing whole. There was a huge, ancient desk with a pedestal top bearing a mountain of notes and a computer screen which Alice knew, without needing to look, would not be turned on. The examination couch was antique, upholstered in burgundy leather and once owned by James's grandfather, who, he liked to say, had been physician to the Earl of Broomhill's bowels. The window had heavy velvet curtains rather than the slatted blinds the surgery used elsewhere. James Ferguson did not hold with slatted blinds – he considered them left wing because he had seen them on TV adorning the windows at a Communist Party conference in Beijing. On the wall were a set of photographs of his children and grandchildren, plus etchings of the fifth and eighteenth holes at St Andrew's and a watercolour of his Alma Mater, St Alupent's College, Cambridge. In the air was the delicate but unmistakable hint of pipe tobacco, which had been soaked in rum and treasured like best caviar.

'Sit down, Alice. Sit down – and tell me, how are you feeling this morning?'

Alice knew at once what he meant. It wasn't about Roland this time. James might be getting on a bit, he might be rather worryingly forgetful at times, he might sport the kind of half-moon spectacles that made you want to pat him on the arm and bring him his slippers, but beneath the veneer of geniality burned the piercingly acute intuition and impossibly elephantine memory of a true GP. It might have bypassed the rest of the world, but James never forgot a date, even though he seemed to forget a lot of other more recent things these days. James had been at her wedding and seen her through sixteen anniversaries before Rob died. He would understand the significance of today.

'I'm fine, James. Really. It's just another day, now. Time passes.'

23

It sounded as limp as it felt, and James looked at her over the top of his spectacles, a look he had perfected over years of asking seriously pregnant teenage patients exactly when they had indulged in the unprotected sex and being told, 'Honestly, absolutely never.'

'Really?'

Alice felt her calm front crack slightly, just a hairline. They don't teach that one at medical school, she thought. That one takes decades to acquire. 'Anniversaries are always difficult,' she said reluctantly. 'It's another separation on top of the others – another year gone by. And even now sometimes I just want to curl up in a corner and howl my eyes out, and I should surely be over that by now.'

James raised an eyebrow. 'Should be?'

'Well, you know,' said Alice, finding the role of patient rather hard to assume when she knew there were already half a dozen of the real thing in the waiting room, 'there should be some sort of resolution of the feelings I have about Rob. I mean, I expected to miss him – but I don't want to just be *angry* for ever, James. It's exhausting.'

James Ferguson smiled a little sadly, and it struck Alice suddenly that he looked tired.

'Would you like to come round for a chat? I know Marjorie would be delighted to see you.'

Alice got a grip on herself, thinking, if Marjorie pats me on the head and offers me angel cake I shall weep, and that won't help at all. 'No. No, but thank you. I must go and see some patients. There's a big emergency surgery building up this morning.'

James smiled benevolently. 'And doubtless none of them needs treatment that can't wait five minutes. I remember the last outbreak of smallpox, you know, when I was a trainee in Yorkshire. Now that *was* an emergency surgery. We were there till midnight inoculating people who hadn't come down from their smallholdings for years.'

Alice, who had heard this story slightly more times than

24

she could remember, got up to go. Does he remember he's told me before? she wondered. 'I'll see you later, James.'

'Of course. Marjorie would be so pleased to see you. I'll get her to give you a ring.'

Damn, thought Alice. Getting out of that now will be like cancelling an appointment with my maker. Not that Marjorie means any harm, but I just don't want to talk about it today. I don't even want to make plans to talk about it on another day, in case it all pours out again and overwhelms me with embarrassment. Perhaps I'll just go to—

'Before you rush off,' said James, 'there's something else I'd like you to think about . . .'

'Oh yes?'

'Our locum, young Tom Lovejoy. Seems a decent enough fellow. Jolly good CV and I know Ian thinks very highly of him.'

Just because he plays golf, thought Alice fondly. 'I don't think we've had any complaints,' she said aloud.

'Well – he asked me about his chances of a partnership here, and it struck me, Alice, that it would save all the fuss of looking for a replacement for me.'

'But you're not retiring yet,' said Alice, reflecting that when James went there would only be herself and Ian left to do battle with Roland. But . . . to take on Tom Lovejoy? An untrustworthily handsome man who clearly – you only had to look at him – had made his life a series of conquests and abandonments. Didn't put those on his CV, did he? Why else was he still single, looking like that, as handsome as . . . as Rob?

James sighed. 'Alice, I'm overdue for retirement, you know that – I always meant to go at sixty. If we took Tom on as a partner now, instead of keeping him in this temporary post, then when Ian gets back from the jungle I can retire. I don't want to leave you in the lurch, my dear, and this way Tom would have job stability and there would be a smooth transition for the practice. And, more importantly, there

25

would be someone else here as support for you, Alice. Rob always said Roland would want this place from us to put it to more profitable use, and it's beginning to look as if he may have been right. There may be trouble ahead.'

Alice sighed, thinking: Rob's opinions are managing to influence us even from the grave.

'I don't know, James. I think we should wait. After all, Ian isn't terribly easy to contact in Papua New Guinea – we've only had once postcard so far and it took a week to get here. He might not appreciate coming back to find that a new partner has been appointed without asking him.' It was a poor effort and she knew it wasn't true – Ian had had nothing but praise for Tom Lovejoy. It was she, Alice, who didn't want him as a partner. Not another handsome hero with a toothpaste smile. If one more person whispered how like Rob he was when they thought she couldn't hear them she'd go bananas.

James looked mildly perturbed. 'It seems to me permanent partners are just what we do need here. You know, in my day people didn't expect to be able to abandon their patients and gad off round the world investigating shrunken heads. In my day people didn't charge their partners an extortionate rent for their premises either.'

Alice sighed. 'This still *is* your day, James – and the research that Ian's helping with could turn out to be important; could be a breakthrough in the study of CJD.' Sometimes, she thought, I feel I'm the only thing holding this practice together.

'And when did you last see a patient with CJD? We need Ian here with us for the asthma and the heart disease, not conducting his personal investigation into the dangers of cannibalism.'

'We all have to do what we have to do,' said Alice, thinking how much she missed Ian's cheerful, down-to-earth personality and wondering if perhaps a few months in Papua New Guinea wouldn't be such a bad thing for her next. Anything to escape Roland and his foibles. But then you never can run away from your problems, can you?

'Well, right now commitment is what we need,' said James, patting her hand, 'and GP recruitment is at an all-time low. Good partners are like gold dust.'

Alice frowned, not liking James's criticism of Ian, who when he wasn't in Papua New Guinea, was really the rock she relied on. 'In which case,' she reasoned, 'why on earth would Tom want to join *us* as a partner, with Roland possibly intending to evict us and leaving us to pay millionaires' rents in the centre of town? If Roland really wants us out of our surgery there'll be no partnership. There are loads of other places where Tom could work without any such trouble.'

'Alice, dear, do promise me you will think about the suggestion. If we were to advertise my post it is entirely possible that no one decent would apply. Candidates of Tom's calibre don't come along in twos.'

Calibre? Makes him sound like a shotgun, thought Alice darkly as she went to her own room. The trouble with Tom Lovejoy is that he's just too good to be true. It wouldn't surprise me if the next thing to fall out of my Rice Krispies is him.

Chapter Two

Alice switched on her computer and watched it warm up. 'ENTER PASSWORD' it said, and, as she had done ever since the bloody thing had been installed four years ago, she entered 'ROBERT', the password she had never quite brought herself to change.

The morning's appointments flashed up a list of the usual suspects, with only a couple of names she did not recognise as regular attendees – and you could bet your life they'd either want a good moan or a good weep. Mornings were often like that. Just when she could have done with a few unusual or challenging medical problems to take her mind off the abiding image of herself in her white frothy dress, skipping down the aisle to where Rob waited with that handsome Colgate smile. She rifled rapidly through her post – a heap of medical magazines crammed with unappetising pictures of rashes and genitalia and a warning from the committee on safety of medicines. Apparently a new blood pressure tablet was being withdrawn because it had been giving people orgasms. You'd think that would be an unexpected bonus, she thought, but then maybe it would be a bit inconvenient in a board meeting, or whilst taking out someone's gall bladder. Maybe I should have taken it myself, she thought. Still, time to put personal thoughts on hold . . .

She dialled into the intercom for her first patient.

'Miss Tinkler, please.'

Tabitha Tinkler was a charming old lady from the Fir Trees with a muscular inflammation, which rendered her aching and tired from time to time. It had been well controlled recently with the aid of steroids, but these tablets had resulted in her already huge volume reaching a level that might give even the King of Tonga a nervous twitch. Otherwise she was pretty well. Indeed, she only chose to live at the Fir Trees, she liked to tell Alice, for the company – 'although not for the men, my dear. There's only one and he tells me he's six hundred and eighty.' She did like regular check-ups, believing that through such thorough and repeated examination she could keep any serious problems at bay. Tabitha and Alice had long since reached an unspoken understanding that apart from the steroids Alice would not intervene with Tabitha's body and its physical functions, she would merely examine each proffered anatomical part with an expression of deep interest. Alice called it the non-interventional prod.

'Are you all right, dear?' she asked Alice now, attempting to heave herself up onto the examination couch. 'You seem a little preoccupied?'

'I'm fine,' replied Alice brightly, wondering whether she should remove Tabitha's corset to examine her and thinking that if she could get her hands on the man who designed it she'd happily throttle him with it. And to think, she thought sadly, that after millions of years of evolution a whale can end up like this.

She unhooked the corset with determined resolution. There was always the terrible fear, if you risked removing these contraptions, that that which poured out of them with such obvious relief might never go back in again. Miss Tinkler's steroids had expanded the contained flesh con-siderably without any compensatory give from the whale element of the corsetry equation. Perhaps, Rob had once said, they ought to have a whalebone lacing display at the Royal Tournament, with great gangs of burly Royal Marines cramming delightfully round elderly ladies back into their body shapers whilst the band of the Dragoon Guards played 'A Life on the Ocean Wave'.

'Everything seems fine. I think we need to begin to bring the steroid dose down,' she said aloud after a prolonged struggle with laces and hooks. 'We don't want you on them for too long and we should be able to reduce the dose now without any trouble.'

Tabitha Tinkler looked smug. 'If you think that's best, dear. As you know, I'm never unwell – but I want to be my best this week. I'm expecting a visitor from Armenia – that's Eastern Europe, you know. Oh, and Dr Alice, that reminds me, I must tell you, I've been doing t'ai chi, and it works wonders for the internal organs. My prolapse has quite gone away. Would you like to see?'

Alice suppressed a smile but shook her head. Her surgery was already overrunning and her next patient was schizophrenic Mr Sykes with his delusions of grandeur, come for his monthly injection. If they were unlucky it would have worn off early and he would be Elvis again. The mums in for baby clinic got very twitchy last time, particularly when he started on 'Love Me Tender' in the waiting room.

'Is it troubling you, Tabitha?'

'Oh no, dear, but I thought you might be interested.'

'There's no need this time, really,' said Alice hastily, thinking: when other people seek entertainment they go and see the Spice Girls or St Alupent's College choir. Why does anyone imagine that a doctor might be any different? Do they think we go home and watch loop videos about wombs? 'Was that what you were all doing earlier? When I drove past the Fir Trees I thought it looked like t'ai chi.'

'It was,' said Tabitha Tinkler proudly. 'You should try it, dear – it's a martial art, you know. It's marvellous for your energy lines. Your dear son, Fergus, suggested it to us a week ago. He said it would be excellent self-defence – and you can't be too careful at our age.'

Alice sighed inwardly and wondered if perhaps Fergus would next have the residents of the Fir Trees auditioning *en masse* as extras in a martial arts film. *Fu Manchu and the Kick Boxer's Granny*, perhaps. 'Maybe I will. Am I seeing you next week?' she said aloud.

'Oh, yes dear. Matron has booked me appointments every Wednesday for the next few weeks. Don't want to be always troubling your nice receptionists on the phone. By the way, I do love your frog collection. I used to collect frogs myself, you know, I had all sorts at one time. I always meant to tell you. I must bring you one next time I go somewhere unusual.'

'That's very kind,' said Alice, thinking that the chance of Tabitha going anywhere even remotely unusual – indeed, anywhere more unusual than the Marks and Spencer's cream cake department – was only slightly greater than the chance that Elvis-impersonating Mr Sykes turned out actually to be, in fact, Elvis.

How did I end up here? she wondered, as the door closed behind Tabitha.

She let her gaze drift around her room, a room whose shelves were lined two to three deep with frogs of all sizes and shapes. The frog collection had been part of her life since early teens, beginning with a frog an aunt had given her and becoming a collection of hundreds from all over the world. It never failed to fascinate her that despite the variety of frogs that exist in nature, the ones she possessed – from as far afield as Thailand, Australia, South America and Africa – were all basically the same. They were not biologically accurate copies of frogs; they represented everyone's idea of a frog – which doesn't look quite like any particular frog, from Japanese bullfrogs to Senegalese tree frogs, yet manages at the same time to look quite like all of them. Rob used to joke that when he married her he married all the frogs as well (he'd been unfaithful to an awful lot of people then, hadn't he?). Actually he had given her several. Now they seemed to look at her sadly, as if they were shaking their little green heads in disbelief at her self-pity, her lack of momentum.

31

Where did my life go? she wondered.

The answer was there on her desk. The photograph of Robert Vane, trapped in time, gazed up at her from the silver frame, the mane of red hair giving him a faintly Scandinavian look. I'm older than you now, she thought. I remember how you laughed when we raced one another across the meadows at Grantchester and said I'd never win because you were oldest. I'm forty-two now. I overtook you in the end.

After seeing Mr Sykes (whose problems were unchanged apart from the fact that he was having trouble with the high notes in some of Elvis's earlier numbers) Alice made herself a hasty cup of tea, ate two biscuits in less than ten seconds, drank the tea and scalded her lip and called for her next patient, Heather Bunberry.

Heather was an odd girl. She reminded Alice of heroines of those newsagent romances in which girls who are actually extremely pretty go out of their way to look plain by scraping their hair back and wearing unflattering spectacles until discovered by Mr Handsome, Rich and Perfect. She was not actually registered with the practice, as she lived in Bury St Edmunds. However, she worked in Cambridge, and had been coming in to be seen as a temporary resident every now and again over the last few months. Alice had done her best to dissuade her from this, feeling it was a rather fragmented approach to medical care, but Heather had proved rather difficult to convince. Her problems were never terribly convincing either, and Alice was certain that she had not yet got to the real reason for Heather's repeated attendances. Today her complaint was weight gain, although she had not in fact gained any weight at all. Alice had tried the usual 'is anything else troubling you?' and 'I get the impression there's something on your mind?' but they had failed to strike gold. Even so, she was sure that Heather was working up to something . . .

Whatever it was, today was not destined to be the day for

it. You'd think, thought Alice, that with the amount of training I've had in uncovering people's hidden agenda, patients would be banging on the door begging to tell me their most secret worries. But as she tried another tack – 'Heather, what made you come about this today in particular . . .' – her telephone rang, and Heather gathered up her bag, any rapport she might have established clearly shattered.

'There's a woman at the front desk,' said Norma cheerfully, 'says you've blocked her in the car park and says she was only five minutes.'

'That can't be true. I've been parked there since ten past nine, and it's now eleven o'clock.'

'I said that. She says she had to take her disabled mother to the Citizens' Advice Bureau where she's gone for help because her pension had been stopped and there was nowhere else to park.'

'Oh, what nonsense,' said Alice, exasperated. 'Heather, I'm sorry, would you mind hanging on a mo –'

'No, no, it's OK . . . I'm just glad about . . . the weight. So sorry to have troubled you,' and Heather scurried out. Alice followed her, annoyed with herself, with the telephone, and with the parking offender.

Outside she found a middle-aged woman laden with a single carrier bag from Martha's, the exclusive lingerie shop in The Close run by Alice's best friend, the perfectly groomed Martha Coleman. This woman looked like a Martha's customer. She had perfectly arranged hair (cut, set and blow-dried within the last ten minutes, Alice was sure), and the sort of coat that no one ever manages to find in a sale except on TV makeover programmes. If she's got a disabled mother living off a pension, thought Alice, then I'm Marilyn Monroe. She raised one eyebrow carefully in the way Rob had taught her years ago. The woman, unperturbed, tapped her foot with an annoying absence of appropriate humility, and sighed loudly. She was, Alice realised, one of Roland's private patients. They weren't all awful snobs, of course – some of them were just normal people who wanted to pay for the privilege of having more than seven and a half minutes at a time with their GP. On the other hand, if you wanted to lay bets on any particular one of Roland's private patients being an awful snob you'd not get very long odds. This was partly a function of its being a private service, and partly a function of their being friends of Roland in the first place.

'Do you know,' said Alice with sudden resolution, 'I think I'm actually going to finish my surgery before I move my car.'

'What do you mean? I'm a personal friend of Roland, you know, and I must –'

'You shouldn't have parked in my spot whilst you had your hair done,' said Alice loftily. 'I'll move when I'm ready.'

The woman glared. 'If you'd been in your surgery at eight – as all doctors should be in my opinion – you'd have been fine. Roland says you're all jolly slack and that's why he had to go private.'

'Well, if you think my hours are too short it will doubtless please you to know that my surgery is now so busy that there is no prospect of it finishing until one o'clock,' said Alice defiantly, 'which is when I shall have time to move my car. Goodbye.'

She got back to her room enveloped in a healthy glow of righteous indignation to find Lisa, the junior receptionist, waiting for her.

'Sorry,' she said in wobbly tones, 'I've sneaked in before your next one.'

'Don't tell me,' said Alice, 'she's got you to tell me to move my car too.'

Lisa burst into tears. Determined not to look at her clock Alice sat her down. 'Do you want to tell me what's wrong?' *Please, just tell me, don't make me drag it out of you. I'm already*

34

running fifteen minutes late, and dragging things out of people takes a full four minutes longer than just being given it straight . . .

Lisa Prescott had worked at the Lammas Surgery for a year, ever since she had left school. Alice had known her before that as she lived in Fox Colne with her mother, a completely shapeless woman who made the simple belt look like an instrument of torture. Lisa, though, was curvaceous, blonde, blue-eyed and pretty, and usually smiling. She worked hard, tried hard, and never left early, and these three attributes had kept her job for her after her six-month trial period, despite the fact that she was absolutely and completely dippy. She was also rather more curvaceous than before.

'It never occurred to me, Dr Vane, that I'd get caught pregnant. I wasn't in the right position.'

'What do you mean?'

'Well – we were standing up,' said Lisa, blushing furiously, 'and Dean said it wouldn't take that way, you know, what with gravity and all that.'

'Sperm,' Alice told Lisa gently, 'are astonishingly determined creatures. If a man can get to the top of Everest, defying gravity for an entire five miles, with nothing but a team of Sherpas and a pair of crampons to get him there, a sperm in its natural environment should have no trouble with three inches.'

Lisa was mystified. 'Do you mean I should have used tampons, Dr Vane?'

Alice sighed. 'No, crampons. You know, what mountaineers wear on their shoes.' And, as Lisa looked increasingly mystified: 'I was speaking metaphorically. Don't you remember my talk? I did give a contraception talk to your year at the High School two years ago, didn't I?'

Lisa looked shamefaced. 'Dean and me didn't go.'

Alice raised a brow. 'Behind the bike sheds?'

Lisa nodded. Alice wondered how many others had

known so much by the time the sex education lesson came along that they didn't bother to go and listen to those few, crucial bits they had actually missed out on. If only they'd let me go in and do that talk at twelve – but look at the fuss the parents made when we wanted to show twelve-year-olds what a condom looked like . . . 'So when did you find out?'

'I only just guessed.'

'When was your last period?'

Lisa looked sheepish. 'About seven months . . . well, I've never been . . . I've never been regular, you know, and I thought it was just all the chocolate I've been eating that had made me a bit tubby.' Lisa started to snivel again. 'I was going to go to Weight Watchers.' Alice fumbled for fresh tissues. There were none left, but there was a free box of vaginal hygiene wipes in her top drawer. She fished them out, thinking: I hope they don't sting. Still, what's safe for the vagina ought surely to be safe on the face.

'And what does Dean say?'

'He says it's great. He says at least I hadn't paid the joining fee, and it'll be fun being a dad and he'll take him to see Ipswich Town.' She began to cry even harder, mopping at herself with a wipe, which didn't appear to be stinging despite the redness and puffiness of her eyes.

Alice patted her shoulder. 'Come on, Lisa, call me an old ignoramus but isn't that what every girl wants to hear?' Alice tried to cheer her up. 'Things could be worse.'

'What do you mean? Worse how?'

'Well, you know. He could support Norwich.' She smiled hopefully. Lisa's family's fervent support of Ipswich Town was such that all their doors were decorated in the team colours. Every time the team changed its strip Lisa's father went straight to Do It All for paint.

Sadly, as a joke it made a slightly worse landing than a multi-storey car park might if dropped out of an upstairs window.

'I'm so upset,' said Lisa tragically, blowing her nose musically on a vaginal wipe. 'I mean, I'd never have wanted to get rid of it, Doctor, not even if he weren't going to stand by me – it's not that – but . . .'

'But what?'

'I want to be married,' said Lisa. 'Me mum wasn't married when she had me, nor was me gran when she had her. I wanted to be the first one of us Prescotts to be married when she has her first baby. A lovely white wedding like the ones in *Yes* magazine, with bridesmaids in peach and a bunch of flowers that reaches my feet.'

Alice nodded sympathetically. Ambition, she thought, what a funny thing. Some of us are completely greedy and want the moon. I wanted to be a doctor, marry Rob, and live a happy but interesting life ever after with an adoring and faithful husband and a garden that looked as though the BBC had spent six months working on it with thirty-six extras and a limitless budget. One of my friends wanted to have six children and climb Everest . . . Tony Blair wanted – well – to change history and build a giant white tent in Greenwich, presumably . . . but Lisa? Lisa just wants to do a couple of things in the right order. It doesn't seem an unreasonable demand, not when set against Everest – not even when set against the giant white tent.

I don't see what I can do about it, though. Lisa's got a feckless man, that's all. Another feckless man to join the endless procession of feckless men who have made women cynical and capable over the ages.

And I can feel the pressure of Roland's friend's eyes boring into me through the surgery walls . . .

'You just sit for a minute,' she told Lisa. 'I have to move my car, then I'll be back.' So much for being a woman not to be trifled with.

It seemed a long morning. By the time Alice had promised Lisa that she would talk to Dean (What am I doing? I shouldn't get myself involved in the personal lives of my staff. *Peak Practice* must have gone to my head), and prescribed two lots of antibiotics on shaky grounds because it was easier than arguing with expectant middle-class Cambridge parents who felt their time spent coming to the surgery would have been completely wasted if all she was going to say was that it was a virus, Alice was feeling tired. The only redeeming feature was the immenseness of a small patient's belief that the loan of one of Alice's frogs would make him better. It was a tradition so well established that Alice sometimes thought there were some patients who really just came in to see her for a frog, and binned any prescriptions they might be given in the process. Still, she generally got them back. Rob had always said it was the power of placebo, but Alice preferred to think of it as the triumph of hope.

'Norma?'

'Yes?' Norma was cheery down the telephone, unfazed. She enjoyed her job. It was so nice to feel useful to the patients – she could always squeeze them in as extras with dear Alice. Alice never complained . . .

'Is anyone else seeing any extra patients? I seem to have been snowed under with emergencies.'

'Well, James had a headache and I sent him home, poor man.'

'Oh dear.' I don't suppose he has got a headache, Alice thought, suddenly uneasy. I expect he's upset, having forgotten who someone is again, or tried to refer to another consultant who retired years ago as he did last week. She put James's increasing forgetfulness and his clear distress about it to the back of her mind again, where she generally tried to keep it locked away. 'What about Dr Lovejoy?' She couldn't call him Tom right now, she was feeling too cross. And if she did, Norma would think she was getting familiar and news would ring around the practice that Alice was taking an interest in a man at last . . .

38

'Oh, Tom has just had to go out on an errand but he has seen an awful lot of—'

'An errand?' asked Alice in her most cynical voice – which was unfortunately her usual voice, slower. Rob used to say she didn't have an ounce of cynicism in her, but she was working on it.

'Flowers for his mother,' said Norma in chastening tones, wanting to tell Alice that the only patients remaining had insisted on seeing her and her alone, but bound to silence by her promise to Tom.

Alice glared at the phone. Flowers for his mother, indeed. You can't expect to be a partner here if you're going to make excuses like that. Rob was forever buying flowers – and look at all they turned out to mean. Anyway, Tom Lovejoy couldn't possibly have a mother. Men like him didn't have mothers – they just evolved out of a set of very white dentures and a Calvin Klein thong.

She clicked on the computer screen, exasperated. Her next patient's notes flashed up – Frances was not a frequent attendee. Alice frowned.

Half an hour later she still felt uneasy. Frances had had a malignant mole – a melanoma – removed from her calf five years earlier and all had seemed well, but now she had a persistent cough and had been sweating at night. There was fluid in her chest – not much, but Alice was worried. Fluid does not belong on the chests of young women and her inner alarm was sounding very loud.

'I think we need to ask for a chest X-ray,' she said carefully. 'Your chest doesn't sound completely clear. If I give you a form they should do it today or tomorrow.'

Frances pulled her cardigan back on. She was one of those single, bright career girls at which Cambridge so excels. Alice knew she was something important in the physics lab, leading the way in an astronomical research project.

'Should I be worried, Doctor?' She had frank brown eyes,

perfect skin, freckled and very faintly tanned. 'I mean, does it need to be this week? I've a lot of work on.'

Alice frowned. 'Well there is a bit of fluid in your chest so I'd like to have a look. If you're stuck we could arrange it for Monday.' It's knowing how much to say that's the problem, she thought. It would be awful to scare the living daylights out of her if it's nothing.

'OK, Monday it is. We've found a new asteroid, you see. I'm planning forty-eight hours glued to the radio telescope to plot its course.'

'Wow,' said Alice, 'I hope it's not going to hit us.'

'No – this one's a long way off us, we couldn't be that unlucky. Neither could I – I've had my bit of bad luck.'

Alice let it pass. 'It's going well, then?'

'Fine. Great, actually.' Frances stood up. 'I've got a conference in the Bahamas coming up next month. Dozens of lectures on asteroid tracking.'

'How lovely. How long for?'

'Two weeks. It should be fantastic – it's such important stuff. I've always wanted to go to the Caribbean. Sometimes think if I could start again I'd forget astronomy and just go and be a beach bum in Nassau. Drink piña coladas and lie under a palm tree all day.'

Alice laughed. 'I can sympathise with that.'

How many of us, she thought, if we could have our time again, would spend more time being beach bums? It's a good job we don't all do it first time round – the beaches would be packed and there'd be absolutely no one running the tax offices . . .

Her last patient, tagged on the end, was Sarah Benjamin, the Labour MP for Cambridge Villages. She had not expected to be elected. Her constituency was made up of swathes of rural Cambridgeshire, an area about as left wing as the player who runs up and down a football pitch on the right-hand side. But she *had* been elected, albeit with a majority of fewer than five hundred, and she was now the darling of the local press.

Sarah looked tired. 'I've just finished my morning surgery in Fox Colne village hall,' she said miserably. 'Those bloody church bells were going non-stop the whole time – and I never knew people could be so unreasonable. I saw a man who thinks he's the reincarnation of Joan of Arc and wants to address Parliament on behalf of the French, and a woman who thinks the Prime Minister is an alien.'

Alice grinned. 'That's care in the community, Sarah. This is the sharp end. They're probably all the same people I saw in my morning surgery yesterday. Mind you, you have to consider the possibility that they are the ones with the better grip on truth. Did you know the definition of insanity includes that what you believe has to be different from what those around you believe?'

Sarah winced. 'So if enough people believe the PM is an alien . . .?'

'Exactly. We open up the long-stay wards and send all the patients out to run county councils. But how's little Jake?'

'Crotchety,' said Sarah. 'To be truthful, I'm tired of breastfeeding, but they've asked me to carry on.'

'They?'

'You know.' Sarah made a vague gesture with her left hand. 'Looks good at question time, trendy lady in fuchsia breastfeeding on the second row – and if it distracts the leader of the opposition when he's just about to go for the jugular, all the better.'

'Sarah, Jake is eighteen months old, he can't breastfeed for ever. Surely you don't have to listen to them?'

'Oh, you know what they say about men bearing whips,' said Sarah. 'They have a way of getting what they want.' She grinned. 'But I didn't come here to moan. I came to ask you if you'd come to our planning meeting on the future of general practice in Cambridge? We're having a bit of a PR drive at local level. The local press will be there.'

Alice frowned. 'To be honest, Sarah, I'd rather not. Everything's got a bit too political for my liking. The new NHS is only the old NHS without the tea ladies.' And, she added silently to herself, I've had quite enough of the press for a lifetime.

'Sounds like the House of Commons,' said Sarah, 'but I mustn't criticise the Pride of our Nation. Oh, please will you do it? Local MP explains Our Leader's Great Plan to local GPs, that sort of thing? Bit of free advertising for you.'

'Unlike you,' Alice smiled, 'I don't have to advertise. People have an uncanny knack of finding me anyway. Why don't you ask Tom Lovejoy? He might well be keen.'

'Gosh, him,' said Sarah, blushing slightly. 'Fantastic.'

Alice groaned inwardly. Not you as well, she thought. Is there no limit to the reach of this man's testosterone?

After that there were far too many patients wanting home visits. Alice saw her own share (which involved an argument with a traffic warden who clearly thought doctors attending to visit patients were demons sent to try him). She then put James's share on hold for half an hour and called into Martha's shop. Martha had been her best friend since they first became neighbours all those years ago in Fox Colne. Alice hoped for a reviving cup of tea and a moan about the workload and the locum.

Martha, however, could not see the problem with Tom Lovejoy.

'You're just peculiar, Alice,' she said, her customary American frankness delivered in her delicate Pennsylvanian drawl whilst ignoring a group of women peering at the négligés on her rails. Clearly they would not be able to afford them – for if they could she would know them already. There is never any truly new business in shops where knickers are fifty pounds a pair. But Martha was a wealthy woman, who had no time for everyday knickers. She had started her own business at the age of sixteen when her English mother died, making American folk art dolls in her aunt's bedroom, and claiming to local shops that her American father's Amish relatives sent them over by carrier pigeon. By the age of thirty she owned this exclusive underwear shop in Cambridge, within sight of King's College chapel. Martha had a heart of gold, a brain like a scythe, the body of a Siren and a metaphorical shell as tough as hardened steel.

Now she leaned towards Alice conspiratorially. 'No one's asking you to marry the man.' And, as Alice winced: 'I think I ought to meet Tom Lovejoy and check him out for you. Actually, I'm surprised we've never met. Have you been hiding him?'

'He's only been here a month,' said Alice darkly, resenting the teasing and what it implied. 'Why would you have met? You're never ill.'

Martha shrugged. 'But I might be one day. I think I should look him over.'

'Charming men are by far the most dangerous sort,' said Alice, leaning against a cushion and inhaling deeply on Martha's placebo cigarette.

'What are you doing? You don't smoke.'

'I'm trying to change myself.'

Martha peered at her, took back the cigarette. 'Take it from me,' she said drily, 'take up t'ai chi. Much better for you than change.'

It was Martha's view that Alice should never have fled Fox Colne on the back of a greedy estate agent (was there, she wondered, any other sort?) and a desire for change. Problems are never left behind, she liked to say, moving house is just a displacement activity – like trying to remember all of the American states beginning with M during particularly unsatisfactory sex. You may manage to forget the thing that is troubling you, but it only gets bigger for being ignored. And not that she had any unsatisfactory sex, of course . . . though she could remember having it years ago. She sighed.

43

'Anyhow, back to Tom Lovejoy. You've admitted he's charming, then?'

Alice frowned. 'Not to me. But I can see it – you know, in the same way that Jeremy Paxman is at his most charming just when he's going for the jugular.'

'Sounds to me as though you're afraid to fancy him,' said Martha, fixing her with an impaling look. 'In any case, a fling would do you good. You're terribly overdue for it.'

'For what?'

'You know. A really good romp between the sheets.'

'I don't need a romp,' said Alice obtusely. 'I romp all the time.'

'Oh yes? Such as when?'

'When the dog got into bed with me and wouldn't get out,' said Alice flippantly. 'I lost and there were hairs in the duvet for ages.' She tried to look as though the flippancy were just a chance thing, as though it had never occurred to her that sex was something you could miss terribly. 'How did you know, anyway?'

'Alice, I'm your best friend, I would know if you romped. God, I'd let off fireworks if you romped.'

Alice frowned. 'I don't see why.'

Martha sighed and tried to stub out the cigarette. 'Damn – I'm sure the stubbing-out is the bit I really miss. Alice, you can't stay faithful to a dead man for ever. You're a young woman.'

Alice winced. 'I've no intention of staying faithful to him. He wasn't faithful to me, after all.'

'If you really count that,' said Martha carefully.

'What do you mean?'

'As unfaithfulness,' said Martha. 'He wasn't unfaithful, exactly . . .'

'Oh, come on,' said Alice bitterly, 'that's not how I was taught to do a vaginal examination.'

'C'mon, Alice. I mean emotionally. Sex like that is just an appetite some people can't help.'

44

Alice was stubborn. 'He had no right to appetites like that. Anyway, what are you standing up for him for? You said he was a selfish git.'

'And he was,' said Martha, 'but I think you need to accept it as his weakness. You're never going to stop repressing yourself till you do. You don't owe him a life of celibacy.'

'I never said I did.'

'No, but you're making yourself a martyr to it all the same.'

Alice frowned. 'Can we talk about something else?'

'You can talk about Tom Lovejoy, if you like,' said Martha in generous tones. 'Has he got good buttocks?'

Alice rolled her eyes. 'I find the thought of Tom Lovejoy's buttocks quite unpleasant. Actually I'm sick of hearing how gorgeous Tom Lovejoy is. The man has more hormones than a sixth form college and he never stops flattering people.'

'You can't possibly have too much flattery at our age,' said Martha, but Alice shook her head.

'Flattery is like Creme Eggs – the first time is great, the second time is pretty nice, but by the time you're on the tenth you want to throw up.'

'When a woman is tired of Creme Eggs,' said Martha mournfully, 'she is tired of life.'

'If you're so interested in Dr Perfect,' said Alice darkly, 'why don't you just pop in to the surgery and ask him for a bonk? He doesn't strike me as the sort of man to say no.'

'I might just do that,' said Martha, 'if I didn't think you needed him more.'

'He's not my type,' Alice said with a sniff. 'Not even slightly. Not any more.'

Alice was still thinking about the conversation with Martha when she got home that evening.

Is Martha right? Is my sexuality deliberately suppressed rather than just dead? Am I still being faithful to Rob out of some perverse sense of self-martyrdom? Perhaps I should make an effort . . . but not with Tom, of course. So who? It isn't as if they're queuing in the street, after all.

The house looked welcoming, reminding her oddly of Pipe Tree Cottage, which had always glowed with cottagey charm beneath its thatched hat. And for a moment the pain of Rob not being there squeezed her heart so swiftly and efficiently that she put a hand to her chest to check there was nothing there, no metal vice with teeth on it, gripping her ribcage . . . But this house was neither thatched nor cottagey, but square and modern, with windows that were absolutely symmetrical and walls that met at right angles. It was as different from Pipe Tree Cottage as a house could be. Inside it was painted absolutely pure white. No pearly white or mushroom white or warm and friendly not-quite-white – and absolutely no blood red or Georgian blue or deep interior-design terracotta. It was not Rob's house in even the smallest way. It didn't even have a name. It was 23 Herne Road – but somehow that welcoming glow had sneaked in anyway. Somehow there was an air of Pipe Tree Cottage about it, something Rob would have recognised.

He wouldn't have recognised the hebes, though. Some flash of longing for the more beautiful past had made Alice transplant three of the hebes here when she moved, three of those that they had planted when they'd first moved into Pipe Tree Cottage all those years ago, but now looking so sad and bedraggled. She had planted them, in the garden that turned into a jungle, whilst Rob laughed and made cups of tea she never remembered to drink.

Pipe Tree Cottage had been their dream house, hers and Rob's – and the children's too, in the way that young children's dreams are assumed to be those of their parents (only in the teenage years is the awful truth revealed). Perhaps, Alice thought uneasily, I should have stayed and confronted the house, rather than running away and leaving it three miles off in Fox Colne. Would I still have sold it, she wondered, if Rob's heart had given up in the middle of Broomhill, whilst he was shopping in Marks and Spencer for some beautiful, feminine underwear for my birthday – so that I'd never have known it was all a lie?

We had Widor's 'Toccata' at the wedding. I remember walking down the aisle with him, beaming from ear to ear, thinking this was a day we'd look back on when we were old because we'd be married for ever. We got outside and the six Fox Colne bells pealed, and we laughed and laughed because it was supposed to be 'All Things Bright and Beautiful' but it sounded like the theme music from *The Magic Roundabout*. And after that it always did, every Sunday when the bells woke us up, and I thought it always would. It's just one more thing that should still be happening that's gone for ever. Like when he bought his bloody parrot. I remember him saying if it lives to be seventy we'll all three have a party and he and I will dance around the kitchen with our zimmer frames . . . Only I'll be dancing solo now, won't I, in a kind of mad senile *pas-de-une*?

Alice bit her lip in an effort to stop the familiar cycle of thoughts, slammed the door of her car and stalked up the drive blindly, transported back to that dreadful day for the two hundred millionth time. The policeman and police-woman at the door, the words she could not remember them saying but which she knew they must have said – for otherwise, how could she have known? Ridiculous to keep harping back to it – but if only, she thought, if only I could go back to the day before it happened. Not to bring him back – I know I can't bring him back – but couldn't I just have had a few minutes to shout at him before he died, to make him realise what he did to us – to me? A few minutes to ask him what Marcie Crombie had that was worth betraying me for?

Later that evening, when she went to the grave to remind Rob about their anniversary, the churchyard was quiet, gently introspective, the air soft and velvety like a gloved hand on her cheek. For a moment she felt him there beside her. If she just turned her head she might catch a glimpse of him smiling – such clear memories of him sitting in just this spot, watching her sketch, teasing her about those great big glasses she used to wear. She had always liked sketching, then.

Never now, though, she thought – I've lost the heart for it. I lost the glasses too. Well, no, that's not strictly true. I put them in with Rob before they nailed the lid down over him. It seemed the right thing to do when I'd obviously not used them to see what was right under my nose. No one knows except the undertaker and me. And Rob, of course.

She walked slowly to the grave, trying not to imagine it not being there. The grass, recently cut, smelled of life and movement, but Rob's stone was solid, lifeless, settled, absolute proof that memory is only a reflection of the truth, not a truth itself. Because she couldn't remember him dead.

A bunch of wilting chrysanthemums lay on the lump that was Rob's eternal quilt, and Alice touched them gently, wondering if one of the children had been today – not worried that they might come, but worried that they might feel a need to come surreptitiously. Hard to know. She often found flowers on Rob – from patients, she supposed, he had been a much-loved doctor, after all.

The church clock chimed nine, creaking a little because the church council couldn't agree to spend the money to get it serviced, even though they had a fortune stashed in a trust fund and hardly anyone attended the morning service any more because the clock was always thirty minutes out and people weren't sure when the service began.

On Rob's grave another hebe grew, this one lush and young and strong. They had planted it together, she and the children, because she had thought it a good idea for them to do something constructive when the stone went in. You have a funeral, you have a burial – but the stone goes in so

48

much later that its final erection seems rather disjointed from the death. The ground had to settle, they had told Alice, for about a year, and she had thought this rather gruesome, imagining Rob wriggling a little to make himself more comfortable, as he used to do in bed, before adopting his position of final repose. The hebe was flowering, thriving, its roots reaching down to Rob gently, hungrily. Perhaps some of Rob's atoms were already recycled into the white feathery flowers . . . Alice touched one gently, caressing, half a tear in the back of her eye.

Why doesn't my garden grow? I must have spread more compost on that garden than there was soil in the first place, but everything looks sad. Yet Rob just lies here doing nothing and his bloody hebe grows like a triffid.

Far above her head there was a white trail in the sky: an aeroplane, in the world yet out of it, carrying a hundred or more people to . . . who knows what? Different destinations, different stories, different dreams, all bound together briefly by their sharing transport in a metal cigar. For an odd moment Alice imagined that Rob was up there, strapped into a seat next to a well-bosomed *Fräulein* and a skinny Frenchman, on his way somewhere she could not follow. She took a deep breath, controlling a tightening constriction in her throat and fighting the onion which was lodged behind her eyes, meaning to talk to Rob about their wedding and discovering that, now she was here, she could think of nothing to say to him at all.

The plane finished circling and began its descent.

The customs officer watching the CCTV screen at Heathrow as the passengers off the last Hamburg flight came through was thinking about his wife's breasts. Tingling, she had told him they were, and you didn't become a father of six without knowing what that meant. So when an elderly man with a grey beard of unremarkable size looked a little uneasy as he passed the camera the customs officer did not press his buzzer. Why should he? The poor fellow obviously had indigestion. He'd probably had an airline meal. There are times, even in Heathrow customs hall, when a shifty look merely indicates a problem with the bowels and a beard is not held on by glue. Or Pritt Stick, as a Macedonian smuggler had recently tried. (Sadly for him Pritt Stick loses all its powers of adhesion in Heathrow's arrivals lounge due to an odd property of the air-conditioning system.)

So life in the customs hall went on in the usual way. Two documentary crews from rival TV channels continued to attempt a fly-on-the-wall record of the day's events, three very elderly nuns with suspicious waddles underwent a total body search which revealed them, unfortunately, to be three very elderly nuns with arthritis, and a Danish au pair coming to work for a family in Hampstead had her bacon sandwich confiscated.

Outside, at the taxi rank, Herman Banescu, still looking uneasy, hailed a cab, and tried to ignore the niggling feeling of indigestion he had had ever since his flight took off.

'King's Cross,' he told the driver, in perfect English. 'I need to catch a train to Cambridge.'

'You'll not get one till early in the morning now,' said the cabbie. 'Your flight's in too late.'

'Then I shall wait at the station till morning,' said Herman, 'if you wouldn't mind.'

Chapter Three

Alice awoke on time the following morning, sliding into consciousness with a contented sigh. Even as she opened her eyes she could tell that she felt a little better, that no oppressive weight of memory lingered on her chest from the night before. Today was not an anniversary of anything in particular – well, it was the anniversary of waking up late with Rob the morning after their wedding to discover that they had been so exhausted by their wedding day that they had completely forgotten to have sex – but somehow that didn't seem to count for much.

There was only one letter on the doormat, although there were also three bills, two offers of entry to a competition apparently guaranteeing to win her a holiday in the Seychelles, a flyer from a firm offering to clad the front of her house with pink textured gunk, half a dozen envelopes from drug companies trying to persuade her to prescribe the latest extract of pickled tree frog (or wherever they got their ideas from these days) and five medical magazines extolling the virtues of general practice, all filled with detailed tips on how to avoid seeing too many patients, and decorated with gruesome photographs of ingrowing toenails and sore bottoms. All of this Alice knew without actually looking through the mail, since it was the same every day.

The letter, though, was unexpected, and Roland Liversill's home address curled and squiggled ostentatiously across the back of the envelope. It was on expensive paper (obviously) and the header carried all Roland's qualifications in embossed scroll. Alice shivered. She could feel it boring a hole in her skull as she put her contact lenses in. What did he want now? Some complaint about NHS bottoms wearing out the private cushions in the practice waiting area, no doubt.

My Dear Alice,

I have decided that the time has come for me to retire (*frankly, thought Alice, you retired years ago. The rest is just a formality*), and I shall bow out of practice at the end of September. After much thought and with some sadness (*ha, thought Alice*), I feel I am no longer able to support the Lammas practice by allowing you and your partners the use of the premises at a rate so substantially below that which the market justifies. I realise that you will need a certain amount of time to find alternative premises, and I am prepared to allow you until the end of this summer to move out. I must advise you, though, that on 30th September the practice's lease will be terminated and I will regard any fixtures and fittings you have left in the building at that time as my own property.

I both hope and trust that you will soon find an acceptable site for your NHS practice.

Yours ever fondly,

Roland Liversill, MA, MB, BChir, etc.

'Bastard,' said Alice to the letter.

'Bloody bastard, bloody bastard,' said Mordecai cheerfully from his perch up on top of the kitchen dresser, and for once Alice felt inclined to agree with him.

She was still staring at the letter when Anemone came down the stairs behind her, her beaded plaits clacking together like executive toys. She was wearing a T-shirt that looked as though rats had been gnawing on it for weeks, and the sort of roughly ripped jeans that give young men wild dreams.

'Hi, Mum. Are you OK?'

'Fine,' said Alice automatically, thinking, I was till I saw your clothes. Then, when Anemone waited expectantly, added, 'Why, do I look ill?'

Anemone frowned. 'No, it was just – well, I didn't see you when you came in last night.'

Alice headed towards the kitchen. 'Melancholia,' she said. 'I was having a melancholy evening. Don't worry about me, I'll be fine. At the moment I'm more worried about eviction.'

'What do you mean? This is our house. We're not going to be part of a road-widening scheme or something, are we?' Anemone's tone rang with hope. She was a rebel with, as yet, no cause, and would quite have enjoyed a good road protest – particularly in the summer, which is surely the best time to dig a tunnel and live in it with hairy men called Hobbit and Butterfly Joe.

Alice shook her head. 'No, it's the practice. We're being evicted from the surgery building. Roland doesn't want to play with us any more, and now he wants his den back. He's given us only till the end of September to find new premises.'

'Well, that's loads of time, isn't it?' Anemone shrugged. 'You could rent somewhere in the middle of town. Somewhere on the marketplace would be brilliant – really busy. All those American tourists see doctors for every little thing, don't they?'

Alice put the kettle on. 'Are you trying to wreck my day? I don't want to be really busy. Anyway, Americans are the last things we want. We're not insured to treat Americans but we're not insured *not* to treat them either. If they walk into the surgery gasping their last you get sued whatever you do. Your best bet if you see an ill one is to disguise yourself as a Muslim extremist and clear off.'

'Wow,' said Fergus, entering the kitchen with Daisy behind him. 'So what happens if you're on a plane and an American needs treating?'

'You can pretend you're a pathologist,' said Alice, 'that usually works. Mind you, you have to spend the rest of the flight telling grim jokes about body parts and dropping your airline meal messily all over your front just to keep up the disguise. In any case, Americans are the least of our problems. The practice can't possibly move into a new surgery before the end of September. It's completely impossible and Roland knows it. There's nowhere we could rent – we'd have to build. To buy a site and build our own premises would take two years at least, and it would cost . . . Well, it doesn't bear thinking about.'

'So what will you do?' asked Fergus.

'Talk to James. Send a telegraph to our man in the bush, Ian, Lord of the Jungle Tribes. The trouble is, everything takes a week to reach him, so I can't get his views on it just like that. We could offer Roland more rent, but if he doesn't want it I think we might have to start thinking about winding up the partnership. James is due to retire soon anyway, and Ian can always find something else to do. As can I.'

Maybe it will be a relief, she thought, tipping coffee beans into the grinder. I shouldn't see the practice as a last link with a decent part of Rob. Maybe it's time to start afresh . . . I could go into business with Martha. Open a little shop next door to hers, selling sex aids, perhaps – become Cambridge's answer to Dr Ruth . . .

The children were staring at her as though she were Saddam Hussein and Swamp Thing rolled into one, complete with anthrax warhead. Could she have spoken aloud? 'I'm sorry, people, I didn't mean –'

'I should think so too,' said Anemone with indignation. 'Wind it up? Wind up the practice? Mum, what are you *saying*? You can't wind it up and give in to that . . . that creep Roland. He dyes his hair. You can't just give up to a man who dyes his hair, not after all you've done there. Anyway, perhaps he doesn't mean it. You could talk to him, appeal to his better nature.'

'I wonder where he keeps that, then,' said Alice drily. 'In the lost property cupboard together with his sense of personal space and his spiritual generosity, perhaps.' She'd have no chance with his better nature – even if she could find out which year and continent he'd misplaced it in. It was also likely to be an unpleasant experience. Roland had that non-awareness of personal body space which is otherwise found only in dentists, together with a very pronounced halitosis. Alice had always tried valiantly not to mind, as she presumed he could not help it. After all, one can always hold one's breath. (Like Japanese pearl divers she had practised till she could manage a whole ninety seconds, but after that her eyes began to bulge.) She had even tried to like Roland on the basis that it is particularly unfair to dislike a man with such a distressing personal problem. In this, though, she had failed.

But the difficulty was pressing. The premises were entirely owned by Roland Liversill. Many GPs in partnerships jointly own their premises (to which they are usually attached by mortgages the size of the Third World debt) but it is not uncommon to find surgeries entirely owned by one senior partner. In the days when doctors were wealthy and property cheap, actual ownership of the building was not much of an issue in the average partnership – but those days, Alice reflected, were long since past. Particularly in a place such as Cambridge, where the price of real estate was beginning to rival that in central Manhattan and so many people are doctors of one sort or another that landlords and estate agents completely fail to be impressed by mere GPs and are never likely to offer them any sort of special deal.

Rob had once hoped that Roland would sell them the premises at a fair market price when he retired. There had been a gentleman's agreement to that effect for many years – but the failure of the transaction actually to take place had begun to worry Rob eventually. After all, he had told Alice, a partnership in which one partner owns the building can be on shaky ground if that partner turns out to be a slimy rat. Unfortunately Roland Liversill was well and truly that rat, and the premises were in a prime spot to be converted to bedsits and rented at a premium to hard-pressed Cambridge students.

'You could move into the branch surgery,' said Daisy. 'Roland doesn't own that.'

'Don't be daft,' said Anemone. 'It's far too small.'

Alice couldn't help agreeing. It was certainly less than ideal, a tiny listed building in central Cambridge rented from St Alupent's College, with one consulting room and a reception area divided from it by a wall rather less sound-proof than a feather. And it wasn't terribly secure. It had been broken into earlier in the year and the insurance premiums were sure to rise as a result. Although perhaps as a last resort it might act as a stopgap . . . It was something to bear in mind.

'You could move into the Fir Trees,' said Fergus cheerily, whilst shovelling vast quantities of cornflakes into his mouth. 'Fred says you spend most of your free time there anyway.'

Alice shook her head. 'No I don't. They're all pretty healthy – although since you started recommending they took up martial arts I suspect I'm in for a few sprained ankles.'

Fergus looked indignant. 'T'ai chi is supposed to be good for the elderly.'

Alice smiled. 'How did you know that?'

'I read it in one of your journals. The one with the silly horoscopes. It said it was good for strength and balance.'

'I didn't know you read medical journals,' said Alice, surprised, as Daisy muttered, 'What a swot,' into her Rice Krispies.

'It was interesting,' Fergus said crossly, flushing slightly, 'and I thought Fred might like to know about it. He says he lives in a rest home with a load of women but he gets no rest because they're all unbalanced.'

Alice suppressed a smile, then watched him thoughtfully whilst she swigged coffee far too fast. His abiding friendship with Fred Ramsden, one of the Fir Trees' elderly residents, was something she was secretly rather pleased about, given his lack of either father or grandfathers. True, the very greatness of Fred's age made him oddly boyish, but the cross-generational friendship seemed to give Fergus something special.

But then he was special, as his father had been. Was he going to turn into Rob? Alice's heart lifted at the thought. It would be wonderful to see Rob again one day, have him come back in his children. Perhaps Fergus would be a doctor, like his father, the one that everyone loved and admired. But how much of Rob do I want him to inherit? she wondered. After all, for reasons that I've never understood, being Rob turned out not to be as simple as it looked.

As it happened, it was Alice's morning to work in the branch surgery, so she didn't have to face Roland yet. (He had taken to breathing on her hair recently in a manner which just could be casually accidental but, knowing Roland, was certain not to be. Sometimes the thought of molecules of exhaled Roland caught up in the twists of her plait haunted her for hours.) Instead she headed into the centre of town to see a list of patients who would probably all be students wanting either contraception or the kind of vaccines required only by those off on geology field trips to deepest Amazonia. It certainly made for variety and was one of the things Alice had always loved about working in a university town.

Cambridge was bustling the way that a town can when every day is market day, when the fish man has just arrived from King's Lynn with an indecent quantity of turbot, and the bells are chiming in a cacophony of song. Alice parked in her allocated parking space a few hundred yards from the surgery and cut through King's College cloisters, enjoying

57

the play of the shadows in the early summer sunshine. This was such a lovely place to work. What a shame that Roland was part of the package.

The branch surgery was next door to a tea shop, opposite the entrance to Great St Mary's church, and was there ostensibly to provide a convenient point of call for students, but actually to try to score a winning number on the annual Cambridge GPs' league tables for numbers of new students registering with each, something of a competition each year between the practices, whose income was largely based on numbers of patients registered.

She was early. As she cut through King's College she passed the St Alupent's College choir heading back the other way. She smiled and nodded, and they grinned back, the head choirboy doffing his cap rather charmingly. The master with them looked rather harassed – he was desperate to get them out through the Backs before King's College choir emerged from their own chapel and attempted to engage in a clash of personalities of hat-damaging proportions.

As she crossed Kings Parade Alice noticed that the flyposters had been out the night before. The flyers were advertising the latest art exhibition at the Pavilion, Cambridge's answer to Tate Modern. Sadly, the exhibits at the Pavilion provoked similar outrage to those at Tate Modern, but none of the admiration from art critics. Pausing to look at the latest poster Alice could see why. 'Two flakes in mine please – ice-cream kiosks as art', it said hopefully, 'a challenging exhibition of the art of the ice-lolly men for the Third Millennium.' Challenging. You could say that again, thought Alice, but Anemone would doubtless argue its merits in the same aggrieved tones that she had used to defend the exhibition of sausages last summer, the one that had closed early because a heat wave had rendered the smell unbearable.

She smiled to herself and carried on, past the silver shop

and the home-made biscuit place, round the corner by Ryder & Amies, where Rob's name had once appeared on the lists of college sports teams pasted up on their windows, past the tea shop where foreign tourists went to gorge on scones and cream under the misguided impression that they were behaving like generations of Cambridge students (who are, of course, far too poor for cream teas), and completely failing to tip.

As she reached the surgery front door, Jean, the receptionist who had come over earlier to open up, was waiting, holding it ajar. Jean was a dour Scotswoman in her mid-fifties, who always dressed entirely in black and who had so far refused all offers of HRT on the grounds that it was the work of the Devil. Usually she wore an expression of such sombre foreboding that Martha had said there was a real risk of her being mistaken for the Grim Reaper and nailed to a cathedral door. Today, though, she looked even grimmer.

'Jean, what's wrong?'

'Oh, Dr Vane, I'm so glad you're here. I found this old man outside. He arrived on the early train from London, apparently, and has nowhere to stay yet – but he doesn't seem very well. I hope I did the right thing, but I've got him inside. I've already called an ambulance . . .'

Herman Banescu was sitting on the waiting-room floor, propped against a large plastic dinosaur. Intermittently, because of the way he lay on it, the dinosaur drew back its head and said, 'I'm a brontosaurus, ROAR,' in cute American English. It had been known to drive toddlers screaming into the arms of their mothers, and was one of the few toys not to have been destroyed by the ADHD children, whose uncanny ability to wreck everything from toilet-roll holders to blood pressure cuffs rendered most waiting-room toys into bits after a few days. Jean had been unable to reach the off button owing to Herman's slumped person, and he did not look well enough to get off it of his own accord. He had that grey colour that doctors come to recognise very early on in their careers as a cardiac look.

Herman's indigestion had become a little worse on the King's Cross train, and then a little more so – so that by the time he had reached Great St Mary's front door his left arm had seemed twice the weight of the right and his chest had felt as though it were being crushed in a giant vice. He had been unable to reach his final destination, and had found instead a doctor's surgery.

Alice kneeled beside him, opening her bag upside down in her haste, and scattering trial packs of HRT, latex gloves, prescription forms, biros and several ornamental frogs of mixed parentage across the carpet. Fishing in the medley for her blood pressure cuff and stethoscope she put a hand on his wrist. Pulse racing, sweaty, pale . . .

'Jean, could you bring me the oxygen cylinder? Can you tell me your name?'

'I am Herman,' he said, 'Banescu, the museum curator. I have come from Armenia. I see you have many . . . frogs.'

Oh dear, thought Alice, mental confusion, a bad sign. Behind her Jean flapped about trying to find things without knowing what it was she was looking for. Alice rifled through her chaotic bag and found an aspirin and a nitrolingual spray. 'How long have you had the pain?'

'It began – last night. On my flight from Yerevan.'

'I've got a long neck. ROAR,' said the toy behind him, and Alice made a mental note to lose it at the first possible opportunity.

'Here – open your mouth. I'm going to spray something under your tongue, and I want you to chew this aspirin. Have you had any trouble with your heart in the past?'

Herman Banescu managed a rueful chuckle through the pain. 'But yes, I have had much trouble with my heart. Not, I think, though, trouble of the kind you mean. So now I am a dying man and you want me to chew an aspirin? It is true what they say about the British.'

60

Alice smiled slightly. 'Nonsense, it will do you good. Now, you're not going to die. Don't let it be said about Armenians that they give up without an effort.'

'Huh. You have the Mary Poppins syndrome. When can a man be morbid if not when he is having an attack of the heart? And why do you carry frogs in your bag? For what do eccentric English doctors use frogs?'

'Interior decoration,' said Alice brightly, drawing up the cyclimorph injection, and inserting it deftly into the skin at the top of his buttock. 'Why, what do Armenians use them for?'

'Ah,' said Herman, 'many things . . .' He was drifting already. Some people are more affected by morphine than others.

There was something of a commotion as the paramedics rushed into the room with that dramatic and attention-catching kind of rushing-in that only paramedics and six-year-old girls ever manage to perfect. Paramedics love blue-light calls to central Cambridge as they have a special key to lower the anti-traffic barricades to allow them to drive safely yet alarmingly over the cobbles with both blue light and siren going full tilt. Paramedics also love a cardiac case, mainly because they know they are better than anyone else at resuscitating cardiac patients. It gives them a chance to practise their most macho skills, particularly if the patient obligingly goes into cardiac arrest and needs defibrillation. They had arrived, therefore, in a state of excited anticipation.

They were not particularly pleased to find Alice there. When you are expecting to be the first hero on the scene there is nothing more dampening than finding some doctor with an impressive bag and a practised bedside manner has beaten you to it. Still, they swallowed their disappointment admirably. After all, what had they really lost? It was too early for much of an audience, apart from the man outside with the turbot and that receptionist who was doing a

61

passable imitation of the Presence of Death. It wasn't as though they were likely to have got on to *999 Emergency* on ITV from this call, either. These days you have to shin two hundred feet up a steeple or perform mouth-to-mouth whilst waist-deep in active quicksand before a TV crew will even get out of bed for you.

'Morning, Doc,' they said now, with casual heroism.

Alice was relieved to see them. There is nothing a doctor hates more than being alone at a cardiac scene. GPs just don't carry the equipment that's needed, and paramedics bring such an air of efficient coping with their big orange jackets and their state-of-the-art defibrillators.

The toy behind them continued to roar about its identity, much to Alice's chagrin, as it did not do to look foolish in front of the macho end of the medical spectrum. She pushed her blonde plait back over her shoulder and sat back feeling rather helpless by contrast. The paramedics thought she looked gorgeous, looked appropriately macho themselves, and forgave her at once for being there.

It seemed to take no time at all to get Herman Banescu onto a stretcher.

'Thanks,' he murmured at her from behind his oxygen mask. The paramedics lifted the stretcher.

Alice squeezed his hand. 'Don't worry – you'll be fine . . .'

The paramedics were not into allowing patients time for conversation. Time was of the essence, especially in view of the snooker-room competition for the fastest cardiac turnaround time. Of course they were caring professionals and would not dream of trivialising serious illness – but a ploughman's lunch at the Rupert Brooke in Grantchester with Dolores from the switchboard hung in the balance . . .

'MsssTinkaaaaaah,' managed Herman, rolling his eyes.

'I'm sorry?'

'I do think,' said Jean, who had once been a dentist's assistant and who therefore understood the things other people did not, 'he said "Miss Tinkler".'

As Alice saw the now semiconscious Herman being raced out through the door she frowned. Miss Tinkler. Could he be a friend of Tabitha Tinkler? She had said she was expecting a visitor from Armenia. Surely it was too much of a coincidence to think that this could be him? Should she get in touch with her? Or might Jean have completely mis-understood and he said 'It's a stinker' or something? It was odd sometimes – the things that sick people came out with. The things they suddenly felt had to be said. I wonder if Rob said anything before he died. What were his last words?

The question shook Alice like a thunderbolt. Rob had been dead for three years and it had never occurred to her to wonder if he said anything before he died! She should have asked her, asked Marcie Crombie. But how could she have done, when she hadn't even been able to bear looking at her picture in the paper, let alone speaking to her, meeting her face to face? It had all been far too raw for that – and, in any case, the risk was always far too great that he might have died saying, 'You're much more fun than my sad wife.'

But what if Rob had said something profound? The coroner had said he died instantly, of cardiac arrhythmia. But then they always say that. Instantly is just one of those things they say to comfort you because it doesn't make any difference once they're dead. What if he had actually gasped out, 'Tell Alice I'm sorry and I love only her'? Would it make a difference now? In any case, anyone would be sorry if they died whilst they were having sex with a prostitute. As divine judgement goes, it's pretty extreme.

I should have spoken to her, Alice thought now. I should.

She began to put her scattered belongings back into her medical bag – drugs, blood pressure cuff, stethoscope, ENT kit, several frogs. She always had a few in her bag as well as at the surgery, to lend to patients who required them – and those in the bag now were mostly recent library returns, so to speak, awaiting recirculation.

'Nice man,' said Jean from the door. 'Handsome.'

Alice smiled, thinking: I am immune to handsome men, but yes, I did like him. Mind you, he was in his sixties. No threat to me.

The medical bag would not shut when she finished. It would not shut even when she tried to repack it. There were just too many frogs.

When Alice got back to Lammas Surgery at the end of the morning there was a huge heap of papers waiting by her pigeonhole to be sorted out, and there was no sign of Tom Lovejoy. James was in his room, ploughing through the last of the urgent extras who had needed 'on the day' appointments. On the staff notice board was a piece of paper saying, 'Would the Partners and Staff of the Lammas Surgery partnership please ensure that NHS patients do not use the private waiting-room chairs? These are for use of Dr Liversill's private patients only, but on one occasion last week a chair was moved across due to a shortage of seating on your side. Your help in this matter would be appreciated. Roland Liversill.'

Alice wondered if other practices' disputes ever came down to arguing over chairs. No wonder someone had borrowed one. Roland had about twenty chairs on his side of the waiting room and only ever one or two people waiting, whereas at times the Lammas side was crowded to overflowing with nowhere left to sit. She rifled through the papers. The majority seemed to be test results Tom had ordered. Most of the patients they had been done on seemed to be James's. She frowned. There were one or two new diabetics here, from the looks of it. Had James been slipping up and missing them? Was he just stressed, or were these memory lapses a sign of something more serious?

Norma heard her muttering. 'Oh, Dr Vane. Thank goodness you're back. It's been so busy and young Phoebe Hamilton's mother has rung for an emergency visit. Dr Lovejoy had to go out . . .'

64

'Oh, did he?' Tom Lovejoy, she reflected, seemed to have to go out far more than your average, hard-working, nose-to-the-grindstone GP. Far more, actually, than your average hormonally charged wolf in an area where lady wolves are particularly plentiful. Alice wondered whom he had said he was buying flowers for this time. 'And did he see any extras before he gadded off?'

Norma looked reproachful. 'He saw nine extras because James got behind with his surgery, and then he got called to the Fir Trees. Now he's gone to the hospital for that planning meeting with the MP that none of you wanted to go to. James thought someone ought to go and he was rather tired.'

So even Norma's joined his fan club, thought Alice. Mix testosterone with HRT and you get a result Guy Fawkes would have been proud of.

She was obviously meant to feel guilty for suspecting Tom of base motives. Well, OK, he had easily his share of the work and more, and in truth she had no evidence of his womanising behaviour, just her instinctive mistrust of his looks – but why go to the meeting? He wasn't a partner in a Cambridge practice, so the future of general practice in Cambridge was none of his business. So what was he doing at a meeting about local development plans? Perhaps he was networking. Perhaps she should have gone to the meeting herself.

But there hadn't been time, and she wasn't keen on the management side of general practice anyway. Neither was Ian, nor James. Perhaps eventually they would need a partner who took an interest. But not Tom – she couldn't handle working with another handsome doctor.

She was probably being paranoid. Maybe he'd only gone for the free lunch anyway. Or for the women. You got a lot of rather alluring nurses at these primary care meetings – the ones who went into nursing because they thought it would be glamorous, then discovered that stockings were banned, bedpans were unpleasant, theatre work meant wearing blue hats that made your hair flat, and that the only way to look sexy was to jack in the ward work and enter medical management.

'Dr Vane?' Lisa was looking slightly less red-eyed today than yesterday, but only slightly. Dean obviously hadn't come up trumps on the wedding ring front yet. 'Mrs Hamilton is on the phone again – d'you want to take it in here? Oh, and Dean's going to come and see you later this week.'

'I'll take it in my room,' said Alice, thinking: I am, honestly, sympathetic to human misery, but my judgement in the marriage stakes, perfect as it seemed for all those years, turned out to have been appalling. So how on earth can I hope to advise anyone else?

She picked up her phone, 'Hello. Alana?' Alice was rather fond of the Hamiltons, who had bought Pipe Tree Cottage so seamlessly and nicely when she had been so desperate never to see it again – even though they had turned the garden into a neat suburban patchwork plot with nail-clipped edges and topiary chickens and a real garden gnome, and even despite Alana's calling her every time Phoebe had a cold.

'Oh, hello, Dr Vane. I'm calling again about Phoebe. She's had frightful tummy ache all day and I'm afraid it might be her appendix.'

'Whereabouts in her tummy is the pain?' asked Alice, reflecting that those diagnose-your-own-child books had a lot to answer for when it came to increasing parental anxiety.

'It started off around the belly button,' said Alana, obviously upset, 'and now it's on the left. No, the right. Her right – my left – you know – the appendix side. And she's crying and she's been sick and she won't let me touch her. And Duncan's away at an advertising conference in Harrogate, learning how to promote the useless rubbish he

66

sells even more effectively . . .' She was plainly crying.

'Don't worry,' said Alice, reflecting that this is surely one of the most pointless instructions doctors ever give their patients. There were, she felt, some mothers who coped well in stressful situations, some who managed less well – and then there was Alana, who fell to pieces every time she ran out of kitchen roll. It was no good asking her to come down to the surgery – she'd be unable to find her car keys for half an hour, then would almost certainly find a bollard to crash into. 'I'll be over shortly.'

On the way out of the surgery Alice almost fell over Roland, who seemed to be inspecting the back door minutely. Her heart sank. He was going to find something else to be unpleasant about.

Roland was a tall man with a rather military bearing, rangy but surprisingly muscular, with smooth, rather pale skin and a thick growth of positively funereal hair, which Alice was sure owed its colour to a bottle. Many women found him handsome but his way of touching her with his eyes had always made Alice's skin creep.

'Ah, Alice, my dear . . .'

Alice shuddered inwardly. You're meant to be appealing to his better nature, she told herself. Make an effort, Alice. It's obviously important to the children that I don't let their father's practice go.

'Hello, Roland. I was meaning to catch you some time about your letter. I'm not sure that we will be able to—'

'Ah yes.' Roland leaned over her and exhaled overwhelmingly. 'I'm glad you have received it.'

'Well, I was a bit concerned,' said Alice, valiantly trying not to breathe. 'I think moving out before the end of September is rather optimistic. I wondered if you would consider extending the deadline, giving us a little more—'

'Ah, no, I'm afraid it's out of my hands,' said Roland, putting a slightly inappropriate hand on her shoulder. 'We have already agreed that Fawkes College will have the building on the first of October. It was my old college, you know . . .'

'I know,' said Alice, thinking wearily: there are so many photos around the place of Roland at his old college – Roland as president of the Fawkes College Real Gin Society, Roland holding an oar, Roland at a debate, Roland with a pair of horns on his head, looking important amongst a group of other horned students in college colours – how could one not know? 'I just thought you might reconsider in view of the fact that—'

Roland patted her shoulder and then, to her horror, applied a slightly lascivious kiss to her left cheek. '*Dear* Alice,' his lips approached the right one and she fought the urge to duck and run, for Roland had that unsettling way of devouring one with a kiss, 'I am truly sorry to put you in this position.'

The second kiss docked and pressed her skin with what she was sure Roland saw as a seductive graze. She fought the urge to wipe her cheek.

'I have been as generous as my financial adviser will allow to the NHS practice. However, I do feel that your situation deserves more chivalry than good business practice allows, so, my dear girl, if there is any way I can help you *personally* . . .' the lips hovered alarmingly in front of Alice, 'then we really need to talk about things over dinner, you know, on a more *intimate* level . . .'

Alice could stand it no longer. This was not the first time he had propositioned her. Does he do it with all widows, she wondered, or is it because he knows I don't like to slap him?

'Absolutely no need,' she said with Mary Poppinsish briskness. 'I just thought I'd ask you for the sake of loyalty,' she ducked under his arm and headed for her car, 'but you've made things very clear, Roland. We'll sort something out. Goodbye . . .'

'Very well. But I'd still like to discuss this back door.' He sounded rather sinister as she attempted to increase the distance between them by several light years, and she knew he was annoyed at the rebuff. 'There is a small patch of damp on it and I feel that as it has been an NHS door for so many years your practice should shoulder the burden of its replacement . . .'

Alice's car door cut him out and she sighed with relief. So much for appealing to his better nature. What now?

She drove out to Fox Colne with the window open which only slightly increased the volume of air moving into the Morris Minor since it was not a particularly draught-proof car, enjoying the sun and flower scents of summer, of warm air and of well-rotted manure spread on a hundred gardens. But the past is everywhere, waiting to stage small ambushes, and as she entered the village she remembered how she and Rob had planned their lives here when they were students, cycling out from their digs with a French stick, a chunk of Brussels pâté and a bottle of fizzy apple juice to picnic by the church, talking about the future and listening to the bells, daydreaming on the spot where Rob now daydreamed for ever.

They had been happy in Fox Colne – although the village had its problems. It was on the main road into Cambridge, and was frequently the scene of minor traffic dust-ups as unfamiliar motorists took their eyes off the road to gaze at the liquorice all-sort cottages lining the road. Occasionally they were so taken by the wooden sign imploring them to watch out for the baby ducks, that they completely omitted to watch out for anything else, and consequently missed the bend and drove straight into the pond. It was noisy too. The church's six bells were famous amongst campanologists, who came from all over the country to try, with varying success, to make the peal sound out 'Frère Jacques' or 'A Life on the Ocean Wave'. But Alice and Rob had loved the bells – she smiled at a flood of pleasant memories released by a whiff of cut grass, the evocative call of the Fox Hall peacocks and the sparkle of broken sunlight on the rippled waters of the pond. Rob used to say that whatever the bell-ringers intended to play the cacophony always sounded like the theme tune to *The Magic Roundabout*. No one else could ever hear it. No one else ever would, now.

Pulling up at Pipe Tree Cottage was no longer such a wrench. She had been here many times since the Hamiltons moved in, even unexpectedly delivering Phoebe's baby brother Zachary on the hall floor whilst her mother huffed and puffed like the big bad wolf and her father rifled frantically through their Miriam Stoppard book and insisted that the second stage of labour couldn't possibly be due yet because Alana hadn't even started to listen to the Vivaldi. Averting her eyes from the manicured front lawn (it did still pain her to see her beloved jungle trimmed into the shape of ghastly topiary chickens) she knocked firmly on the door – which was still pillar-box red, so those were still Rob's actual brush strokes – and pushed it open.

Inside was completely different from before. The Hamiltons favoured the minimalist look and the house was New England beach house pastel, although Alice could never quite throw off the feeling that the operatic colours Rob had chosen were still there beneath the duck-egg blue, pulsating with life and memory.

It was, she told Alana a little while later, whilst waiting for the hospital to answer the phone and arrange admission of the tearful Phoebe to the children's ward, very fortunate that there was such a helpful armoury of Miriam Stoppard-sourced wisdom available to parents these days. It was marvellous that Alana had spotted what was probably wrong . . .

Phoebe was not impressed. She might look like a delicate blonde angel who wouldn't say boo to a gosling, but she had the lungs of a fire-eater and a streak of obstinacy reminiscent of men who complete the London marathon disguised as the back end of a pantomime horse. Now she

70

howled and howled, and no amount of suggesting that nice nurses bearing ice cream, and play leaders wearing Minnie Mouse costumes might well feature large on the hospital agenda could placate her. It was only when Alice opened her medical bag that Phoebe seemed prepared to negotiate. She would go in the ambulance with the nice men, she said, and she would promise not to bite the nice nurses or the Minnie Mouse play people – just as long as she could take those frogs out of Alice's bag with her.

Alice was delighted at the compromise – one she had reached many times before with other children and other tummy aches. However, if there is one single rule in the whole of medical practice it is that you should never, ever let a six-year-old girl at the same school as your children think that she has got the better of you. So she negotiated back.

'One frog,' Alice said, 'is enough for anyone.'

'Two.'

'One and a pear drop for later.'

'If I can choose my own.' Honour satisfied, Phoebe allowed her mother to brush her hair and arrange it into two pigtails, whilst she contemplated the choice of available frog. There was a wooden one with a pink tongue, a wooden one with jointed legs, and a rather cheerful-looking china one with a wild smile.

'The smiley one,' said Phoebe. 'I'll have him. What's his name?'

Alice smiled, playing the frog game she always played. 'Do you know, I don't think he has a name. Would you like to choose a name for him?'

'Jeremy,' said Phoebe without hesitation and with relentless unoriginality, 'Mr Jeremy Fisher. Can I have ice cream as soon as I get there, then?'

When Alice got back to the surgery, to her consulting room and its hundreds of frogs, most of whom were called Mr Jeremy Fisher, Tom Lovejoy was waiting for her. Treating him to a cool glance she made for the treatment room and rooted in the drug fridge for her lunch, delivered daily by a man in a van who had made a small fortune supplying doctors' surgeries with sandwiches, ready to blame him if there was only one sandwich left and it was cheese and coleslaw again. She was slightly deflated by the discovery of a giant French stick absolutely blossoming with prawns and avocado. Her favourite.

Tom followed her in. 'Alice. Are you OK now?' He beamed his toothpaste beam. God help us, thought Alice, a man with a smile that beautiful could surely not be trusted – as surely as a wolf amongst sheep. She took a stubborn bite of the sandwich. Two prawns and a slice of avocado shot out of one side like bullets and splayed onto the floor. There is mayonnaise on my chin too, she thought, but I don't care.

'Fine,' she managed discouragingly, ruthlessly resisting the urge to find her tissue.

Tom Lovejoy moved a step closer. 'I wanted to speak to you about the planning meeting. They're talking about the expansion of Cambridge practices . . . here, let me,' he whisked out a pristine white handkerchief – what kind of men have ironed hankies? Alice thought. Ones surrounded by pathetically adoring women, surely – and dabbed at her chin with cavalier chivalry. She smelled his sandalwood with reluctant appreciation, and remembered that Rob used to wear citrus. Perhaps citrus masked the scent of Marcie Crombie rather better than sandalwood. She sniffed.

'Alice?'

'What? Oh, sorry. Run that by me again.' Alice knew that it didn't suit her to try to sound like Anita Roddick, but a businesslike manner can be a useful defence against unease, even when you're five foot two, with the kind of fringe that truly only belongs on a pelmet, and you are trying to eat a sandwich shaped like a penis.

'I went to the meeting,' said Tom earnestly.

He makes just the right amount of eye contact, thought

Alice, I'll give him that. She bit the sandwich again. 'Why?' This time three prawns fell out. This is becoming embarrassing, she thought. Perhaps I'd better—

'Here, let me mop up.' Norma scurried in with a J-cloth. 'There's a cheese and coleslaw sandwich left if you'd like it, Dr Lovejoy, although it's only small.' She eyed Alice's sandwich pointedly. Clearly it had been intended for Tom. She obviously thought he was a prawn and avocado man, thought Alice guiltily, so it's probably also she who's been responsible for ordering in my coleslaw-only diet.

'That would be marvellous, Norma,' said Tom, beaming again. 'I missed the lunch at the hospital – I was too long at the Fir Trees.'

'Who did you go to see?' Alice rather regarded the Fir Trees patients as her property.

'No one specific. Mrs Tebbitt was in a twitch because two of the other residents went off in a hurry and didn't tell her where they were going.' He smiled self-deprecatingly. 'Charming ladies of a certain age seems to be one of the few things I'm good at, I'm afraid, so she asked for me.' Behind him Norma sighed, not only audibly but also visibly. Alice winced.

'Where were they?'

'Oh, they'd gone off up to Addenbrooke's to look for a friend of Miss Tinkler – old foreign chap with a heart attack. I gather you sent him in this morning.'

Herman, thought Alice. But what was Tabitha Tinkler's connection to Herman? Old lover? No – he's young enough to be her son . . .

Tom was still speaking. 'Anyhow, after that I went to the meeting.'

'Oh yes . . . ?' Alice was reluctantly curious.

'I went to the meeting,' said Tom, 'because I'm interested.' He twinkled at Alice but she blocked him stonily. 'I thought you might want to hear what was said.'

'So ought James,' said Alice, suddenly remembering that

73

she had meant to catch Anemone at lunchtime and make sure she wasn't going to have a navel stud.

'I did want to speak to James about it,' said Tom, 'but he told me that as he's retiring soon he doesn't feel it really concerns him. The thing is, although I'm only here as a locum I would like to settle down in Cambridge, which is why I went.'

Alice felt her heart sink slightly. This wasn't the first time she'd heard James hinting about retiring soon, and she'd always assumed he'd go on till sixty-five – another five years.

'You don't have to explain why you went,' she said, hoping he wasn't about to ask her directly about a partner-ship. 'What you do in your own time is your business.'

Tom smiled. 'Quite – but I wanted you to know about it since I'm working here at the moment. I wanted to make quite sure I'd told you myself so you didn't think I was manoeuvring in some way.'

Alice was slightly taken aback. 'Well, I appreciate that, but I think you're wasting your time. Planning meetings are all very well, but at the end of them they say, "Oh, we need another surgery in central Cambridge, and we need more doctors to have more appointments," but they don't look at the price of central Cambridge real estate and there's never any money to follow the ideas anyway.'

'I couldn't agree more,' said Tom, and flashed his teeth.

That's me played right into his hands, thought Alice. She raised one eyebrow cautiously and tried to keep the seg-ment of her brain that was worrying about Anemone's potential navel piercing separate from the rest.

'So what's the point?'

'It's the principle of what they want,' said Tom, becoming slightly excited. (Alice had to glare Norma from the room at this point lest she fluttered so much that she took off and hit the strip light.) 'I mean, in principle they're interested in practices opening up in the centre of town.'

God, thought Alice, finding herself liking him suddenly

despite her reservations, was I ever this enthusiastic? I suppose he will make quite a good partner for someone. She nodded cautiously at him. He was only echoing what she thought herself. On the other hand, that 'we' was rather repeated. It implied some sort of jointness between him and Alice other than the shared Hippocratic oath.

'They always are, in principle,' she said, 'but no one can afford to do it. Have you looked in a Cambridge estate agent's window lately? I mean, have you seen the type of cars estate agents drive round here? That ought to tell you something about Cambridge prices.'

'I know. Look, Alice,' Tom smiled earnestly, 'have you had any thoughts about premises once your lease runs out? I mean, four months isn't long . . .'

He never gives in, thought Alice. *I didn't want you to think I was manoeuvring*, indeed! She'd bet James had told him that Roland was calling in the lease. James thought so highly of Tom he'd probably told him her life history too.

'I've had several thoughts,' she said cautiously thinking, unfortunately the most appealing one is to murder Roland, 'it's just a matter of the partners sorting out the options.'

'Obviously,' said Tom smoothly, 'but if you draw a blank on what to do, and given the attitude of the meeting today, I had an idea.'

'Tom, we're fine. Look, I don't want to discuss this. Really. This is a particularly bad moment.' Alice didn't like him trying to sweep her off her feet. She could sense him doing it – not in the romantic sense, admittedly, but in the sense of trying to take it all on, sort it all out. She had met that personality before, believed it, married it. You let them take it all on, you let them solve it all for you, you trusted them . . . and where did it leave you once you were betrayed? Starting again, that's where!

Alice took a huge defiant bite out of the sandwich and the rest of its contents hit the floor, leaving her trying to chew the crust of a French stick with dignity.

Tom offered a Gallic shrug, effectively conveying the feelings of a man who is only trying to help, a man who feels that if his efforts are not appreciated then that would not be a problem, because he and Gérard Depardieu are cast in the same, phlegmatic mould.

'I just wanted to let you know I'm on your side, Alice. Tell me,' he hesitated briefly and looked a little abashed, 'what do you like to eat?'

Alice tried not to look at the trail of prawns and mayonnaise gracing the linoleum. 'Most things,' she mumbled rather weakly through a mouth full of crust.

'Well then, I just wondered . . .' he had awkward shyness off to a tee, she thought, 'whether you might like to have supper with me.'

You must be joking, thought Alice. She swallowed her mouthful without chewing it properly. 'I'm . . . sorry. Baby-sitters, you know. I don't like to . . .'

'Well, in that case, why don't I come and cook for you at your place?'

Alice gasped mentally, trying to find a way of saying no that was unambiguous and yet not too rude. Whatever did I do, she thought, before I met Rob, about unwanted invitations and attempted pick-ups? What socially acceptable get-lost lines did I use? I don't remember any. In my adult life there was only ever Rob. Is Tom Lovejoy asking me out? I'm not sure how you tell.

Indigestion seized her, as sudden and ghastly as if ten giant Marks and Spencer sales staff had rushed through the door, pinned her to the ground, and forced her to eat an entire dish of ready-to-microwave sprouts. 'I . . .' she floundered.

Tom looked contrite. 'I'm sorry. Of course. You're busy. I should have . . . I do tend to let my enthusiasm carry me away. I don't know many people in Cambridge, you see. I did ask James and Marjorie over for supper but I think James must have forgotten to pass the invitation on.'

76

He's lonely, thought Alice with a jolt of guilt compounding the pain in her stomach, and I've hurt his feelings. I suppose he might just be a person underneath the charm. Now I feel a heel.

She heard her own suddenly reassuring tones. 'Look, why not come for supper – come tomorrow evening. I'll be cooking for the children anyway.'

Why can GPs never resist the urge to reassure? That's why they endlessly come out with useless pieces of advice for panicking patients, like 'Don't worry', and 'Drink plenty of fluids.' What else would you drink, for heaven's sake? Alice was aware of Norma beaming wetly from the doorway, and fought a serious urge to throw a box of elastic support hosiery at her. 'I was going to say, actually I'm cooking anyway, as a friend is dropping over.' Please, Martha, be free tomorrow, because if you're not I might actually kill you.

'Oh goodness, I wouldn't want to intrude. Perhaps another –'

'A female friend,' said Alice, thinking darkly: Don't push your luck, matey, or the deal's off. 'And you won't be intruding.'

'I don't think I should come,' said Martha on the phone half a minute later. 'It's time you had a man. I don't want to play gooseberry.'

Alice felt sudden sparkles of defiance in the backs of her eyes. 'He's a colleague, not a man. I don't want a man,' she said tightly, 'and if I did I'd rather have Rasputin than him.' I want Rob back. I don't care about any of the rest of it. If only he hadn't been to that woman. There was nothing wrong with our sex life. *I thought I knew him better than that.*

Martha heard the voice. 'I'll bring the starter,' she said, 'you do your meringue thing.'

She hung up, leaving Alice staring at the phone. My meringue thing, she thought. Now there's something I haven't made for years.

Chapter Four

Alice finished at five on Thursdays, so she drove up to Addenbrooke's, Cambridge's hospital and the place where she and Rob had trained, on her way home, steering with one hand whilst attempting to retune the radio to something playing music. Unfortunately there seemed to be absolutely no music on it at all today – just a mixture of news and the kind of phone-in programmes that send people to sleep in traffic jams on the M25. There must be, Alice felt, having been listening to a particularly painful phone-in, a special bank of tame callers kept at Broadcasting House and fed on bland food and decaffeinated coffee, ready to be put on air to fill the gap whenever a producer had to use his cut-out button because a real person had phoned about something unacceptable. General practice had taught Alice that most people's problems are unacceptable, especially for airing on local radio, so when they got through they were inevitably cut out and replaced by Pauline from Braintree with her question about getting a rash on her hands whilst arranging hyacinths. As she gave up and turned off she thought, are we really meant to believe that people only ever phone live radio shows with problems about hands and hyacinths? Surely dozens must ring in with worries about foreskins and incontinence, and the difficulty inherent in inserting suppositories when wearing a truss.

Miraculously, there was a parking space at Addenbrooke's. The only place more difficult to park than Addenbrooke's, Fergus had said recently, was the surface of

Mars, which had no proper car parks at all and had thus proved extremely inhospitable to computerised exploration vehicles.

Phoebe ought to be awake by now.

Not far away, Herman Banescu lay on the coronary care ward connected to a drip, a drug infusion pump, a monitor and his bed. The monitor beeped annoyingly every so often, reminding him that there was something that he had lost. He had no idea what it was. The staff would not let him leave his bed, not even to pee. This was very frustrating when he had been, for all of his life, a healthy man.

'You don't understand,' he tried again to the ministering angel in blue, 'I have lost something, and it is essential that I find it. It is very important.'

The nurse, although young, was quite senior, as all the older nurses had retired through stress. She had modelled herself on the giant and intimidating *Carry On* matrons and was both authoritarian and impassable. Indeed, the combined mass of the elderly residents of the Fir Trees had been unable to get past her to see Herman, not even when Tabitha Tinkler suggested she herself had a bad heart and should be wheeled into the next bed on that account. The nurse was called Sister Annette Goodenough, and she had heard that one before.

'Mr Banescu,' she boomed, in the kind of voice which could well have caused a blip on the seismic activity readouts at the earthquake monitoring centre in Stoke-on-Trent. Indeed, he thought whimsically, if a butterfly could flap its wings in the Caribbean and thus cause a hurricane in the Far East, it was dreadful to contemplate the effect that Nurse Goodenough's voice might be having upon some distant corner of the world. At the very least one might expect a tidal wave sufficient to submerge Fiji. 'You are on a coronary care unit, and you are confined to your bed. This is a peaceful, low-stress environment. We do not make telephone calls. We do not leave the room. We rest, Mr Banescu, and we recover. And it is time, Mr Banescu, to see if we can pee.'

Herman Banescu had withstood years of totalitarianism and cabbage soup through having a patient mind and a defiant spirit. But Sister Goodenough was a different kettle of fish. He would defy her too, of course. But later.

A short distance from Herman, Phoebe Hamilton lay on D3, the children's ward, surrounded by soft toys and get-well cards. Her two blonde plaits lay across her pillow where she had arranged them for maximum princess-like effect. There was a bowl of Mars bars beside her bed, and her mother had instructed the nursing staff in no uncertain terms that Phoebe was not to be expected to eat prunes.

She put a cautious hand down to the dressing on her abdomen, and wondered how many stitches she had, numbers of stitches being something of a glory count at St Alupent's School. She was pleased to have had her appendix out because this, Mummy had explained, meant that she could now go to the moon. Mummy said that astronauts had to have their appendix out before they went to the moon, in case the appendixes went wrong when they got there – and Phoebe was off to the moon – just as soon as she was a princess, because she was going to be the first princess on the moon.

'Hello, Phoebe, how are you? Hello, Alana. Where is little Zachary?'

'Oh, hello, Dr Vane.' Alana looked up from her book. It was, Alice noted with interest, *Passion in the Library* by Esme Smuts. Wasn't that the outrageous one about the vicar who seduced the librarian in the mobile library? I wouldn't have had Alana down as a lust-and-ripped-bodices type, she thought, but then I've already proved in a big way that I'm no judge of other people's romantic appetites. 'He's at my mother's; I couldn't possibly cope with him now that Phoebe is so poorly.'

Alice suppressed a smile, surprised that Alana could cope with any children at all. 'Oh, I see,' she said.

'It is nice of you to come. Dr Lovejoy popped in earlier as well. He brought Phoebe a lovely stuffed rabbit.'

Alice raised an eyebrow, then hastily lowered it. It would not do to look disparaging about a partner, even a temporary one. Actually, she had often reflected, doctors are so loath to criticise one another to patients that even if you discovered you had been working for fifteen years in partnership with the Beast With No Name, then as long as he did his fair share of cervical smears the accepted norm would be to explain to patients that a little halitosis can be caused by gland trouble and excess bodily hair is often associated with stress. You certainly wouldn't express any doubts about which species, precisely, he belonged to. Not to a patient.

'Dr Lovejoy wears perfume,' said Phoebe, in the archly observant tones that six-year-old girls are so particularly good at, 'and all the nurses like him. They went all goofy when he came in. It's *so* yucky.'

Hooray for a bit of serious appraisal, thought Alice smugly, whilst Alana flapped her hands like a hysterical Victorian and gasped an apology.

'It's because she's annoyed that he didn't send her into hospital when he saw her last night,' she explained anxiously, 'but he was awfully nice.'

'Don't worry.' It struck Alice that some women spend their entire lives trying not to offend. Not me, she thought. 'I'm sure Phoebe didn't actually have full-blown appendicitis when Dr Lovejoy saw her. In the early stages it can mimic other things.'

Phoebe arched a brow. 'I liked your frog better. Dr Vane, did you really used to live in our house?'

'Er – yes.' Alice was caught off guard. 'But it was a long time ago.'

81

'Before I was born?'

'You were a baby.'

'Why didn't you want to live there any more?'

'I thought I'd try somewhere different for a change.'

'Is it nicer?'

'It's – not as pretty,' said Alice, surprising herself.

'Why don't you move back to our house, then?'

'Phoebe,' said her mother firmly, 'tell Dr Vane –'

But Phoebe persisted. 'Why don't you? I'd like you to.'

'Well, there isn't really room for me with you in it,' said Alice, smiling.

'But we're moving,' said Phoebe. 'Daddy says we're going back to Dubai.'

'Phoebe. Tell Dr Vane why Dr Lovejoy said you needed your appendix out,' said Alana, wincing visibly.

Phoebe was diverted at last. 'Cherry stones,' she said proudly. 'He says I got it from eating the stones in my cherries. And,' she paused for effect, 'he says if I don't stop then trees will come growing out of my ears.'

'Does he now?' So he's got Phoebe eating out of his hand, thought Alice. It's impressive.

Phoebe looked proud. 'I'm checking every day for leaves.'

'How's your tummy?' asked Alice, deciding to ignore any possible ethical problems involved in supporting this glaring untruth.

'Sore.' Phoebe looked coquettish. '*He* said ice cream and Smarties would help.'

No need to ask who he is. 'I'll tell you what, I'll ask him to come and see you again tomorrow.'

Phoebe beamed.

'I'm sorry, Dr Vane,' said Alana, walking with her to the door of the children's ward, 'I was going to tell you. Duncan has been offered a job in Dubai for two years – we're all going. We're putting Pipe Tree Cottage on the market.' She hesitated, before adding, 'That is, of course, unless you want to move back.'

82

'Oh goodness, no,' said Alice, as automatically as if someone had asked her if she would like her gall bladder removed without anaesthetic. 'We're quite happy where we are.'

Is that true? she wondered, as she walked back through the hospital, and even if it is, is *quite* happy honestly fair to the children? Don't I want more than that for them? Don't I want more than that for me?

Alice drove back towards Cambridge trying to chase all conscious thoughts out of her head and throw them where they belonged, in the ridiculous thoughts bin. On impulse she pulled into Sainsbury's car park, wrestling with her conscience. So Pipe Tree Cottage would be for sale. Well then, that would mean that someone else would live in it, and that would be fine. Perhaps they would paint over the red front door at last, then all of Rob's handiwork would be gone. There was no need to tell the children – there was nothing worse than knowing something you could do nothing about. Nothing. Because they couldn't possibly move back.

They could afford to. Since Rob died they could afford to. Life insurance may be a peculiar joy in such circumstances, but it brings security. It was a mad idea, though. Mad. She had too many other things to worry about. The practice, to begin with. With Roland's current attitudes to his former partners, and the absence of any suitable property in Cambridge, it was difficult to see how things were going to be resolved for the practice. That was what she needed to concentrate on.

Yet Pipe Tree Cottage was for sale. Alice knew what the children would say. She knew they would want to go back. When she had left there had been no shortage of people telling her what a mistake it would be to move, how sorry the children were, how they used almost their every breath to tell her so. Alice had ignored them all, citing a need to move on. But then, nothing truly had moved on, had it?

Throwing away her specs hadn't changed her one bit and moving house had simply moved all her Rob-based misery and disbelief with her. You couldn't expect anything else, really. Maybe it would be a relief to go back, to stop trying to prove to everyone that Rob was gone and forgotten, to admit that she still couldn't quite believe it had been him she had lost that day.

Carefully she allowed her mind to go into idle, like a punt without a pole, drifting gently over the idea of moving back to Pipe Tree Cottage, to waking there in the morning and remembering Rob, to being back where she was last truly happy. Of course, he was still dead, whether they lived in Herne Road or in Fox Colne. Maybe moving back would make it easier to see that.

Or do I secretly think I can get nearer to him again that way? she mused. Am I afraid he's drifting away with the years? That getting angry with him is actually all that's left?

Fergus had stopped at the Fir Trees on his way home from school, as indeed he did most evenings, and found his good friend Fred Ramsden, the oldest resident, sitting in the back garden contemplating a pair of peacocks as they trawled his flowerbeds for slugs. Fred was the sole man living at the Fir Trees. There was a long waiting list for places, and he was the only man who had ever got to the top of it. Fergus had never really understood why he'd wanted to be there – Fred certainly didn't need looking after and he did just as much gardening now as he had during his employed life. He particularly fascinated Fergus because he claimed to have made his fortune from turning peacock dung into gold.

'My delphiniums,' he said, as Fergus drew up a chair beside him, 'will be popping up shortly. If you like I could teach you about the secrets of my delphiniums. Let you have some fertiliser for your mum.'

Fergus, though, was not easily impressed by delphiniums. For him they came somewhere a long way down in the priority order of everything – lower, even, than sorting out his sock drawer and giving Daisy back the calculator she thought she had lost. He had, however, a fair idea that for Fred delphiniums were right up there along with breathing, eating and surfing the Internet, his newest hobby, so he said, 'That would be good. Nothing grows in our garden.'

'Why's that, then? Doesn't your mother like gardens?'

Fergus looked sage. 'She used to do the garden a lot when we had our dad. Anemone thinks it's because he died.' He gazed solemnly at the soil, sensing that more things had changed with the loss of his father than could be counted with the seeing eye, without fully understanding why. 'Actually,' he added wistfully, suppressing the slight feeling that he was being disloyal to his mother, 'we had loads of fun in that garden. We used to play hide and seek, and Dad said he'd build us a tree house. He never did do it, though.' It was the first time, he realised, that he had consciously thought of something Dad had not been great at. But then, you can't do everything, and tree houses take time.

'That's what gardens are for,' said Fred. 'You should sort your mum's garden out. Give it a mulching. I make the best mulch in the world, you know. How did you get on with the Internet?'

Fergus sighed. 'I tried a search on alchemy. Mr Blackwell says that alchemy would be how you turn dung into gold. There were billions of references on it, but some of them were pop groups and loads of them were weirdos. I couldn't find any formula for making gold, though, so I think you're teasing me.'

'Ah well,' said Fred, 'that just goes to show.'

Fergus was frustrated. 'But you said you got rich from turning dung into gold and you said it was on the Net. You have to give me a clue.'

'Ah,' said Fred inscrutably, 'perhaps I'll tell you how I do

85

it one day. I'll tell you what – I'll let you have some of my compost for your mum's garden. That'll do the trick.'

It must be great to be as old as Fred, thought Fergus, from whose vantage point of twelve the coming teenage years looked fraught with dangers and humiliations. It must be great to be old enough to have passed all that girlie stuff and not have to spend your days worrying about whether one of the girls fancies you or that you might suddenly find you fancy one of the girls yourself. Instead you can just sit around designing compost and being cheerfully nutty. I hope I'm cheerfully nutty, thought Fergus, when I'm his age. I wonder how old he really is. How old do you have to be to get into the Fir Trees?

When he got home Fergus found Daisy examining her abdomen in the living-room mirror. This involved her standing rather precariously on a soft chair and leaning heavily to the left.

'Hi, Fergus, what do you think?'

Fergus regarded her thoughtfully. 'You look like a refugee from a Turkish bordello who's put on only half her disguise.'

Daisy sighed. 'I should have expected you to be juvenile. When you want a sensible, considered opinion it's always best not to ask a square-eyed computer nerd who keeps all of his brains in his clarinet.'

'If you could play the Elgar,' said Fergus, with as much blazing scorn as he could muster – which is, sadly for twelve-year-old boys everywhere, so much less than girls of the same age can manage – 'then perhaps you wouldn't be so jealous.'

'You're the jealous one,' said Daisy, stung into childishness by the echo of truth in his words. She did struggle with the Elgar. The trouble with being fifteen is that it's old enough to notice the truth in other people's arguments without being old enough to formulate a swift withering reply.

86

'I don't see why you think I'd be jealous of you having a bit of coloured glass embedded in your navel,' said Fergus rudely. 'Like I said, you look like Aladdin's mistress. I hope that was a sterilised emerald.'

Daisy sighed. 'It's for my belly-dancer costume and it's only glued in. Trouble is, I used your stupid model glue and now it won't come off.'

'Serves you right for touching my stuff,' said Fergus territorially. 'It'll probably never come off.'

Daisy was accustomed to Fergus. 'I expect it'll wear off.'

'It won't,' said Fergus, 'or my Thunderbird Five would have fallen apart by now. Why d'you want to belly-dance, anyway?'

'It's for auditions at school,' said Daisy, who secretly hoped a more exotic look might get her where she wanted to be on the boy front.

'Mum might have something to say about it,' said Fergus dubiously, wondering if his fantasy *Baywatch* babe would have been to belly-dancing classes when she arrived to beg for a date.

Daisy shrugged. 'Promise you won't tell her? It's a surprise.'

'Oh yeah? Like you said not to tell her because it was a surprise when you spilt blue ink all over the bathroom carpet? That sort of surprise?'

'That was different,' said Daisy, 'and you know it. Come on, Fergus, I know you can keep a promise.' Appeal to his better nature – he just might be old enough for it to be functional.

He wasn't. 'What's it worth?'

'A pound.'

'Three.'

'Two.'

'OK.'

'Good.' Fergus accepted with a show of reluctance. He would have settled for one. It would go into his fund for the new clarinet – the brilliant one in the music shop. Then he remembered what he had meant to say. 'D'you think Mum can't grow stuff in the garden because she's sad?'

Daisy was startled. 'I don't know. Perhaps. But she can't help being sad.'

'But maybe she's sad because of the garden. Maybe if it was nicer she'd be happier. Fred said we could have some compost for it . . .'

'Don't be daft,' said Daisy dismissively. 'It's not something you can fix with compost. You have to want to do it and she just doesn't. Oh, look. She's back. You'll have to stop talking crap now.'

Fergus sniffed. 'Well, I'm going to try. Fred says . . .'

But Daisy wasn't listening, she had gone to open the door. 'Come on. Shopping to fetch in. There might be chocolate biscuits.'

'If you get any more of a belly,' said Fergus, trailing sulkily after her, 'you'll have to give up belly-dancing in case you knock people out with it when you swing it around.' He expected a reaction but Daisy had shut her ears.

Some distance away in Fox Colne the bells were clanging unnaturally as a group of campanologists from Staines tried to manage a six-way chime. Martha Coleman unwrapped a Marks and Spencer's salmon hollandaise and put it into her microwave to warm whilst she poured a glass of Chablis and slipped her feet into the kind of high-heeled mules that drive young men wild. Running an eye along her CD collection she hovered briefly over a Rachmaninov piano concerto – but no, that sort of thing could put you in a dangerous mood, and look where romance had got almost everyone she knew. Martha was no romantic. True, *Brief Encounter* was her favourite film – but that was absolutely not because it was romantic, it was because her mother had watched it endlessly whilst Martha was in the womb. And look what romance had done to her mother.

She frowned and instead chose Jacqueline du Pré playing the Elgar Cello Concerto. And for a brief moment, as she sank into those passionate opening chords with a tingling sense of tragedy and bliss, she wondered whether Alice really did fancy Tom Lovejoy. He sounded quite presentable – although not on her scale, of course. Available men were rarely presentable on Martha's scale, and in Tom's case he was particularly not presentable since he worked with her friend and could well be sticking around for a while. She might therefore have to see him more than once, which ruled him out on the sex front. Still, it was interesting to wonder what he would be like.

'I thought I might get my ears pierced again,' said Anemone casually, chopping onions for supper, 'instead of my navel.'

'Gross,' said Daisy, from the depths of a peanut butter and fish finger sandwich. She never, on principle, ate with her family on the days when Anemone cooked. It was all far too vegan. Daisy would have a burger any day, even if Fergus was right and they were made from cows' udders.

'That's only your opinion,' said Anemone, who was not too old for a good bicker. 'We all have to project our own image.'

'Don't you ever wonder,' asked Fergus cheerily, 'whether the one you project might look better on someone else? Someone out of *Star Trek*?'

Anemone shrugged and shook her hair beads smugly. 'What would you know about fashion? Your idea of trendy is having Godzilla on your pyjamas.'

'Well, I think you look stupid with all those holes in your ear,' said Daisy, secretly glad to have Anemone riled. 'Just imagine how it'll be when you're old. You'll be sat in an old people's home looking like a used tea bag – all floppy and wrinkly and full of perforations.' She found Anemone's eccentricity peculiar. She herself aspired to look like the young Jacqueline du Pré, all intensity and passion.

89

'That'll be fine,' said Anemone, stung, as Alice sidled through the kitchen door half concealing a carrier bag, 'because all the other old ladies will have three holes in their ears too. Except you, of course; you'll be the miserable one in the corner complaining about old people nowadays and refusing to pull crackers on Christmas Day.'

'What's this?' Alice dropped her bags and put her car keys somewhere that she would almost certainly forget about later. She had pulled herself back from the brink of melancholy and cheered herself up by buying a wonderfully tasteless furry frog from a craft stall on Cambridge market.

'Anemone's having more holes in her ears,' said Fergus.

Alice shrugged. By the time your children reach seventeen you have long since realised that you have no control over them whatsoever. 'No tattoos, then?' she asked brightly.

Daisy glowered, expecting more – but at least Mum wasn't all miserable like yesterday. She'd gone off in the car last night and then come in and gone straight to bed, even though it was only ten o'clock and there was a *Red Dwarf* repeat on in half an hour. They'd all known she'd been to the churchyard – but when Granny rang the unspoken agreement to say she was in the bath had surfaced and so no one had told the truth.

'She'll look stupid when she's old,' Daisy said grouchily.

'Won't we all,' said Alice happily, 'and some of us don't have to wait to be old. Anyhow, if it's any consolation I'll probably be sitting in the next chair to you, Annie—'

'Anemone.'

'Anemone. Sucking my pureed beans on toast through my toothless gums and cackling at Daisy when I glimpse her through the holes in your ears.'

'Ugh,' Daisy shuddered, 'is that what it's like at the Fir Trees?'

Alice peered over Anemone's shoulder at the developing dinner and wondered about a takeaway kebab. Shared chores were all very well, but they started to lose their appeal when they resulted in an evening meal of alfalfa and tofu every third day. 'Actually, no,' she said, 'not at all. They've all got more about them than most patients I see. They do t'ai chi, gardening, go to Alton Towers – more than most of them did when they were young, I should think. What's that?'

'It's an adaptation,' said Anemone happily. 'I took a Delia recipe and made it vegan.'

'Did that leave anything actually in it,' asked Fergus, 'other than the olive oil and the onions?'

Anemone sniffed. 'And the garlic. Then I added tofu and alfalfa. And you'll thank me,' she added darkly at Fergus' expression, 'when everyone else in the whole world collapses with vitamin deficiency and you don't.'

Fergus rolled his eyes. 'I'll look forward to that, then.'

'I'm going out for a burger,' said Daisy, 'I don't suppose someone else would like to pay?'

'Ha,' said Alice, thinking, I could almost fancy a burger too, whatever Fergus says about them.

'You mean an udder burger,' said Fergus, on cue. 'They have bits of udder in them, you know, and Daisy glared and left the room noisily.

'Oh dear,' said Alice, 'I wish you wouldn't argue with her.'

'I don't argue with Daisy,' said Fergus, 'ever. They warned us at school about PMT so I keep very quiet and Daisy just moans at me. That's bad enough – it's like being nibbled to death by budgies.'

Alice was curious. 'What else did they tell you about PMT?'

Fergus shrugged. 'That women go bonkers once a month and it's better to agree with everything they say. I said it would be difficult to tell when my sisters didn't have PMT

91

in that case, and Mr Blackwell laughed and said he could well believe it.'

Alice smiled. She liked Mr Blackwell, even though he had a perfectly ridiculous beard (there was, she felt, no other sort). She liked the way he seemed to give Fergus a little of that something that was missing since Rob . . . It's rotten for Fergus not having a father, she thought. More rotten than for the girls, in many ways, since they only had to learn to be women, like her, whereas he had to learn to be a man like his father. Perhaps not too like his father.

'That art exhibition's still on at the Pavilion,' said Anemone, who was doing A level art and liked to feel her taste was rather avant-garde. 'It's brilliant.'

'What is it this time? Another giant heap of disposable nappies and a pile of recycled compost, like the last one?' Daisy, sidling back in as no one seemed to have noticed her going off in a huff, had a very low opinion of what Anemone thought constituted art.

Anemone looked superior. 'That was a statement about the way a society's waste defines it. And anyhow, that was ages ago. This is the one about commercial art . . .'

'Oh, the ice-cream kiosk exhibition.' Daisy was still not impressed. 'That's not art. Elgar is art. That's ice cream.'

Anemone glared. 'Well, Elgar isn't art the way you play it.'

'That's true,' said Fergus smugly. 'She should have learned the clarinet . . . Ouch!'

'Don't throw alfalfa,' said Alice mildly, 'it might set seed and you know how fast it grows. I'll tell you what, Anemone, I'll buy you a ticket if I can borrow your astrology book.'

Anemone folded her arms. 'You're not doing astrology again for that *Doctor* magazine of yours? That's awful. You're such a fraud.'

'Why? It's only a joke column.'

'People might believe what you say and make life

decisions based on it. And you know I'd be much better at it. I know about planets and birth charts.'

'You wouldn't, you'd be rubbish. You read my birth chart and said I was going to be a crappy cellist and ought to train as a kangaroo tamer.' Daisy was up in arms.

'That was a joke, stupid.'

Alice shook her head. 'I'm only doing it for a few weeks to fill in till they find someone else.'

Anemone waved her arms excitedly, as teenage girls do when they spot a chance to earn money for very little work. 'I could do it. At least I'd be a proper astrologer.'

Alice smiled. 'Well, I'll ask them if you can do it. You never know – this could be your chance to change the world.'

Later that evening Martha called round and sat at Alice's kitchen table trying to draw her on the subject of Tom Lovejoy and regarding the ghoulish collection of medical journals upon it rather warily.

'Shouldn't I bring a bloke of my own? We'll be a man short . . . Honestly, Alice, how on earth can you read this stuff?'

'It's very important,' said Alice, stirring things in preparation for tomorrow's supper, 'to keep up to date. That one is particularly good. And no, I admire your constant flow of handsome devils but one smoothie is quite enough in this house.' And one smoothie was quite enough to last me a lifetime.

Martha leafed through. 'Oh my God.'

'What?'

'It's got a giant picture of a penis in it. That's disgusting.'

Alice looked. 'Well, yes, it is, rather, but in articles on genital diseases you have to show these things. That's a diseased willy.'

'God, I wouldn't have your job,' said Martha, 'looking at all those bottoms.'

'It's much the same as selling underwear, I should think,' said Alice cheerfully, 'but at least I don't have to pretend to admire them.'

'You should read the horoscopes,' Anemone said, rooting in the fridge in search of a perfectly grilled aubergine topped with yogurt and chopped tomato, her portion of the tofu and alfalfa having been surreptitiously consigned to the bin. There wasn't much hope of finding one, of course, but she did find a leek. She took a huge bite, crunching the layers and releasing its sweet fresh smell to pervade the kitchen. Martha winced, and turned to the horoscopes.

'Dr Iphigenia Probe? What will they think of next? Probably some miserable old bloke in a grey suit making it all up. Listen to this. "Taurus. The appearance of Venus and Mars in your sign means that love is on the horizon but should be viewed with extreme caution. In particular, avoid Sagittarians, and do not on any account enter into business with anyone called Tom." God, Alice, that is just so weird. You're a Taurean. That could be written for you.'

Alice said nothing; she was deeply absorbed in thickening a sauce.

'What about Pisces?' asked Fergus cheerfully. 'Anemone's a Pisces.'

Martha read, ' "You may feel the urge to have an extra earring inserted somewhere this week. Resist it, or you risk contracting acute fin rot and developing a permanent list to the left." '

'I could do much better,' said Anemone. 'Mum's got no idea about astrology.'

Martha raised a perfect eyebrow. 'Alice Vane, are you writing these horoscopes? You dark horse . . .' There's hope for her yet, she thought.

Alice grinned apologetically. 'I started doing it a few years ago when they needed an astrologer at short notice. Rob was a proper columnist for them, you see – he wrote serious articles about liver disease and piles. He suggested

94

me for the lightweight stuff.' And, as Martha frowned at that, she added quickly, 'I stopped doing it when he died, but they occasionally ask me to do another one. Their regular woman had gall bladder trouble and has given it up.'

'You'd think she'd have seen that coming,' said Fergus brightly, 'her being an astrologer. What does Daisy's say? She's Cancer.'

'"Cancer,"' read Martha drily, '"your diet is seriously deficient in everything. Remember that your mother's cooking is the ultimate yardstick by which all else should be judged and avoid udders at all costs."'

Daisy sniffed. 'Why do they print such tosh?'

'Some people,' said Alice, offended, 'think Dr Probe is funny. I used to get letters, you know.'

'So does the Secretary of State for Education,' said Anemone, 'but I don't think it means they think he's funny.'

'It's all stupid,' said Fergus, suddenly cross. 'You should hear what Dr Patrick Moore thinks about astrology. He says it's all complete rubbish.'

'He'll see things differently when he gets fin rot,' Martha grinned. 'I think it's brilliant. They should use you all the time, Alice.'

Alice was uncomfortable. 'They asked but I said no. I didn't really feel like taking it on again. Anyhow, Anemone wants to do it.'

'She'd be rubbish,' said Fergus meanly, as Martha frowned at Alice. 'Hers would be all about mascara and spots.'

Anemone looked offended. 'You're such a worm. At least I'm going to do it properly.'

Afterwards, when the children had scattered to their various hobbies so that the house reverberated to competing clarinet and cello, and they were alone, Martha eyed Alice seriously. 'You're like my grandfather's clock. You know, in the song, it stopped short, never to go again, when he died. Life can't end, Alice. You know that isn't what Rob would have wanted. You can't just live for your kids. It's time you picked up the threads of your own life again. You owe it to yourself and them.'

Something went twang in Alice's heart. Well, not really in her heart, really, more around her left recurrent laryngeal nerve where it looped beneath the aorta – but you could see why the Victorians might have thought it was the heart. What *would* Rob have wanted, exactly? She had sometimes wondered, since his death, if he'd actually planned to stay with her at all. That they would always be together was something that she had taken completely for granted when he was alive. It's a luxury, she thought, taking things for granted. You don't know how much so until you lose it.

'I didn't say it *had* ended,' she said. 'I just don't want to write stupid bloody horoscopes any more.'

'Well, fine – but don't you think there ought to be more for you now?'

'I suppose you mean I need some man on the scene to prove I've got over Rob,' said Alice crossly.

'No, of course not.' Martha was indignant. 'You ought to know me better than that. Since when have I ever thought no woman was complete without a man? But, Alice, my mom did nothing but reflect once Dad left her. Reflect and drink, of course, and hang around US bases seeing him in every man in uniform even after she knew he'd left the air force and . . . well, you know the rest. It destroyed her in the end.'

Alice sighed, put a hand on Martha's arm. 'I know, I'm sorry. But don't you think I have started again? I mean, I went back to work full time, I moved house, changed my colour schemes . . .' she attempted flippancy. 'Don't they say if you want to change your life you should redecorate your bathroom?'

'No they do not,' said Martha, smiling reluctantly. 'You made that up.'

'I didn't – it was on one of those home improvement programmes.'

'You're changing the subject again, Alice,' said Martha sternly. 'My point is that you haven't started again. You've made a jolly good job of pretending to, I'll grant you that, but you haven't actually made a break. Why don't we just examine what you've really done?'

'I don't think I want to,' said Alice, fidgeting and looking at the kettle. 'I never win when you go into your New England psychobabble. Shall we just have another nice cup of tea instead?'

'No, we shall not. Come on, Alice, a little analysis won't hurt.'

Alice sniffed. 'I bet all the really rich analysts use that one.'

Martha smiled. 'I'm no analyst, I'm your friend. I'm trying to help.'

'I know you are and I love you.' Alice hugged her. 'Go on then, you win, fire away – but if they take me away screaming you have to look after my children—'

'I adore your children.'

'I hadn't finished. And breastfeed them – so watch out.'

Martha smiled. 'I get your drift. But look at the job first, Alice. It's still Rob's job you're doing, even now. I know general practice is pretty conservative – but this Tom business has made me realise you actually can't bear to change a thing about that practice to make it your own.'

'Oh, come on! It's my job now – and I'm a jolly good doctor. I'm better than Rob, actually. I'm—' Alice stopped short and put a hand over her mouth. 'Oh.'

'Aha!' Martha pounced. 'We're getting somewhere at last.'

'You're tricky,' said Alice. 'It's like having tea with Woody Allen.'

Martha shrugged. 'Enough of the flattery. So, you're better than Rob. I'm sure you're right. But you're still locked in doing his job. You don't want James to retire, you hated Ian going off to the Far East, you treat this Tom Lovejoy as if he were launching a hostile takeover – it's your practice, not Rob's. You can change it, take it forward – you don't have to preserve it for him.'

'Is that really what it looks like to everyone else?' Alice was shocked. 'As if I'm just treading water and waiting for him to come back?'

'Of course not,' said Martha, 'but I've known you long enough that I'll see something happen when you start going forwards again. And I haven't. Oh, you're not like my mother who spent the last part of her life hanging around the US air base asking people where my dad was and writing sad letters to Pennsylvania begging his mother to send him back to her. But you're still Rob's Alice.'

Is that what I'm doing? wondered Alice, startled to recognise herself in all this. 'What are you suggesting? That I should be Tom's Alice?'

'Alice's Alice would be better,' said Martha. 'And before you tell me I'm wrong, just think what Freud would have made of all your white paint.'

Alice smiled, reluctantly accepting it. 'OK, point taken. If I promise that the next time I paint the bathroom it will be purple and I also promise to try to be nicer to Tom, will you stop analysing me and let me off writing the bloody horoscopes?'

Martha grinned. 'It's a deal. Actually I think you should let Anemone do it. She'd be great.'

'I might just do that. Now let's talk about this blasted meal I've invited Tom for. Casserole for the main course, meringue for pud – what about the starter?'

'I said I'd get it,' said Martha, satisfied that she had got somewhere at last. 'Leave the starter to me.'

Chapter Five

Martha did not use cookery books, which she felt were for insecure women, the kind who needed to look at a picture to check that their sticky toffee pudding was of the right consistency. Martha did own a set of books by Marc Gastoffier, which she kept beautifully on show in her perfect Shaker kitchen, but as every one of Marc's recipes began with boiling a pig's head for two hours with a bay leaf, she did not actually follow any of the recipes in them. If you weren't going to do things perfectly, Martha felt, you should pay someone else to do them. It kept the economy going far more effectively than the endless training posts for the unemployable the present government seemed to delight in. Martha was as cynical about politics as about men.

Now she walked with her elegantly measured stride through Cambridge's busy market square, absorbing the sights and smells of the city she loved, having left the shop in the hands of Philomena, her assistant. Every day was market day in Cambridge, apart from Sundays, when the bells seemed to take over the town completely. Today the striped awnings and strong smell of fish were as much a part of the atmosphere of the place as the drifting river and mellow stone buildings more familiar to those who have never visited the lands of the Fens, but who nevertheless have a set of place mats depicting Cambridge college gateways on their dining-room table. There was a hubbub of chatter split by the multiple cries of banana men trying to outdo one another – 'Sixty pence a pound! Best bananas!'

'Even better bananas, two pounds for a pound!' – and the jingle of bells on the hippy stalls, stirred by the wind and the ponytailed hair of curious tourists. T-shirts bearing the University coat of arms jostled for space with cut-price sweets and mountains of chrysanthemums. Water swirled on the cobbles where the fish man had hosed his stall, but Martha passed without getting her feet wet – hers were instinctive feet, the sort that never slipped nor stumbled.

On the central island where the old town signpost stood, a group of Japanese students observed her with mild but brief curiosity, omitting to photograph her as she was not wearing a voluminous black scholarly gown and could not therefore, in their eyes, be a true local. She smiled at the cheese man, and nodded a greeting at the lady on the sheepskin stall.

Martha's two-inch heels suited her perfectly and her beautifully applied nail varnish and long curved nails sang of spare time, a steady hand and a certain sensuality. She wore the kind of clothes that women with children never wear, for children are always sick on such garments within ten days of purchase and they certainly can't go into a coloureds wash. Although Martha had godchildren, and although she adored them, she was somehow not the sort of person they were ever sick on. Children, even babies, have an innate sense of direction in such matters, and invariably manage to be sick on their mothers instead.

As Martha walked she turned heads – male heads of all ages, assessing, admiring, desiring, female heads envying, trying to find fault and failing. She did not notice particularly, as she always turned heads, and had never truly appreciated that others do not find themselves followed by such eyes during the everyday chores of life. She was extraordinarily beautiful – but she had always been beautiful, and had learned to eye her perfect features in the mirror with the kind of detachment that an artist might apply to the final touches of his greatest work. People said that she looked like Michelle Pfeiffer, but with longer hair and fuller breasts.

Yet Martha Coleman had never married. This was a constant source of amazement to those who met her, as in addition to her unusual looks she was wealthy, successful, intelligent, and blessed with the uncanny ability to persuade apparently sane women to pay fifty pounds for a pair of wispy knickers that would take a silk worm merely half an afternoon to produce, and only then if he knocked off early. Probably, in the way that the advertising industry has utilised so effectively, they thought that they could buy a piece of the person selling the knickers along with the wisp, that a little of her presence and gorgeousness came with it. Perhaps, all advertising implies, the product is itself responsible for the looks of the model, rather than a blessing of genes and many hours at the gym.

Despite her perfection, Martha was at the age of thirty-four, truly unattached. The combined package of her beauty and self-assurance so often proved a little too intimidating for men of her own age, who rarely approached – whilst the sexual education of younger men whose less well-developed self-doubt did not inhibit the odd attempted pick-up was not, she felt, an acceptable alternative. She simply didn't want to waste time on sex with men who needed teaching where the clitoris was on the first date – and she didn't really trust the men who knew already.

So there was no permanent man in her life. Occasionally, when the need for sex became all-consuming, she rang the number of a very discreet woman who ran a very discreet agency in London. A very handsome, charming and discreet man, already well-versed in the location of clitori, was then dispatched to her door for an evening's company. It was always made very clear by the discreet woman that should the escort wish to provide any more than the specified services of companionship and charm that was for him to decide. Sex, she liked to say (rather untruthfully) was not what she was selling.

None of Martha's escorts had ever left without sex. Most of them had wanted to see her again, but Martha was not interested in starting a relationship with a man who could be bought. So for her the male sex was separated absolutely into the kind you have sex with and the kind you get to know socially. And that was fine. She had seen what happened when you mixed the two, seen it in her mother, and everyone had always said she was so like her mother to look at. Which, she believed, surely meant that beneath the surface she was a seething mass of her mother's vulnerable and self-destructive genes. She just had to keep them firmly under control, and she would be fine. She did not have to become her mother. Not even given that she looked so like her. Not even if everything is in the genes.

Of course, she told her friends when they teased her, she had been in love, many times. She would say this with a toss of her golden head, a mysterious smile in her green, slightly slanted eyes – but in truth Martha knew that she had not, nor did she wish to fall like that. She did sometimes wonder, in the very private part of her brain that she rarely examined too fully, if this meant she had not really lived yet – that she was just perfect at everything without actually being truly alive – but this was only the very slightest self-doubt, and easily crushed. After all, she had seen several friends through marriage, through betrayal of one sort or another, through divorce, even through widowhood, and was not sure that she had identified in any of them the life-long passion so beloved of romantic novelists, the greetings card industry and the film *Titanic*. Not even, she thought deep down but absolutely privately, in Alice and Robert Vane.

Now Martha cruised the aisles of Marks and Spencer, and selected an appropriate starter for Alice's dinner. The vichyssoise – with the garlic bread. Alice could serve it cold – keep things simple.

She was on her way out of the store, loaded with bags of shopping, when it happened. She had found the starters in the food section downstairs – but women like Martha are unable to venture into M&S without being sucked relentlessly up the escalator by the magnetic pull of sensibly priced knitwear, unable to leave without three jumpers, a pile of stockings, a set of pasta plates, a new duvet cover and a really rather lovely ceramic jug. There was no time now to wait for the store's carry-to-car service so she stepped carefully through the automatic doors, fielding a couple of glares from old ladies who clearly thought such doors for their exclusive use, and, unrushed, out onto the pavement, where the flowers she had bought for Alice fell from the top of one bag onto the feet of someone. And wow.

He was tall, beautiful and neither too young nor too old. As Goldilocks (to whom Martha had frequently been compared in her youth) would have said, he was just right. If he were on an escort agency's books she'd pay double. What a shame men like him always proved so disappointing in real life.

Seeing Tom Lovejoy prevented Martha from seeing the bacon, lettuce and tomato sandwich recently deposited on the pavement by a passing child who could still be heard screaming about its loss from a departing buggy. Less than a minute later the sandwich made contact with Martha's elegant heel, and sent her flying across the pavement.

'I . . . oh my goodness . . . I'm so sorry,' she gasped as she careered into Tom Lovejoy and he caught her with almost flamboyant expertise, steadying her effortlessly as she wobbled against him, Martha finding her footing carefully whilst inhaling the delicate scent of sandalwood that came from his warm, lightly tanned skin.

'Goodness, are you OK?' Scottish. Lowland too. Oh God.

'Y-yes,' Martha was flustered out of her usual composure. This just wasn't her. She fought not to look like the sort of inelegant housewife who might have gone into M&S for underwear and come out in shoes she is unable to walk in. She was so accustomed to knowing that her poise was unrockable that she had absolutely no idea what to do when it was not. Incredibly, she felt herself blush. She hauled herself upright (thanking God for the Alexander technique) and took an even breath.

'Tom, I'll be off.'

Martha barely noticed the voice of the other man, the companion, except to register the public school accent. Lawyer, she thought, and I'm never wrong. The ability to judge a man's profession and likely income band from a single spoken phrase is a valuable one in lingerie sales.

'Remember what I said, though, and take your property back. I'll be in touch.'

'OK.' Tom was still looking at Martha, smiling. Too good to be true. Perfect teeth. He's probably gay, she thought.

'I'm fine, really.'

'Can I give you a hand with all those bags?' His eyes had that come-to-bed twinkle.

'No, thank you.' She was cool now, at last contained, and she was not that easy. 'I must go, I'm running late.' I'll despise him if he offers again. Real men don't need to push.

He was cheerful, unworried. 'If you're sure. Here – your flowers. Take care – watch out for random lunch box rejects.' And by the time Martha had translated lunch box the correct way rather than the Linford Christie way, he was gone. Bastard. He might have tried a bit harder.

Alice had a half-day, which meant that she had an entire afternoon in which to mess up cooking the evening meal, rather than just a couple of hours in the evening. She spent a relaxed hour wandering through Cambridge's market buying free-range eggs and imagining how much nicer life would be if she had her own market stall and sold hot soup. It was an idea she and Rob had come up with long ago when she had idly said that an outdoor life on Cambridge's daily market would suit her, and he had said that no job which involved getting even slightly cold fingers could possibly suit her. She had replied that she'd be fine, because she'd sell soup, and when she got cold she could hug a mug and drink it.

The market was wonderful, full of colour and life and good humour, and for a while she was able to forget Roland and the practice, and just enjoy the good weather. As she drove home through the edge of town afterwards she noticed Fred Ramsden and Tabitha Tinkler. They didn't see her – they were sitting drinking tea outside one of Cambridge's many coffee bars, and seemed to be talking intensely. Tabitha didn't look very happy – she must be worried about her Armenian friend. Alice almost stopped to talk to her, but patient confidentiality would have stopped her saying very much, and, in any case, this was Cambridge, if you pulled up to talk to anyone wheel-clamping vans appeared from all directions and fought for the right to clamp you. Anyway – she had cooking to do, and she wanted it done before the children got home.

It wasn't, of course, even though they were all late back. Anemone had apparently been in the art room finishing off some self-portrait she was being rather smug about, and Fergus had been at the Fir Trees waiting for Fred, who had, he said in rather offended tones, been gadding about Cambridge with Miss Tinkler when he should have been gardening. Alice thought he sounded rather like a boy whose best friend has just started dating. Daisy got home latest, as she had just taken part in the school's annual audition for one of the great honours of the year – the right to be in the steering seat of the St Alupent's School bed in Cambridge's annual street bed race, a somewhat wild charity event involving the pushing of wheeled beds around the city streets by teams of volunteers, each ridden and steered by one person. The bed trials had involved a quiz (so that the representative of St Alupent's School should not be, as the Head Girl had put it so succinctly, a total goon), a bicycling obstacle course (to test steering ability), a race around the school hall (to test competitiveness), and appearing in the proposed costume (to suggest general jolly good fellowness). Daisy had excelled at all tasks, and her belly-dancer costume had impressed the judges – who were, she had ascertained in advance, seventy-five per cent male. The adherent emerald had particularly intrigued Mark Blackwell, school cricket captain and all-time heart-throb. Even being the son of Mr Blackwell, Head of History, could not dim his appeal. Daisy was on cloud nine.

No one in her family knew that she had won this much-coveted honour yet, and she wasn't quite sure how she should tell them. Whatever she did, she was certain to end up being teased by someone, and that was just . . . typical, that was. So should she be smug, nonchalant, delighted or proud? She was, of course, all four of these, and she also wanted to crow, but Anemone was bound to be pissed off if she was proud and Fergus would manage something awful if she was smug . . . She edged around the back door and decided to play it as overwhelmed.

'Hi, everyone. Guess what? You'll never guess, really.'

They were all in the kitchen. Her mother was getting something out of the oven and trying not to fall over stupid Paddy, who was lying in front of it. Was it meringue? Fantastic – she never made meringue and it was Daisy's favourite. Mordecai was hanging by his beak and one claw from the Welsh dresser. Anemone was playing with dolls' house furniture on the table (isn't that mine? thought Daisy. I'll make something of it in a minute – but I'll pretend not to notice for now so as not to spoil my entrance), and Fergus was practising his clarinet – that bloody Mozart again, just because he could, when he knew she couldn't manage the Elgar on her cello. If he got into the BBC Young Musician of the Year finals before she did she'd just have to commit suicide. She'd been planning what to wear (bright red strapless silk dress, blonde hair flowing free on shoulders, a simple silver cross at her throat) for years.

She tried again, abandoning overwhelmed in favour of happy. 'You'll never guess who's been chosen to ride the school bed this year?'

Fergus took his lips from the clarinet for just long enough to say, 'Not Meryl Streep again?' before returning to the Adagio, whilst Anemone sniffed and said, 'Didn't anyone else audition for it, then?'

Alice, though, put her oven gloves down, turned round and cried, 'You didn't! That's great – I had no idea you wanted to do it – it doesn't seem like your sort of thing. You never said the trials were today. Are you sure it's safe?'

Daisy shut her cheeriness channels with the speed of a Venus flytrap. 'Of course it's safe. And why shouldn't it be my sort of thing? I don't only want to play the bloody Elgar, you know. There are other things in life.'

'I'm sorry, darling, of course there are – although your Elgar is coming along splendidly. And I'm delighted for you. When is it?'

That was the trouble with Alice, thought Daisy, glowering at Fergus and reflecting once more that, well, the clarinet was obviously so much easier than the cello, it just wasn't fair. Her mother was immune to being grumped at. If only she had a dad as well. Maybe they'd have rowed a bit and then she could have got a rise out of both of them. What do you do when your mother insists on being a saint? But then, maybe when something so bad as widowhood has already happened to you, minor things just can't get you going any more. Mind you, she did once ask a plumber to leave for being far too miserable to work on their loo. 'Bed Race day, of course. Bank Holiday Monday.'

'Golly,' said Alice, 'that's only a week on Monday!'

'Fancy choosing a girl!' Fergus was trying to conceal envy. To be selected to ride the St Alupent's School bed was honour indeed, but being the little brother of the *girl* who'd got to do it – well, that was plain embarrassing.

Daisy looked smug. 'I thought I might wear my new Doc Martens.'

'What new Doc Martens? Mum, is she having new Doc Martens?'

'You said I could have some if I did well at school,' said Daisy, with sudden sullenness, 'and I have. What did you think I'd wear – a milkmaid's costume and daisies in my hat?'

'I assumed you'd wear a crash helmet.' Alice was a little unnerved. 'The bed races are awfully fast, Daisy. And when I said do well at school, the end of term report was kind of more on my mind.'

But nothing could burst Daisy's bubble. 'It will be brilliant,' she said. 'It's what I've always wanted to do. It's like playing the cello, really – you get to be the star. And I'll put all my pocket money towards the Docs, honestly . . .'

'Whoever heard of a belly-dancer in Doc Martens?' said Anemone nastily. The only starring she had done had been as Gwendolen's speechless maid in *The Importance of Being Earnest*, which didn't hold a candle to riding the bed. In her year a dreadful girl called Sally Persimmon had done it, and only because she, Anemone, had had a virus on audition day. 'You'd think they'd choose someone older,' she added, 'who was already learning to drive.'

'If I can ride a bike then I can steer the bed,' said Daisy, stung, 'can't I, Mum?'

'You can do anything you put your mind to, darling,' said Alice, 'you know that.'

'She couldn't be a model on page three,' said Fergus, suddenly a little more interested, interested enough to use more words than he could fit between two clarinet-breaths. 'She'd be useless.'

'Now, Fergus,' this contravened Alice's philosophy of rearing children without limits on their horizons, 'Daisy could be a page three model if she wanted to.' She hoped that as tones of maternal encouragement go, these were not too encouraging.

Daisy glowered resentfully. 'Oh sure, just the small matter of needing some breasts.'

Anemone looked up from her furniture. 'I've got none either. You may as well give up hoping – it's genetic.'

'Hallelujah!' said Fergus. 'The Lord is merciful. I could have been doomed to grow up surrounded by giant breasts.'

'I thought that was what your class all dreamed of,' said Anemone, sticking her tongue out at him.

'God, no,' Fergus was genuinely shocked, 'not on sisters. That would be sick.'

Alice frowned. I should stop all this blasphemy, she thought guiltily – but me and God, well, we've not exactly been mates these last few years. Not since He smote my family. Smote Rob from above like Sodom and Gomorrah. Even so . . .

'You're juvenile,' said Daisy, thinking, but not saying, that what Fergus really needed was a stepfather to sort him out. Might stop him acquiring his sexual obsessions from that group of voyeurs he shared a classroom with. She herself would quite like a stepfather too, actually. He'd have to be handsome, of course, and he'd have to throw her up into the air and, still smiling, catch her as she fell. She wasn't sure why this was so important, but it was all tied up with what her mental image of what a proper father should be. She must have seen it on a film somewhere. 'What are you doing with my stuff, Anemone?'

'It's feng shui,' said Anemone, arranging dolls' house furniture carefully on the table, 'the art of arranging your surroundings to harness the energy lines. I went to my third class today.'

Fergus started to take his clarinet to pieces. 'Why?'

'Because it's interesting. I thought I might do it in my year off. People pay you loads to do it.'

'How much?' Now she had his attention.

'Tabitha Tinkler said they'd pay me fifty pounds to do the Fir Trees.'

Alice stared. 'Fifty pounds for turning the sofas sideways and putting a fish tank in front of the telly?'

Anemone glared. 'At least I'm not making up horoscopes. I do it properly.'

'We should call you Astral Anemone,' Fergus grinned.

Anemone decided not to be riled. 'You could – and, anyhow, it pays better than the sausage factory at Fox Colne.'

'I suppose it does,' said Alice. Fox Colne's sausage factory, somewhat aspirationally named 'Camelot Luxury Meats', did not pay its employees well. Even sixteen-year-old schoolchildren regarded its hourly rates with some scorn.

'Mr Blackwell worked out,' said Fergus, 'that to buy one game of Donkey Kong you'd have to make four thousand sausages, eight hundred black puddings or two hundred and twenty-five luxury haggises.'

'Donkey Kong? What on earth is Donkey Kong?' Daisy poured maximum derision into her voice.

'It's a brilliant computer game,' said Fergus, 'about this kung-fu donkey.'

'Thank God for that,' said Anemone. 'The alternative was too awful to contemplate.' She finished rearranging the furniture, then looked in her book at the answers page. 'Damn. The zimmer frames will deflect the energy in the wrong direction. I wonder if they really need them.'

Alice felt a sudden sadness drop onto her like a wet flannel. With it came an old memory of Rob, in the garden of Pipe Tree Cottage, throwing a toddler-sized Daisy into the air and catching her as she chuckled in delight. It was all so bloody unfair. She looked at the meringue she had so recently removed from the oven. It was the first time she had made it in three years and it felt like another step away from him. Rob had always liked her meringue. She couldn't not make meringue for ever just because Rob had said she made the best meringue in the world. Because he had once fallen asleep into one after a night on call. How we laughed about that, she thought. I wonder if he and Marcie laughed together? God, they couldn't have done. Not laughed, that would be even worse than . . . than whimpers of passion or moans or intimate whispers . . . Laughter is far more intimate, far more precious.

She shook herself a little, mentally, and moved to look at Anemone's furniture arrangement. 'So that's meant to be the Fir Trees then?'

'Uh-huh.' Anemone brushed long blonde plaits back from her face. 'The common room. I went there to see Tabitha this afternoon. She was a bit upset, actually. Worried about a friend of hers from Armenia.'

'Oh goodness.' Alice was startled, remembering Herman and that she hadn't been to see him when she'd gone up to check on Phoebe. Mind you, she thought, I can't visit all of my patients who're in hospital – I'd have no time for the ones who aren't.

She left the children to their own devices briefly to phone coronary care, but a rather stroppy nursing sister refused to tell her anything about Mr Banescu on the basis that she could be just anyone phoning in and it was all confidential. Alice sighed; it was true, really, but most of the hospital staff were familiar with local GPs and would answer the odd question.

She rang the Fir Trees instead, and got the cook, who told her that Tabitha had indeed been to try to see Mr Banescu, who was a very old friend, but that visiting had been refused and she was desperate for information. Reluctantly Alice had to say that she couldn't tell them anything either.

She wondered again as she hung up, what Tabitha's connection to Herman could be – it wasn't as if she was likely to have been to Armenia, after all. She was a typical elderly spinster, kind and familiar, it was hard to imagine her ever having been further than the annual Fir Trees outing. Mind you, they had rejected Frinton-on-Sea last year and gone for Alton Towers instead. They were an active lot – apparently the only one of the party who had refused to go on the big dipper had been the driver who took them there. Alice often reflected that most of them lived at the Fir Trees purely for the company, because they certainly didn't need looking after.

She returned to the kitchen and eyed the meringue rather mournfully. It was exactly as she had always made them. A total disaster.

'What's that meant to be?' asked Fergus – somewhat unhelpfully, under the circumstances. 'Food?'

'It's my meringue,' said Alice sorrowfully, 'but it hasn't worked properly.'

'You haven't made that for ages,' said Anemone, 'not since Dad died.'

Alice jumped inwardly, slightly shocked that Anemone could use those words so easily, that 'since Dad died' had suddenly become an acceptable conversational phrase. It seemed to say that Rob's death had become something unchangeable in the course of life, something that was a fact. Which it was, of course.

'No,' she said, in a slightly odd voice, 'I suppose I haven't.'

Daisy glared at Anemone, angry at her insensitivity. 'Perhaps you've forgotten the recipe.'

'Perhaps I have,' said Alice, staring at the meringue, which seemed, suddenly, a metaphor for her punctured dreams. 'Perhaps you need more than just a recipe to make meringue.'

'That's rubbish,' said Anemone soundly. 'It's because you had the oven too hot. And you're out of practice – you never cook fancy things any more. You're always too busy painting everything white.'

'I'm not. I haven't painted anything for ages.'

'You touched up the bathroom last week,' said Anemone stubbornly. 'I smelled it.'

'That was just touching up,' said Alice, 'it doesn't count.' She remembered her promise to Martha about the purple and wondered what the children would say. Perhaps she wouldn't do it for a while . . .

Anemone appealed to Daisy: 'Have you ever known there not to be a pot of white paint on the go since we came here?' but Daisy shrugged, unwilling to be sucked in on Anemone's side.

Later, Alice wandered around the upstairs of the house, ready for dinner but not ready to come back down again. Anemone was right. It was all, really, very white, very deliberately empty of vibrancy. Apart from the children's rooms, which weren't white any more, of course. She peered in through Anemone's door. Her bedroom, Fergus liked to say, looked like a Moroccan brothel. No one was sure how he would know, but it is well recognised that boys of twelve have particularly fertile imaginations in some directions. It was a strong, deep red, with a ghastly purple carpet bought from a charity shop and incense burners in every possible nook and cranny so that the oxygen content of the air was rather less than at Everest Camp Four. The jasmine, terracotta and sandalwood content was stiflingly high, though. A photo of Rob sat discreetly on her dressing table in a dark wooden frame.

Daisy's room, on the other hand, was yellow, a colour she believed to be conducive to cello practice, and more obviously teenaged. She had stencilled big orange daisies all over it, and her cello sat in a corner, wearing her woolly school hat and scarf. On her dressing table was a double photograph frame – Rob in one side, Alice in the other. Alice had to turn it face down every time she hoovered.

Stepping into Fergus' room was like being jettisoned unexpectedly into deep space. Model planets hung from the ceiling. All surfaces were dark blue, his giant poster advertising *Star Wars* took up most of one wall, and all of his socks lived in a slightly threatening heap underneath his bed.

Alice swallowed. Rob was clearly coming through in his children. You expected them to look like him, smile like him, maybe lift a brow like him in the middle of an argument and send a painful lurch down into your deepest gut – but can you genetically bequeath the tendency to acquire purple carpets and midnight-blue walls? Or could it just be a reaction against the white that Alice had introduced so thoroughly to their lives?

She had tried to become a minimalist after Rob had died, to clear away everything, including the colour. In truth she hadn't been much good at it, surreptitiously retrieving most of her belongings from the skip. Martha had said you couldn't really be a minimalist when you owned five hundred frogs.

Even so, Alice thought now, maybe I threw away too much, even taking the frogs into account. Maybe it's like when you put some tiny, minuscule piece of computer information into the computer wastebasket, and suddenly the whole thing absolutely won't work properly any more. Perhaps when I was so busy throwing Rob away, I threw away some part of me that I needed to keep in order to function in a wholesome and healed way. Some bit of me without which I can't grow hebes.

And what was white anyway? A rejection of the past, a blank page? Or was it like snow, a featureless blanket which covers all the colours of the world until they're ready to burst out again?

As Alice worried over her dessert, at the Fir Trees Tabitha Tinkler rocked gently back and forth and dabbed a tear from her cheek.

'What's the point of living to be so old if everyone you love is gone?'

Fred sat beside her, his usual rather bland expression quite understanding. 'Longevity,' he said, 'is a blessing. And you don't know he's gone.'

'I do, I do. That has to be why Herman has come here to see me.' She sniffed and blew her nose. 'How old are you, Fred?'

'Older than my teeth,' said Fred, 'a little. A few hundred, actually.'

'Oh ha. Mind you, it would explain how you got in here – no other men have beaten the waiting list.'

Fred shrugged. 'Shame there's no discount for age.'

'Who pays your fees, then? I had to sell my house for mine. My nephews have never got over it. Every time I see them they're desperate to know if I've heard when I'm going yet.'

'Going where? '

'You know. Over to the other side. It's their inheritance, you see. Haven't you got any family?'

'All gone,' said Fred sadly, 'ages ago. This place is my family now, and I pay my own fees. I've a bit put away.'

'You're a dark horse, you are, Fred Ramsden,' said Tabitha, 'you and your silly peacocks.'

'Ah,' said Fred, 'well. So tell me about Herman.'

But Tabitha wasn't ready to talk about Herman. 'There's nothing more to tell. As I said, I had a postcard saying that he was coming over from Armenia to see me, then the call from the hospital yesterday to say he was carrying my name and address and did I know him? Could I tell them if he had a history of heart problems? Then that stupid nurse wouldn't let me in to see him and said she couldn't tell me a thing because I'm not a relative and it was confidential. Confidential! You don't have to be Einstein to work out what's happened when they put a man into coronary care. That's all I know.'

Fred sighed and patted her arm. 'I'll try and phone them again, shall I?'

'Oh, would you?'

'Coronary care, Addenbrooke's,' said Sister Annette Goodenough in her singsong telephone voice.

'I am inquirink after Mr Banescu,' said a voice. It sounded like Peter Sellers doing Inspector Clouseau.

'Oh yes,' said Sister acidly. 'And are you a relative?'

'Da. From Armenia. Ve are asking is he vell? Haf he all vot he needs? Haf he his luggage with him?'

They had picked the wrong nurse to try this one on. Annette Goodenough had made it her mission to give nothing away on the telephone, not today, not any day. 'Mr Banescu is not receiving visitors and if you're an Armenian then I'm a monkey's aunt. Goodbye!'

She hung up. She'd bet it was that ridiculous crowd of old people from the Fir Trees again, trying to pump her for confidential information about her patient. It had to be the sixth time they'd rung. Feeling quite belligerent she settled down at her desk with the latest six-pack of medical romances from Mills and Boon, and wondered when a handsome surgeon would propose and what colour roses she should carry at the wedding.

'Alice . . .' Tom treated her to a pair of kisses when she answered the door, so unexpectedly that she almost felt charmed. A warning bell sounded with deafening familiarity in her inner ear. 'It's so kind of you to invite me – actually, I've the terrible feeling I've invited myself.'

'Of course you didn't,' said Alice, thinking: you bloody did too, and so don't think you've charmed your way out of it now, either. 'Come through and meet Martha and the kids.' It will be interesting to see if you can charm my kids, she thought. I think you've more chance of grooming a dead hedgehog with a pair of silk knickers.

'Oh – I didn't realise you . . .' began Tom in a surprisingly awkward voice, then he was in the living room.

Martha, looking her elegant and poised best in a simple cream dress and hardly any jewellery, turned to say 'Hello', blonde hair fanned across her shoulders in the way, Daisy observed, that other people have to *arrange*. As she turned she caught her heel on an invisible thread, and was immediately spread-eagled onto the carpet at Tom's feet with the studied grace of an octopus on roller skates.

Alice stared. She had never seen Martha lose her poise for a moment, not in all the time she had known her.

Tom moved first, bending over her, helping her to her feet. 'Are you all right? I'm so sorry, I must have startled you. Let me refill your glass.'

'Er – thank you.' Martha was flustered by the unaccustomed clumsiness. 'I just caught my heel – oh goodness, it's you again.'

'Well, hello,' said Tom, recognising her. 'We meet for a second time in one day.' He flashed his handsome-devil teeth in that devilishly handsome way that Alice knew Martha would never fall for. 'D'you think it's time we were choosing china?'

Martha smiled weakly. 'I'm Martha Coleman, an old friend of Alice. And you're the locum – Alice has told me all about you. I was expecting more of a villain.' Alice winced, thinking, Martha, how could you?

'You were? Well, actually, I will be popping out in a minute to beat up a few old ladies and desecrate a church. What gave me away?'

Martha dimpled. 'Anyone who could work with James and Alice would have to be an angel or a devil,' she said impishly, 'and I hope you're not an angel.'

He twinkled with just the right level of boyishness. 'There's something of each in us all. I'm delighted to meet you, Martha.'

'Likewise. Would you just excuse me? Alice, I must just pop upstairs and dry my dress. Don't want to have to take it off, but I spilled a little tonic water.' She beamed at Tom and hurried off.

God, thought Alice in disgust, if she keeps looking at him like that she'll have digested him before the first course. She's probably gone to put her diaphragm in. It's a bad idea. He's not a man to trust. Let's hope he's terrified to bits like most men she meets.

'So,' Tom watched Martha go, followed Alice back to the kitchen, 'Alice. I do apologise if I've said anything untoward – that is – I mean, I had no idea you were gay. How long have you – er – known Martha?'

For the rest of the evening Tom, Alice observed rather grudgingly, was excellent company. It would be easier to dislike him if he laughed like a drain, told filthy jokes or chewed with his mouth open, but you couldn't fault his social skills. She still didn't want him as a partner, though. He was just too . . . good to be true. That was it. And when you think a man is too good to be true, you're generally right. *Aren't you, Rob?*

At least he wasn't flirting with Martha, despite her obvious efforts to entrap him. Nice to see that even he had the decency not to try to steal her lesbian lover from under her nose. He also seemed to be able to converse with Anemone about feng shui and Eastern mysticism quite convincingly. Don't you dare rope her into your fan club, Tom, Alice thought. I hear enough of your virtues at work, without having to listen to the same thing at home. Even Daisy seemed quite impressed, even though she was usually about as vulnerable to charm as a particularly irritable triffid.

Alice wished Fergus was downstairs – Fergus wouldn't like him, surely – but Fergus had retreated upstairs with his clarinet in some disgust at being sent to bed at ten, and could still be heard playing 'Stranger on the Shore' mournfully in his room, demonstrating his inability to get off to sleep early, even if it honestly was way past his bedtime.

Still, thought Alice a little grimly, let's see whether you pass the meringue test, Tom.

Martha was beginning to feel a little discouraged. She had tried every flirtatious line in her book, every come-on sign that was acceptable at a dinner table at which two teenagers were sitting, but she wasn't getting the vibes in response. Yet when she first saw him she had definitely felt a spark, a *frisson* . . . Her usual escorts didn't give her that feeling, that spark of excitement, this zing of uncertainty; the feeling that all might not go exactly the way she planned. It had been deeply enticing, as if it was the something that was always missing with the smooth, groomed men who were quite happy for her to be on top, whose desires always took second place to her own. Face it, Martha, she told the woman in the mirror, when she went to check her lipstick, you were simply wrong, he just doesn't fancy you. The fact is, only the men whose company you pay for respond to your signals, and they'd probably respond if your signals involved putting on a hard hat and asking them to help you build a shrubbery.

In the end Alice served the meringue. She had toyed with the idea of serving up the M&S tarte tatin she had as emergency spare instead, but that would have been giving in, and Alice never gave in any more. She hadn't given in since – well, not for years.

The meringue was just the way Rob had liked it – still just a bit too gooey despite an hour in the freezer – and cracked in several places. She was horribly reminded of the first time she had made it, under instruction from Rob's mother, who had insisted that it wasn't right. Rob had let her complain, failing to leap to Alice's defence. He had always found it impossible to displease his mother. It was after that that he had started overcompensating by insisting he liked it better gooey. He was never very good at confrontation, come to think of it, never very good at displeasing anyone. Well, he displeased me in a really big way by dying, she thought.

That had been the ultimate escape for the man who hated confrontation.

'What are your future plans on the job front?' Martha was asking Tom as Alice came in with dessert plates. 'I mean, after your locum with Alice is over?'

Tom smiled. 'I've no plans,' he said, rather disingenuously, Alice thought. 'There's always lots of locum work in general practice, so there's no real need to worry.'

Alice, returning with the cream jug, was curious. 'Don't you find it a little frustrating,' she asked him, 'always moving on? I mean, being a locum is such a peripatetic life, and it's not difficult to find good practices these days.' Unless you've got some dark secret in your past, she thought, and wondered suddenly if he knew about Rob. He must know. Someone must have told him. She always knew someone must have told everyone, because no one ever mentioned it. No one ever said, 'Weren't you in the papers a few years ago just after your husband died whilst he was in bed with a tart?' They didn't say it. So they obviously all knew.

But Tom shrugged nonchalantly, unaware of the churning in Alice's brain. 'I've just never felt the urge to settle down,' he said, 'at least, not until recently. I've always been a bit of a drifter, I suppose, and I do have a few business interests that keep me occupied. Maybe I've been too much of a loner.'

Alice heard Martha sigh. God, she thought, pass me the sick bag, Clint Eastwood.

'What sort of business are you in?' Martha was asking now.

'Just family stuff,' he said, 'this and that.' He seemed a little embarrassed, 'I've actually –'

'Tell me,' Martha was still trying to make the conversation flirtatious, the business could wait, 'what's your star sign? I bet you're an Aquarian?'

Daisy and Anemone exchanged glances. When she

started talking star signs rather than business interests – well, Martha had clearly got it bad.

'Alice, that was absolutely wonderful,' pronounced Tom as she served second helpings of meringue. 'I don't remember when I last had as terrific a meal.' And if Rhett Butler had spoken to Scarlett in such admiring tones the very first time they met she would never have bothered with Ashley, the world would have lost a very long film, and millions of people would have thought that Gettysburg was the town the Getty family lived in. He was, Alice thought, exceptionally charming, just as Rob had been. But I'm immune to charm, thought Alice. I loved Rob in spite of his charm, not because of it. Because he had no control over it and he was forever charming people I really didn't like – people he didn't like either. I loved Rob but I hated him being so bloody charming.

The thought gave her such a mental jolt that she dropped her elbow onto her plate and sent a glob of whipped cream sailing through the air and straight onto Martha's shining curtain of blonde hair. It was, unfortunately, quite a large blob. Yet Alice barely noticed the ensuing clean-up, orchestrated by Tom with another of his virgin hankies.

I really have to do something about myself, she thought, before I end up finding things about Rob to hate. I don't want to hate him. Martha's right. I've got to try to move on.

She watched them all with detached eyes. Martha, her wet hair recalling the stars of those gratuitously damp American beach soaps, was quite flushed, with that sparkle in her eye that meant that letting Tom Lovejoy think she was a lesbian hadn't been entirely a fair thing to do. Anemone, who affected to be more cynical about men than an entire olive grove full of Corfiote grannies picking olives by the ton, was offering to wash his handkerchief. Daisy was gazing slightly wistfully at him, as though wondering what sort of impression he might make at the school gates. I suppose, Alice caught herself thinking with the very edge of her mind, I could do a lot worse for a practice partner, given that I actually don't fancy him in the slightest myself . . . but, oh, I wish Ian were here, big warm Ian with his good sense and his endless jollity. I wish he'd even ring, but I suppose it's not that easy. Instead I just get these postcards with 'wild time, wish you were here' on them, which is no blooming help at all.

Is it normal not to fancy someone like Tom? Alice wondered later, alone in bed. One day I might recover my old self and fancy someone wildly again, but when will 'one day' be? How exactly do I resolve my feelings about Rob and move on? I go to the grave, but Rob and his hebes just lie there and wait for me to sort myself out. Nothing happens to make me. I'm stuck.

Daisy sat in her bedroom in the darkness. The house was very quiet. She wondered if Mum was crying – she had certainly seemed odd and quiet when she went to bed. Maybe she fancied Dr Lovejoy. It was pretty strange to think of your mother fancying anyone really – but then, he was quite like Dad. He was a doctor, he was handsome . . . Perhaps once you were as old as Mum you always fancied the same sort of person. They were your type.

Daisy had always been unsure as to what her own type was, other than that it was bound to be dishy, and quite possibly royal. Now, though, Mark Blackwell was much in her thoughts. He was the school heart-throb anyway, but since he had smiled at her in her belly-dancer costume . . . Just better not let Fergus guess. He'd wreck everything.

It would have been nice to ask Mum about it, about how she got to go out with her first boyfriend. The trouble was, how could she ask? After all, they all knew that Mum's first boyfriend had been Dad.

'Daisy?' There was a hiss from the door.

'What?'

'Are you awake?'

'Obviously.' Daisy was rather proud of that one – and if Anemone was going to ask fatuous questions in the middle of the night she deserved all she got. Her door opened and Anemone crept in.

'What did you think?'

'What of?' Daisy switched her bedside lamp on and blinked owlishly in the light. Giant daisies seemed to float out of the darkness from her walls, an odd optical illusion which happened because she had used gloss paint for them against a matt yellow background.

'Of him, of course. D'you think Mum brought him home for our approval?'

'No. You don't think so, do you? I mean, you surely don't think she and he are –'

'Well, they might be,' said Anemone. 'They're not that old. Anyhow, even old people have sex, you know.'

'I guess so.'

They sat in silence for a moment, sharing the feeling that sex ought to stop well before your offspring were old enough to know what it was. Mind you, thought Daisy, I knew the ins and outs when I was six after I saw next-door's dog. She frowned. 'D'you think she expects us to tell her if we like him?'

'Well, we do like him . . . don't we? I mean, he's a bit of a dream to look at,' said Anemone. 'I could almost fancy him myself . . .'

'Oh yuck!'

'. . . *if* he were a bit younger. I think we should tell her we think he's OK.'

'He's quite like Dad,' said Daisy, suddenly dubious. 'I mean, he's a doctor, he's tall, he's dark . . .'

Anemone frowned. 'Isn't that good? I mean, you wouldn't want Mum to go out with a . . .' she sought for an example which would not make her sound class-conscious, '. . . a teacher.'

'Ugh, no. Imagine if it was one of ours! Maybe she wouldn't want someone too like Dad, though. Not . . . again. I mean – well, you know.' Marcie Crombie hung between them, rarely spoken of (especially not spoken of in front of Fergus), together with the uncomfortable but also unspoken realisation that Dad, who should surely be their hero, had hurt Mum more than just by his dying. Alice had told them the bare bones of it at the time. There was no way of not hearing about it back then, she had said, so it was best coming from her.

'I suppose you might be right.'

The door opened again.

'Go away, Fergus. This is girl talk.'

Fergus ignored them. 'What are you whispering about?'

'Periods and things,' said Daisy nastily, 'actually – so bog off.'

'Oh no you weren't,' said Fergus, 'you were talking about Mum.'

'So what if we were?'

'Well, the two of you are daft. Even I could tell she's not interested in Dr Lovejoy.'

'How could you tell?' Anemone liked to feel she had the patent on intuition. To be upstaged by a twelve-year-old boy was humiliation in the extreme.

Fergus shrugged. 'She told me in the kitchen. She says he's probably falling in love with Martha.'

'Oh dear,' said Anemone, 'poor bloke.'

There was another long silence.

Then Daisy said, 'But how would we feel if Mum had found someone else? I mean, she might. She's not exactly ugly.'

'She's got two nightmare daughters, though,' said Fergus, and ducked to avoid a pillow.

Daisy sighed. 'Well, I'd like a stepfather.' The intimacy of the semi-darkness made her add her secret dream: 'A handsome one who'd throw me in the air and catch me.'

'God, you'd crush him.' Anemone rolled back onto the bed, creased with mirth. 'The best you could hope for would be that he'd push you on a swing and sing to you like the one in *Chitty Chitty Bang Bang*.

Daisy sniffed. 'You know what I mean. I'd like her to meet someone else. She's probably lonely.'

'She's got us,' said Fergus, 'how could she be lonely?'

'It's not the same, Fergus,' said Anemone. 'She's an adult. She needs someone to go for walks with her in the rain, to watch films like *Gone With the Wind*, and to sit next to her and talk about *Panorama*.'

'God,' said Fergus, 'I see what you mean. Someone to listen to Wagner with.'

'Must be miserable,' said Daisy, 'being an adult. All that and then you die as well.'

'It's OK,' said Anemone with cheerful blinkeredness, 'that's just her generation. We'll be different.'

'She could always marry Mr Blackwell,' said Fergus cheerfully. 'He hasn't got a wife,' and, as Daisy rolled her eyes, 'Why, what's wrong with him?'

'Facial hair,' said Daisy kindly. 'One day you'll understand.'

Ah, thought Fergus heading back to his room, so facial hair was the thing that put girls off. In that case he would start growing his beard now. With a bit of luck it would reach his knees by the time he was twenty. Then he could stay at home and look after Mum. That way she wouldn't be lonely. He could be brave. He could manage *Panorama*, as long as it wasn't a special long one – and as for the Wagner, well, there were always earplugs.

The coronary care unit in Addenbrooke's Hospital was meant to be a calm, hushed place – and particularly so at night. It was intended as a peaceful haven for the start of recovery. Patients talked in whispers, had only one or two visitors, rested a lot, ate a little, stayed in bed in a dimly lit room and recovered. They did so, Sister Goodenough liked to remind them, quietly.

Herman Banescu was not quiet. Herman was giggling. He had been giggling since seven o'clock that evening, when he had been given another dose of morphine. Worse, his was the kind of infectious, penetrating and self-perpetuating giggle that is the worst sort to develop when the nurse who holds you in the palm of her hand is about as warm and friendly as an iceberg.

The junior doctor on call was tired and cross. Coronary care bleeped her every bloody minute all through the night, and the second she had sat on the lavatory the bloody cardiac crash bleep went off and she had had to go tearing through the hospital with her knickers in a twist – *and* she'd lost all of her biros. Male doctors didn't get this level of harassment when they were on call. Male doctors got, 'Would you like us to put the catheter in for you, Doctor? And would you like to feel my boobs?' That's what male doctors got. All the female doctors knew it.

She answered the phone. 'Hello. Dr Underwood here.'

'Doctor, this is Sister Goodenough on coronary care. Can you come and see Mr Banescu?'

'Why?'

'Because he can't stop laughing.'

'Surely that's not so bad?' said Amy Underwood. 'If I could laugh even once it would improve the quality of my evening by a factor of thousands.'

Sister Goodenough knew exactly what factors were – she just couldn't remember right now, and she didn't like doctors trying to be clever. 'Dr Underwood, Mr Banescu should not be giggling.'

'Absolutely not,' said Amy, 'not with you on duty.'

'I beg your pardon, Doctor?'

'Nothing, Sister Goodenough. Have you given him anything?'

'It is precisely because we have given him so many things

126

that he is giggling,' said Sister Goodenough. 'He is intoxicated and disturbed. His urine output has fallen. I think you should pass a catheter.'

'Oh, OK, I'm on my way.' Sleep, thought Amy Underwood, who needs it when there are catheters to be passed? Why didn't I become an accountant?

But when she reached the coronary care ward she called for her registrar, and at this Sister Goodenough thawed so substantially that if she had been Antarctica, Easter Island would have been submerged. Annette Goodenough had fancied the senior registrar for, well, as long as he had been the registrar (he had not been nearly so attractive when in a more junior post) and she welcomed the chance to impress him.

'Poor Herman's been like this all evening,' she said now, 'and he's talking nonsense. We thought he was in acute retention, but Dr Underwood passed a catheter and it's not that. It must be the morphine.' The leaping flame of delight she felt at having his attention was revealed in the unaccustomed warmth of her tone. Sister Goodenough was usually fairly cool with the medical staff. The trouble with doctors was that if you caught them too early in their careers you might end up with one who turned into a GU clinic doctor or, horror of horrors, a GP. In the Hero-Doc world of the hospital, only a GP seems less heroic than a GU specialist. Two sets of doctors overwhelmed by trivia and the unpleasant, she thought.

'All patients talk nonsense,' said the registrar now. His elegant carriage and curly hair made him a dead ringer for Alexander the Great (unfortunately for Sister Goodenough, so did his sexuality), 'but he could have a morphine psychosis. I'll ask the psychiatrists to have a look at him.'

The psychiatrist, when he arrived, was very keen and enthusiastic about being on the coronary care ward, even though Sister Goodenough had reverted to her former, frozen subcontinent state (in her view psychiatrists were beneath consideration – not nearly the cachet of surgeons, and they all go bonkers in the end). He questioned Herman Banescu long and hard, before wandering into the nurses' room to find that pretty sister, the one he'd been eyeing for months.

'Very interesting,' he told her. 'It's probably the morphine. He keeps saying he has lost something, then he giggles and tells me to go and ring the frog. He's got no idea who he is and how he got here.'

'Sounds potty to me,' said Sister Goodenough, unwilling to show interest. 'I just want him to stop laughing. It makes me nervous.'

The psychiatrist smiled and tried his intellectual chat-up line. 'Don't you ever wonder about really mad patients – that maybe they're the sane ones and we are the ones who are crazy?'

Sister Goodenough looked at him suspiciously. He was a psychiatrist, it was true, but they weren't usually bonkers by this age. 'No,' she said.

The psychiatrist was not discouraged. 'What I mean is, the acute psychiatry wards are full of people who think they're the reincarnation of King Arthur, and we treat them as mad. But what if one of them really is King Arthur? What if he really had come to save the world and we put him in a strait-jacket and filled him full of haloperidol? I mean, we think we're so clever but one day we might be wrong.'

Annette was slightly interested, despite herself. He did have nice eyes, and it was appealing to be talked to as an intellectual equal by a doctor. And he did seem to care about her nice Armenian patient. Perhaps a psychiatrist wouldn't be so bad. After all, the trouble with surgeons was they never heard a word you said unless you were the one telling them that they were a pair of scissors short just after they had closed up the patient.

'So what should we do with Mr Banescu?'

'We just have to sedate him for now – can't do much else

– he's probably quite distressed. Imagine waking up and not knowing where you are or how you got there.'

Annette blushed. That was exactly what had happened to her the morning after the last mess party.

'I'll be back to see him in the morning, Sister. I'm Simon Frobisher, by the way. Tell me, do you ever go to the theatre here? I understand there's an Oscar Wilde play on next week . . .'

Behind them Herman continued to giggle softly until he fell into a drug-induced and dreamless sleep.

Chapter Six

'So,' said Anemone over breakfast the following morning, by prearrangement, 'd'you fancy him?'

'No,' said Alice, without bothering to ask who, 'of course not.'

'Why not? He is a real dish.' Anemone poured enough muesli into her bowl to keep a dozen Alpine goatherds marching to the pastures for months. 'I'd fancy him if he was ten years younger.'

'D'you really think he's falling in love with Martha?' asked Daisy.

Alice looked uncomfortable. 'Probably not now.'

'What do you mean?' Anemone was intrigued.

Alice had the grace to look uncomfortable. 'He thinks we're gay, Martha and I.'

'What? Why on earth does he think that?'

Alice shrugged. 'He just assumed it, and I didn't put it right. I'd rather not have him leering at me or my friends.'

But Anemone disapproved. 'Oh, Mum. Poor Martha. She'll think she's lost her touch. It's time she found herself a nice bloke.'

'You mean you think I should correct his false impression,' Alice sighed.

'Definitely,' said Anemone. 'What a waste. You must be the only woman on earth not to fancy him.' She sensed Daisy crossing her eyes at her and added hastily, 'At least of your age.'

'All right. I'll say something.' She's right, thought Alice, chewing slowly on her Frosties. It's not fair on Martha. She *was* virtually dry of drool by the end of the evening. It's me that's lost my appetite for men. Is it because I still expect Rob to come back and I want to be able to say, 'Look, I've been true to you. Even though you weren't true to me'? Because that would be really pointlessly stupid.

'Maybe,' she said aloud, 'it's because I work with him. It's a mistake to fancy people you work with.'

'It didn't stop Antony and Cleopatra,' said Fergus, coming in to the tail end of the conversation and pouring Frosties into a mixing bowl. 'Mind you, look what happened to them. And it would be a bit sick, fancying someone your own daughter fancies.'

'Easy mistake to make,' said Daisy, 'specially when the daughter fancies everything in trousers.'

'I do not.' Anemone was indignant. 'And I said I'd fancy him *if* he was ten years younger.'

'OK.' Fergus faced her squarely across the breakfast table. 'Name one man you don't fancy.'

Anemone met his eyes. 'Mr Blackwell,' she said, pleased with herself.

'That doesn't prove much,' said Fergus, then yawned widely.

'Don't worry, Anemone,' Alice grinned at her, 'you're at your sexual peak now. You're programmed to fancy everything in trousers.'

'I don't have to take this abuse.' Anemone stalked out of the kitchen. She had, though, finished her muesli.

'Course you do,' shouted Fergus after her, 'you're a girl!'

Rather smugly, Daisy watched Anemone go. It was not often that she got to play the part of the reasonable sister. 'Take no notice of her,' she told Alice kindly. 'She's a bit disappointed that you're not in love.'

'Why?' Alice stared at her daughter, slightly shocked at the undercurrent of truth she could sense there. 'Do you want me to be in love?'

'Of course we do,' said Daisy as airily as she could

131

manage. 'We think it's time you got off with some bloke, you know.' It was a daring thing to say, but the others had agreed that she should, and anyway the opportunity for grown-up conversation arises so rarely at fifteen.

'Got off? Got *off*? I'm not going to get off with any bloke,' said Alice crossly, 'and if I was I'd make darn sure you didn't know about it.' Underneath a knife twisted. To get off with anyone would mean finally accepting that Rob was no longer watching, was no longer in a position to care.

Daisy shrugged and twiddled a long strand of her hair. 'You can't seriously believe that. Why do adults always think they can keep their sex lives secret? My friends always know when their parents are at it. Veronica says her whole house creaks, and Lucy says when her parents do it in the bath the water slops down the overflow in a bonking sort of rhythm.' She was slightly overstepping what she and Anemone had agreed to, but she was enjoying the conversation too much to stop.

Alice poured coffee, hiding her discomfort. 'Well, I would have thought you'd be relieved that I didn't spend the night sloshing down the overflow with Tom Lovejoy, then.' And, as Daisy and Fergus exchanged glances: 'What?'

It was Fergus who came out with it, sitting at the table to do it properly, suddenly earnest beyond his twelve years. 'Well, actually we've been talking about it, and we do think it's time you looked for someone. After all, we're going to leave home one day, you know; you need a life. And I really don't like Wagner, although I could manage *Panorama* now and again.'

Alice sighed. *Grange Hill*, she thought, has a lot to answer for. I could do without my children being taught to be sensitive. 'Have you been talking to Martha?'

'No. We just think you're too young to be on your own.' Fergus, being both twelve and male, had no qualms about saying the things his sisters felt were unspeakable. 'And Mr Blackwell told me all adults need sex.'

132

'He said what?'

Daisy nudged Fergus, alarmed that the conversation was running out of control like a Teletubby on speed. 'He did not say that, Fergus.'

Fergus shrugged. 'He did, too. It was in social biology. Sebastian asked him why people did it when they weren't trying to have a baby, and he said sex was a natural function, just like eating and breathing. Well, you can't live without those, can you?'

Alice took a deep breath. I can't believe I'm having this conversation with my children, she thought. I'm supposed to be the one worrying about their sex lives, not the other way round. 'That's not quite true, Fergus. I'm very touched that you're all concerned about my love life, but believe me, when I find someone I want to have a love life with, I'll tell you.'

'You never will,' said Daisy, 'if you don't look.'

Anemone reappeared at the table, not wanting to miss too much. 'Well,' she said, 'if you ask me . . .'

'Which nobody is,' said Fergus, 'thank you.'

Anemone ignored him, as dignity demanded. 'If you ask me you need to have some fun – preferably with someone dishy. Saturdays are for relaxing, Mum, so promise me you won't spend the rest of this one reading some ghastly article about bottoms.'

Alice slid the medical magazine she had privately earmarked out of sight and promised.

Is that really how I seem to them? she wondered later, after the children had dispersed to their various weekend activities. Joyless? Well, I'll show them. I can have a good time without a man to provide it. I can enjoy myself with the best of them.

Later that afternoon, though, after spending a depressing few hours in a Cambridge beauty salon being told that her pores needed steaming and there was a lot that could be done with collagen these days, Alice made her way to

133

Martha's shop for coffee and gossip.

'D'you think I'm middle aged and joyless?' she asked.

Martha, who was fighting an inner battle between the Martha that wanted to ring Tom Lovejoy and offer him her body and the Martha that thought he ought to offer his own to Alice, frowned. 'Who's told you that?'

'No one as such. My children just seem to think it. They're trying to find me a bloke.'

'I got the impression you'd found one last night,' said Martha, trying not to mind, but Alice shook her head.

'Absolutely not. He invited himself that was all. And I don't need a bloke to enjoy myself. I can have a perfectly good time by myself.'

Martha shrugged. 'It's not me you have to convince.'

'I know. It's them.'

Martha thought it was herself Alice needed to convince, but forbore to say so. 'I'll tell you what, let's rent a film tonight. Have a girls' night in. Unless of course you'd like me to set you up on a nice blind date . . .'

'I don't need a blind date,' said Alice, and Martha reflected wistfully that she certainly didn't, not with Tom Lovejoy practising his bedside manner in her surgery every day. Not that the thought of Tom Lovejoy at the bedside made that much impression on her . . .

The door opened and an expensively dressed middle-aged woman breezed in. She was clearly a good customer. Martha greeted her like an old friend and Alice watched, slightly flabbergasted, as the woman spent an outrageous sum of money on a scrap of a silk nightdress and breezed out again with a sparkle in her eye.

'You see,' said Martha, when the door shut, 'she's having a good time.'

'It involves a man. It doesn't count.'

'Actually it doesn't,' said Martha, 'she's gay – but I take your point.'

Alice sighed and paced the room, not noticing the door

opening again behind her. 'It must be possible to have fun without having sex,' she said crossly, then blushed bright pink when a voice behind her said, 'Good afternoon, Alice,' and she turned to see the vicar of Fox Colne smiling and holding out his hand in greeting.

'You shouldn't be so surprised,' said Martha later, as she locked up and counted the day's vast profit. 'Vicars are no different from the rest of us. He's actually having a wild romance with that nice lady from Grantchester who played the organ at his wife's funeral.'

'You know more about people in this town than I do,' said Alice, impressed. 'It must be over a year since his wife died.'

'It is,' said Martha, figuring that no more needed saying; Alice could make the obvious link.

'You gave him a huge discount,' said Alice, imagining the reverend presenting the frothy creation he had purchased to his new partner. 'Considering you always say you're as hard as nails when it comes to business.'

Martha looked defensive. 'He is a vicar,' she said, 'and anyway, this isn't just a business, it's a social service.'

'Oh ha ha. Fifty-pound knickers?'

'You should buy some,' said Martha. 'Believe me, there's nothing that gives you a twinkle in your eye like knowing your knickers cost fifty pounds.'

But Alice shook her head. 'Wasted on me,' she said.

In the end she and Martha spent the evening wrapped in a gothic horror comedy called *The Mummy* in Alice's living room whilst her children hid behind cushions and shrieked deliciously at the gore. It wasn't exactly what they'd had in mind for her, she felt, but it was probably the best she could do for now. At least none of them, Martha included, yet knew that Pipe Tree Cottage was going to be for sale. She'd get no peace once they did.

As Alice and Martha drank Pinot Noir and giggled at the dark secrets of the pyramids, Herman Banescu had recovered a certain degree of lucidity on the coronary care ward.

'Where am I?' he asked in Armenian.

Sister Goodenough, who could manage a few simple Armenian phrases taught to her by her Armenian cousin Tanya (notably 'I'll have a rum and coke,' and 'Go out with a dog like you? You must be joking!') managed to struggle a reply, and it was only an hour or two more before he could speak English fluently again too.

'The doctor,' he said to Annette, 'I must see the lovely lady doctor again. She is my saviour.'

Annette was a little miffed. True, you got used to doctors getting all the credit in this job, but bloody Amy had done sod all. She, on the other hand, had sat here all night, the Florence Nightingale of CCU, bloody well adopting a nurturing role. She had even said, 'You are in hospital in Cambridge' in Armenian, when being bilingual wasn't in her job description. 'She's not on duty,' she said, rather icily. 'Doctors only work the odd night, you know.' The fact that they also worked on the days in between was not something she was prepared to credit them with.

'Oh,' said Herman, 'will you tell her I must see her. It is very urgent.'

Annette smiled meanly. 'Well, I could always bleep her. I'm sure she wouldn't mind.'

Amy Underwood was not impressed. 'What the hell are you bleeping me for? I'm not on call.'

'You should have turned your bleep off then,' said Annette smugly. 'The patient is most insistent he needs to speak to you.'

'What for?' Amy was impatient.

'He says it's personal.'

'I only put his catheter in, for God's sake.'

'Well,' said Annette, 'in my book you can't get much more personal than that.'

'Look, if some chap gets a kick out of me gripping his

thing with a pair of rubber gloves it's not my fault, and I'm not bloody coming!'

'I'm sorry Mr Banescu,' said Annette, smiling like a sorely tried angel, 'I think we'll have to hang on till tomorrow. Did you know you had visitors today – an elderly lady named Tabitha, wants to see you when you're awake.'

Herman sighed and shook his head miserably. 'I cannot see Miss Tinkler. I will not.' He could not possibly see Tabitha Tinkler when he had lost the most precious thing he had ever touched. Because he had remembered what he had been bringing to her, the thing that was so important that he had had to come in person – and it wasn't with him, it wasn't in his stuff. Where had he put it? Where had he been after he arrived at Cambridge station? Why did he keep dreaming of frogs? Who was this vision of a lady doctor he kept having, the one with the beautiful golden hair? If only he could remember . . .

Alice, unaware of the extent to which she figured in Herman's dreams, spent the Sunday morning writing to Ian. She had tried to get some swifter message to him than a postcard, feeling seven-day letters were rather slow, given that they had only four months till eviction. Unfortunately the British Embassy in Papua New Guinea did not feel they could send a consul into the Highlands to find Ian because of an eviction order. 'We do have more important things to do,' said a voice rather huffily, and was unswayed even when she tried to suggest that the entire future of the NHS might be in jeopardy.

'Diplomats,' she said darkly to Fergus, as he appeared to forage for lunch, 'give a whole new meaning to the word "diplomatic".'

Fergus was cheerful. 'Did he tell you to go and boil your head?'

'In effect,' said Alice, 'although he didn't use precisely those words.'

'It's probably being in Papua New Guinea,' said Fergus, breezing away with half a pound of cheese and a tomato, 'the local traditions have rubbed off on him.'

It was difficult to know what to write to Ian, particularly as he had warned her that postcards got through more reliably than airmail letters, which had a habit of dissolving in the rain on their way through the jungle. Eventually she wrote, 'Roland calling in the lease. Have to get out 30th Sept. No prospects at the moment. Please get in touch,' in large letters, which hopefully wouldn't run too much in the downpour, then sent Fergus out with his cheese to post it.

After this she spent a peaceful Sunday with several pots of emulsion in different shades of white touching up barely visible marks on the walls. It was quite a good way of not actually thinking about anything else, particularly when her children had forbidden her to read anything medical on the basis that this would be too sad.

Unfortunately, though, the sound of distant church bells kept making her think about sex. Perhaps, she reasoned, it was because she and Rob had so often had sex to the sound of church bells. They had had sex more often on Sundays, she was sure of it. Perhaps, she mused, people need sex more on Sundays. Perhaps that was why so few people wanted to be vicars – after all, it's not a day you want to be too busy on.

At Addenbrooke's, Herman Banescu had remembered a little more.

'Frogs,' he said to a mystified Sister Goodenough. 'There were frogs where I was taken ill. Lots of frogs, all around me.'

'He wasn't found in a pond, was he?' asked the student nurse who had called her over. 'I mean, where else would you find frogs?'

'He was found in central Cambridge,' said Sister Goodenough reading his notes, 'by the paramedics.'

'No,' said Herman, 'there was a beautiful blonde woman. I think her name was Poppins.'

'Wow,' said the student nurse, 'perhaps he saw an angel. I've heard about those sorts of experiences. I saw this film with Nicholas Cage where . . .'

Sister Goodenough rolled her eyes. 'Bedpans,' she said, 'and you, Mr Banescu . . .'

Herman gulped. She reminded him uncomfortably of the mother superior of the convent in Yerevan, and you wouldn't cross her. '. . . must get some rest. You are remembering Dr Amy Underwood who put in your catheter. She will be here tomorrow.'

'Yes, sister.' Herman sat back rather miserably, sure that that wasn't it.

Sister Goodenough warmed slightly. 'It will come back to you,' she said, patting his hand, 'just give yourself time. Maybe if you saw your friend Tabitha – she rings twice a day . . .'

But Herman shook his head emphatically. 'No, I can't see her. Not until I have remembered. Not until then . . .'

Alice awoke on the Monday morning unable to remember her dreams but quite sure that whatever they had been she didn't approve of them. That would teach her to eat cheese at bedtime; it always gave her funny dreams.

It was an uneasy start, as it turned out, to an uneasy day.

'Oh listen,' said Fergus, in the car on the way into school, 'that's your phone.'

'Answer it then.'

'Hello? Fergus Vane speaking . . . Mum, it's Jean.'

Jean's distress echoed from the mobile, her particularly wailing lilt giving it an almost musical quality. Although she was normally slightly dourer than the Grim Reaper with an attack of colicky abdominal pain, she was capable of a range of dramatic emphasis which even the great Maria Callas managed only at her best. Alice often wondered if perhaps Jean had only been put into this life in order that she might become a particularly theatrical spectre in the next.

'Aieee, Dr Vane, I dinna ken hoo tae tell ye.' Jean's Glaswegian was the slightly sinister accent of a soprano Billy Connolly.

'What on earth is the matter?' Have Rangers lost at home? she wondered, or has she had too much of that ginseng tea again?

'The branch surgery, Dr Vane, I've never seen such a state. The surgery is desecrated.'

'It's what?'

'Desecrated,' howled Jean, 'and all yon mess all over the floor. Who's going tae clear this one up, that's what I want tae know?' The line went dead.

'Damn,' said Alice, 'I forgot to change the battery. Now I'll have to worry till I get there.'

'When she says desecrated, d'you think she means decimated?' Fergus liked to be correct.

'Well, unless a dozen Anglican nuns dressed in nothing but red corsets and black mitres have been in there overnight sacrificing a Nubian goat then I think you're probably right,' said Alice, 'but I didn't want to nit-pick. I expect the trouble is that Gladys the cleaner didn't come in last night. Jean's always like this if she has to hoover. I suspect she needs medication but she's not my patient, thank God.'

'You ought to look after all the staff,' said Fergus. 'Then you could put them on all sorts of drugs to make them work faster – and smile more.'

'It's a tempting thought,' agreed Alice, 'although I'm not sure that the General Medical Council would entirely approve.'

'No one would notice,' said Fergus, 'apart from Jean. If she smiled it would be on the front page of the *Cambridge Evening News*.'

'Hmmm.' Alice was only half listening. She felt a little worried about Jean. Perhaps she ought to be referred to someone. She pulled up in her doctor's space and opened the doors. Fergus climbed out and shouldered his giant sack of school books. It always amazed Alice that a boy who claimed he needed to take so many books home apparently needed to do so little with them when he actually got there.

'Have a good day. Is it your clarinet lesson today?'

'Yep. Bye, Mum. Good luck.'

'Have a good day,' said Alice, thinking: I really must tell him Pipe Tree Cottage is for sale. If I'm not careful he'll find out at school and rush home and spring it on me joyously.

Fergus waved her off. His was a pretty good mother, really, he thought, in that she could still climb trees and she knew about the moons of Jupiter. It was a shame she was still so sad about Dad. Fergus was sad about Dad too, of course, but in a slightly abstract way now. It had been a while. Dad was gone and Fergus had the rest of his life to do things with. Dad wouldn't have wanted him to give up and mope – but perhaps it was different for wives?

Alice waved Fergus off and set out along Kings Parade herself, quickening her pace at the thought that a patient might arrive before she did and find Jean histrionically refusing to hoover. As she rounded the corner of Market Hill there was a police car, blue lights flashing in that 'just two handsome burly types saving the world so please don't stare' way that they have. The surgery door hung open – the lock had clearly been smashed.

Inside was a mess. Leaflets, post, newspapers, cushions, chairs – all were scattered about the place. The filing cabinets had been forced open, Alice saw, as she walked through to the reception area, and the desk looked as though it had been attacked with something blunt and heavy. Her frogs had been swept onto the floor – and some-one had even pulled the stuffing out of the consulting-room chair. Well, that wouldn't make it any less comfortable, anyway. Alice stood in the doorway, vaguely aware that Jean was bemoaning the state of the place somewhere out of her line of vision. All she could think was: that's the second time this year. I must have been mad to think we could move the practice here, even temporarily. It's too small, too insecure, it was never designed to be a surgery. You can't practise medicine from a rented front room any more. And anyway, after this it's going to be uninsurable. One more nail in the practice's coffin.

'Ma'am. Inspector Hammond of Cambridgeshire CID. And you are . . . ?'

'Oh. Hello. Alice Vane. I have a surgery here this morning – those are my patients waiting outside.'

'I'm sorry, Dr Vane, it may be some time before you can clear this up – we're waiting for the fingerprint boys. Can you tell if anything has been taken?'

Alice focused on him briefly. His resemblance to Inspector Morse began and ended with his being male. His resemblance to a tub of lard, on the other hand, was fairly pronounced.

'I can't say. There's nothing really worth taking.'

'Most people who break into doctors' premises are after drugs, Doctor,' said Inspector Hammond officiously. 'We'll be rounding up the usual suspects later.'

'There's very little in the average GP's surgery that a drug addict would find useful,' said Alice, sighing. 'They all know that, I'm sure.'

'Indeed, ma'am, but these villains will stop at nothing,' said the inspector. 'It is my belief, ma'am, that the violation of property is a heinous crime. The perpetrators should pay heavily. Rest assured that we will do everything in our power to apprehend the miscreants.'

Alice wondered if Inspector Hammond had had a thesaurus chip inserted into his head at police school. She shook his hand. 'Thank you, Inspector, that's very reassuring.'

He kept hold of her hand a little longer than was strictly necessary, pinning her with interested blue eyes. 'Isn't your husband a GP here?'

'He's dead,' said Alice, certain that he knew.

'Oh, I'm so sorry. I didn't mean to . . .'

She took pity on him. Perhaps he didn't know, and he did, after all, have the misfortune to be one of the least charming men (bar Roland) she had ever met. Particularly with that cigarette.

'It was three years ago. Don't worry.'

'Ah. Right.'

He definitely knew that, she thought, so why . . .?

'Perhaps you'd be free at lunchtime? I often take a squash and a light lunch at The Mill.'

'I – er – it may be a busy day,' said Alice, thinking: do I have an availability tag illuminated on my head, or something? *Desperate widow needs bonk*, perhaps? 'I don't think lunch is likely to be on my agenda today.'

She was saved by Jean. 'Aye, Dr Vane, I've told yon patients tae go tae Lammas Surgery in half an hour. You go over, dear. I'll stay here and sort oot this mess.'

'Oh, Jean, I couldn't let you –'

'Go on, dear,' and Alice realised that Jean was now actually thriving on the drama. Well, let her get on with it. So some silly boys had broken in, thinking there might be something worth taking. They weren't the first surgery in Cambridge to have this happen, and they wouldn't be the last.

When Alice reached the Lammas Surgery Tom bounded out of his consulting room, concerned anxiety etched perfectly onto his tan. 'Alice, I just heard what happened – you must be dreadfully shaken. Sit down, have a cup of coffee, let me see the rest of your patients for you.'

Alice gulped, unnerved by the sense of being looked after. The temptation to accept, to ask Tom's help, loomed like the urge to give in when drowning. Morning surgery would already be running appallingly late. If he didn't mind seeing one or two of the patients . . . It would be nice not to have to sort all this out by herself. James couldn't be asked. You couldn't ask James to do anything now, not if you minded doing it yourself in the end, because he never got round to it, probably never remembered. Wouldn't it be much simpler to offer Tom a partnership? To have someone to help with insurance and new locks and finding somewhere else to practise from?

Norma and Tom were still looking at Alice as though she were a particularly fragile china doll, and she swallowed. 'I . . . It would be marvellous if you could help me catch up. Thank you, Tom,' and he smiled like a sudden floodlight, making her blink. If Martha doesn't fall head over heels for this one, she thought suddenly, she's made of sterner stuff than even I realised. He's perfect for her.

Norma followed her into her room a moment later with a cup of tea. She was positively glowing with oestrogen. 'Oh, Alice, he is such a splendid young man, don't you think? Such an asset to the practice! It would be nice is he could stay!'

Alice smiled non-committally. 'I don't really know what's going to happen at the moment,' she said, wondering if perhaps Norma's HRT patch needed reducing. Hadn't that been Sacha Distel playing in the waiting room?

'Well, you know, Alice,' Norma was in motherly mode, 'I do worry about you. You've carried such a burden lately – with Ian away, and especially now that James is – well – getting on a bit.'

Alice let the euphemism pass. They all knew that James was a little too absent-minded for all their good at the moment, but it wasn't anything she felt able to discuss with the staff. 'I'm fine, Norma, really.'

But when Norma had finally gushed back out to reception she found herself thinking: that *was* a significant moment. I've accepted help from Tom. I've given in.

Rubbish. Tom was merely seeing a few extra patients for her on a bad day. Wasn't that what locums were for? She glanced at her computer screen. Tom was about to see Mrs Entwhistle, whose flatulence was a constant problem, not only to her but to all those who came into contact with her, followed by Annabel Froggitt who always brought all five children with her without actually making appointments for them, then expected all their multitudinous complaints to be sorted out within her allotted ten-minute slot. But two patients does not the offer of a partnership make. Not even when both James and Ian clearly thought he was wonderful. Alice needed to be surer than that to trust someone these days.

She felt drained, suddenly missing Ian terribly. Could she really carry the practice and the staff, and try to move surgeries, and pacify Roland when he tried to charge them extra for breathing his air, and worry about James and his odd moments and cope when the lock got smashed and the frogs got broken? It would be nice to have someone else to shoulder the burden – but how could they even think about taking on a partner until she had spoken to Ian? Together they needed to address her concerns about James and work out whether there would even be a Lammas Practice in three months' time. She had sent that postcard – perhaps she hadn't said enough – but there had been no reply yet, no indication that Ian had received it. No, this certainly wasn't the time to be making decisions about Tom.

The insurance company had bad news when she rang them about the break-in. Although nothing of value was missing, and they confirmed they would pay for the broken door, they were going to review the surgery policy and 'update' it. They could not promise that, in view of the obvious security problems with the premises, they could continue to insure them next year.

This, Alice surmised, meant that far from being the answer to the practice's problems, the branch surgery would probably have to close. It was an impractical building anyway for a town-centre surgery. During lapses in the waiting-room conversation the finer details of the problems of the patient being seen were audible throughout the ground floor. Unfortunately it was a listed building, rented from Fawkes College, who would allow no changes to it whatsoever, not even the replacement of the window locks. Alice sighed. It was all her problem – because it obviously wasn't Tom's problem, James was being particularly absent-minded today and Ian was quite stunningly unavailable. It was one more thing to add to the next letter she wrote him. What was it Ian had said when he left? 'Treat Tom Lovejoy as if he were me. He's a great guy, I've known him for years, he can take it if you kick his shins,' and Alice had laughed, rather liking the sound of this Tom Lovejoy, sublimely unaware that Tom Lovejoy would be the most handsome, charming man she had seen since Rob, the sort of man she'd sworn for ever to avoid.

The only slightly redeeming feature of the whole thing was that the insurance company's man on the phone had a glorious Scottish accent and managed the near-impossible feat of flirting with her even whilst telling her that her insurance was a complete waste of time.

'You're absolutely right, of course,' he said when she expressed this opinion, 'but, you know, insuring doctors' surgeries is a bit of a fool's game. The only ones worth taking on are the purpose-built surgeries and the really good conversions. These old Heath Robinson places are too far behind the times – more trouble than they're worth. Expensive, insecure, far from ideal . . . I should look at new premises if I were you.'

'Very expensive option,' said Alice, wondering whether he could possibly have second sight, 'particularly in Cambridge.'

'Ah well,' said the man, 'Cambridge is rather a law unto itself. Wonderful city. I suppose you're one of those horribly bright young things who simply couldn't leave the city of perspiring dreams for the lands we lesser mortals inhabit. You should come up to Scotland – I can recommend my little corner of Aberdeen. Great people and I might even show you a good time.'

'Gosh,' said Alice, perplexed, thinking: I'm not sure I've been called a bright young thing for a few years, 'I don't know that I'd call myself young. You'd have to ask my children.'

'Ah,' he sounded suddenly cooler, 'well, I'll put the forms in the post.'

Alice bade him farewell, surprised to realise that she felt very slightly piqued at the sudden cessation of flirting. Perhaps it was a sign things were changing. Perhaps, she thought, I do miss feeling wanted, flirted with, desired. Perhaps my weekend of sexual reflections ought be telling me something. But it's not so easy to find a date, though, when every time you turn a street corner you see someone who is either a patient, a member of your staff or a medical secretary from a rival practice. Still, she mused cautiously, Martha did say she could arrange something for me – I know she could find someone suitably charming and discreet. It would do me good to feel I'm a woman again.

'You could go on TV and get a free holiday out of it,' said Anemone, excited, when Alice hinted to her children that evening that she was considering a blind date. 'You know, they ask you what sort of men you like, and you'd tell them, and then you'd get an evening with Cilla Black and a week in the Seychelles with a Sean Connery lookalike.'

'Oh God,' Daisy put a theatrical hand to her forehead, 'you wouldn't? I mean, how would we ever live it down?'

Alice was puzzled. 'I thought you liked *Blind Date*? I mean, you always watch it.'

Daisy rolled her eyes. 'I know, but you'd be one of the golden oldies. Imagine the shame of it.'

Fergus grinned. 'We could think of three questions for you to ask the men. Something like: "I really like going out on dates with complete plonkers. What makes you a complete plonker and how would you prove it?"'

'I think it's a useless idea,' said Alice. 'I'd probably get a Gary Glitter lookalike who smokes Rothmans, and a weekend living off the land in Swindon, and afterwards half my patients would try to set me up with their dreadful sons because they'd think I was obviously desperate.'

'Don't tell Fergus,' said Daisy, 'or he'll set you up with Mr Blackwell.'

'Heavens,' said Alice, 'life gets more dangerous by the minute. Although an evening trying to find Mr Blackwell inside his beard would probably be safer.' I shouldn't be rude about Mr Blackwell, she thought, I like him, and it's not his fault he has more facial hair than Rasputin. Well, actually it is: he grew it. Yet I've often suspected that he was rather good-looking under the beard. 'Well, if you really think I should – I mean, if it wouldn't upset you – I might go on a sort of a date. I might ask Martha if she knows anyone.'

'I should stop rabbiting on at us,' said Anemone, 'and just do it. We're not your keepers, you know. You don't need permission.'

Alice smiled. 'I know. I'll think about it. Look, you three, I have to talk to you about something else,' she smiled apologetically. 'I've been thinking about things since this break-in, and it feels like the final straw. I don't think there's much chance of the practice carrying on with only me effectively running it. I know how you feel, but I need to be realistic. I still have to speak to Ian, which is no easy thing at the moment – but I think I'll have to close it all down.'

'Mum, you can't. You can't just give up. Dr Liversill hasn't been and breathed on you again, has he?' asked Daisy rudely, whilst Anemone pulled a face.

'Daisy, don't,' said Alice. 'You shouldn't be rude about people's . . . physical afflictions. Not even his.'

'He hasn't got a physical affliction,' said Daisy darkly, 'he's just so revolting that he even breathes ghastliness.'

'He might just have ill-fitting dentures,' said Fergus, who knew about such things from the Fir Trees, 'or gland trouble. Fred Ramsden says you can blame most of the world's problems on glands.'

'Either way,' said Alice, 'I can't work in the same building as the man any longer. Perhaps it's no bad thing that he's throwing us out. But I can't sort the whole mess out alone, there are too many insurmountables. The branch surgery was broken into today and we'll probably have to close that down soon. We have no other premises to go to, Ian is out of the country and James – well, I've been worried about James lately, I think he's just really tired of it all . . . Look, I know you think I should carry on but . . . I don't have to work, I mean, not financially. I could just do the odd sessions for someone else, without all the hassle of partnership. I just don't want life to be this difficult any more.'

Anemone was regarding her coolly. 'What's the alternative to hanging up your hat and giving up?'

'I wish you wouldn't be so negative about it. I can't really see a manageable way through.'

'What about Dr Lovejoy?' Anemone looked like a headmistress questioning her charges.

I feel as though I should shuffle in my seat and look uncomfortable, thought Alice. 'Well,' she said aloud, 'he's just a locum, he has no part in it. One option would be to offer him a partnership, if he wants it, and to look for new premises together – but I don't see the point when I already know there's nothing suitable we could move into at such short notice. There's no time to build afresh – we'd be lucky even to see planning permission by Christmas.'

Anemone fiddled with something in her bag. 'Maybe you should just ask him if he can help? I mean, he might have a perfect solution up his sleeve.'

'I doubt that. Oh, I agree he's a nice bloke, but . . . Oh no,

Anemone, I'm not basing all this on a tarot reading.'

'Go on. Just draw one card. You know it always tells the truth.'

'I do not know that. Oh . . . all right.' Alice drew one reluctantly, knowing she had a superstitious side, knowing that Anemone knew too. 'Well, that's a lot of help.'

'The lovers,' said Anemone in some satisfaction.

Alice sighed. Blooming omens, that was all she needed.

She dreamed that night again – vague, disturbingly erotic dreams which she tried but failed to put down to too much cheese before bedtime as this time she hadn't had any cheese. They might, or might not have involved Rob, she thought, but secretly knew, when she woke in the early hours, hot and tangled, that they had not; that Rob had not been in those sort of dreams for quite a while. Rob was gone, and her body no longer yearned for him. She knew that now – had known it, in truth, for a long time. She missed him, that was true, longed to hear his voice again other than in a dream, to tell him of her problems and to have a hug when the worst of the day had done its bit – but she didn't ache for him in that awful throbbing way that had so disturbed her nights at first. Something had changed. Somewhere in the confusion and pain of the last three years she had accepted that he wasn't coming back. Somewhere along the line he had become untouchable, someone you should not, could not ache for.

But the ache itself was not gone – and sometimes, when she consoled her sleeplessness with vague fantasies and her own touch, sometimes she thought it was stronger than it had ever been. That was proof itself that she was still a sexual being. When had that begun again? Slowly at first, perhaps, for comfort, to help her imagine better times – but it had morphed into a longing, a demand for something more than thoughts of the past to warm her to the core.

I actually have a need for sex, my dreams are born of a

150

burning need, she realised, sitting bolt upright in bed at the surprise of the thought and staring blankly at the opposite wall, the one on which there had been a strategically placed bronze-tinted mirror when they had moved in here. A thick-set and unhandsome builder had removed it for her and taken it away as payment with a nod and a secret smile.

'I need sex,' she said aloud, quietly so as not to shock herself too much, 'and it's not even Rob I want any more.'

Either, she thought, she had changed – or she was like this all along and never knew it because she had been Rob's Alice so completely and without question. Rob's Alice had never needed sex. Wanted it sometimes, enjoyed it often, gone along with it an awful lot of the time – but demanded it? Never. Sexually demanding women had always meant leather and whips and riding high wearing stilettos and a lot of blueberry lipstick. That had never been the way Rob wanted her.

He'd wanted Marcie Crombie to be like that, though, hadn't it? Obviously Rob had needed more than his prudish Alice – yet he had never given her the slightest sign that anything was lacking in their intimate life. He had never shown the slightest urge to have her handcuffed to the dishwasher or chained to the dining table by a dog collar. How could she not even have had an inkling . . . ?

No wonder it killed him, she thought – it must have given him ten times the excitement he ever got with me . . . Was I prudish and unimaginative with Rob, or was I simply being the woman I thought he wanted? Well, maybe I want more than that too. Maybe it's time I got it somewhere else. It's just such a stupid shame Rob had to die before I found it out. Before he found it out. Bastard.

Alone in her bed at the darkest hour of the night, Alice began to cry.

Chapter Seven

Alice rang Martha early the following morning, before she was properly awake and well before her cortical common sense zone kicked into action. Rob had always said that in a woman's brain the common sense zone is right on the other side of the brain from the sex-drive area, so that the sex-drive area cannot influence it at all, whereas in men the two are very close and the sex drive area of the brain swells regularly and totally obscures the common sense area. Sadly, in his case, this had proved to be all too premonitory – but then perhaps Rob's Alice had been so fundamentally unfulfilling that even the Pope would have had to look elsewhere. Well, thought Alice hastily, not the Pope perhaps (sorry, your Holiness, slip of the brain) but even an honest and faithful man . . .

It didn't matter any more, because it was time she had sex again. It was obvious from the dream – Anemone said that dreams were your more sensible thoughts, the ones you were too self-censoring to think when awake, and Alice thought there was probably something in that. She wasn't looking for romance, or love, or even prolonged flirtation – that might still seem a betrayal of Rob who, despite everything, was still the only man she had ever loved – but straight sex would be simple enough.

'Alice, this had better be good. I'm supposed to be out of the door in half an hour, and I look a fright,' said Martha.

'Rubbish,' said Alice, who was fully aware that Martha awoke looking as though thirty-two Hollywood beauticians had been working on her for a fortnight. If there had ever been a living advert for Oil of Olay, it was Martha. 'Martha, I need some help.'

'You certainly do,' said Martha cheerfully, suppressing her disappointment that it wasn't Tom Lovejoy on the phone. 'What had you in mind?'

'A date,' said Alice, quickly enough that she couldn't stop herself halfway through, leaving the word 'a' hanging in the air like a sneeze that never happened. 'You were right – about the sex. I feel as though I'm shrivelling up. I've had these dreams.'

Martha felt an odd palpitation in her chest. Was she being asked to matchmake for Alice and Tom Lovejoy? Tom Lovejoy, who had stirred something in her which completely excluded thinking of him with Alice. Something wildly exciting. Something that made her heart beat faster. Something that . . .

Obviously Alice wanted Tom Lovejoy. Who wouldn't? And what are friends for? Alice saw him first, and her need was certainly greater.

'I think that's fantastic, Alice. If you take my advice you'll invite Tom over for drinks – but this time, just the two of you, then the theatre. Or opera. Isn't *La Bohème* coming to the Corn Exchange this week? Puccini is easily the best for sex.'

Alice shook her head at the phone. 'No, no, not Tom Lovejoy, Martha. I just need – a body to practise on. I mean,' she blushed furiously, 'you were right about me needing a man – but Tom Lovejoy is far too close to home.'

Oh dear, thought Martha sadly. She's never going to get over Rob this way. She's not the type for casual sex. I should find her someone she can feel comfortable with.

Aloud she said, 'So you want my advice on how to pick up some strange chap?'

'I want you to organise it,' said Alice bluntly. 'I don't want to discuss it, I don't want to plan it, I don't want to . . . to choose someone from a photograph. I just want you to

153

arrange a . . . a blind date. No one too strange. Please?'

Now, I've said it. A slight sound made her jump suddenly. Surely the children weren't down . . .? But no, it was just Mordecai, eyeing her – mournfully, she felt – across the kitchen.

Martha was staring at the phone. 'A blind date. Are you sure?'

'Yes, I'm sure.' Mordecai always was on Rob's side.

'Have you got knickers?'

'What are you talking about? Of course I've got knickers. Why?'

'I know you. I bet you go to M&S. I'll find you a nice pair from my stock.'

'Nothing wrong with M&S,' said Alice indignantly. 'I always go there for them. I hear the Queen goes there too.'

'The queen's not planning a night of wild but blind passion,' said Martha drily. 'At least, not as far as I know.'

'Mine are fine.'

'Just promise me they're not knee-length thermals with a double elastic waist and a reinforced gusset.'

'Martha!' Alice was laughing, despite her discomfort at the realisation that these knickers of hers might actually be on show to someone of Martha's choosing. Someone extremely sexy who would remind her that she was a woman again.

'Promise.'

'They're white.'

'I knew it. Lacy or plain?'

'Lacy – look, I've got to go. Daisy's here.'

'I don't believe you. Anyway, when is this to be?'

'Soon. I don't know.'

'Tomorrow?'

'Er,' Alice was slightly taken aback, 'OK – if you can. Before I can think about it and change my mind. Bye.' She put the phone down. 'And you can shut up, too,' she said to Mordecai.

Mordecai eyed her with an evil glint. 'Knickers,' he said clearly. 'Knickers, knickers, knickers.'

In Fox Colne Martha sighed. A blind date. Just like that. Alice would be shocked if she knew how she, Martha, arranged her own dates, and just how blind they were. That wouldn't do for Alice, who was far too proper to pay, and who would almost certainly bottle out of the sex anyway. Thoughtfully, she fished out her address book and ran through the list of names. The advantage of reaching your mid-thirties as a single woman was that the men started to free up again, as divorce flung them back into the market-place. A man unmarried by forty almost always has something wrong with him whereas a man divorced may simply have been guilty of poor judgement and therefore could be worth a look. Unless crippled by alimony, of course.

Oliver. He would be perfect for Alice. He was a doctor. Martha made the common but incorrect assumption that doctors always socialise particularly comfortably with one another, thankful to be rid of the fear of slipping into talk about piles and pubic lice to those for whom such things are not commonly encountered. What's more, he met the criteria for being defined as unfortunate divorcé as his wife had been both faithless and ugly. She had also been conveniently wealthy, so Oliver had kept the proceeds of his Harley Street practice to himself. And Alice wouldn't know him already – why would she know a gynaecologist from Hampstead? Martha picked up the telephone, hoping Oliver hadn't acquired some floozie in the meantime.

Alice, unaware that Martha had taken quite such swift action, arrived at Lammas Surgery on time. Lisa was waiting for her when she got in, with a pile of results from the hospital and a 'having a great time so far' postcard from Ian, sent four weeks ago when he arrived in Port Moresby.

155

It just went to remind her how very distant he was. If only I could ring him, she thought again.

'Dean's coming in to see you in a minute, Dr Vane.' Lisa looked nervous. As well she might, thought Alice. After all, my own husband was an adulterer and yet she thinks I've got a magic wand for sorting Dean out. I get all of the problems that ought to be taken to the vicar. Morals and marriages. Oh, and infidelity, of course. I wonder if the vicar gets presented with piles and indigestion? Why *do* people always assume that their doctor, expert though he or she may be at feeling people's prostates through their bottoms, has any more of the answers to life's problems than the woman next to them in the chip shop or the man driving the number 23 bus?

Oh well, she thought, I've made an entire profession out of interfering in other people's lives despite being trained only in simple physical things like how to spot a diseased gall bladder and how to tell if a limp is faked (other than by kicking the other leg, that is). Why get nervous about it now?

Dean Grabber was twenty years old and well over six feet tall. He ought to have worn braces, but didn't, and so also had the scruffy, rather shuffling gait of a man whose trousers are balanced on his hips more by luck than tension. He also ought not to have wet-shaved – several small red scabs and two little bits of tissue paper bore testimony to the sharpness of the blade. It was a mystery to Alice how anyone who looked like Lisa could have chosen him, until she saw the charm of his smile, which lit up his face like a beacon. In any case, she thought, perhaps it's better to avoid good looks and fine muscles. Look what happened to me.

Lisa ushered Dean into her consulting room personally, settling him into his seat as if he were the chairman of British Airways about to fly to Barbados. Dean accepted this, Alice noticed, as no more than his due.

'Hello, Dean,' she said, wondering where to start.

156

'Hello, Dr Vane.' Dean looked moderately uncomfortable. 'I don't normally come to see doctors. Lisa wanted me to come and talk to you but I don't know what I'm supposed to say.'

Alice fixed him with her blue gaze, looking for truth. Failing that, clarity would be something. 'Did she say why she wanted you to come?'

Dean blushed and shrugged. 'A bit. I know you've been good to her – about the baby 'n' all. I appreciate that.' He stared at the executive toy on her desk, a plastic prism filled with a mixture of water and blue gel. When you turned it upside down the gel fell through the water in blobs, an effect rather reminiscent of jellyfish attempting to sprint through syrup. Even amongst the vast number of moderately useless objects drug reps had given her it was, Alice felt, a particularly pointless one – and for that reason she felt a certain affection for it.

She watched his slightly mesmerised discomfiture. 'Lisa is a lovely girl, you know, Dean. You won't find another one like her.' She didn't add that no one else as helplessly dippy could possibly exist outside a Jane Austen screen adaptation. 'She needs you right now. Being pregnant for the first time is very hard, both physically and emotionally. She's very vulnerable.'

'I know she is,' said Dean, brightening and rising to the conversation with obvious pride, 'but we're very fertile in our family too.'

Alice frowned. 'I mean she's vulnerable now. She needs your support.'

Outside Lisa paced the corridor, taking the occasional five-second break to check her make-up. She didn't want anything to be out of place – you never knew, after all, whether Dean might propose. It might be any minute, and the way she looked at that moment would be etched on his brain for ever so it wouldn't do to erupt with a zit. She had been looking at *Yes* magazine all yesterday evening. No one in *Yes* magazine ever had a zit.

'Sit down, Lisa, you've got ants in your pants.' Norma had no patience with agitated juniors.

'I can't. I'm too nervous.'

'Well, make some tea or something, and for God's sake remember to take the Borax out of the kettle this time.' Lisa had made Dr Vane's tea with the Borax still in it last month, but fortunately the surgery had been so busy that Alice had forgotten to drink the tea, and a possible stomach pumping had therefore been avoided.

Inside Alice's room Alice felt that at least the ice was now broken. 'So do you know why she wanted you to talk to me?'

'Yep, of course, but I don't want to get married,' said Dean, laying his cards on the table completely. 'Marriage is crazy. No offence, Doc.'

'None taken,' said Alice, reflecting that hers had hardly turned out to be a glorious exception to Dean's rule anyway. She leaned back in her chair and watched him, thinking: not that much older than Anemone. So young to be a father. But then, Rob and I weren't much older than Dean when we met.

'Look, Dean, it's not for me to tell you whether to get married – I wouldn't dream of it – but Lisa wanted me to tell you how she feels, because she doesn't find it easy to tell you herself. You see, she feels insecure and alone, and she hoped to be married before having a baby. You have to decide whether you can give her what she wants. And if you can't, you need to work out what you *can* offer her, and talk about it.'

Dean blushed. 'Um – if she hadn't have got herself in the club we'd be fine.'

Alice smiled. 'She didn't do it by herself.'

'I can manage without sex when I have to,' Dean shrugged. 'I work with a pneumatic drill.'

I'm not going to ask what that has to do with it, thought

Alice, although unfortunately I can imagine. Aloud she said, 'Dean, why are you and Lisa together?'

He was embarrassed. 'She's OK. I mean I – well, you know . . .' He blushed deep beetroot. 'I do love her, Dr Vane. I'm not a bastard, whatever she says.'

'She doesn't say any such thing. You'd not find anyone more loyal,' said Alice. 'But I think you need to talk this through with her – you're both going through a difficult time.' Did Rob and I talk enough? she wondered. Her clock clicked on to the hour, catching her attention. Time was passing. Patients would be building up in the waiting room in a tidal wave of viruses and depression.

'I don't want to get married,' said Dean, oblivious to her unease. 'My parents are married and they're a couple of miserable buggers. I don't want me and Lisa to finish up like them. They virtually only speak when he wants her to pass him the ketchup.'

'Maybe you should tell Lisa that's why you don't want to get married,' said Alice. 'She's afraid it's because you don't love her.' Hopefully, she thought, a few of my patients will just have coughs. If anyone is depressed I'll probably be here all night.

Dean spread his hands. 'I would – but she won't move in with me unless I marry her. My dad says that's when the rot sets in.'

Alice sighed. 'We don't have to repeat the mistakes our parents make,' she said. 'We all start out with a clean slate.'

'How do you mean?'

'Life,' said Alice, suddenly inspired, 'is like an empty building site. OK, someone may have had a go at doing the foundations, but all the rest is up to you.'

Dean stared, absorbing this slowly. 'Wow,' he said eventually, 'that's brilliant. I really like that. Lisa said you were clever.'

'So you will talk to her?' Alice stood up. 'Try to agree on what to do?'

He shrugged, standing also. 'Course I'll talk to her. But I still don't really want to get married.'

'I'm not asking you to, Dean. That's not my place. But if you can't compromise – both of you – then you'll both be losers.'

'I can compromise,' said Dean, 'as long as I don't have to get married. She's from a big family, you know. She might want ten kids.'

'Has she said so?' Alice put her hand on the doorknob and gave it a slight rattle in case Lisa should be leaning on the other side and, caught unawares, should come hurtling into the room when she opened it.

'No. She says she wants two, but it might not be true. My dad says women will say anything to get you to marry them.'

'So don't you trust her? She's taken quite a chance on you.'

'How do you mean?'

'Well, she is seven months pregnant with your baby, Dean. That's taking quite a chance on you, isn't it?'

'I s'pose so. Look, I will talk to her.'

'That's great. It's amazing what you can solve by talking.'

'Maybe. It didn't do much good in Munich,' said Dean darkly, edging out, 'and look where it ended up. Virtually led to all-out war.'

'Er – no.' Alice was taken aback, wondering if Dean meant Chamberlain's attempts to appease Hitler or the recent Middle Eastern peace talks.

'No,' said Dean, 'they talked for days and in the end Griggs signed for Milan. Scored three times in his first match, you know. The Germans have hated him ever since.'

It was not, Alice felt as she closed the door behind him, a huge success. Indeed, any optimism that he might go onto one knee in the corridor outside was almost certainly misplaced. I can't turn this into my problem, though, thought Alice. I've got enough problems.

Outside Lisa waited on edge, but Dean emerged looking shifty and, far from dropping onto his right knee at once merely said grumpily, 'D'you want to come out for a pizza tonight?'

Lisa, nodding joyfully, refused to allow the thought to cross her mind that she could think of more romantic places to be proposed to than watching Dean demolish a giant-sized crusty-base four-seasons-with-everything washed down by two lagers and a knickerbocker glory.

Alice's morning slipped relentlessly from her grasp from then on as it set out to remind her of how very often people have everything taken away from them, and of how sometimes she was doomed to be the first to know. It's always hard when you open your results pile from the hospital and discover that your next patient is going to die. Frances' faxed CT scan report was burning a hole in her desk. She knew before she read it, for she had asked for only an X-ray on Monday morning, and they had followed it up with a CT scan on Monday afternoon; a CT scan with a long report. Long reports are always bad news. After all, how many lines does it take to write 'normal anatomy'?

It was the number of places Frances' tumour had reappeared in that made the report very long.

We're all going to die – Alice frequently had to remind herself of that in these situations – even though in the Western world people are beginning to think death is optional. But dying young? Frances was almost certainly going to die by forty-three – and she was forty-two now.

'Hello, Dr Vane.' Frances came in bright, glowing even. At first glance no different from when Alice had last seen her, but Alice could see now, with the benefit of the report in front of her, that her cheeks had that look that only malignancy can give. Caving in. Like the earth when something terrible is exploding deep down below. 'I went for the X-ray and they did a scan as well. Have you had my report through?'

'Yes, I've had the report.' Alice chose her words carefully. 'Frances, I'm afraid it's not good news.' She watched Frances for signs of having guessed, signs of a routinely pessimistic turn of mind, or of things let slip in the CT department.

But Frances' smile did not falter. She was a warm, cheerful woman who lived alone, as far as Alice knew. One of Cambridge's bright young things. 'Oh dear,' she said, 'does this mean you can't get rid of my cough?'

Alice kept her body language open, kept her eyes on Frances'. 'We might be able to help the symptoms a little bit,' she said, 'but we can't treat the cause.'

'So I'll just have to live with it indefinitely, then?'

Sometimes, thought Alice, people just aren't even slightly primed to hear this. It's always so much easier if they say, 'D'you mean it's the cancer, Doctor?' Aloud, she said, 'Frances, I've known you for a long time, and I think you'd like me to be absolutely straight with you. You see, I'm afraid it is really bad news. Had you realised there was a chance it might be serious?'

'Serious?' Frances frowned. 'Well – yes, I suppose it's always a possibility, and of course I'd rather know. But it's not the cancer back again, though, is it? I mean, I know you wondered about it when you said there was fluid on my lung, but I thought I was clear after five years.'

Alice swallowed. 'So did I, but I'm afraid it is that.' And then she saw it happen, the shadow of dawning fall across Frances' face as though her internal temperature had just dropped by forty degrees. The darkness of contemplating no future, of starting to wonder when, how long . . .

'It is that. Do you mean I'm going to die?' Frances swallowed, lifting her chin to defy the unknown enemy. 'Me?' She was looking for a denial, waiting for it; it was her obvious right, at forty-two, to receive a denial. But Alice's face gave her the answer. 'You do mean it, don't you? I'm going to . . . I can't believe it . . . I'm dying. Cancer. That bloody cancer . . . How long? Months? Years?'

162

'I can't tell you. Everyone is so different, Frances. You can never guess. We have to see how things go.'

'I want to know when.' Frances was suddenly, surprisingly stubborn.

Alice put a hand on hers. 'If I could answer that for you with any meaning, any accuracy, then I would – but I can't. The closest I can say is that it's going to be months to a year or so – but not years. Not lots of years. You've not been well recently, but now the chest infection has been treated – well, it depends how you are over the next few weeks. That will give us an idea what to expect.'

Frances held on to her arm. 'But I don't want to. I'm forty-two – I'm well enough for any treatment that's going, you know. I'll try anything . . . It's not . . . Can it be wrong?'

'No,' Alice shook her head, 'not wrong. It's spread, I'm afraid.'

'All from that mole?'

'I'm afraid so.'

'But it was years ago. They said it was clear. For God's sake, I even used sunscreen when I went to Normandy in April. It can't be true. It can't be hopeless, surely it can't. Can't anything be done? Chemotherapy or something?'

'I don't know. I'd like the oncologists to see you,' said Alice. 'There are some experimental treatments for melanoma. I'll contact the specialists in London today. And I'd like to ask the Macmillan team to make contact with you too. They help with –'

Frances smiled bitterly, a twisted attempt. '– dying. They co-ordinate dying. You'll be telling me not to give up hope yet, next.' She was still stunned, refusing to meet Alice's eyes.

Alice rubbed her arm. 'They don't, Frances. They co-ordinate living. They help you with living. You're not to give up, Frances. I won't let you.'

Frances looked up. 'How will I tell Gareth?'

'Gareth?'

163

'My partner. Gareth. Didn't you know? We've been together for about six months. We don't live together – we'd thought of it but . . . it seemed too soon.' Her voice began to break. 'We thought there was plenty of time for that. God, it's like James Bond – you remember – "We've got all the time in the world." It always makes me cry, that bit, when they shoot his wife . . . Dr Vane, will you tell him? I don't know how.'

'I . . . of course I will, if it's what you want.'

'I – yes. No. No, it's not what I want. It's down to me.' Frances pulled herself upright in her chair. 'I owe him that. I'd better . . . I'm sorry, Dr Vane.'

'Whatever for?'

'It can't be nice, doing your job. Not when it's like this. I'm sorry not to just have . . . a sore throat. Especially when . . . I mean, I know you lost your husband.'

Alice blinked. 'I'm here for you, Frances. This is about you, not me.'

'I don't know how you do it. I couldn't . . . I . . . don't know what to do. Should I give up work? I mean, I'm not ill, not really. I just felt as if I needed a good holiday. Can I come and see you next week, when I've had time to – you know – to think?'

'Of course you can. Would you like me to call someone?'

'No . . . No, not now. I just need a few days to decide what to do. And can I – I mean, this is going to sound stupid and I know it's silly but we all know you have this thing about the frogs . . .'

'A frog for luck,' said Alice, trying not to cry. 'Please take one. All my best patients do.'

Poor Frances, she thought as Frances left, clutching a small wooden frog with a serene smile. Poor, poor Frances. Is it better to know in advance? Or is it better just to have a heart attack whilst you're having the time of your life, *in flagrante delicto*? She sat at her desk for a minute or two, feeling slightly drained. How do I switch from that

164

consultation to seeing someone complaining about a cold, or wanting me to write a letter asking the council to rehouse them because they found a cockroach in the pantry? She rubbed her eyes wearily and felt one of her contact lenses slip out of line. Damn it. At least she was nearly at the end of surgery.

The next three patients had sore throats, and the first complained because he'd had to wait twenty minutes. 'Another five and I'd have recovered spontaneously.' Alice felt like telling him to grow up.

Her next patient was Heather Bunberry again, doubtless with another trivial complaint. Alice fished out her temporary resident's card and resolved to ring Heather's GP and see if he knew anything about her. Why did she come so often? GPs are conditioned by their training to believe that those consulting repeatedly with trivial problems are generally concealing a deeply significant hidden agenda. Even Alice, who tried not to spend too long looking at the two billion books written for GPs on The Hidden Agenda was sure Heather had such a problem.

'Hello, Heather. What can I do for you?'

'Hello, Dr Vane. I've come to talk about my cervical smears.'

Not again, thought Alice. She's forty, she's been having smears for years. What can there be that she doesn't know about having smears? What does she really want?

Whatever it was, it was not revealed over the following ten minutes, even though Alice used every technique she could think of from the 'Tips for uncovering the Real Problem' article she had read in the *Journal of General Practice* last week. Heather left, leaving Alice convinced that she had not listened to a word of her explanation of the cervical screening programme. Odd girl. Very pretty face, very curvaceous – yet always dressed so frumpily and wore a terribly obvious wig, the sort of thing that would make most men run a mile. Perhaps that was why she did it.

Perhaps she was gay. What if her secret is that she fancies me? Better get a chaperone in here the next time she gets on to cervical smears.

Alice's last patient was Tabitha Tinkler, starting to speak even before she had wedged her impressive frame into the consulting-room chair.

'I'm terribly sorry to have used an emergency appointment for this, but –'

'That's all right, Miss Tinkler,' said Alice, thinking: I am my own worst enemy. No wonder I've never got any free appointments. 'What can I do for you?'

Tabitha's face was creased with anxiety. 'I had to come and talk to you, dear. You see, I am so very worried about my dear friend Mr Herman Banescu.'

'Have you been to see him?'

'No dear,' said Tabitha sadly. 'I have tried but they say he doesn't want to see me. Yet he came over here particularly to see me, so there must be something very wrong with him. They won't tell me a thing. Those nurses are like dragons, you know. They'd have made great East German border guards in the old days.'

'Does he know –'

'I feel responsible,' said Tabitha, as if Alice hadn't spoken. 'I feel as responsible for Herman as if he were my son. I have to find out how he is. I wondered if you would see him for me.'

Alice was intrigued. 'How do you know him?'

'His father, Tamas,' said Tabitha, suddenly wistful, and Alice felt as if she had intruded into a very cherished place, 'was the love of my life. The only one, dear. In my day you only had one chance at it all – marry the first one or become a dried-up old prune. It was prune for me,' she sighed. 'I think he must be dead. That'll be why Herman has come to see me. To tell me.'

Alice frowned. 'But he's Armenian, isn't he? Were you ever— I mean, how did you meet him?'

166

'In Armenia, dear. I travelled there a great deal when I was a young woman.'

'Goodness, I didn't know that.'

'Oh yes, well, we old folk had lives once too, you know. I worked in Eastern Europe for some years – I have the languages, you see. I read Russian and Armenian at Girton just after the war.'

'Really?' Alice was fascinated. Her Miss Tinkler, who she had thought could never have been further than Alton Towers. 'Then what did you do?'

'Oh, this and that. Commercial contacts, banking, you know the thing. There were a lot of commercial travellers in those days – business was done face to face. But things eventually got a little awkward – you know, fuss with the Soviets – and I was recalled. In a bit of a hurry, actually.'

Alice stared, in spite of herself. 'It sounds as though you had quite a time.'

'Oh, I did, dear, especially when I met Tamas. He had eyes as clear as the clear green sea, and a heart of pure gold.'

'So what . . . ?'

'It just wasn't meant to be.' Tabitha stood abruptly. 'And I never looked at another man, the more fool me, from then until now. Believe me, my dear, if you sit around being mournful you end up with nothing but moonshine in the mustard pot. Tamas had sense – he made the best of it. Got himself a fat Armenian wife and had a life.'

'You've never seen him since?'

'No, dear,' said Tabitha, 'never. We agreed to forget one another. I wrote and told him I had a good English husband so that he could get on with his life.'

'Gosh,' said Alice, 'how brave of you – and sad.'

'I lost him,' said Tabitha, her eyes bright, 'but even so, I always knew that somewhere he lived and breathed. Until now. You can lose someone more than once, you know. I'm sure that's what Herman has come to tell me. I had a postcard to say he was coming, you see, and the hospital called me because he was carrying my address. But he won't see me. He refuses to see me.'

'I'll speak to him if I get the chance,' said Alice, 'I promise.'

After Tabitha had gone Alice sat for a long time, staring at her photo of Rob, thinking of Frances, Frances' boyfriend who hadn't got round to moving in yet because they had all the time in the world. And Tabitha, who had spent her entire life keeping faith with one man. Now she was just another fussy old lady with nothing but memories of her one great romance, and she had lost him twice over.

I lost Rob twice over, she thought, because the day he died I discovered that I had already lost him before that. I just hadn't known it. What the hell did you see in a woman like Marcie Crombie? You weren't that sort of man, I'd have bet my life on it. I suppose I did bet my life on it. After all, for the first sixteen years the gamble paid off.

Rob gazed out of the photo, younger now than she, smiling and bold. I'm forty-two and he's not even forty. He's gone for ever. But I'm still young and Martha is arranging me a date. I wonder whom she has in mind?

Martha was having an unsuccessful time when Alice arrived at her shop, her American accent for once counting against her.

'I could not possibly wear one of these . . . contraptions,' a Jaegered woman with bouffant hair and enough face powder to roll out an entire batch of scones in was telling her. 'It's just revolting.'

Martha smiled. 'Thongs are very popular now, but of course they're not everyone's preference,' she said smoothly. 'The matching full knicker is terribly popular.'

'Knicker?' Her customer was not easily mollified. 'And what, might I ask, is a knicker? I am a professor of linguistics, and in my opinion you can either have knickers or you can have nothing.'

'Oh, I know just what you mean,' said Martha smoothly and conspiratorially. 'American English. It's taking us all over, isn't it? But I can have the longer-line knickers here for you tomorrow if you would like to see them.'

'I should hope so,' said the woman pompously, adding, mysteriously, 'I shall return when they are here. I'm not Judith Chalmers, you know.' She swept out of the shop.

Martha met Alice's eyes and they both got the giggles.

'What can she mean?' asked Alice.

Martha grinned. 'Judith Chalmers went on a chat show a few years ago and said she never wears knickers when she's on location. It shocked Middle England. Didn't you know?'

Alice smiled. 'Obviously the really major bits of world news somehow pass me by. I get all hung up on the trivia – earthquakes, pestilence, rivers of blood, that sort of thing . . . do you think she really is a professor of linguistics?'

Martha shrugged. 'Probably. This is Cambridge – some people are far too lacking in social skills to be anything other than academics. What brings you in here? Not enough people being ill today?'

Alice's smile drooped a little. 'Too many. That isn't why I've come.' (How do I broach this?) 'So. How are you this morning?'

Martha's grin lost a little quality. 'Fine. Not that your Tom Lovejoy thought much of me.' She turned and stared at herself rather disconsolately in the mirror. 'I'm getting older.'

'Don't be silly.' Alice watched her peering at her laughter lines minutely (and they were particularly minute). 'Men watch you wherever you go.'

Martha shrugged again. 'Men are always watching women.' She had never, Alice knew, realised that they watched her far more than any other women. But then, how does one judge these things?

'No, they're not, Martha. It's just you. You're the only woman I know who doesn't get accosted by beauty

169

consultants on the ground floor of John Lewis. I think they know there's no point.'

'Tom Lovejoy wasn't interested in me. D'you know, Alice, when I first saw him outside M&S I was sure there was a spark. I must be losing my judgement.' Martha sighed wistfully. 'Still, he's probably too intelligent for good sex. Intelligent men are hopeless – they're too good at self-censorship and they consistently underperform, even with the lights out.'

'You could always drug him,' said Alice cheerfully, 'knock out a few brain cells and drag him upstairs.'

'No point,' said Martha, thinking: if only I could. 'Intelligent men are particularly useless at oral sex. I think they never lose sight of the inherent silliness of the situation.'

'Rob was intelligent,' said Alice, 'and he wasn't useless.' She felt a sudden pride in Rob, even now, that in one way at least he had been better than Martha's rules predicted he would have been. 'At least I don't think he was.' What have I got to compare to, after all?

'Rob was not intelligent,' Martha told Alice. 'If he had been he wouldn't have been where he was that day.'

Alice sighed. 'He was a doctor, Martha. You can't just say he was stupid. It doesn't explain it.'

'I can,' said Martha. 'Some of the stupidest people I know are doctors. Not your Dr Lovejoy, though, he's sharp. You know, he'd be perfect for you.'

No he wouldn't, said a fierce voice in her head, surprising her, he'd be perfect for *me*.

'Oh, thanks,' said Alice. 'Don't you think I know anything about oral sex either?'

'You're starting to sound normal,' Martha grinned. 'So what made you decide you were ready for a blind date?'

Alice felt guilty. Martha was trying to help her get her life together, even pushing her towards Tom Lovejoy when she clearly fancied him like mad herself. But it wasn't going to happen because she, Alice, had ruined Martha's chances and switched off Tom Lovejoy's oozing charm by letting him think she was gay . . . she brought herself back to Martha's question. 'I just thought it's time I made some changes. I've finally realised they're not going to happen by themselves. I mean, maybe it's bad for me, being so . . .'

'Celibate?'

'No – yes – I mean, not in the sense you mean. I mean, I should at least try, just to see.'

'You mean,' said Martha knowledgeably, 'that maybe you're celibate purely because you're celibate, and that's why you've asked me to fix you up?'

'Ugh, don't put it like that. You're worse than Anemone, who wanted me to go on *Blind Date* in pursuit of the opportunity of a week doing assault courses in Herefordshire with a man named Craig. I don't want eternal romance. I just need to see if I'm dead through and through, or just on the surface.'

'Look, you don't have to explain it to me – I think it's a good idea.'

'It is. I've been having funny dreams lately. Even the children think I should get myself a life.' Alice bit her lip. 'Although they still think the sun shines out of Rob's glorious memory too.'

'Don't you?' Martha was quick.

'Of course not. You know how I feel.'

'I know you blame him,' said Martha gently, 'but that doesn't mean you honestly think anyone else can hold a candle to him, does it?'

Alice shook her head vehemently. 'The less like Rob my date manages to be, the better. But it is time I made an effort – you know, see if I can stir up an interest, improve my emotional health. I shouldn't still feel so . . . empty.'

Martha was glad to hear it. 'I've just the man in mind,' she said. 'He's exactly your type. You did say tomorrow.'

Alice was cautious. 'It needs to be soon, so I can't think

about it too much and back out.' She frowned, wondering what Martha had in store. 'What do you think my type is?'

'Not too tall, not too hairy, no serious psychiatric diseases,' said Martha. 'You're forty-two years old, Alice, the best men are taken, you can't be fussier than that. You could always leave your contact lenses out.'

'Just so long as he's not gay.'

'Trust me,' said Martha. 'I know what I'm doing.'

Chapter Eight

Alice had a fair idea where Martha got her sex from. Actually, you only had to take one look at some of the men she turned up to the theatre with to realise that those sort didn't sit around on the shelf unless it was the shelf of the very expensive men shop. It didn't appal her – actually, oddly, it didn't even surprise her. It was, after all, impossible to imagine Martha ever compromising on the quality of her men, impossible to imagine her waking to a man who farted or smelled of garlic – and even the best, most perfect of men feel they have earned the right to those slight lapses of personal manners after a night of the utmost intimacy, particularly where good oral sex is involved. Not so a gigolo, though, a gigolo would never allow himself to fart. Alice could see that. It was all about being on your best behaviour. Martha wouldn't arrange that for her, of course. Not a gigolo. Not after Rob doing exactly that.

She tried not to think, on returning to the surgery, of exactly what Martha *might* do. Sometimes in life thinking can be a bad idea.

Sometimes reading your mail can also be a bad idea. The note she found on her desk quite clearly said that Dr Liversill objected to patients of the Lammas Practice using the designated private patient parking spaces. Someone's car had leaked motor oil on the private spaces and this clearly would not do. He had also just learned of a recent and appalling problem, the letter added, when one of his valued patients, visiting him on a matter of utmost urgency, had parked for a second or so in one of the Doctor spaces, and had been blocked in by one of the doctors. Roland was now having to counsel her for post-traumatic stress following the ensuing altercation. It was, pointed out the letter, actually Roland's tarmac, even if Dr Vane's name was painted on that particular spot.

For a moment Alice nearly yielded to the temptation to take Roland's letter and stuff it into his supercilious mouth. But no. The fact that it was her car that had leaked oil onto the car park didn't help. Roland would know the culprit was certain to be the Morris Minor, and his interpretation would be that this had happened because she didn't have a man to keep an eye on her big end, and then he would offer to check her oil level with that same kind of patronising flirtatiousness that ruined Tess of the D'Urbervilles. Better to let this one pass. There wouldn't be a Lammas partnership for much longer, anyway. Perhaps she ought to send another postcard to Ian, telling him it was all over bar the shouting.

Her telephone rang as she doodled imaginary tribesmen with bones through their noses onto a pad marked 'Canesten – first for vaginal thrush.'

'Dr Vane,' said Norma when Alice picked up her phone, 'could you pop out here a minute?'

Alice frowned. What now? Another pregnant secretary, perhaps? She put down her pen and walked through.

There was a hushed atmosphere in reception, and she frowned. No patients were in yet – but then afternoon surgery wasn't due to start for another hour.

'Tell me,' said the voice of James Ferguson, clean and crisp as a lettuce over the intercom, 'do I not have any patients in the waiting room? Or is it perhaps that they are there but are being entertained by a bevy of Egyptian bellydancers with rubies in their navels?'

Norma sighed. This was something she did a lot, and it was a rather horselike sigh which vibrated her lips and gave her the look of a woman who had spent too long trying to play a didgeridoo.

'D'you see what I mean? I think James is ill.'

'I'm sure you're wrong. You know James. He's just showing a little humour,' said Alice. 'I don't think you should worry. He probably thinks the speaker system isn't working. I'll have a word with him.'

But when Alice popped in to speak to James he said he was fine, he had just been joking, and she retreated to her room, concerned. True, James had always had a peculiar sense of humour, but he had been worse recently. There had been that odd affair the week before last when he had reported his car stolen after dropping it in at his usual garage for repair, and she had seen him waltzing around the car park with Gladys the cleaner last Friday evening. It was probably stress – she hoped it was just stress – but was he actually safe to do his job? Should she speak to Marjorie? Should she write to Ian? If she wasn't careful when Ian got to read his bunch of postcards he would turn tail and flee deep into the Papuan jungle and never be seen again. She picked up the phone.

'Norma, have you seen—'

'The hospital have just rung,' said Norma brightly. 'They said that Mr Banescu in coronary care has been asking for you. They wondered if you could go up there and talk to him.' Norma enjoyed passing on messages and pleasing people. She also enjoyed getting patients seen by doctors at the patients' convenience, even when the doctors were fully booked and almost at the chewing-the-wall stage. This meant that as a dragon receptionist she lacked a certain something.

'Didn't you tell them I had a surgery to do?' said Alice wearily.

Norma beamed helpfully. 'I said your next patient wasn't for an hour.'

Alice ground her teeth. 'Very well. I'm just popping up to Addenbrooke's to visit a couple of patients. I may be gone for quite some time.'

'Right you are, Dr Vane,' said Norma, who at times seemed to fancy herself to be an extra off a sixties Yorkshire police drama and who had a complete immunity to irony in any form. 'Dr Lovejoy is due in at any minute so I'll tell him to call you on the mobile if he needs you.'

Hopefully he won't call me now that he thinks I'm a lesbian, thought Alice, a little guiltily. I really ought to tell him the truth about that. If I do he'll make a beeline for Martha, I'm absolutely sure of it, but that's none of my business. In any case, any romance between Martha and Tom would be short-lived: if Martha ran true to form she would eat him alive, Tom would be used and then dumped. Martha was highly resistant to being possessed, and possession always moved swiftly onto the agenda of the men who orbited her for any length of time.

Alice found Herman Banescu sitting up in bed delighted at having finally located his Mary Poppins thanks to Sister Goodenough finding the paramedics for him and giving them a grilling.

'Ah, the lady doctor,' he said as she approached his bed. 'It is true what they say about the English. They have no idea how to make tea. This tea tastes of slippers and cabbage.'

Alice smiled. 'You are on the NHS now, you know. Slippers and cabbage is the coronary care unit treat. It's tarmac and old socks on the general wards. How are you feeling?'

'I've been worse,' said Herman, 'but only slightly.'

'I heard you'd been a bit confused. Is that any better?'

'Ah,' he said, 'I did get a little muddled. It was the morphine, they tell me. I became quite strange for a while. Now I am almost myself, but I have lost something. I was hoping you could help.'

'If I can.' Alice pulled up her chair. 'What do you want to know?'

'I brought a gift with me,' said Herman, 'a very important thing for an old family friend. To lose it would be a tragedy. The shame . . . I cannot begin to explain the shame. St Gregory would never forgive me. I cannot see her till I have found it, and I'm sure I had it when I was taken ill in your surgery. I remember thinking I had dropped it somewhere.'

'What did it look like?'

But Herman was still confused, could not remember. It was in a box, he said, he had hidden it in some sort of a box, and brought it through customs. Then he had been in Alice's room and surrounded by frogs, and that had seemed very important. 'All the eyes,' he said anxiously. 'I remember all those frog eyes looking at me.'

Alice thought he was probably still rambling. 'Could you have hidden it behind my frogs?'

But Herman shook his head. No, that wasn't it. His mind, he said apologetically, seemed to have lost a bit of time at the moment. All he could remember was the pain in his chest and those frogs.

As Alice and Herman were talking, Martha was closing up her shop, still conscious of a ridiculous sense of relief that Alice was not entertaining lustful thoughts of Tom. Ridiculous because he'd made it plain he wasn't interested in her either. Martha, despite displaying the same immaculately groomed exterior that she always presented to the world, felt as though someone had taken her confidence and given it the tiniest little shake. Tom Lovejoy simply didn't fancy her. This was a good thing, she told herself, because she did not need a relationship with a man who made her fall over and spill things. It undermined her poise and turned her into a swooning Cartland heroine. And that wasn't her at all. She just needed to get him out of her system. It wasn't as if she had fallen in love. She was immune to that sort of disaster.

Having reached this firm conclusion Martha drew deeply

177

on her fake cigarette (no real ones in the shop) and reached for the phone. Cigarettes, she liked to tell her dates, were her only vice, but of course that wasn't quite true. She had two vices – sex was the other one, and the rejection by Tom Lovejoy (not rejection, just lack of mutual spark) had left her a little hungry.

'Hello. Laura Morgan speaking.'

'Hello, Laura, it's Martha Coleman. I need a date for tonight.'

Laura was smooth, you could give her that. Without seeming to do anything more than take a thoughtful breath into the phone she had reached for Martha's file, flipped it open, checked which of the current escorts on her books had not dated Martha already (Martha never repeated a date) and said smilingly, 'There's a charming man I know called Greg who's free tonight and who would love to escort you. Shall I introduce you?'

'Is he . . . my type?' Martha sounded a little unlike herself and Laura stared at the receiver, surprised.

'I'm sure you'll like him,' she said, quickly but carefully – for even a regular client could turn out to be Inspector Knacker of the Yard, so you shouldn't let your guard slip. 'Would you like me to charge our introduction fee to your usual card?'

'Yes, of course,' said Martha coolly, poise recovered. 'I'll expect him at the usual place around eight.'

Alice had an extraordinarily busy afternoon surgery, and began to run late after half an hour with a patient from Warsaw who needed to talk about viruses in sign language. Then an emergency call came in about a fitting child and Alice abandoned her waiting patients to rush there, only to find that, far from having a fit, Kirsty Grainger was having a tantrum. The mother was apologetically defiant, a state which is all too familiar to most GPs. 'Well, I knew you wouldn't come if I didn't say fit, but I've never seen her in

178

such a strop, Doctor. It isn't like her, and I'm sure it must be a food allergy.'

Alice kept her cool. 'Mrs Grainger, Kirsty isn't allergic to food. She's just an angry frustrated child.' Just like I'm an angry frustrated adult.

By the time she got back to the surgery after delivering the standard manipulative child talk to Mrs Grainger, a woman who was as putty in her children's hands anyway, her last afternoon patient had gone in to see Tom Lovejoy and there were no more waiting to be seen. Tom had tidied up for her again and had seen six of her patients, including Mrs McTaggart, whose sinuses were a constant source of despair to all who encountered her, both medically and otherwise. You really couldn't fault Tom. He had even seen three of James's patients, Norma told Alice with huge smugness.

James, it seemed, had gone home early with a headache. He had left his car keys on his desk, which must mean Marjorie had come to fetch him. Or that he had forgotten them again and caught the bus.

Evening comes slowly to those who long for it, but swiftly to those who have forgotten all about it. It was dusk by the time Alice finished her paperwork and she was surprised, therefore, to find Tom Lovejoy still in the reception area when she took her patients' notes out.

'Alice, I wonder if I might have a word?'

'Yes, of course.' Alice felt a little warmer towards him because of Mrs McTaggart. 'And, Tom, thank you for helping out today.'

'Think nothing of it. Listen, thank you so much for supper the other night . . . Alice, I've been trying to talk to James, but he seems a little . . . odd.'

Alice frowned, torn between the need to talk to someone about James and the loyalty she owed him. The loyalty won. 'I . . . I'm sure James is fine. He's just a little tired at the moment.'

Tom looked unconvinced. 'Well, if there is anything you want to talk about – you know it wouldn't go any further.'

Alice bit her lip. 'Thank you, but I can't.'

'I wish you'd let me help, Alice. You're trying to do an awful lot all by yourself. You don't have to be a loner all the time.'

Alice felt her hackles rise rapidly. One minute he was jolly nice and she started to feel quite mellow towards him – the next he was coming out with one of those things which Rob used to say. Well, she didn't need taking care of, not any more.

'I'm fine.' She picked up her pile of forms requesting information on patients taking out insurance policies, topped by the pile of letters from insurance companies asking why she hadn't completed and returned them yet as the insurance companies had sent them a whole twenty-four hours ago and everyone knows GPs have absolutely nothing else to do with their hours of spare time and are particularly eager to spend their leisure hours filling out insurance reports. 'I must be off.'

Getting into the car, though, she was suddenly, horribly aware that there were tears of self-pity in her eyes. A loner, he had said. Was that what she was now? Once life was about partnership – partnership with Rob, partnership with James and Ian and even Roland – and now she had become a loner. Was that honestly what she wanted to be?

As Alice drove home, up at the hospital Phoebe lay in her bed on the ward, allowing her mother to tempt her with jelly whilst her father retied the red ribbons in her pigtails to make them exactly symmetrical. Phoebe did not know the word symmetrical, but nevertheless had a powerful and parent-wearying sense of symmetry when it came to hair. She was pleased that her baby brother was still at Grannie's, as she had not yet forgiven Mummy for having him. On the table beside her stood Alice's frog, Jeremy Fisher. Phoebe had decided that Jeremy was stupid. The boy in the bed opposite, who was called Lawrence, had an Action Man whose arms went round and round, and the girl with both legs in plaster had a doll which sang 'Ring-a-Ring o'Roses' when you held both of its hands at the same time. Mummy said she couldn't have one because it might be electric – but all Jeremy did was rattle when you joggled him about, as if something had got loose inside him.

Her nurse, a blonde siren called Lucy, appeared beaming. 'It's eight o'clock. Time for bed now, Phoebe,' she said. 'Lights out.'

Phoebe sniffed. 'That's silly. At home I can stay up till half-past eight.'

'Ah, but you're a poorly girl.'

'I'm not going to sleep,' said Phoebe, 'till I've got an Action Man like Lawrence.'

Her mother frowned. 'we haven't got any Action Men, darling. You've never wanted one before.'

Phoebe glared. 'Well, I can't sleep without an Action Man.'

'Sounds like some nurses I know,' said Lucy cheerfully to Alana. Alana glared and Lucy wilted fast. It didn't do to be pulled up for making inappropriate jokes when you were only a second-year student. 'I'll see if Lawrence will lend it,' she said hastily.

Lawrence, it turned out, was prepared to swap his Action Man for Phoebe's frog, so that was settled. At least for now.

Eight o'clock was also the time that Martha met Greg, so by half-past ten they were dancing gently around her elegant living room to the music of Edith Piaf, and a sense of anticipation was starting to build in her. He was every bit as handsome as Tom Lovejoy. He was attentive, he was charming, he was polished. It was almost enough to overwhelm and submerge the sense of frustration which had lingered ever since the dinner at Alice's house – almost, but not quite.

181

Edith trilled in her gloriously evocative voice. *'Non, rien de rien . . . Non, je ne regrette rien . . .'* and Martha wondered if Greg used Viagra. Of course, most of the escorts surely would, most of the time – but it was less than reassuring to think he might need it with her. Still, she thought, running her hands over the broad torso, the flat stomach, feeling the outline of the flatteringly firm erection beneath the expensive cloth of his trousers (obviously tailored, Laura had excellent taste), still, if he had used Viagra you could take the view that he thought this would be an experience worth prolonging.

'It's been a lovely evening,' he murmured softly in that gorgeous public school accent that was almost as much of a turn-on as Scottish.

She met his eyes boldly. 'I hope it's not over yet . . .'

He smiled.

Outside, far above, the moon shone, non-judgmental, on Martha and Greg, on the Fir Trees where Tabitha Tinkler sat on her bed in the pale silver light and wept, the tears catching in the lines on her pale and furrowed face and dropping onto the crumpled picture in the small silver frame. She could have had it copied or enlarged – but that would have meant leaving it with a photographer and she had never been prepared to do so, for it was the only picture she had of him. Outside a peacock cried, then another. No wonder I can't sleep, she thought. Stupid bloody birds.

There was a knock at her door.

'Yes?'

'It's me.' Fred Ramsden.

'What do you want?'

'Can I come in?'

I hope he doesn't want sex, thought Tabitha. That's the trouble with old people's homes. There are so many women that the men think all of us are panting for them all of the time. And here there's only Fred. I wonder how many of them he's servicing.

'All right,' she said suspiciously, 'the door's open.'

Fred, ridiculous in a nightshirt and pointed striped hat, appeared suddenly in her vision, as people do when you wear aphakic spectacles. Tabitha's cataracts had been removed years ago, long before decent lens implants, and she had become accustomed to the thick lenses which made things suddenly loom at her from nowhere. It added a sense of surprise to life, which was a good thing most of the time. Now Fred loomed, and sat on the end of her bed. For a while he said nothing, and she blew her nose several times, sounding to her own ears like an African elephant issuing a challenge.

After a while she said, 'People think old people don't cry, you know. They think we expect death at our age.'

Fred leaned over and took the picture from her. 'As time goes by,' he commented cryptically, 'the sense of death wears off. It all becomes a little unreal as you get older.'

Tabitha peered at Fred, momentarily disturbed out of her sorrow. 'How old are you really, Fred?'

He shrugged. 'You know. Older than my teeth. Older than you are.'

She smiled in a watery way. 'He was ninety. It's a good age, they say.'

Fred waited. 'D'you want to talk about him?'

'We had to say goodbye. I've always wondered if there was another way.'

'You kept in touch?'

'No. We agreed to forget one another. I wrote and told him I had married someone else. I got a letter back from him wishing me luck and saying that he too had married. Faithless bastard. And now he sends his son to tell me . . .' She wept anew.

Fred put an arm round her. 'No point sitting around. You do nothing but get older.'

Tabitha straightened immediately, shook him off. 'Don't you dare try it on with me, Fred Ramsden. Don't you think just because I'm old it means I'm desperate.'

Fred jumped to his feet. 'Old? You wouldn't know the meaning of the word.'

'Oh, I know, you're as old as the dinosaurs and twice as wealthy. Well, go and have your way with some other old bird. I'm off for a cocoa. And if you've nothing better to do than wander round the Fir Trees in the middle of the night then why don't you go outside and throttle those bloody peacocks? I don't know where you get your money from, Fred Ramsden, but it smacks of no good to me!'

Fred watched her thoughtfully as she stalked out and headed for the kitchen. Nice behind when she took her corsets off.

As Tabitha made cocoa, in a fury at Fred, Alice was sitting in the garden at Herne Road with a glass of wine, gazing rather sadly at the garden. The garden was neither thick nor lush. The hebes were scrappy, lavender no larger than when she'd planted it, and she had rather lost heart when it came to the roses. Everyone knows roses won't grow unless your heart is in it, and hers looked as though they felt particularly unloved. Only the big stone sundial looked sturdy, a monument to the pretentiousness of suburbs, even those in Cambridge. Rob would have laughed at the sundial. It isn't even lined up right, he'd have said, and it's too new. He would have been right too. He was sometimes right.

Should she move back to Fox Colne? Should she abandon this poor sad garden that she had obviously never been able to love properly? Could she take up her old life again and go back to deep red dining rooms and gardens in the country? Should she even start bringing men home for breathless dates and evenings of checking out their souls before sex? As she once had with Rob . . .

She could do it gradually. Try a date, check out sex again,

try a pot of slightly not white paint, try to feel her way forwards through the gloom of adversity a step at a time. She was ready for that, at least.

Would the children really be keen to go back, or might she precipitate some return to melancholia? Can one really ever go back, in order to go forward?

The sky was dark velvet blue, the moon the stunning, flooding white that makes all the whites that have ever gone before seem a pale reflection of the one, true whiteness. You could look at the moon, Alice had found over the years, look at it and ask it questions, and its gentle face would seem to listen and understand.

'Penny for them.' Anemone, coming out with cocoa, liked the moon, which was, she felt, womanish and menstrual. The moon, she had worked out from her tables, had been full when she was conceived, and so it must have an affinity with her now. Paddy trailed out after her, hoping for a walk, and sat on Alice's feet with resigned dogginess.

'Not worth a penny,' said Alice, sighing, and Anemone knew she had been thinking of her father. She sat beside her mother. 'Do you ever feel as if he's up there?'

Alice smiled. 'I suppose I do. I talk to him there sometimes. In the eye of the moon. The left eye.'

Anemone gazed up at the smiling face, the mountains and seas of a barren rock, imagining her father there in a white space suit, clutching the long-planted American flag and jumping up and down in slow motion, like Buzz Aldrin on those old black-and-white clips they showed in modern history. 'Does he talk back?'

But Alice shook her head, pressing her lips together painfully. There is a void between Rob and me, she thought, a gulf, a chasm so vast that Rob cannot hear me speaking to him, cannot be reached, will never be reached again. It's far wider than death, far more impassable than the river between heaven and hell. I just don't know who he was, don't understand how I could have got him so wrong.

185

'Fergus says Tabitha Tinkler is awfully upset about her friend. Even my feng shui doesn't help. Is he going to be OK?' Anemone sounded concerned.

'I hope so.' Alice put an arm round her daughter. 'I do hope so.' She thought back to her conversation with Herman, earlier. He was convinced he must have dropped his gift for Tabitha at the surgery, but she didn't remember seeing anything unusual – and he was absolutely adamant that he wouldn't see Tabitha until it had turned up. Until he could tell her exactly what they were looking for there was nothing more she could do.

Some distance away the same moon lit Bury St Edmunds, where Heather Bunberry also gazed thoughtfully up at its gentle face. She had once been Marcie Crombie, but had reverted to the name of Heather Bunberry, the one she had been born with in the first place. She had felt it to be a rather stupid name and it had not sat well with her former career. Now, though, she was a bestselling novelist, writing romantic bodice-rippers about dastardly marquises and virginal brides which set the hearts of female England fluttering even more effectively than Leonardo DiCaprio. So Heather Bunberry she was again – but no amount of erasing her past (she had even had the penis tattoo on her left buttock altered. They had made it into the leaning tower of Pisa – an incongruous object to display on the left buttock, it's true, but better than the alternative) could ever quite take away the guilt. She loved living in Bury St Edmunds. She had a lovely house near the cathedral, a marvellously suitable fiancé who was going to marry her and cherish her for ever . . . and there was even parking at the back of Marks and Spencer for when the urge to buy sensible underwear overcame her reassuringly on rainy days, as it now so often did.

But money, fame, success, and the incineration of every pair of crotchless knickers she had ever owned had failed to exorcise the demons of her past. Even the trio of psycho-therapy, tattoo alteration and sensible knickers had not put her guilt behind her. She had killed Robert Vane – it was as simple as that. She had, by luring him to that hotel room, taken him from his wife and children – and worse, even, than that, she had left them bereft and mystified. She had fled in her pain and shock, and yet now, after all this time, she had come to see that she needed to talk to Alice, explain how things had been. It was the only way she would be able to move on.

Unfortunately, though, she was plagued by the same problems teenaged boys face in pharmacies – in that every time she went in to see Alice to *tell* her, she found herself uttering the medical equivalent of asking for toothpaste instead. She would make another appointment, and this time she would tell Alice the truth. That was what she would do.

In Fox Colne, bats sang sweetly at walls and hedges as they flitted blindly from church to yew. A dog barked, a car drove quietly away – there was something about the village that intimidated the revving of engines. In Hall Cottage Madame Butterfly sang a poignant lament as Martha lowered herself gloriously onto Greg, neck arched in pleasure, digging her nails into his hard, tanned abdomen like a cat as she felt him penetrate, rigid as a gun barrel in a velvet pouch. She leaned back, ground her pelvis down and sighed. This was the best part. She could never understand women who liked to lie there and get squashed. What was the point of letting some chap work you as an instrument for his own pleasure, as though you were a creature of Plasticine for moulding at a whim? Martha preferred to be on top – indeed, it was essential to her orgasm to be in control of what went on. She knew from experience that men were like trains – if you let them get up a head of steam then they rocketed off like a brakeless locomotive and before you knew it they'd reached the station home and dry. It wasn't that they all suffered from premature ejaculation, it was more that she herself, like a perfectly trained racehorse, needed plenty of time and very careful handling. It took a lot of concentration too, to make the perfect orgasm – controlled, blossoming, unfolding like the petals of a giant, glorious, tropical flower, perfumed, and honeyed, and warm. Orgasm should be all-encompassing, like swimming through tropical waters to lie stretched and damp and exhausted beneath cloudless skies on coral sands.

Martha often liked to watch a man's body as she took pleasure in it. A good body was essential so she could enjoy watching him react as she felt her own climactic spasms building in waves and surges to squeeze her tight – but she rarely watched his face. She might watch his lips sometimes, if they were particularly good lips, or his chest, if it was smooth and tanned – but she watched them with the detached admiration of an art critic, as things of beauty worth admiring. And more often than not, as now, she threw back her head, closed her eyes and thought of someone else entirely. This way if she wanted someone specific, someone from real life, she could use them for her sexual pleasure without their ever needing to know. Adultery, betrayal, guilt – none of those things were relevant. A married man was fair game since he would not actually participate and need never know about it. This way Martha had sexually enjoyed dozens of men whose eyes, bodies or voices had caught her attention. Some were unattainable – Alexander the Great, Che Guevara, Tony Blair, Bill Clinton – often men whose power would add a particular *soupçon* to the position of domination. Others were men she had met, many of whom would, had they known about it, desperately have regretted not having being present in person during Martha's glowing fantasy. One had been Robert Vane, although she had never told Alice that, of course. The fantasies were as essential to the orgasm as the riding position – and Martha had honed them to a fine art. Now, using Greg as an instrument of her own pleasure (although, fair to say, he seemed to be getting a great deal out of it too, as he was groaning like a drowning man) she focused physically on his hot, thrusting organ as it pierced rigid between her thighs and, smiling beatifically, focused mentally on the handsome features of Tom Lovejoy.

She had been right about the Viagra. Greg had not been expecting Martha Coleman. His usual clients were fat-diamonded tennis-club wives with hairdos harder than his erection and skin which, like elephants', moved independently of the muscle layer beneath. It generally took immense concentration on his part, both on the magazines that he had invariably viewed earlier and on mental images of real women he had actually chosen to enjoy in the past, to produce a believably solid erection and to manage to appear to climax convincingly at a suitable moment. Sometimes, if things were particularly difficult, he thought of Hillary Clinton, but he liked to save her for times of real adversity. Besides, it often didn't take these women long to come, as they weren't used to men like him, and he was particularly good at managing the afterglow. That's what they were mostly missing out on. There they were, sexually revitalised on their HRT, with husbands who had forgotten that women have an afterglow at all, and who treated them only to the occasional quickie when the secretary was having her period or in Marbella with her boyfriend.

Actually, Laura had told him that this client was different, more attractive than the rest, but he had assumed that to be sugar on Laura's part to get him out of London and into the sticks at such short notice. And even if he had believed her, he would have assumed she meant attractive in relative terms – relative to the typical client, which didn't have to be much, not attractive like a sex goddess. But Martha Coleman was unbelievable. He hadn't been this rock hard since that first time with his father's mistress in the office car park.

He groaned gorgeously, scarcely able to believe his luck. To think he was getting paid for this . . . and his moment of fulfilment approached rather too rapidly as he felt the surge of uncontrollable climax. Even when he closed his eyes in an attempt at delay he could still see Martha on the backs of his eyelids, riding him like a Valkyrie. Her glorious round breasts were etched on his retina like golden orbs. He hung on valiantly for as long as he could, trying desperately to think of cold chip fat, of the fact that he had run out of cat litter and of trips to the zoo with his incontinent great-aunt – but eventually it was impossible, and his moment seized him and shook him in violent and groaning release. And then he had to withdraw so as not to lose the condom, even though he would have preferred to remain buried in her for hours, for days, for weeks – at least for as long as it took to do it again. If only he hadn't looked at those magazines on the way up. If only he had read something on pig husbandry instead . . .

Martha, who had had similar experiences on many occasions, coped well. She knew what she liked, and although she was paying for it there was plenty of the night ahead.

But she was troubled. It wasn't Greg's inability to hang on troubling her, for the Viagra did its job and within half an hour he was seriously desperate for more – it was the fact that, far from enhancing her orgasm the image of Tom Lovejoy seemed to have ruined things completely. I can't even get past first base with him in my head, she thought, letting Greg trace her nipples with his tongue, pull them into his mouth, sliding back onto his eager hardness with demanding pressure. She usually avoided breast contact. True, it always worked with her, like being turned on at the mains, but it seemed a little too personal a thing with a stranger. No, the thought of Tom Lovejoy had given her the oddest feeling. The feeling that she didn't want to be doing this with Greg when he wasn't the one she was thinking of. And that was ridiculous. You can only sleep with the available men, after all. And she enjoyed it so much more when it was on her terms.

But by the early hours of the morning Martha was more worried than she wanted to acknowledge. She had worked on herself and Greg all night, pulling out every sexual trick at her disposal, even trying the unthinkable and allowing him to mount her and drive into her with all the force he could muster, his face contorted with lust and delight, his energy and flexibility second to none. She had built up and built up and built up her orgasm – but the peak had never been quite within her reach, the shore of that coral island was never quite within her stroke. Tom Lovejoy's face swam between her and the unreachable explosion so effectively that by four o'clock she had decided to switch images to Richard Branson, an unheard of ploy and almost like being unfaithful, as it was like sleeping with two men in a row.

By five o'clock they both gleamed with baby oil, and Greg, drained dry, was beginning to wonder if friction burns made it bigger, because it certainly felt that way, whilst Martha had discarded all her inhibitions about familiarity and had him bury his face in her pubic hair. At least that way her climax was guaranteed – and it was modestly spectacular in the end. Nevertheless, she knew that all had not been well. A body like Greg's, an erection that popped back up on demand for six hours, his obvious delighted enjoyment of her energetic ride and her welcoming body, all of these should have made it a night to remember. But it had not been, because in the end she had only reached the climax by the deliberate and sustained action of forgetting Tom Lovejoy completely.

Chapter Nine

When Alice got home the next day she needed an hour in the bath with a whole bottle of Sexy Banana Invigorating Bath Oil in order to convince herself that she could face the evening. 'Use one capful in the bath for a sensual soak,' said the bottle. So if it's effective, she thought, then with the amount I've put in I could soon be a complete nymphomaniac. One can, after all, be invigorated too much.

It had been an emotionally draining afternoon, and the notification of planning approval that had come in for her from the local council had not helped. Roland, it seemed, had applied not only for permission to convert the building into bedsit accommodation, and to convert the car park into a communal garden, but also to install a bicycle rack and a small fountain. Doubtless it would be a peeing cherub – that would be Roland's style.

Alice had shown the letter to James, but James had not seemed interested.

'You know, my dear, I have always thought that tarmac patch a bit of an eyesore. It's a real suntrap at the back there – you could grow some nice bay trees and maybe even a magnolia. It could be a real asset to the practice.'

'James,' she had said, exasperated, 'I think the magnolia and the practice are mutually exclusive.'

But James had not seemed to be taking it in – or even terribly interested – and eventually Alice had watched him leave, chewing her lip. Did he see that they were going to have to close down? Did he care? She had the terrible feeling that his disappointment in Roland was so great that he'd simply lost heart.

She was still standing in the reception area looking tired when Tom Lovejoy found her. 'Alice?' He sounded concerned. 'Is everything OK?'

'OK? Oh, yes . . . I mean . . .' Why not just tell him? Everyone will know soon enough. She showed him the letter. 'Well, this, actually. It's a reminder of how precarious things are. Roland's given us till the end of September to find somewhere new, and now look – he's planning to put in a fountain where my parking space is.'

'I'm sure he can't evict you as easily as all that. You have rights as tenants . . .'

'He can,' said Alice. 'He can make things so bloody unpleasant that we simply have to go.'

'Surely not,' said Tom. 'The law is rarely on the side of the landlord in these kind of disputes, you know. What can he do to you? '

'He can just be here,' said Alice bitterly, 'that's all it takes with him. He can be so impossible that we'd all rather be anywhere but here. You wouldn't believe the rows we've had with him recently – I've had with him, actually – about trivia. Rows about light bulbs and biros and whether we should be paying him nuisance money because the NHS phones ring so much more than his does. Rows about whether NHS patients expose private patients to lower social-class viruses and whether our receptionists ate his chocolate bloody digestives. Today it's loo roll that's on his mind, tomorrow it will be fly spray or air freshener or the condensation on the windows first thing in the morning . . .'

'I get the idea. So you want to move the practice to new premises?'

Alice sighed. 'I don't think it's an option, realistically. Even if such a thing were possible, James doesn't seem interested – and with Ian away . . .' It was suddenly easy to tell someone. Tom was smiling, friendly, didn't have the kind of halitosis that would set off the gas attack sirens in an Israeli street. 'Anyway, we've really got nowhere to go. The cost of real estate in Cambridge makes anything central completely impossible, and if we go too far out we'll lose our patients and then . . . well, you can imagine.'

Tom was politely persistent. 'But if there were somewhere available, a suitable building in the centre of town, you'd think about it?'

'I'd consider it,' said Alice wearily, thinking: the last thing I need is pedantry. 'But it's not going to happen.'

'Why don't we put our heads together on this tomorrow? I might have a few ideas. We could brainstorm?'

Alice shook her head, suddenly feeling bamboozled. 'It's very kind of you, Tom, but I have to think this through and I so need to talk to Ian. Things are . . . a little confused at the moment. I'm also going out tonight and I'm a little late.'

'Oh dear, I won't keep you, then. Actually, I must go – I'm on call for BASICS at the moment.'

'Oh.' Bloody typical, thought Alice uncharitably. Why do male doctors get such kicks from being on road accident call-out? Some people will do anything for the chance to put on one of those fluorescent yellow jackets and look important. She'd bet his aftershave was called Hero and he played Bonnie Tyler CDs in his car.

She was about to leave herself when the call came in. Five to seven, she thought, bane of my life. There's always a call at five to seven. It's as if they know we put the phones through to the answering service at seven o'clock. If this is a drug rep I will never, ever prescribe his product again in the entire history of time. If this is someone at the Fir Trees I shall say it's James's on-call day and then sneak off. If this is Martha I shall cancel tonight. Why hasn't she returned my message yet? I've told her answering machine three times that I can't go through with it. She knows I wouldn't just fail to show up, that's the trouble. With the time I spend moaning about Did Not Attends on the NHS I couldn't stand her up.

'Yes?'

'Dr Vane?'

Alice's heart froze. If Frances needed her she would go right now. 'Frances. How are you?'

'Dr Vane, I'm ringing to tell you I'm cancelling my appointment with the specialist.'

'Oh. I mean – why not wait till after your holiday? I mean, I thought you wanted to explore the possibilities.'

Frances was silent for a moment, and then said, 'I think you and I both know that's pointless now.'

'Well, we don't know that for sure, Frances. They're trying new things all the time.'

'It's all on the Internet, Dr Vane. Patients are impossible to deceive these days, you know, even when you mean well. I've got zero chance, with my tumour histology and at this stage.'

'Frances, I think we should talk about this. I could come over and see you.'

'Well – actually, I'm just off out. Look, don't think I'm stupidly brave – I'm not in denial, you know. I – we – just don't want to waste what's left. So I'm packing. We've booked tickets – we're off to the Bahamas together. We're going to get married there, actually.'

'I don't know what to say.' Alice was stunned. 'I mean, congratulations, of course, but—'

'That's the trouble,' said Frances, 'there isn't anything you can say. I know it sounds like something they'd put into *EastEnders* to get the viewing figures up, but this is what we want to do. I could sit around and wait till I'm really ill and it's horrible, or I could have a really good time and say no to being pumped full of poison on some near-hopeless drug trial they can't bear to turn me away from. So say nothing, just wish me luck and see me when I get back.'

'I . . . I do,' said Alice. 'I do wish you luck. Is there anything you need? What about your travel jabs?' Oh, what a bloody stupid thing to say.

'No, not now. I'll take my chance on hepatitis A – but

thanks for asking. I'll see you as and when. The way we see it today, now, life's for living, Dr Vane. The clock's ticking for everyone, really – it's just I can hear mine. You know how they always say you could be run over by a bus any time? Well, this is like knowing the bus is coming, and I'm just standing in the middle of the street. I might as well do something nice whilst I'm waiting for it to hit me, especially when it might be later than everyone thinks.'

Frances' words echoed around Alice's head as she drove home. What a contrast, she thought. There's me, putting my life on hold for years as if it's not worth having, as if it needs to be saved up for later when I'm ready to live it again – and there's Frances, determined to wring something out of every drop that's left. Which of us actually has more life in them?

And when Martha rang whilst she was in the bath, Alice had forgotten her earlier thoughts of cancelling. It was time to feel alive again.

It took an absurdly short time to get ready, even when having to negotiate the goldfish Anemone had placed in the middle of the bathroom, leaving slightly less available floor area than there is inside a washing machine.

Surely, thought Alice, applying red lipstick which Martha had put through the letterbox this evening, it ought to take much longer as we get older. When I was twenty and Rob and I were first together I used to spend hours getting ready. I suppose once you're married to someone there's no point; once they've seen what you look like first thing in the morning, it seems silly to coat yourself in skin-coloured Polyfilla and pretend you haven't got spots. Rob always said he didn't like me in heavy make-up. Or was that what I wanted him to say? Maybe I stopped trying and he would have liked a bit of lipstick from time to time. Well, I've got lipstick now. Harlot Scarlet.

She considered specs briefly but decided on the contact

lenses. Perhaps, on balance, it would be better to be able to see all night.

She emerged into the kitchen slightly nervous of her children's likely reaction to the lips. She need not have bothered. Fergus was elbow-deep in the biscuit tin whilst reading the TV listings for the evening. Anemone was plotting a birth chart, and Daisy was mixing something rather gruesome and green in a tub. No one seemed to notice that Alice smelled like a banana cream pie.

'Anemone, can we talk about those fish in the bathroom?'

Anemone clattered her beads expressively. 'It's good feng shui.'

'Since the only other explanation for a bowl of goldfish sitting in the middle of the bathroom floor was madness on someone's part, I'd worked that out. But it's not very safe.'

'It's not very safe having all the family's chi pouring down the loo either,' said Anemone.

Daisy looked up from something she was stirring. 'Toilets are bad feng shui, apparently,' she said, in the dry tones of one who had already had the same conversation.

'It will be bad feng shui,' said Alice, 'if I trip over Percy the fish in the night and break my ankle. What did the ancient Chinese do about toilets then?'

'Well, they didn't have flushing ones –' Anemone began.

'What she means,' said Fergus, 'is that if we went out and dug little holes in the garden whenever we wanted to go we'd all be prosperous and healthy and we wouldn't need fish on the bathroom floor.'

'We'd have very cold bottoms,' said Daisy, 'so you can forget that idea.'

Alice raised a wry brow. 'It could certainly cause a bit of a stir in Herne Road. How must the fish feel about this, Annie?'

'Anemone.'

'Sorry. Anemone. How must they feel about watching us

197

enthroned one at a time, gloriously magnified by the curves of their bowl?'

'Pretty crap feng shui for them,' said Fergus, who thought (and indeed had already said) it was all a load of old cobblers. It was women again, that's what it was. He had a mother who wrote horoscopes, a sister who arranged goldfish and the other one had a jewel glued to her navel. She was probably barmy too; this was easy to believe when you heard the noise she made with the last movement of the Elgar.

'Isn't that my avocado?' asked Anemone suddenly, as Alice cleared her throat to announce her imminent departure for an evening of sin. 'Mum, she's put my avocado into her bloody face pack again!'

'It was overripe,' said Daisy defensively, 'and you weren't going to eat it anyway. We're supposed to be ordering in pizza.'

'I'm only eating it if it has pepperoni on it,' said Fergus at once, 'and I'm not watching *Friends*. He sounded as entrenched as the Germans in 1914.

Alice sensed civil war. 'I'm off in a minute,' she said. 'The pizza money is on the hall cupboard. Er – if anyone rings, tell them –'

'We'll tell them you're out on call,' said Anemone. 'Don't worry. And I'm not eating anything that's even *seen* pepperoni, so you'll just have to give that idea up.'

'Well, if anyone needs me urgently, I've got the mobile phone switched on . . .'

She left them to their squabbling, half relieved and half disappointed that they were exactly the same as every other night. It's only a date, after all. It's not as if it's a big deal.

As Alice drove off the children relaxed.

'Who d'you suppose she's meeting?' Daisy voiced the question they'd dared not ask her.

'Some friend of Martha's.' Anemone didn't want to imagine.

'Did you smell that stuff in the bathroom? Yeugh. I hope she doesn't meet any hungry monkeys.'

'I thought it smelled nice. I hope he's not slimy,' said Daisy, looking down her nose at Fergus. 'Slimy would be awful.'

'That would be weird,' said Fergus, drawing a black line through several items on the TV listing. 'Slimy, I mean. It would get on his car seats and everything.'

'Don't be silly. I mean, I just hope she's going out with someone nice.'

'Well,' said Fergus, suddenly and surprisingly, 'I think it stinks.'

'Why? What's the matter?'

But Fergus just glared, his freckles standing out starkly against a pale face. 'Nothing.'

'No, what? You can't expect her to wait around for ever.'

'I don't want another dad.'

'Oh, Ferg,' Anemone gave him an unfamiliar hug and he tried to shake her off, horrified, 'you won't get another dad. But you and I and Daisy, we all have our own lives to lead, and Dad dying didn't take that away from us. It didn't change us wanting to grow up and get married.'

'Yeugh,' said Fergus.

'Yes you will. Get married and be a famous musician or start a rock band or whatever. You can still do all that. But what about Mum?'

'She doesn't want to start a rock band,' said Fergus, refusing to see it. 'And if she did she'd be crap. She'd call it Snotty and the Stethoscopes, and she'd sing soprano and the lyrics would all be about viruses.'

'You know what I'm getting at.'

'No, I don't,' said Fergus.

'Neither do I,' said Daisy, 'and I've got brains where he's got computer games.'

199

'You two are just so dense,' Anemone sighed. 'What I mean is, we all have plans – you know, things we want to do when we grow up. Yours and my plans aren't really much different, even though Dad's gone – but Mum's plans – well, her plans were to grow old with Dad. Her plans are all gone. Don't you think she ought to make some new ones?'

'She's got us,' said Fergus. 'She doesn't need some slimy bloke oozing on her. She could just stay at home with us.'

'She needs a life of her own to look forward to,' said Anemone. 'She's just letting life pass her by now. She hasn't been on a date since Dad died. That's why she should move back to Fox Colne. Get a fresh start.'

'She hasn't even mentioned it yet,' said Daisy dubiously. 'She doesn't even know we know it's for sale.'

Fergus shrugged. 'It's probably not for sale – stupid Phoebe Hamilton's probably been telling porkies. I bet they're not going to Dubai at all.'

'Look, Fergus,' said Anemone, 'I know you like it here, but it would be good for Mum. You know how she is: creeping off to the churchyard all the time; sitting in the garden staring at the moon. She's just waiting.'

Daisy nodded enthusiastically. 'She's like Sleeping Beauty waiting for something to start her living again. I mean, look at the state of the garden, for heaven's sake. It's barren and sad. Doesn't that tell us all something?'

'It tells me teenage girls are crap at psychology,' said Fergus to no one in particular, 'and she's a bit old for Sleeping Beauty. Anyhow, Fred and I were going to fix up the garden. He says it needs a good manuring.'

'Charming. But, Fergus, I know she seems quite old – but you know Joanna Lumley is older than Mum.'

'Wow,' said Fergus, impressed despite himself. 'Just think, if *she'd* stayed at home and knitted there'd have been no *Absolutely Fabulous*.'

'Tragic,' said Daisy.

'OK,' Fergus said reluctantly, 'I get the point. Maybe

you've convinced me. Look, why don't we order two pizzas – one with pepperoni and one without?'

'Go on then. You do it. And you'll back us up when we talk to her?'

'OK. Give me the phone . . . One extra large bomb blaster with extra pepperoni and extra chilli,' said Fergus into the phone a moment later, 'and one teenage girl special. You know, lots of rabbit food and cheese and no calories at all.'

Oblivious to the conversation that had followed her departure, Alice chugged down the A14 towards Bury, trying not to use the fast lane. The drive there from Cambridge could be particularly fraught for Morris Minor drivers, as the road has only two lanes for the most part, and the sight of the back view of a Morris Minor moving into the only overtaking lane seems to issue a particularly provocative challenge, inspiring even the oldest and rustiest white panel van to accelerate at the speed of sound in order to sit furiously two inches from the bumper. Unfortunately using the slow lane meant sitting between immense lorries, shaken by their vibrations and cooked in their exhaust fumes. Whoever thought of Bury St Edmunds?

It was Martha who had thought Bury a suitable venue for what she termed an evening of necessary vice. Alice had been paranoid at the thought of running into one of her patients or, worse still, one of her children's friends, if they used a Cambridge hotel. You never knew where you might find girls from Anemone's year waitressing or chambermaiding in order to earn their university fee down payment. Imagine emerging dishevelled from a steaming shower with a dripping and obviously satiated man to discover someone to whom you'd fed jelly and ice cream at eleven birthday parties in a row gawping at you over the top of a pile of fluffy towels. Besides, Bury seemed somehow more appropriate. Its air of complete propriety just *sang* of hidden scandal. Martha had often thought of opening a lingerie branch there, but suspected that the good folk of Bury might turn out to want more racy intimate apparel than she could comfortably provide.

The Angel Hotel stood, ivily benign and reliable as a trusted great-uncle, more or less opposite both the great gate of the Abbey Gardens and St Edmundsbury Cathedral itself. On summer days the gardens were ablaze with roaring colour and teaming with townspeople, their flowerbeds so matched and colour-coordinated that they would set the teeth of a floral anarchist on edge; lawns so symmetrical and well trimmed that even Alan Titchmarsh could surely find absolutely nothing to do at all. Aviaried birds sang songs of exotic places they never saw but of which they often dreamed genetic dreams, and pale-skinned lunchtime girls dozed idly in the sunshine with Marks and Spencer sandwiches, and magazines full of articles about orgasms to fill their private hour.

But on summer nights the gates closed firmly, shutting the middle classes out and the no-leeway St Edmundsbury perfection in. Then the Angel Hotel was freed from competitive niceness and whispered from beneath its ivy-clad exterior of secret meetings, debauched dates and naughty nights. All was carefully camouflaged by sensible couples having anniversary dinners, and drug company-sponsored medical conventions sitting down to free salmon à l'Ecosse in return both for listening to lectures on impotence and subtly agreeing not to specifically avoid prescribing the latest treatment for scabies. But beneath it murmured the secrecy, like molten lava beneath a volcano, which boils smugly and keeps everything else just that little bit warmer than you might otherwise expect.

Alice pulled into the car park through the old brick arch. Ahead of her executive achievement cars were lined up in a row – silver BMW, silver Lexus, silver BMW, silver Mercedes . . . this last was Martha's. Alice was oddly glad of the Morris Minor's apparent daftness next to such grand illusions of power and potency.

The foyer of the Angel Hotel was bustling in a slightly clandestine manner, as though it had sensed that the Abbey Gardens had shut both its gates and its eyes – or was that just her imagination? Alice caught sight of her own expression in a floor-length mirror and shuddered inwardly. At moments of particular guilt or unease, she felt, it was better not to be confronted with the whole of herself at the same time.

'Alice, this is Oliver Cameron. Oliver, Alice Vane.'

Alice didn't know whether to be relieved or furious. OK, he wasn't too hairy, and his eyes weren't too wildly staring . . . but she knew even before he opened his mouth that he was a gynaecologist, and that was almost as bad. It wasn't the bow tie that gave him away, although it is often said the gynaecologists avoid the more traditional neckwear for fear of what it might dangle into, nor was it the gratuitously smug expression that assumed an intimate knowledge of women that not even women have themselves. It was simply the fact that she had met him before.

'Hello, Oliver.'

'Alice.' He kissed her hand. Alice darted a swift look at Martha, who had that aren't-I-clever? expression you see on the faces of shop assistants when they've noticed your credit card has just expired. Thank God, she thought, I've met him here and not at home. Imagine what Anemone would have to say about a gynaecologist. 'I'm delighted. Have we met before?'

'It was ten years or so ago,' said Alice, 'at a medical conference. I don't suppose you'd remember me.' But I remember you, she thought. I remember thinking: how on earth can you ever have sex if you spend your entire life lecturing on and showing slides of women's whatnots illuminated in a state of pathological unpleasantness?

Oliver frowned. Clearly he could bear to leave no stone

203

unturned. 'Was that one of my talks on pelvic pain?'

'I think so,' said Alice, hoping to avoid a discussion on vaginal discharge but feeling a deep sense of fatalism over her chances of success. 'In that place in London – you know . . . the hotel where they served that amazing cream tea.'

'Ah yes – I remember it well. My talk was called "The Discharge Detective".' Martha winced, but Oliver beamed. 'I have done a lot of work in the field of vaginal discharge. I –'

'Oh, I know,' said Alice hastily. 'I haven't forgotten a word. Tell me, what do you think of –'

'How splendid of you to remember. You're a GP, aren't you? It has always been my theory that GPs should be able to diagnose infective vaginal organisms by smell, and I have recently published . . .'

Alice smiled tightly and switched her ears off, remembering that Rob had been there that day and they had both sneaked out of Oliver's lecture because it had been just too revolting for a nice Saturday, and had ordered a huge cream tea at the Ritz followed by a quickie in a hotel bedroom just off Piccadilly. That was why she remembered it all so well. Crazily expensive but deliciously wild . . .

Well, the Angel Hotel was pretty risqué – and far enough from home that no one was likely to recognise her. And the kids seemed OK with the idea that she might be very late home. They'd better not wait up . . . Now that she was here, she might as well do her best to see if there was any life in her still, and if the moment arose to see if she could forget Rob and the touch of his hands, and take some pleasure for herself again without any guilt or regret . . . It was what she needed – and a gynaecologist wasn't so bad. At least he ought to know his way around.

Late that evening, as the stars appeared over Bury St Edmunds and the lights of the Angel Hotel gradually went out, Fred Ramsden wandered out across the garden of the

Fir Trees to talk to his peacocks, for their guano was the essential key to his compost mix, the one that helped the best delphiniums in Cambridge reach their maximum bloom. Tabitha might complain about the peacocks' noise, but without his peacocks, well, where would he be? He never would have got started, never would have made his fortune. And if you don't keep peacocks happy, they just fly away. Still, nice ankles, that Tabitha . . .

As Fred wandered, Martha Coleman drove back to Cambridge alone. She and her escort, Bart, had partnered Alice and Oliver for supper, but halfway through the evening she had felt the pizzazz drain out of her completely. Bart simply hadn't had what it took to keep her interest. He hadn't been quite tall enough, had been a little too smooth shaven. His teeth hadn't been quite the right shade of white and there had been something rather effeminate about the scent of his cologne . . . Of course, Martha told herself, the problem really was that it had been Alice's evening, not her own.

She wondered how Alice was getting on with Oliver. In Martha's opinion life without sex was an arid thing. A woman without sex was surely like a garden without fertiliser – things grow after a fashion, but they're not lush, they cannot be verdantly stunning. She felt it was no wonder that Alice lived her life in a daze of Rob memories – her garden simply couldn't grow. She hadn't allowed anything to happen to her since Rob. There was no touch, no caress, no sensual moment to overlie the memories of him. Martha felt guilty for not having realised this before – but then her own sex life was so completely separate from the rest of her social life that she could perhaps be forgiven for not thinking about Alice's absence of one. After all, to a casual observer she herself might appear celibate. Indeed, for tonight, she was. It must be the first time one of her escorts hadn't been suitable.

Of course, she told herself as she stopped at the lights on Northgate Street, she was an exacting woman. Every so often Laura was bound to choose a chap who wasn't quite what she wanted. And she was entitled to not feel like it from time to time, wasn't she? There didn't have to be a reason.

Still, she had been quite relieved to see Bart get into his car and head back to London, was quite glad that now, nearly midnight, she was heading home alone. It made a pleasant change, proved she was her own woman, that she wasn't conforming to anyone's expectations of her sexuality, least of all her own . . .

The car behind her at the lights had a green light on the roof. It must be an on-call medical car, she thought. Hope it's no one I know . . .

But even if there had been no green light flashing on the roof Martha would have noticed Tom Lovejoy sitting in the front, next to the driver. She could feel him there, like a magnetic field, crackling around the bits of her that Bart had not made any impact on at all. Please God make him not notice her! If he waved she would almost certainly crash her car. She was clearly jinxed around him.

He didn't see her, thank God, his car disappearing off into the night towards some other medical crisis. Imagine having Tom Lovejoy turn up to swab your infected tonsils! Patients must swoon when he arrived on their doorsteps. Imagine going to him for your *smear*! It was a good thing he didn't fancy her, really. A man like that could cause problems for the peace of mind. Indeed, if she was the sort of women to fall in love – which she obviously wasn't – she might think herself at real risk.

Alice's mobile phone was under the pillow but it rang insistently. It must be the children. What could be wrong? Had the house burned down? Her heart was thudding as she pressed receive, trying not to let Oliver see that she was distracted. She didn't know him well enough to let him see her worry, even though he wasn't currently concentrating on her face.

'Hello? Is that Dr Vane? This is Tabitha Tinkler. I have been thinking about Mr Banescu and I wondered if he was any better. I cannot sleep for worrying about him, you see. Your children very kindly gave me your mobile number.'

Why did I have to bring my mobile? Alice cursed inwardly. I could have given the children another number. 'Tabitha,' she said aloud, flabbergasted and slightly desperate, 'I know you are worried about him, but I really can't do anything till morning. We can talk then – but you know I can't really tell you anything. That's up to Mr Banescu.'

Oliver was working quite valiantly, she felt, on her left nipple. It wasn't his fault that Tabitha had been seized by insomnia, but it wasn't helping the sexual ambience. Neither was the overpowering smell of chocolate, which was actually rather grim in these quantities. Mind you, it surely took a rather insensitive kind of man to carry on with the body chocolate whilst she was clearly talking to a patient. Poor Miss Tinkler – I shouldn't be uncharitable. After all, she's spent her whole life waiting for one man.

'Oh, I know, dear, but I thought if you rang coronary care for me again . . .'

Alice sighed. 'I can't do that right now, Tabitha, not in the middle of the night. Perhaps we could talk at a more reasonable hour.'

Tabitha sounded affronted. 'Oh, very well. I'll speak to you tomorrow. I'm sorry to have bothered you. I do hope you weren't asleep. I wasn't. Bloody peacocks were keeping me awake as usual. Good night to you.'

I might just as well be asleep, Alice thought, for all the animal abandon I'm managing to muster up here. Actually, I'd rather be asleep. Come on, Alice, try a bit harder . . .

She put the phone down. Oliver had moved on to her

cleavage. God, she thought, at this rate it will take all night to get anywhere interesting. I should have left my contacts out. It would have at least injected a little mystery into the proceedings. Rob used to love me looking myopic. I must get back into the swing of this.

She wriggled slightly. 'Oliver?'

'Mmhh?'

'That's really nice. Can I . . . do anything for you?'

Oliver took a deep breath and moaned slightly. Gosh, thought Alice, surely I can't have excited him that much.

'I'm sorry,' he said, all in a rush, 'I don't feel very . . .'

He had gone, of course, before dawn – but now she had to get herself home, past the smiling good morning glances of the Angel receptionist, who informed her with the overwhelming smugness of front desk conspiracy that the room bill had been paid by The Gentleman. Past the Abbey Gardens, peaceful in the early sunshine, where poor martyred St Edmund lived and breathed before learning the true unpleasantness of the invading Danes and coming to a ghastly end. Out onto the A14 and back to Cambridge. She wondered how often people sneaked out of the Angel Hotel with clandestinity written all over them at four in the morning. Once she would have thought the whole scenario funny. Actually, it *was* funny. Rob would have found it hilarious. Alice began to laugh.

She laughed all the way to the Newmarket turn-off, which was just about as long as it took for her to realise what she had really done, and for the deep and sickening feeling to get into the car with her, like a bucket of creeping ooze. It had immobilised them both, woman and car, by the time she reached the Histon Road traffic lights, even though they were on green.

What was I thinking of? I've destroyed something for ever. It's as if I've thrown away my virginity. I can't ever undo it – there's been someone in me since Rob. Another man has written on me, has known the things that I kept for Rob. I've taken Rob's *me* away.

The car behind her hooted, and Alice looked indignantly into her rear-view mirror. What sort of a person would be out at this time of the morning, hooting? And in the rear-view mirror she clearly saw the green flash of the doctor-on-call light, the proper one the BASICS doctors use rather than one of those rather naff magnetic ones that would-be hero-docs plug into their cigarette lighters when they want to pass all the other traffic in order to get to Cambridge United before kick-off.

Tom bloody Lovejoy, that's who it was. On call for BASICS. Bloody show-off. Please God, don't let him have recognised me. What on earth would he imagine I've been doing at this time in the morning?

Sadly, a Morris Minor is a recognisable car, and Tom waved cheerfully at her as he zoomed by. On the way to some urgent hero stuff, no doubt. What business of his was her private life anyway? Nosy bugger. Alice wriggled uncomfortably as Tom tore away into the middle distance. Her neck felt sticky. Her entire body felt sticky. Bloody Oliver. Bloody chocolate. And it was Belgian. She put the car into gear with a crunch, the lack of synchromesh on first in the Morris proving oddly satisfying at this moment of transience and mental discomfort.

Bloody Tom. Rob used to work as a BASICS doctor too, tearing off out of surgery to head for the M11 every time the call went out. And if it wasn't that he was dashing off to Mildenhall air display every May Bank Holiday for a bit of hero practice. Of course he'd been very sincere about it, but that's what it was, all the same. And for a moment – a tiny weak moment, the sort of moment that you should never let in through the crack in your mind that is the border with insanity – for a moment she allowed herself to see Tom Lovejoy's disappearing taillights as Rob's, to imagine that the warmth of her body, the early morning tiredness, was because of Rob, rather than because of Oliver and his intense self-worship.

Her thoughts ran on, one on another like lemmings struggling for the edge. How could I have slept with Oliver, so meaninglessly? It's not like me at all – so meaningless. But then perhaps it needed to be meaningless for me to have managed it; needed to be more like a fantasy than a true act.

Some fantasy. Odd that Martha, of all people, should choose for me someone with the charisma of a case of trench foot. Still, I am an adult woman. I can accept that I still have a sexuality, can't I?

Can't I? *Could I ever?* Perhaps I was never cut out for fantasy. Perhaps Rob was. Did that make him a pervert, or does it make me a sexual failure? And which would be worse?

On the radio a cheery early morning presenter was discussing the relative temperatures of England and Gibraltar. England was warmer today, apparently, but Gibraltar had more apes. Alice smiled suddenly. More apes. Perhaps every deficiency has its compensations. Just because I didn't share all Rob's fantasies doesn't mean we weren't good together, she decided.

I don't feel guilty about last night. I feel sad. Sad that it was a waste of time. Sad that I'd rather have been watching TV or waxing my armpits. Sad that it's another milestone between me and Rob, another step on in life that he can't share. But not guilty. And not sorry.

She got home to a quiet house, the children not awake yet, and so she made herself coffee then took it to her room, then sat on her bed with Rob's photograph. Rob looked out of the frame, ever so slightly past her, like the Queen in last year's Red Cross Christmas card, the one showing her obviously waving at someone else. That slight squint he had always had gave the impression that the photo-Rob was watching for someone other, different.

Her body still remembered Rob – Oliver had not erased

that. Rob had been good at oral sex.

Oliver hadn't. Not even with chocolate body paint. With Oliver the chocolate had seemed to take precedence over the sex. Even before he was sick.

'I miss being in bed with you,' she told the photograph. 'I've never told you that before.'

Chapter Ten

Martha didn't know whether to laugh or cry when Alice told her the whole story the following lunchtime in the shop. 'Oh Alice, you've been celibate for three years – don't you think a whole pot of body chocolate was a bit ambitious for your first time together?'

'It was his idea,' said Alice. 'I was never that keen. To be honest, I only like After Eights and I didn't suppose he'd fancy peppermint cream on his thing. I was quite relieved in the end when he rushed into the bathroom – although it was embarrassing for him.'

'His thing? What are you, woman? Doctor or nursery school teacher?'

'Prude, I suppose,' said Alice, with a flash of sadness. 'At least, I've begun to wonder about that. Maybe that's why Rob –'

'Rubbish. You're no more a prude than I am. Did he stay all night?'

'He said he felt fine after a glass of Alka-Seltzer, but the atmosphere was gone and after he left I had a shower and came home.'

'Oh, Alice, you must have felt wretched – abandoned and rejected.'

'Oh no,' said Alice, 'it wasn't him going that upset me. It was quite a relief not to have to watch him put his underwear on in the morning, actually. The worst thing was being stuck to the sheets. That chocolate is never going to come off, and I don't know what the hell they'll think of it in the hotel laundry.'

'That it's body chocolate,' said Martha, running a hand through her blonde hair. 'The nicest hotels probably see the most extraordinary things. They'll just think – wow, couple of doctors, look at them.'

'They'd be wrong,' Alice frowned. 'Everyone thinks doctors have a wild and adventurous sex life. They think we must know everything so how could we possibly get it wrong? But we do. I did.'

'That's silly,' said Martha, who had always thought exactly the same. 'Mind you, doesn't everyone always think everyone else must be having better sex than them?'

'I suppose so. Except Sean Connery's wife.'

Martha nodded, understanding. 'Oh yes. Except her.'

Alice sipped her drink and then, suddenly serious, said, 'Perhaps it's me. Perhaps I'm not a very sexual person. I mean, poor Oliver did try,' she stirred her coffee guiltily, 'but it just didn't – do anything for me, really.'

'Well, it can't be technique,' said Martha. 'He is a gynaecologist, after all.'

'Maybe that was part of the trouble.' Alice shuddered slightly at the thought. 'Just because you know where to find the clitoris still doesn't mean you know what to do with it when you've got it. He wasn't technically hopeless or anything, but I didn't exactly go into orbit. Maybe I just need to be in love.'

'God, you don't expect much, do you?' Martha was impressed. 'You were jolly lucky he even knew the geography. I have this theory, you know, that if you asked a hundred men to walk across a gigantic model of female genitalia, ninety-nine of them would trip over the clitoris and shout, "What the hell is that supposed to be?" Believe me, the only way to go into orbit is to have it away with an astronaut.'

'Well, OK,' Alice was defensive, 'but it would have been nice to get off the ground. With Rob I at least went up in the elevator even if I didn't reach the penthouse suite.' She clapped a hand to her mouth and stared at Martha, shocked.

Martha looked satisfied. 'That's the first time you've ever suggested that Rob wasn't perfect in every way.'

'I didn't mean . . .'

'Leave it,' said Martha wisely, 'you don't owe me any explanations. Or him. Forget the gynaecologist, though.' And I'll strike him out of my book, she thought. One can clearly know too much about clitori. This had never struck her before. 'You could do worse than trying out Tom Lovejoy, you know.' *Please do, then perhaps I could get him out of my mind.*

'Oh God, no,' said Alice immediately, 'I couldn't.'

'Why?' Martha fought off the gigantic feeling of relief that she wasn't obliged to matchmake the two of them then sit back and watch them roar out of the atmosphere.

'Too charming, I've told you,' said Alice, 'and I don't fancy him. He's not my type.'

'He's a bit like Rob, though – I mean, physically.'

'I know. Maybe that's the problem. Or maybe Rob wasn't my type either, but I loved him so it didn't matter.'

'It wouldn't be because he's a doctor?'

'Certainly not. Anyway, he doesn't fancy me. He – er – actually he thinks you and I are gay.'

'He *what*?'

Oh no, thought Alice. I should have told Martha before. I've let myself get sidetracked, and it obviously matters a lot. Glaringly obviously, now that I've noticed it. 'Well, you see, he misunderstood things a little, the other night at dinner.'

'Misunderstood? How?' Martha stared piercingly at her. 'Something about me? Something you said? Alice – tell me what you said!'

'Nothing,' said Alice guiltily. 'He thought it all by himself.'

Martha's jaw dropped briefly before she remembered to neaten it up. 'Why would he . . .?'

'I'm sorry.' Alice was full of remorse. 'I mean, not that I've got anything against lesbians, but . . . I didn't mean him to. He just assumed it, because you were there, and it seemed rather funny at the time. I didn't know you'd be so bowled over by him.'

'Bowled over? By Tom Lovejoy? I didn't say that. I admit I was – attracted.'

'Martha, you fell over when he moved into your scent zone.' She's fallen, thought Alice suddenly, fascinated right out of her former self-contemplation. The unassailable Martha has fallen and she doesn't even know it.

Martha shook her head emphatically, 'Coincidence. Well, OK – I did find him very attractive. My God, I must be losing my touch. I came on to him like Mata Hari and he thought I was gay!'

Alice sighed. 'Look, I'll tell him we're not gay as soon as I next see him. I'll make a point of dashing straight up and saying, "Tom, just for the record, Martha is not gay." Then he'll probably race over like a speeding bullet and sweep you into the back room and seduce you on top of the cupboard where you keep all the thongs.'

Martha glared, tempted despite herself. 'You can't just – tell him. What will that look like?'

'Guilt,' said Alice, 'I expect. Look, I'll be subtle.'

Martha sniffed. 'You're a doctor; subtlety is anathema to you. Look, please forget it. I'm not that easy, you know.'

'No, but I bet he is,' Alice grinned.

'Why do you think that? Because he's a charming, gorgeous man?'

'Maybe.'

'Your trouble,' said Martha bluntly, 'is that you expect every man you meet to let you down. But you're not thinking about marrying the man. You could do worse than throw in your lot with him. You need a partner – he wants a partnership.'

'Certainly not,' Alice glared, feeling now that Martha's

motives were clear. 'Stop trying to *have* him vicariously. Your trouble is you're too scared to go for him because you're used to holding all the cards and knowing where you stand. You've fallen at his feet, Martha Coleman, hook, line and sinker like a landed trout, and you can't bear to see it. And now I've got a baby clinic to do, so I've got to go.'

She left with the distinct feeling of a point struck home, even if the metaphors had been a little mixed. If I can't sort myself out, she thought, I can at least sort Martha. It's about time she had a man she didn't have to pay for.

'Well,' said Martha to the whispering silks on the rail, taken aback by the sudden and unexpected truth, 'it's progress – of a sort.'

'Tom,' said Alice a short while later and in her firmest voice, by-passing Roland who was clearly trying to speak to her about something – she could tell from the way he raised his nose and flared his nostrils at her approach, as if he intended to hoover her up with them – and striding into Tom's office with the resolute step used both by the supremely confident and the extremely embarrassed. 'Good afternoon.'

'Good afternoon.' Tom treated her to a brief tooth dazzling. 'How are you?'

Alice shut his door behind her. 'Tom, er – I just – I actually just need to tell you something.'

He took in her awkwardly embarrassed face; pushed his chair back. Oh dear, thought Alice suddenly, he thinks I'm going to tell him I fancy him. He looks as though he feels sick at the thought. God, have I aged so much?

She took a deep breath. 'You misunderstood the situation at dinner the other night,' she said bluntly. 'I'm not gay. Martha isn't my lesbian lover. That is, she isn't gay either. You see, the – um – the children were upset when I told them what you thought, so I . . .' Damn it, I'm making it worse. Now he thinks I'm throwing myself at him. 'Look, I . . .'

216

'It's fine, really.' Tom got up from behind his desk, came round towards her in Mills and Boon slow motion (how does he do that?). 'It's very good of you to tell me. I –'

'I'm not making a pass at you, for heaven's sake,' said Alice, fed up with the social rules which said you conveyed such messages only subtly. Martha was right: doctors spent too much of their lives asking to see people's bottoms and feel their breasts without any preamble whatsoever to have a talent for subtlety. 'I'm telling you Martha Coleman's not gay either. Just in case you should have thought that she was as well. As well as me, that is. If I was – which I'm not.' And before he could reply she had left the room.

Roland was waiting for her outside.

'Alice, we really do have to talk about our lavatory problem, as another aspect of it has struck me.'

Alice glared at him with intense fury. Even given that I'm a mere woman, she thought, a lesser man would have backed off from this look. A sensitive man would have been reduced to a small steaming heap of carbon-based waste products – but Roland merely beams in an oozing kind of way.

'Due to water metering, there is, of course, an added cost per flush whenever the lavatory is used. Clearly it is unfair that the private patients should bear an equal share of the practice water bill when the NHS practice is reimbursed for its share of expenses.'

'I really don't think it matters,' said Alice drily, wondering if Roland could actually be flushed away himself, were she able to get the whole of his head into the lavatory pan at one time. 'We won't be here much longer, will we?'

Roland shrugged. 'It's all money, Alice dear, and much as I admire your NHS work I really can't let my own financial position support it. In any case, I have come up with an interim proposal for the lavatory.'

'Look, Roland, can I suggest –' (Can I suggest you spontaneously combust?)

'A flush counter!' said Roland triumphantly. 'We install a flush counter on the lavatory, and measure the use. That way I can bill your practice a proper sum per event, as it were.'

Alice, overcome by curiosity despite her outrage, had to ask, 'How will you know which is a private flush and which is on the NHS?'

'Ah,' said Roland, like Merlin during King Arthur's first lesson in becoming the future King of England, 'my secretary will ask the private patients entering the small room to sign an elegant visitors' book. We can then simply count, and will assume the other flushes are yours. I feel we can be reasonable and overlook the number of non-flush usages, which I'm sure will arise from NHS patients.'

'Roland,' said Alice, suddenly exasperated beyond even pretended tolerance, 'do whatever you bloody well like. Just tell me about it afterwards.'

'Thank you, Alice dear. I knew you would understand. After all, one cannot get much sense out of James these days, and as for that young whippersnapper . . .'

His voice trailed away expressively, and he wandered off towards the private half of the building. One could tell where it began, as Roland had recarpeted the private part of the reception area with a rather gruesome Axminster, just as far as the line. The pile was so deep that little old ladies walking across it looked as though they were trying to heave their zimmer frames through treacle. On this side of the reception area, though, the friendly but practical blue looped berber still provided basic comfort for NHS-funded feet. As she watched him go Alice felt a surge of warmth towards Tom Lovejoy, simply for being a man that Roland disliked.

'Dr Vane?' Norma, looking rather harassed. 'There's a call for you from the hospital. That foreign man.'

'Oh, thanks.' Coming from Norma, Alice reflected, that could mean anything from one of the ENT registrars to

Saddam Hussein (should he be in Cambridge having his gall bladder done, that is). Unusual for Norma to look harassed, actually. Mind you, they did seem to be a little short on reception staff today.

'Where's Lisa?' Suddenly noticing her absence Alice felt a guilty lurch that the problem of Dean and his views on marriage had slipped out of her mind along with everything else.

'Antenatal clinic.' Norma managed to say it on a half-sneer. People in her day, said her facial expression, had not expected time off for clinics when they were pregnant. People in her day had felt lucky to have a job and thought nothing of working till midnight on Saturdays. Indeed, when she was twenty-three she was shovelling sugar beet on a farm in –

Fortunately Norma's sneer did not have time to say any more than this, as Richard Clayderman began to play the Moonlight Sonata, her favourite, and she was rendered instantly mellow.

Alice picked up the phone.

'Dr Vane. It is I, Herman Banescu.'

'Oh – hello, Mr Banescu.' Not Saddam this time, then. 'How are you feeling?'

'Much better,' said Herman, 'always bearing in mind that a man can only feel so good when surrounded by Gorgons.' In the background Alice could swear she heard Sister Goodenough snort.

'What can I do for you?'

'Two things. I wish to leave here but I have nowhere to stay. They do not let me go early unless I have somewhere to stay, but I cannot stay here another day – it is like water torture. I don't know anyone else to ask. I have taken my own discharge from the Good Nurse Annette and am even now standing beside her desk with my toothbrush.'

'Oh. Goodness. I – er – what about your friend Tabitha Tinkler? Why don't you go to her? I thought you had come to see her, and she's very anxious to see you.'

'I cannot go to see her whilst I have lost the gift,' said Herman, an oddly Eastern stubbornness creeping into his voice. 'I have to find it before I see her. It was Tamas Banescu's last wish that I should deliver it, you see, and I would be so ashamed. But now I have remembered that I hid it inside a frog.'

'A frog?'

'Absolutely. And you have many frogs in your surgery rooms. It must be there.'

Alice remembered suddenly Herman's mutterings when he was ill on her floor that day. He *had* said something about frogs. And she felt responsible for him – after all, where else could he turn?

'Mr Banescu –'

'Herman. Call me Herman.'

'Herman. I have hundreds of frogs. You'll have to come and look.'

'It was a frog,' said Herman, 'with staring eyes. Have you seen it?'

Alice frowned. I'm sure I have, she thought, but I'm not sure I have a frog without staring eyes. Now when did I see a china frog . . .? 'I'll have a good think, I promise.'

'That is very kind,' said Herman, sounding agitated, 'but it is a valuable thing. I cannot hang around here.'

Alice sighed. There was something deeply persuasive about his tone, something emotionally stirring about his passionate need to find this bloody frog and give it, whatever it was, to Tabitha Tinkler. Old people are just so complicated, she thought suddenly. Perhaps we all just get more complicated as we get older. I feel as though I'm getting more and more complicated as time goes on – whereas perhaps Rob was, simply, simpler. Perhaps –

'Dr Vane? I wonder . . . Can you recommend a hotel that would take me? I am not a rich man but I—'

'Don't be silly, Mr Banescu,' said Alice, her resolve suddenly firmed, her sense of her own culpability in this saga of frog-loss and her curiosity as to what secret a frog could hide (other than the possible consequences of it being kissed by completely the wrong person, of course) combining into an offer she might later regret. 'Why don't you come and stay with me? We can look for your frog together.'

'And you promise me you will not tell Tabitha where I am?'

'If that's what you want. You are my patient, after all. I won't tell a soul.'

Whilst Alice worked out whether or not she would have time to get Herman from Addenbrooke's before evening surgery (no, bearing in mind that it took twenty minutes to get there but easily an hour to find somewhere to park), Lisa was at the hospital, arguing with Dean Grabber in the antenatal clinic waiting room. An interested audience of women in leggings and rugby shirts tried to look as though they were concentrating hard on the pages of Miriam Stoppard which swam before their eyes, whilst mentally lapping up every word.

'My mum always said you were no good. She said you'd use a girl, then throw her aside like old . . . old candyfloss. You're a rotten bugger, Dean Grabber, and I wouldn't marry you if you were the last man on earth!'

Dean was looking faintly stunned. He always looked faintly stunned, as it happened – it was the way his face was made – but on this occasion the expression was appropriate to the emotion beneath.

'All I said,' he said with astonished carefulness, 'was that we couldn't get married on a weekend when Ipswich Town are playing at home.'

A barely audible hiss (by far the most effective kind) went through the waiting room, a couple of the men cringed into their seats as if expecting blows, and the massed pregnant psyches of half a dozen large women homed in on Dean like the Midwich cuckoos, and wished him Bad Karma.

Dean, who was not sensitive to atmosphere, smiled hopefully.

Lisa revved her engines. 'I don't know why you don't just . . . change your mind and marry the goal post! You don't want a wife, Dean Grabber, you want a football supporter. And don't think I want you at my antenatal appointments now either.'

'But it's my baby too. I want to be a supportive partner. I said we could get married if you really wanted to. What more do you want, woman?'

Lisa drew up to her full five feet one. 'A bit of romance, that's what I want.'

'But you said you didn't need a white wedding. You said –'

'She's pregnant, mate,' volunteered a brave fellow two seats along. 'What she says has got nothing to do with what she means. Take it from me.' His girlfriend nudged him. 'Shut it, Gary. Don't show me up.'

Dean frowned at his unexpected mentor. 'You mean she really does want a white wedding?'

Gary shrugged. 'Don't ask me, mate, more than me life's worth. Already off privileges for nine months because of this little lark.'

Lisa started to cry.

'Oh, come on, love. Don't get upset.' Dean didn't like tears. At every building job he had done there had always been someone in tears – if not beforehand then certainly afterwards. 'Just tell me what you want me to do.'

'I don't want to have to tell you. I just want a proper wedding. I want it with bridesmaids and flowers and a fat happy vicar with a beard. I want all my family sitting at the front and I want my mother to cry and my dad to be proud, and I want photos and a reception and a car with tin cans tied to the back bumper. And I want it on a Saturday and I don't care if Ipswich Town are playing bloody Lazio at bloody home!'

222

Dean's face softened with a deep and compassionate sympathy. 'Look, love,' he said, in his gentlest, kindest, most romantic voice, putting a soothing hand on her arm, 'they wouldn't be playing Lazio at home this year, see, because even if they got into the super league, to get into the Cup Winners' Cup again they have to –'

'Mate' said Gary kindly, 'I should just give in.'

And Dean, whose sixth sense was slightly less well developed than Namibia, was suddenly swamped by a profound feeling of fatalism.

Not far from the antenatal clinic, Phoebe was experiencing emotional upheaval that made the removal of her appendix seem a minor thing. The boy in the bed opposite had gone home and had been replaced by a handsome but gloomy teenager who did not speak but simply glowered at her as if she was – well – not a beautiful princess, which she obviously was (Daddy said so all the time). Phoebe thought he looked like Leonardo DiCaprio. The attractions of getting out of hospital and showing off her scar to the gaping admiration of Fox Colne Primary, the headmistress welcoming her back with tears in her eyes, the staff lining up to hug her, Thomasina Johnson finally admitting to the rest that Phoebe must really be very, very brave to have had her appendix out – all these things paled into insignificance beside attracting the attention of Finn. Imagine going back to school and telling them you had a boyfriend.

But Finn was not a happy boy. He refused to speak to his mother, or to the nurses, or even to that stupid Minnie Mouse woman who had laughed when she heard Phoebe sing 'Mummies on the bus are learned and wise' to cheer up the littler children. He wouldn't speak to anyone. Eventually they had got the other doctor to come and see him, the mental doctor the others said he was. The mental doctor came and pulled the curtains, but Phoebe had ears like a big floppy rabbit (that's what Mummy always said) and she heard that Finn was sad because his girlfriend had gone off with someone else and crosser still because he had broken his leg falling off her roof where he had gone to sing to her – and crosser even still because the girlfriend had kept his Eternal CD. The mental doctor had said that Finn was fine and would get another girlfriend and would maybe not then want the Eternal album, and had opened the curtains. That was when Phoebe had seized her chance to go and offer her services as Next Girlfriend-in-Chief.

Of course, he had said to bog off, but boys were like that, Mummy said. That frog of Dr Vane's had been on the table between their beds, because Lawrence's mum hadn't let him swap it for the Action Man and had left it behind, so she had taunted Finn with it, as you do in such circumstances. And he had laughed and quite liked the frog, so she had lent it to him and he had smiled. So that was how the frog got her the prince, even if he hadn't kissed her yet.

Alice's evening surgery, meanwhile, was not going well. GPs have to be prepared to examine thoroughly any proffered part of a person, appealing or unappealing, with a warm manner and an interested heart. Unfortunately, her last patient, a local solicitor who had come down for an afternoon appointment after missing his morning one, was proffering his bottom. Rodney Brascombe walked into the surgery brandishing a pile of papers rather ostentatiously.

'Do you always run this late?' he asked Alice, as if she were the defendant and he were prosecuting counsel.

Alice sighed. She did not like Rodney, who made a point of telling her he specialised in medical negligence whenever she met him at dinner parties, and whose wife, Isobel, a mousy woman with inappropriately enlarged breasts, clearly adored him out of all proportion to his actual worth. 'It's been busy,' she said, adding pointedly, 'I was on time this morning, if you'd made it to your appointment then.'

Rodney shrugged, spreading himself into the seat and eyeing her challengingly. 'You know how it is.'

Alice smiled. 'If you could phone up to cancel next time it would help us here,' she said sweetly.

Rodney subjected her to a slightly lascivious look. 'Busy professional life,' he said loftily. 'One can't remember everything.'

Alice wondered what he would charge a client who didn't turn up. 'I thought you had secretaries for that,' she said, then saw from the suppressed smirk what Rodney regarded his secretary's function to be. Poor Isobel.

'Well,' said Rodney, 'now I'm finally in here, I've got a problem with my back end.'

Damn it, thought Alice, asking the appropriate questions. 'I'll have to examine you, I'm afraid.'

'That's fine,' said Rodney, removing his trousers with alacrity. 'By the way, how was the Angel? I thought I spotted you there last night.'

Bastard! Alice caught her breath. Well, I'm certainly not going to risk being alone with his bottom. 'I'll just have to call a chaperone. Nothing personal, Rodney, we always do.' Perhaps, she thought, I should have taken out an advert in the *Cambridge Evening News*. I wonder if anyone in Cambridge doesn't know I spent last night with Oliver the Prat. Do I need to tell the children before they find out from school? It's probably already on the history syllabus.

And now she knew Rodney had a hairy bottom, which was another bit of information she could have done without. Dinner parties with him and Isobel would never be the same again.

As Alice battled with the tail end of general practice and looked forward to getting home, Martha was locking up with similar feelings and was tempted to ignore her telephone. It had been a busy day, Cambridge was apparently facing a chaos of wedding anniversaries over the next few weeks, and she had used her charm, tact and beauty to full effect to persuade a number of credit-carded men that what they had in mind for their wife's gift was not quite what the average woman of taste and class would actually be pleased to receive. They might have come into her shop thinking they wanted to buy that sort of stuff – but things with peepholes did not feature in her collection, and it always astonished her that men seemed to lose all sense of taste at the sight of a pair of tight black satin knickers of the sort that are only made in a size ten, trying to buy them for their more normal-sized wives even though this risked cutting off the blood supply to their thighs on a permanent basis.

Still, under Martha's guidance the men, to a man, had been impressed enough to part with pleasing sums of credit-card payment for the frothy, silky, woman-enhancing objects that Martha knew no woman would ever want to bring back to the shop. It had been a profitable and satisfying day.

Even so, she was feeling tired, a little jaded, a little dissatisfied with herself. It was guilt about Alice, of course. How awful that she should have set Alice up with a man so unschooled in the art of seduction. Perhaps she had been wrong not to have used the agency. Alice need not have known. There are ways of organising such things so discreetly . . .

But she did answer the phone, for the true business-woman never rejects a call.

'Miss Coleman? I'm so sorry. I failed you. I really thought you would like Bart. I can only apologise. I have always prided myself on –'

'Laura, there wasn't a problem with Bart.' Martha frowned at the phone. 'Please don't apologise.'

'Oh, I got the impression that you didn't find him . . . pleasurable.'

Martha was irritated. 'Look, Laura, I'm just your client, this isn't telesales. You don't have to ring up and find out

226

why I'm not delighted with the service, you know. Bart was fine – he's a nice man, good company . . .'

Laura sounded anxious – Martha was a good customer. 'Well, of course. I didn't mean to pry – but if—'

'Oh yes you did.' Martha was suddenly exasperated – she, who never, ever lost her cool. 'You completely meant to pry. You want to know why I didn't sleep with Bart and it's absolutely nothing to do with you. Now, if you don't mind, I've a business to run.'

She put the phone down, then stared at it in mild alarm. This wouldn't do at all. This Tom thing was making her very odd. She had really got to do something about herself. Perhaps she should have her hormone levels checked. She had read somewhere that you could get growths on your ovary that gave you orgasms every time you thought about men . . .

The telephone again. What now? Just be business, for God's sake. I need something to get my mind off . . .

'Martha? Tom Lovejoy, Alice's locum. We met the other night.'

. . . off him. There, I've admitted it. Martha felt herself flush, then caught the side of her desk hard against her left hip bone as she turned her right heel over and tried to steady herself. Damn it.

'Ouch. Hello, Tom, how are you?' Calm down, Martha. The racing heartbeat had to be because of the pain in her hip, of course. Thank God he fancies me, she thought. I was afraid I was losing my touch. Of course it's not love, it's unrequited lust. I'm just not used to it.

'Fine, I'm absolutely fine.' He sounded slightly breathless, which was extraordinarily erotic. 'Martha, I wondered if you'd like to meet up for a drink?'

'I . . .' All of Martha's danger lights were flashing in her head. She regarded them, startled, for a moment, not having previously realised that she possessed them, then swallowed. Don't be too easy, she told herself, if you lie at

227

their feet they walk all over you. 'Er, I'm not sure.' She tried to keep the tremor out of her voice. 'I've had rather a long day.'

'I'll tell you what –'

God, he sounds *just* like Sean Connery. It's more than a woman can bear.

'I'll cook for you. Tell me where you live and I'll even pick you up. Can you say fairer than that?' Masterful and mischievous combined. Had the man been to classes?

'I don't think . . .' Don't you try masterful with me, thought Martha, now slightly alarmed by her own heart rate. I'm not that sort of woman. On the other hand . . .

'Martha, I won't beat around the bush with you. I have to see you. I shan't stop asking until you give in, so you might as well make it easier for yourself.'

Actually, masterful is OK, thought Martha, capitulating and twisting her other heel as she did so. 'Damn it!'

'What did you say?'

'N-nothing.' I'm like a schoolgirl. This is silly. I need to get this out of my system. 'Just a war wound. I'll see you at eight – Hall Cottage, Fox Colne. Three along from the duck pond on the right.'

'Great. I'll look forward to it.'

'I can't wait,' said Martha with dry lips – but only after the line had gone dead. Maybe, she thought, staring at the telephone in a slightly stunned way, maybe I just need to get him out of my system. Yes, use him and lose him. That would be for the best. She put her hand up to her suddenly hot cheek and pretended it was trembling because she had bashed her hip. She just needed to get him out of her system. After all, it was surely not the time of the month that had made her put her deodorant in the stenciling cupboard and spray stencil fixative under her arms in the bathroom this morning. Even though she had showered at once she could still clearly feel that her silk shirt was glued to her left armpit.

As she left the surgery Alice stuck the flier, inviting her to yet another meeting of interested bodies trying to improve medical services in Cambridge, in Tom's pigeonhole. If he was so interested, let him waste his time. Then she drove up to Addenbrooke's and persuaded the man in the kiosk to let her into the consultants' car park by saying hello to him nicely. She generally issued him with a script for Viagra once a fortnight so he had no hesitation in raising the barrier. She felt no remorse for accepting this favouritism – in the NHS you take your perks where you can.

Having said that, aside from the odd free sandwich in return for listening to a lecture on suppurating diseases of the penis, the only thing she had ever truly had free from the NHS was her ultrasound photo of the intrauterine Fergus. The ultrasonographer had said, 'I don't see why you should pay for your picture. There ought to be some sort of perk for working for the NHS till the day you die,' and had issued it free. Alice had left guiltily feeling as though she had accepted a free stay at the Paris Ritz without declaring it on her tax return.

She found Herman Banescu sitting on his bed in coronary care. Sister Goodenough, who had not wanted him to go because of the repeat psychiatric opinions she had been obtaining on him almost hourly, was at the desk. She was a little mollified as she and Simon, the psychiatric registrar, were going to see *Swamp Thing* at the Cambridge Arts Cinema that evening. It might not be everyone's idea of an arty film, but she wasn't intending to watch much of it anyway.

'Goodbye, then, Mr Banescu, and good luck. '

'Thank you, Sister,' he said gravely, 'and may I say that even the best hospitals in Armenia during our years of Soviet Rule could not better the iron discipline and extra-ordinary level of patient control which you dispense with such generosity here.'

Annette Goodenough was so flattered by the tone that she completely failed to question the meaning. 'Well, thank you, Mr Banescu – and if you change your mind and don't return to Armenia soon, just telephone us and we will make your six-week follow-up appointment here. You must be sure to have that exercise test. And remember in the meantime . . .' they were walking away from her and her voice echoed, bell-like, around the ward where other less lively patients lay attached to drips and monitors, watching Herman leave with a kind of weakened envy, 'no driving, no running and no SEX!' The word 'SEX' escaped from the coronary care ward with them and bounced invitingly down the corridor, past intensive care and into the porters' office, where it almost startled them out of watching *Casualty*, but not quite.

Chapter Eleven

Fergus liked elderly people, who were, he felt, far more interesting than the array of Mum-aged uncles and aunts with whom he was expected to make polite conversation every Christmas. He was pleased to find Herman in the kitchen at Herne Road, and hoped Alice would not stand in the way of a decent exchange of views for too long. The elderly, he had found, are very like the young, in that they return to the belief that all things are possible.

'So,' he said to Herman, sitting at the table beside him with half a packet of chocolate biscuits, 'where do you live then?'

'I am from Yerevan,' said Herman, with some pride, 'the capital of Armenia, which is the oldest Christian country in the world.'

'Wow,' said Daisy without enthusiasm, rolling her eyes slightly, but Fergus was interested.

'How do you know that? I mean, how would anyone know when a whole country became Christian?'

Herman turned and peered closely at Fergus. 'Because,' he said, displaying a remarkable grasp of the twelve-year-old mind, 'it says so on the Internet. In Armenia I look after the museum and the library next to the cathedral, a very important job. Let me tell you a thing or two about Armenia, young man. Our patron saint is Saint Gregory the Enlightener, also called the Illuminator – and thanks to him Armenia became the very first Christian country in the year AD 301 . . . '

*

In Fox Colne Martha was listening to Rachmaninov's Third Piano Concerto (the second being far too romantic for something which was, after all, pure animal attraction) and rubbing herself with perfumed lotion in a state of tightly controlled anticipation. If I let the tension out now, she thought, I'll explode like a champagne bottle, and run naked and shrieking around the village.

Alice rang. 'Martha?'

'Alice. How are you?'

'I'm fine. Considering that Daisy has arranged to ride on the St Alupent's School bed in the bed race dressed as a belly-dancer in Doc Martens – which I have to buy her. I was just ringing to let you know I told him.'

'Who?' asked Martha, knowing very well.

'You know. I told Tom. That we're not a pair of gay girls. I thought he was going to crawl under the table to escape me, until he realised that I meant not only myself but also you. Then I left him trying to scrape his tongue off the carpet.'

'Oh, stop it.' Martha giggled through the clutch of nervous tension that twisted the first part of her duodenum. She couldn't bear to tell Alice that he had rung her already. It was too important to share with anyone. 'He's hardly the tongue-scraping type.'

'He is now. So what are you going to do?' Alice was surprised by the giggle. Martha never giggled, her laughter was of the low sensuous chuckle variety.

'I don't know.' Martha rubbed one eyelid absently and an eyelash detached itself and went into her eye. 'Ouch. Perhaps I'll ring him up and ravish him within an inch of his life.' Of course she was joking, but she still held her breath for Alice's reaction.

'I'm sure you should,' said Alice. 'It's time you had a proper love affair. I've never known you fall over as often as you have since he turned up.'

'What nonsense. You don't fall over just because you find

someone attractive, I'm just – a little tense at the moment . . .
That time of the month.'
    'Have it your way.'

In Herne Road almost everyone had gone to bed by eleven,
after a game of Scrabble complicated by Herman's insistence
that all kinds of Armenian words should be allowed to count
whilst Anemone would not even let Fergus get away with
'BARBIE', even though he had struggled hard with his pride
in order to put the letters down in the first place.
    Only Alice was still up, calling Paddy in from the rugby
pitch behind the house, reflecting on the day. She was sure
that Martha was far more rattled by Tom Lovejoy than she'd
been prepared to admit. It struck Alice now that she had
never known Martha fall for anyone, not really. Come to
think of it, she had never seen her lose her poise like this
either. She was always so self-possessed – but then perhaps
she had had to be, after what happened to her mother.
    Well, even the mighty can fall – but mustn't it be
wonderful to be on the edge of something fantastic? An
unexpected gush of wistfulness broke over her, soaking her
with astonishment. Could she really be envying Martha the
thrill of new romance? Or was it that she was reminded of
those first ecstatic years with Rob? Her mind seized Rob and
tried to pull him into her emotional memory but he
wouldn't come.
    Still, it was no good going all reflective now – look what
happened to Lot's wife. And in any case, she had other,
more pressing, problems. Herman Banescu and his frog for
one thing, not to mention the huge question of whether she
would even have a job to support herself with after the end
of September or a practice to call her own. So she shut
Paddy in the kitchen, locked the front door and bolted it.
There was plenty of time for worrying in the morning.
Morning would come soon enough.

                                *

In Fox Colne morning was still far away. Tom brushed Martha's hip gently, but just enough. Like static electricity the charge was already there, the touch like lightning. All her body hairs stood on end at once, like soldiers at roll call when the general barks.

'How did you get the bruise?'

'I knocked into a desk.' Martha felt too exposed, too fragile, too *vulnerable* to tell him that she had fallen against the table because the very sound of his voice had seemed to unbalance her.

'Here . . . let me kiss it better.' He trailed his lips across her lower abdomen, round, round to the bruise on her iliac crest. Martha sighed. It had been . . . splendid. Fireworks, earth tremblingly splendid. Her heart rate had not calmed yet, and wouldn't for days, she knew. When she thought of the way they had been, the way he had carried her to the bedroom. He hadn't just carried her. He had swept her off her feet . . . Feeling his warm breath on her bruised hip she closed her eyes and allowed herself to enjoy it all over again, in minute detail.

The doorbell had rung at two minutes to eight – perfect, in Martha's book, for whilst a gentleman is never too early it smacks of a slight disinterest to be slightly late, and only Virgos are ever absolutely on time. The thought of any man sitting outside in the street with an eye on his watch, waiting for the second hand to creep round to twelve, is one of the world's ten biggest turn-offs (the others, Martha felt, began with farting in bed and ended with chewing with the mouth open, whilst between lay everything from ingratiating behaviour to physical violence).

At any rate, Tom was perfect from the moment of his arrival. He was carrying a Marks and Spencer carrier bag and a bottle of chilled champagne. Dom Pérignon – Martha's heart fluttered slightly. He wanted her to feel special. That was good. The analytical part of her brain, ever active, had been judging his every move, and so far he was without equal.

'I've brought smoked salmon,' he told her in that amazing Sean Connery voice, as rich as dark chocolate, 'and fillet steak, and strawberries. Point me to the kitchen, and I'll cook for you.'

Then he marinated the smoked salmon, seared the steak and rinsed the strawberries, whilst she sipped a little champagne and talked about her shop, her life, her plans . . .

By the time they ate Martha felt heady as a schoolgirl on her first date. She had barely touched the champagne, feeling his subsequent performance needed to be judged without the clouding of alcohol in order that she might use it to excise him from her psyche. The smoked salmon slipped down like ambrosia, although her appetite was tiny, and the steaks were small but perfect. Rare, which is as steaks should be, served only with Béarnaise sauce and a tossed salad. *She had met a man who could make Béarnaise sauce!* Martha, feeling the meat melt on her tongue, watched him eat. He ate beautifully, poetry in motion. No ghastly chewing or chomping. He talked with his mouth empty, yet managed not to take all night to clear his plate. He cut his food as though it were butter and never once dribbled salad dressing on his chin. Martha, watching him, was suddenly aware that she had dropped half a curly endive into her lap.

The Dom Pérignon was exquisite, even those few sips she dared take made her feel as it she were floating on a warm pool of desire – and then he suggested they took their strawberries into the living room. Watching the way his strong hands carried the tray, Martha was unable to suppress a shiver at the thought of those hands on her skin, touching her, moulding her . . .

And all evening it hung between them like an unsaid prayer. What was it? The power of knowledge, the certainty that, by keeping their hands and bodies apart, the conversation light but neutral, they were simply teasing out the strands of their desire, prolonging the expectation before that moment when the trembling got too much and they tore into one another like creatures created entirely of sexual energy . . . Martha could feel her desire for him glowing out of her skin like the scent of garlic. He must smell it, she thought, it must overpower him soon because it is overpowering me.

But despite all this Tom did not break the unspoken rule, the rule of chivalry, that in a woman's home the first time she must make the move – and so as she devoured him in her mind they ate strawberries delicately and then she offered to make coffee with a tremble in her voice. His eyes had a way of looking right inside her. He will know, she thought with glorious certainty, he will know exactly where to touch, which places react exquisitely to the gentle brush of lips, which to a lingering kiss. He will know that I cannot bear to have my earlobes chewed . . .

'Come and talk to me in the kitchen,' she whispered, and she knew it was too late. She had tried to find fault with him, and had found only her own desire. Now, when she finally saw the danger she was in, it was too late: she could no more resist him than the moth does the flame . . .

They had not even reached the kitchen doorway when she turned to face him, defeated.

Fire gleamed in his eyes as she said, 'Tom . . . if you don't make love to me, I think I'll explode into a shower of a million sparks.' And he took her in his arms as if she were a china doll, oh so carefully, and his kiss was like the whisper of satin on cool skin.

It grew, and grew, and grew until the very air around them burned with the force of it, and she led him to the bedroom – the big beautiful bedroom that was the epitome of elegance, whose sheets were white silk, whose bed was huge enough to sleep in with a stranger – and by then she had been swept up in his arms like driftwood and flung with careful passion onto the bed in one smooth swift motion, and his skin was hot and gently scented. She was almost screaming for him by the time he lifted her forward and down as if he would pierce her through the centre, impale her on the silken rod, neither too large nor too small. It was all she could do to rein herself back from the chasm as he moved, gently at first and then, soon, wildly and with a loss of control that was, in itself, the most exquisite thing she had ever felt, the more so because her own control was so precariously unbalanced. And as she sobbed his name, breaking one of her own rules in the process (she had always felt that names made sex so very personal), and as she begged him not to stop, to go on, and on, and on and on for ever, the tiny part of her brain that had been judging, watching, trying to prefer other men, the ones who had gone before, to prefer them at least in some tiny, insignificant way – the part of her brain that clung to sanity – exploded in a puff of magic dust and was gone for ever.

She pulled him over on top of her, the delicious caress of the cool silk sheets exquisite on her hot back. And as he sank into her he kissed her, over and over and over, sweet as honey, lips like velvet, until she felt that she should open her mouth wide and swallow him all up in the frantic hunger that seized and shook them.

The surging orgasm, when it came, built like a rising tide in her loins, seizing her like the flotsam of a mighty wreck and flinging her, gasping and helpless, onto some far shore where she had never been before, and then exploding with nuclear intensity in a wave of shuddering ecstasy that she was barely aware was mirrored in Tom as he whispered her name.

Alice stirred restlessly in her bed as dawn broke, unable to get back to sleep. Had she been dreaming of Rob? She had dreamed of him vividly at first – night after night: that he was still there; that he was killed and then that he wasn't;

that it was a crazy mistake, a misunderstanding . . . Then, as time went by a little, the dreams had seemed a little more repetitive, familiar to her as dreams and no longer seeming as an altered reality.

But this was different. Just like the other night, if she had been dreaming it had not been of Rob. Her body still ached a little in a disturbingly familiar way. There was still a slight sensation of chocolate behind her left knee – and that was after three showers and a serious scrub in the bath. There was no real chocolate there, of course – she put a cautious finger down to check – it was just the memory of chocolate, not quite washed away. If the chocolate was still there in spirit, though, the same could not be said of something else. Because some aspect of Rob seemed to have left her, something that she had not really realised had still been there. Or if not Rob, exactly, just a part of her link to Rob. She was lightened in a small but significant way, like a traveller loaded with cases who has finally managed to find an airport trolley. No less baggage, perhaps, but a heck of a lot easier to move it around.

Perhaps Martha had been right – perhaps she had been keeping faith with Rob. Well, now she had broken it. There had to have been a next man one day, of course, unless she had remained chaste for ever. It might have been one of life's more forgettable experiences, but it at least proved she was human; it still removed her from that awful pedestal of mourning saint which she had begun to fear she had placed herself on indefinitely.

But would Rob wish her well? Or would he feel she had merely evened the score?

She gave up in the end, thinking, sleep is not sleep when it tangles the mind – and went downstairs to cook useful and freezable meals of the sort that no one in the family would ever actually eat. Perhaps Herman Banescu would eat them. He came from Eastern Europe so he was almost certain to like pie. She wondered if he had slept well, and if, refreshed, he would be able to identify his frog. If there had actually been a frog. He seemed harmless enough – but there was always the vague possibility that he was entirely deluded and actually needed not a fruitful search for a frog but a regular and powerful psychotropic injection into his bottom.

'Morning, Mum.' Fergus appeared at the kitchen door looking mildly shifty, like a boy with nothing to hide (which is always the worst kind), and, by some fiendish means known only to boys, put the entire contents of a box of Rice Krispies into one small cereal bowl. As he added milk they surged ominously up above the rim like rising lava, but held steady. 'Can I tell you something?'

Alice looked up from the pie. 'What? And have you seen Mr Banescu up yet?'

'Mr Blackwell wants to talk to you. And no. I left a note on Herman's door saying that the bathroom would be free once Daisy had glued her face on but that usually took half an hour. I think she's been really weird recently. I think she's sickening for something.'

Alice ignored the obvious red herring. 'Does he now?' Mr Blackwell seemed to want to talk to her rather often – usually it was about nothing much and she assumed he was just a teacher who believed in communication but perhaps he was working up to some terrible Fergus problem. She raised her 'tell me more' eyebrow. One thing that doctors, like teachers, learn very quickly is that silence and an expectant brow draws forth the kind of rapid confessional blabber which can otherwise only be extracted using sleep deprivation, thumbscrews and the truth drug.

Fergus was not a doctor's son for nothing. He affected an airy return eyebrow and a shrug, then headed for the biscuit tin. Alice followed him with her antennae.

'Fergus? Haven't you got something else to say?'

'Don't do it,' muttered Daisy, sidling in carefully so that Alice wouldn't notice what she had done to her nose, and with an uncharacteristic show of Fergus support: 'she's using that tone.'

'What tone?' Alice frowned. 'And what have you done to your nose?'

Daisy fingered the nose ring. 'It's not real. It's a clip-on one. I don't know why you even noticed – it's so small.'

'Why I even noticed? You come into the kitchen looking so invitingly bovine that I'm surprised there isn't a queue of likely heifers at the front door, and you think I might not notice? One thing about eyes, Daisy, is that when you point them at things they tend to send signals back into your head. Or is that just a skill developed by doctors?'

Daisy put her nose in the air, and then tried to catch a glimpse of the ring in the kitchen mirror. 'It's like living with twenty-four-hour satellite surveillance.' She removed the ring deftly and without pain.

'Thank goodness for that,' said Anemone, wandering in, fiddling with her hair beads, which were dripping profusely, 'you might easily have got led off to market. You shouldn't take this belly-dancer thing too far.'

Daisy glared and reattached the ring, this time to the other nostril. It had actually been pinching a bit, but she didn't want to admit it.

'I shouldn't go anywhere near Felixstowe harbour,' said Fergus, not wanting to be left out. 'Someone might rope a container ship to you.'

'Leave her alone, you two,' Alice intervened. 'As long as there isn't a hole in there, Daisy, you can do what you like. Anyway, I think it looks rather fetching. Reminds me of the hippy things we all wore in the seventies,' and, as Daisy snatched the ring away again (*seventies?*): 'you still haven't told me what tone it is that I use.'

Daisy sniffed. 'You know. That doctorish tone – all, tell me more-ish.'

'I'm sorry.' Alice finished assembling the pie and put it in the oven. 'I'll try to be a little less helpful and understanding, shall I?'

'Don't be silly. I just – want to be a bit different, that's all. I'm going to be riding the school bed – I need to be cool. I need –'

'Is this about Doc Martens, by any chance?'

'How did you know that?'

'You're not my first daughter,' said Alice drily, 'and there's a time in every teenager's life when the urge for Doc Martens surpasses all reason.'

'She's in love,' said Fergus, 'and I bet I know who with.'

'No you don't. And I'm not.'

'Bet I know . . .'

'Don't tease, Fergus,' said Alice crossly, 'otherwise when you're in love I shall advertise it on a hoarding in Lion Yard.'

Fergus shrugged. 'I'll never be in love,' but he left Daisy alone. Alice wondered whom her daughter had set her sights on. Hopefully someone not too hairy. I was only twenty when I met Rob, she thought. It's frightening, watching my children approaching that time, and without him to bounce my worries off.

Daisy wanted the subject moved well away from love. 'If that's for tonight, can I have my pie without pastry? It hasn't got mushrooms in it, has it?'

'It has. And it's followed by mushroom ice-cream and mushroom sauce,' Alice grinned.

'I hate mushrooms,' said Daisy.

'Well, this is saturation therapy,' said Alice. 'It works with spiders. I've cured three patients of spider phobia.'

'Was that the day Lisa ran screaming into the street?' Anemone raised her eyebrows.

Alice grinned. 'Well, she shouldn't have opened the box. So anyway, come on, what's wrong with me being doctorish?'

Daisy sighed. 'It's sometimes a bit much, that's all. I could do with being understood a bit less. I mean, look what you did to me. You gave me anti-acne treatment before I even got my first spot.'

'You mean you'd rather have spots?' Fergus was mystified, the Mr Blackwell discomfiture forgotten.

'No, don't be stupid. But teenagers are supposed to be agonised first. How will I ever get to put passion into the Elgar if I don't learn agony?'

'Would you rather I shrieked and shouted and banished you to your room every time you swore?'

'She'd never come out,' muttered Anemone.

Daisy glared. 'You're ganging up on me now. Look, I'm not complaining, it's just I need a bit more conflict. We're doing *Romeo and Juliet* in English, you know. Miss Fitzgibbons says I've got to think of Juliet like a difficult teenager in perpetual conflict – I can hardly say I don't know what that means. You make everything too easy. I mean, everyone else is planning where they're going to hide the pill from their parents, and you keep asking me if I want it yet.'

'I'm just being sensible, that's all,' Alice shrugged. That's me, she thought, the sensible one. When Rob was having a wild time with Marcie Crombie I was the sensible one. Was I too sensible, perhaps? Still, you can't say the other night was sensible. God, I shall never eat chocolate sauce again without blushing . . .

Daisy sniffed. 'You're always sensible. This house is sensible. White and sensible, like toilet roll. Sensible is boring.'

Alice raised her eyebrows. 'So what's this about? You want the pill, or you want me to paint the hall purple?'

Daisy sniffed. 'Purple would be better than white. Do you know Pipe Tree Cottage is for sale?'

Ah, thought Alice, now I see. 'Yes,' she said aloud, 'I do.'

'Well, maybe we should buy it.'

Alice looked at Daisy, at Anemone and Fergus, and it was

clear to her at once that this had been discussed.

'Anemone?'

Anemone was reluctant to cause upset. 'We thought it might help you.'

Alice frowned. 'You mean, help me get over your father? We won't find him there, you know.'

Anemone shook her head. 'No, but here you've only ever been miserable. This house is like white blotting paper and you've stained it miserable. White is the colour of mourning in India, you know.'

Alice was taken aback. 'It isn't that bad, is it?'

Daisy shook her head hastily. 'No, of course not. But perhaps you'd be happy there. You were happy there before, and you're not happy here.'

'We could paint it any other colour you liked,' added Anemone, 'except white.'

Alice looked at their awkward faces. 'Fergus? Is that what you want to do?' Fergus was uneasy. He didn't like family decisions coming to rest on him. Well, apart from when it came to choosing which TV channel they watched. He would have liked to tell Alice the truth – that the more he thought about it the less he wanted to move – but Anemone had threatened to e-mail naked pictures of him to all the girls in form four if he didn't toe the line.

'It had a brilliant garden,' he said eventually. 'Anyway, we couldn't let anyone else live in it. It's bad enough having that stupid Phoebe living there.'

'Don't be mean,' said Daisy. 'You're just miffed because she got your bedroom and now it's pink.'

'I could soon fix that,' said Fergus darkly. There are some things a boy cannot be expected to live with.

'Well, I think it would be good,' said Daisy. 'I mean, Fox Colne is still home, isn't it? And you'd be near Martha too.' She wondered whether she would automatically get her old bedroom back or whether she could bid for Anemone's, seeing as Anemone would be leaving home soon anyway.

243

'I'll think about it,' said Alice. 'Will that do?'

'Look,' said Fergus, 'd'you want to forget the Mr Blackwell thing for now? It wasn't important.'

'Mr Blackwell?' Daisy had missed the first part of the conversation. 'Why—'

'Nothing important,' said Fergus hastily. 'Forget it.'

'On the contrary,' said Alice darkly, 'I think the sooner I see him, the better.'

'Good morning.' Herman came in looking quite bright and sprightly.

'Oh, Mr Banescu, hello, would you like some cornflakes?'

'Yes, indeed. Good morning, everyone.'

'Did you sleep well?' asked Alice. 'That spare room can be rather stuffy so I left the window open. I hope you weren't cold.'

'I am feeling very refreshed, thank you,' said Herman, 'and now that I am not drugged and imprisoned in my bed my head is much clearer. I need to look for my frog.' Alice wondered briefly again about his possible need for a depot injection to calm him down. But then, she had a surgery full of frogs. If Herman was potty, what was she?

'We were talking,' she said on impulse, 'about moving house. Back to where we used to live. What do you think?'

Herman considered this briefly. 'I think,' he said, with surprising gravity, 'that you should follow your heart, and for hearts the best way usually lies straight ahead. Ah, I do like cornflakes. Hardly ever do I see a cornflake. Always bread, bread, bread . . .'

Alice did an early school run, wanting to speak to Mr Blackwell in case something was wrong.

'There's no need to worry, Mrs Vane. Fergus is really doing very well,' said Mr Blackwell, peering earnestly at Alice through a rather lush beard. He had lovely eyes, really green. Deep eyes, the sort of eyes you could lose yourself in whilst you were kissing him. She wondered if he remembered what his face looked like beneath the beard. Imagine kissing a beard like that – it would be like a vigorous facial scrub . . . depending on how good he was at kissing, of course. They could rent him out as an abrasion treatment for scarring. A gentle, hairy rub. It would be much nicer than a facial scrub . . . She pulled her thoughts up sharply (what am I thinking? Perhaps my night with Oliver has left me mad with unfulfilled lust) and smiled at him reassuringly, hoping he had not spotted anything untoward in her look.

Mr Blackwell was a tall man, with a rather sweet face rendered professorish by the beard, and hair whose tight cropping could not disguise the fact that it was almost anarchically curly. Not a smooth man, thought Alice, not a charmer at all. And such clear eyes, the sort you could trust. He didn't generate that feeling of needing to start closing the portcullis. A man like this would be a good safe bet for someone. He wouldn't be passionate, probably – too shy for oral sex – but then too much passion could be . . .

'. . . with his singing voice,' said Mr Blackwell.

'Oh, I'm sorry Mr Blackwell. Just drifting. Night on call,' lied Alice, thinking: well, I could hardly tell him I was just imagining what he's like in bed. She bit her lip. Martha is getting to me. It struck her suddenly that Oliver had been hopeless on the kissing front. How exactly had it felt when Rob kissed her? Romantic? Sexy? It was hard to remember it clearly now. Perhaps I should kiss Mr Blackwell and see how that feels . . .

Mr Blackwell smiled, and his eyes twinkled. 'Do call me Colin.'

Do people usually call their son's schoolteacher Colin? Not if he's called Richard, I suppose . . . Alice's lips twitched in spite of herself. 'Colin.'

Colin Blackwell watched her with well-hidden longing. Fancied her like mad, of course, but then all the male teachers did. There was something about widows. All that repressed passion and wistful air – made you want to hug them and – well . . . he shifted slightly at his desk and cleared his throat. 'I – er – was just saying, Fergus has a splendid singing voice. You should consider lessons.' It sounded a weak excuse to have asked her in to talk to him, it even sounded weak to him.

'But surely his voice will break soon? All those hormones . . .'

'All the more reason to get him some lessons – keep it in control. You never know, he could have the makings of a fine tenor.'

'He wants to be the first man on Mars,' said Alice, 'and to play Mozart's Clarinet Concerto in the Sea of Utter Misery, or whatever it's called, when he gets there.'

Colin Blackwell smiled. 'Didn't we all? Mind you, I was more modest – I planned on a solo. I thought it might be a bit ridiculous, expecting NASA to send up a whole orchestra with me.'

'Did we? I mean, did you?' Alice was curious suddenly. Fergus' odd ambitions, all the things she had attributed to Rob because they couldn't be hers – were they *Mr Blackwell's*? Or do all boys want the same things? How many more of these bits of Fergus which she'd put down to Rob's influence were just *boyness* coming through?

Colin Blackwell blinked, nodded, and then broke about eleven (actually exactly eleven, as he had been planning this for some time in his deepest fantasies so he had counted) of his personal teacher-etiquette rules by saying, 'Er – I wondered – would you like to meet me for a drink at The Mill?'

Alice swallowed. I was right. I do have an availability light flashing over me. Maybe Oliver left a little sign on my forehead that only other men can see – 'Looks like a widow but is actually a total slapper.'

Make nothing of it. Say yes or no fast, or it looks even worse. He's not charming – not smooth – not even slightly

Robbish . . . but he's Fergus' teacher. His *teacher*, Alice, you can't even consider it . . .

'I'm sorry, it's not a very good time for me at the moment.'

'Of course not, say no more, stupid of me.' Damn, thought Colin, mistimed it. Blew it completely. Probably picked her wedding anniversary or something. She probably hates beards. Maybe that's it. 'But I do need a doctor to be on hand on bed race day. I'm organising it all this year, you see. I wondered if you . . . ?'

'I, er . . .' I just keep saying no to him, she thought. I must sound like the world's most useless mother – and Fergus is already losing out, not having Rob. 'Of course I will. It will take my mind off Daisy steering the school bed. Just let me know where you need me to be nearer the time.'

In my arms, thought Colin Blackwell hungrily, in my arms. With all that blonde hair spread across my pillow. He eyed her with a wistful lust. It was hard, anyway, to find the right woman, when you taught in a school full of teenagers. Life gave you a rather haggard look that seemed to put women right off. But Alice Vane was so vulnerably sexy. It made him want to fling her onto his computer console and ravish her within an inch of her life. He guessed she was probably still in mourning for that bastard husband of hers. What sort of a man must he have been to throw away his chance with a woman like that? How can I make her see me? Maybe the beard . . . ?

Life just got more complicated, thought Alice as she left. Singing lessons for Fergus – but where was he going to get the learning-to-be-a-man lessons from? Mr Blackwell and the series of teachers who would follow him? Then Doc Martens for Daisy. Do I really want my daughter wandering around Cambridge looking like a belly-dancer with attitude? The trouble is, I really miss having someone to share the policing of it all with, but I'm just not sure I want

247

to go through all the upheaval in order to find someone. Still, I've enough to worry about at the moment, without adding a date with my son's teacher to it. Herman Banescu for starters.

Alice worried about Herman all the way to the surgery. She didn't really like leaving him alone – although he wasn't truly alone, as today was the day that Mrs Otway came in to clean the floors, tidy the cupboards and nose through the drawers. Actually, the presence of a strange Armenian would cheer up what must surely be otherwise a rather fodderless existence. Alice hadn't exactly provided Mrs Otway with much meat for the gossipmongers recently, after all. 'Dr Vane has been crying again and she still keeps her husband's photo face down on her bedside table,' must rather pall after the first couple of years. But the frog that she had apparently managed to lose weighed on her mind.

Alice knew that she was deliberately using the Herman crisis (uncrisis though it seemed to be) to squeeze the buying-the-house-back dilemma right out of her head. A useless strategy, in fact. Pipe Tree Cottage was bubbling underneath, like lava glimpsed through a crack in the earth.

When she got to the surgery, however, the surgery crisis threw all thought of Herman and of Pipe Tree Cottage out of her head.

Tom was waiting for her there in front of the reception desk, looking, she thought, rather flushed and odd.

'Good morning,' she said, with slight sympathy. She wondered how long it would take him to get in touch with Martha now that she had told him the truth – that Martha was as heterosexual as Genghis of the Ten Thousand Wives. The chances were he'd rung her already. Actually, looking at him, he'd probably already spent the night with her . . . so he deserved sympathy because soon he'd be dumped.

'Alice – I'm afraid we have a bit of a problem.' And then over his shoulder she saw the workman screwing a Chubb bolt to the lavatory door. Roland lurked smugly in the background, arms folded, like Banquo's ghost at the feast.

'Roland? What on earth . . . ?'

'I did warn you, Alice,' said Roland, like an admonishing schoolmistress, 'that I simply could no longer tolerate the misuse of my property by your NHS patients. I consider the lavatory to be private since you will see it lies on my side of the dividing line. Yesterday evening after late surgery one of my titled ladies went into the lavatory to find . . .' he lowered his voice, '. . . Something floating.'

Alice didn't know whether to laugh or shout. Roland's pandering consultations with patients who wouldn't come in during normal surgery hours for fear of being contaminated by the lower orders rather annoyed her, and it was pleasing, in a dreadful, childish way, to imagine the probable scene.

'Oh, Roland, you can't really mean to lock the loo?'

Roland drew himself up to his full height. 'I do think, Alice, that it's about time you realised –'

Beside Roland, though, Lisa got to her feet suddenly. She looked rather pale and drawn. She felt sick. Pregnancy was making her queasy – the baby was growing fast now and pressing on her stomach, and she needed somewhere to be ill. She had had such a craving this morning, and Dean had been so good to her, rushing out to the supermarket like that – but that pâté and jelly hadn't mixed very well and she could feel them now, burbling in a pâté-jelly glob. Now that Roland was locking the lavatory there was nowhere nearer than upstairs to run to. She could suddenly stand it no longer.

'What can you mean, Dr Liversill,' she demanded in furious exasperation, '"something floating"? You're a doctor, for God's sake. If you mean a turd then just say it was a bloody turd!' She rushed past Roland and the reception area and up the stairs towards the staff area, leaving them all staring after her open-mouthed.

Roland glared. 'You should sack that girl,' he said nastily.

'Her bad language will offend.'

Alice sighed. 'Roland, you can't really be doing this. Where are the patients supposed to go when they need to?'

'That, as I have already told Dr Lovejoy,' said Roland, 'is not my problem. The private lavatory was only ever available for your patients to use as a courtesy.'

'You're being ridiculous, Roland. Can't we talk about this sensibly?'

'There is really no more to say.' He turned his back.

Alice glared. 'Well, we'll pay you,' she said desperately, 'loo rental. Just decide how much you want.'

Roland smiled meanly, and she had the impression that victory was far more important to him than money. The sooner we get out of here, she thought, the better. He doesn't care about the lavatory at all; he's just showing us he's in charge.

Tom Lovejoy touched her arm. 'Alice, can I have a private word?'

She nodded. 'Come through. Where's James?'

'James is feeling unwell,' said Tom, when he had shut her door. 'I told him to go home and he went. Frankly, I think the whole thing with Roland is upsetting him terribly. Look, Alice, you can't carry on here under these conditions – it's becoming ridiculous. We have to make a stand – the patients are going to suffer.'

Alice sighed. The fact that James would allow himself to be sent home spoke volumes about how upset he must have been. She felt too worried herself to take issue with Tom's 'we' and all it seemed to assume. 'It takes months to wind up a partnership, Tom. We can't just close down like a shoe shop. Anyhow, it's not your problem.'

Tom looked hurt. 'Well, no – but the thing is, I do know of a –'

The telephone rang. 'Hello? Dr Vane.'

'I'm the house manager here at the Fir Trees. Dr Vane, Miss Tinkler is just not herself and she says only you can

250

help. I think she and Mr Ramsden have had an argument about his peacocks. I thought if you came to talk to him . . . He says if he pens them up in the summer they will pine, but Miss Tinkler says she is positively fading away from the stress of it.'

Alice could not imagine Tabitha fading – it was rather like trying to imagine Ayers Rock evaporating. 'I'll come over after morning surgery,' she promised, thinking: this is the agony aunt thing again. What on earth am I supposed to do about Tabitha and Fred arguing? And actually, if Tabitha is upset it's probably nothing to do with Fred's peacocks. It's probably stress because of Herman. If this surgery has to close down, what will happen to people like Tabitha?

Tom was still waiting when she put down the phone. 'Alice, I wondered if you would consider converting another building.'

'Far too expensive. We could never afford central Cambridge property prices.'

'But if you took on another partner who –'

Alice closed her ears. 'I'm not sure that I even want to stick with the partners I've got. I appreciate your concern Tom, but it's *really* not your problem. I'm sorry – I have to get on now.'

I don't need any of this, she told herself wearily. I just have to resign and find myself an assistant's post somewhere else in the city. There are always jobs coming up. That way it's simply not my problem either. It was better just not to worry about Tabitha and Lisa, and all the people of whom she was really very fond who were the whole reason that she was still here doing this job three years into widowhood. It was just a shame that not thinking about things gets more difficult the more things there are to not think about. Pipe Tree Cottage, the children, Tabitha, Herman, James, Roland, the practice . . . It's as if, thought Alice, life is forcing me down an impossible path, so impossible that I can no longer drift on with the flow.

251

Morning surgery rather dragged afterwards, although a few things were resolved. The medical magazine rang to say that Anemone was welcome to write their horoscopes, and Roland had temporarily unbolted the door without payment, due to Lisa threatening to be sick on his carpet, so patients were at least not building up outside in a horrible state of desperation. Obviously he had just been exercising his authority, but Alice felt quite proud of Lisa.

There were, though, an awful lot of people who didn't need to see a doctor waiting to see her. Some of them were the usual suspects who came to the surgery every time they coughed. One or two were anxious parents with well but hot toddlers. Three old ladies only really wanted a short moan about their knees. She had begun to wonder whether she served any useful function at all when her last patient came in, sat down and presented her with a card and a box of chocolates.

'It's for everything you've done for my Tina,' she said proudly.

'Er . . .' If only I had a photographic memory, thought Alice. I have absolutely no idea who Tina is. The computer gave no clue, as according to her screen the woman was named Brian Hobbs and was aged twenty-seven. 'I'm sorry,' she said, 'you are . . .?'

'Her mum. You referred her up to the fertility clinic.'

'Oh, Tina Hobbs. I see.'

'Twins. She's pregnant with twins,' said the woman, 'twenty weeks. I just had to tell you, Dr Vane. We're so proud . . .' She burst into tears, and it was some time before Alice could escort her, still sobbing intermittently, back out to her car.

Well, she thought afterwards. Doesn't that just about sum it up, really? A surgery full of people who think they're ill when they're not, a woman thanking me for all I've done when I didn't at first remember doing it, and an old Armenian coming to stay with me because he's got nowhere

252

else to go. You wouldn't get this in any other job. I used to think I did this job for Rob but I don't at all. I do it for me.

So how could she give in to Roland without even trying? Perhaps she should throw in her lot with Tom, ask him what this idea of his was. But when she went to his room to ask him, he had gone.

After surgery she called in at the Fir Trees, where she found Tabitha miserable. She wasn't hungry, she wasn't thirsty, she wasn't even bothered about her knees. It was time, she told Alice, that someone found her 'off' switch. Alice was troubled to hear her speak that way.

'Is there anything else that's worrying you?'

'For heaven's sake,' said Tabitha surprisingly, 'stop trying to turn me into the search for the hidden agenda. I know what you doctors do. No, I am simply unearthed. I have lost my earth wire. It's obvious.'

'Would this have anything to do with your visitor from Armenia?' Alice asked.

'Well, of course it does,' said Tabitha. 'I know he's here somewhere – he's not at the hospital, and I was expecting him to come and see me. I think you've got him hidden, and it's making me very cross. And when I get cross my bowels play up, and you know what that means, Dr Alice.'

'I'm sorry, Tabitha. If I could tell you where he is I would – but I can't. I'd be breaching a confidence. Why don't you tell me about him, and I'll see if I can help?'

Tabitha sighed. 'There's not much else to tell. I think he's come to tell me my Tamas is dead. I just wish he'd get it over with. You know, Dr Alice, all my life I kept faith with that man, even though he married some fat peasant and got on with his life. Until recently I couldn't ever see anyone replacing him . . .'

'Until recently? What changed?'

Tabitha shrugged. 'I've seen myself for a fool. A dried-up old spinster. Look at me now. Tamas said he would do anything for me, all those years ago. Catch the stars, he said.

Move Heaven and Earth. And what did he actually do? Died and left me stuck in a blooming rest home with forty incontinent women and an infuriating old codger who keeps birds that scream all night.'

'Fred? Infuriating? Why?'

'He's jealous.' Tabitha folded her arms across her ample bosom. 'He doesn't like me talking about Tamas. He wants me all to himself, you see. Thinks he can manage us all single-handedly.' She pouted in an astonishingly Bardot-ish manner. Alice fought valiantly to suppress the mental image of Fred attempting to single-handedly manage all the female residents of the Fir Trees.

'Tabitha, I'll try to persuade Herman to come and see you.'

Tabitha's eyes brightened. 'Would you do that? Please do.'

But Herman, when she got home to wolf lunch and put this to him, refused point-blank to see Tabitha until he had found his lost frog. Alice had brought all the frogs she could find from the branch surgery and he had looked through the whole lot, but none was the right frog. She wasn't sure that he had a clear memory of what the right frog looked like. Perhaps she had lent it to someone – she had lent out several in the past few days.

'I came to bring her something,' he said stubbornly. 'It was my uncle's last request, and I cannot possibly see her until I've found it again. I am too ashamed.' And Alice stomped back to the surgery in some disgust. Old people. He might be twenty years younger than Tabitha but he was still old. Is anyone ever more stubborn than the old?

At least afternoon surgery began with good news, even if lunch had to consist of Frosted Shreddies because Herman insisted on preparing it and it was all he could do. 'You must let me look after you – you have all been so kind . . . Your breakfast cereals are so fantastic here, why do you even need any other food? Besides, I cannot even boil an egg

254

– my wife does all the cabbage soup.'

At least it was nourishing. Alice knew this because Herman insisted on reading out the vitamin content from the box as she ate ('. . . and look at this – of pantothenic acid – forty per cent of the adult daily requirement!').

When Alice got back to the Lammas Surgery Lisa was waiting to see her, looking much brighter now that she had got through the morning and won access back to the loo. She was heroine of the day, which was rather nice, and it had taught her that being assertive was a jolly good thing. She would have her way about her bridesmaids' dresses using the same forceful approach.

Casually slipping half a ton of medical post, most of which seemed to be about pus, into Tom's pigeonhole (it was a learning opportunity, she told herself guiltily), Alice escorted Lisa through to her room.

'Dr Vane, I wanted to thank you. Dean and me are OK – and it was all because of what you said.'

'You mean congratulations are in order?' Alice was delighted. 'That's wonderful news – and I'm sure it was nothing I said. You and Dean just talked to one another, that's all.'

Lisa sniffed. 'I'd have had ten children and he still wouldn't have married me if it weren't for you.'

'You weren't planning ten, were you?' asked Alice slightly anxiously, but Lisa shook her head.

'One's enough for me. Dr Vane – I wanted to ask you something. I wanted to ask . . . I wondered if you'd be my bridesmaid. Please say you will?'

'I, er . . .' Alice was slightly flabbergasted. 'Are you sure? I mean, I'm not exactly a maid.'

'Oh, don't be silly. Without you there wouldn't be any wedding – and it'll be in Fox Colne, at the church. I know it used to be your local – oh!' She stopped, suddenly horrified, and Alice knew she was thinking of Rob's grave.

'That will be lovely,' said Alice firmly, ignoring the

potential for Rob and his grave to loom into the conversation. 'I'm honoured to be asked – although matron of honour might be a better title. When is it going to be?'

After a quick rundown of her favourite hymns and a firm statement by Alice that if Ipswich Town FC first team were to sing 'You'll Never Walk Alone' in harmony during the signing of the register then she would not be up to providing the descant, Lisa went back to the front desk, beaming. Behind her she left the dawning and ghastly realisation on Alice's part that she was to be expected to wear frilled peach silk with a big cream sash and shoes with little bows on. And a shiny peach ribbon in her hair.

Chapter Twelve

Later that afternoon St Alupent's School had a cricket match against a local rival, St John's College School, and Mark Blackwell was captain of the school team. Daisy was trying to decide on her next move on the object of her desire. The trouble was, she really fancied him – but if he didn't fancy her then she was going to look such a fool. But what else could she do to capture his attention? She had won the competition to ride the bed, she was getting Doc Martens, she had an imitation nose ring for use after the school bell went, Anemone had lent her a really nice blusher – but he still seemed not to have noticed.

She gazed across the school cricket pitch to where he was bowling. Mark Blackwell, cricket captain extraordinaire. He didn't have a girlfriend, even though he was Captain of Sport – but then, he was Mr Blackwell's son. It was pretty naff to go out with a teacher's son, even if the teacher was reasonably cool in himself. It meant that she couldn't tell any of her friends.

It was tough that she couldn't tell Mum. She'd have told her most things – but it didn't seem fair to discuss falling in love with Mum. She'd had such a rotten time – and, anyway, was her advice any good? You could say she'd rather mucked things up herself, after all.

Fergus materialised alarmingly at her side. 'Hi sis. Who are you watching?'

'No one,' said Daisy. 'I just happen to like cricket.'

'Oh yeah, like I like ballet. Who do you fancy, then?'

'No one. Don't be stupid.'

'Must be Hugh Appleton.'

'Certainly not. He's only fifteen.'

'You're fifteen. What about Jeremy Andrews.'

'Stop it, Fergus. I don't fancy anyone.'

'It's Jeremy Andrews, isn't it? I'm going to tell everyone. Shall I ask him if he fancies you?'

'It's not Jeremy bloody Andrews, you little monster.'

'Ah,' said Fergus, who was expert in extracting secrets from girls.

'Ah, what?'

'Nothing. I know.'

'No you don't.'

'Yes, I do.'

'Don't.'

'Do.'

'Don't.'

'Nice one, Mark!' shouted the wicketkeeper, and Daisy looked up automatically.

'Mark Blackwell,' said Fergus, 'I might have known. You should watch where you walk.'

'Why?'

'I have noticed,' said Fergus snidely, 'the problems that most of the girls in year five have with tripping over. They're forever falling onto other people's lips.'

Daisy glared at him. 'If you say a single word about this to anyone, I'll get all the photos that show your willy and hand them around all the girls in your year.'

Fair enough, thought Fergus, she's got me there. Mark Blackwell, heh?

'I think Mum likes Mr Blackwell,' he said, stirring.

'Don't be ridiculous.'

'No, she does. She came to see him this morning.'

'Why?'

'I dunno,' said Fergus untruthfully. 'You'll have to ask her.'

He wasn't sure quite what he hoped to achieve – but with

the number of odd little questions Mr Blackwell had been asking about his mum lately, the wistful way he looked at her, it could be interesting, especially if it wound Daisy up a bit. He wondered what Fred would think.

Fred, when Fergus reached the Fir Trees on his bike, seemed oddly reticent at first on the subject of romance. He looked at Fergus rather suspiciously over the top of his *Financial Times*.

'What do you mean, what do I think of romance in later life? Who had you in mind?'

'I mean Mum. I wondered if I should matchmake her with Mr Blackwell, my form teacher. He made eyes at her this morning.'

'Ah, I see.' Fred folded his paper. 'Now why would you want to do that?'

Fergus shrugged. 'I think he likes her, and it wouldn't half wind Daisy up. I mean, I know she's probably a bit old for that sort of thing.'

Fred grinned. 'Winding up women is excellent justification for most things,' he told Fergus, 'but I think setting up your mother with your teacher is probably the exception.'

'Why?' Fergus frowned. 'It would do her good.'

'I don't know that anyone can be the judge of that,' said Fred, adding rather wisely, 'Romance is like a firework. Once you've lit it you have to be jolly careful with it and if it goes the wrong way it can cause a whole lot of trouble.'

Fergus was lost in admiration. 'That's brilliant. Where does that come from?'

'Chap I knew in the sixteenth century,' said Fred airily. 'Lived in Stratford; wrote plays.'

'D'you mean *Shakespeare*?'

Fred looked coy. 'Maybe. Here, come and help me with these sweet peas.'

Fergus followed him across the garden. 'You can't really be seven hundred years old. Mum says the oldest man in

England is a hundred and seven and that when most people reach a hundred they're so stiff they can't get out of their chairs without creaking.'

'Ah well,' said Fred, fiddling with his sweet-pea canes, 'here, tie this round there . . . that'd be the oldest man with a birth certificate. I've got no birth certificate, so how old I am is anyone's guess. Believe me, young man, if you learn one thing from me it should be that you're as old as you feel and there's an exception to every rule.'

'That's two things,' said Fergus smugly.

'Ah,' said Fred. 'So it is – and here's a third. Between you and me and these sweet peas I'm considering a little romance myself.'

Fergus' eyes were round. '*Are* you? Really?'

'Think I'm too old for fun, do you?'

'Of course not.' Fergus was genuinely indignant. 'But you always said women were a blooming nuisance not to be trifled with.'

Fred grinned. 'Well, I suppose I've grown up since I said that.'

'But it was only last week. You can't have changed your mind that quickly. Unless you've fallen in love, of course. Ha ha.'

Fred turned pink.

Fergus stared. 'Fred? You haven't, have you? You *are* in love, aren't you?'

'I jolly well might be,' said Fred, 'and you'll get no more out of me than that till the lady herself has heard about it. Not a word to anyone, either.'

'Course I won't,' said Fergus, affronted. 'Your secrets are my secrets, remember.'

'Good.' They shook hands, and Fred added, 'Just think of it this way: compared to you your mother may seem old, but to me she's a spring chicken. Now then, once we've finished this we have to discuss preparing that mulch for your garden. I need you to count the weeds.'

'Count the weeds? What, every weed?'

'Absolutely,' said Fred. 'I'm a scientist.'

It struck Fergus, not for the first time, that Fred was probably the wisest person he had ever met.

As Fergus was cycling home from the Fir Trees Martha remained wrapped in the amber glow which had enveloped her all day, the kind of amber glow that only she could see. It made her smile. It put a spring in her step. It had made her give Philomena, her assistant, a long lunch break, and offer two women négligés they had clearly fallen in love with and couldn't afford for only a little more than the cost price. And she put the Rachmaninov Second Piano Concerto, used in *Brief Encounter*, which was secretly her all-time favourite film, on the CD player. Every time she heard it she imagined Trevor Howard and Celia Johnson gazing at one another with a whole world in their eyes. Of course that sort of thing was a fantasy, and even then only so exquisite because it was so very brief. Just like all love affairs it had been at its very best in the beginning, and like all love affairs only remained so beautiful because the participants had very sensibly preserved it by never seeing one another again. If she had been Celia Johnson, and she had met Tom Lovejoy on a railway station . . .

'Ahem.'

Martha looked up to see Roland Liversill in her shop, eyeing the displays.

'What can I do for you?'

'Ah, Ms Coleman, how are you,' said Roland, in his best Leslie Phillips voice, emphasising the 'Ms' in what she thought a rather condescending manner. 'I want to buy something intimate for a lady. Something slightly – you know – risqué. I rather thought something red might convey the right sentiment.'

Martha turned the CD down and switched into business mode. 'Of course, Dr Liversill.'

261

'Oh do call me Roland. We have met at dear Alice's. I recall.'

'Of course . . . Roland. But red is a very difficult colour to wear. Unless the lady is blonde I would recommend black or cream . . .'

'Oh, she's very blonde,' said Roland, and Martha gulped, well aware from long-ago dinner parties at Alice's house, when Rob was alive and Alice had thought it the done thing to entertain his partners with supper, that Roland's wife was grey and mousy. Surely no one else would . . .? With Roland? Ugh, no, surely not – what a thought. Alice would be horrified. Still, you don't turn away good business, and men just as unappealing as Roland had bought from her before and would do so again.

'Well, I have those on the red rail by the wall – they're a Swiss manufacturer, beautiful lace – they're forty pounds . . . and the silk ones next to them, they're French, this season's. They're fifty. Then I have some darker red—'

'I'll take the French,' said Roland. 'This size, I think. I can usually judge. My friend deserves the French – gift-wrapped.' He produced his credit card with a flourish.

After he had gone Martha rang the surgery. She had wanted to talk to Alice, she told herself. She was absolutely sure she hadn't hoped that Tom would answer the surgery telephone – so when Alice responded to her casual 'How are you?' with 'In a bit of a dilemma, actually,' she denied her disappointment to her inner self and moved swiftly from unexpectedly encountered lover mode into best friend mode.

'Go on then,' she invited, 'what dilemma?'

Alice pulled a face at the receiver. 'There are several dilemmas, but only one is personal and moral and minor. The rest are all professional, terminal and huge, so it's pointless discussing them.'

'Don't tell me,' said Martha, thinking: you think you've got problems. Her nether regions were still glowing at the

262

memory. It was hours ago yet she just couldn't help recalling . . . 'You're not still worrying about Oliver?'

'No, I'm not that sad,' replied Alice indignantly. 'It's about Mr Blackwell, Fergus' teacher.'

'Oh, the one with the beard.'

'Yes. He's asked me out.'

'So?'

'Well, I can hardly go out with my son's teacher, can I?'

'So don't,' said Martha, to whom choices were very much a black-and-white thing – shades of grey were for the indecisive, which she never had been.

'I feel sorry for him,' Alice was saying. 'He seems lonely.'

'You don't go out with men because they're lonely,' said Martha sharply, suppressing a sudden thought of Tom. God, she must still smell of him. He had soaked into her like the scent of incense.

Alice shrugged. 'You don't go out with men because they're gynaecologists either,' she said drily, 'except that I did.'

'Do you fancy him? The teacher, I mean?'

'Well, I don't really know. I don't see him with the right eyes.'

'Perhaps,' said Martha, 'he's been eyeing you from afar for years.'

Alice played with a paperclip miserably. 'Perhaps he's anyone's for a pot of tea and a Jammie Dodger. He is a history teacher.'

'Just say no, then,' said Martha. 'Where's the problem?'

'None really. I told you it was trivial. I suppose it's more that I want to *want to* say yes. I just want my life to be normal. I don't want to keep on mourning.' I'm not even sure that I am still mourning, she thought. I miss Rob and I want to talk to Rob, but I want to get away from him too. I really do. Her mouth fell open in surprise at the thought.

'What you need to do,' said Martha teasingly, not sensing

the dropped jaw, 'is make a mental list of his good and his bad points.'

'OK. Er . . . right.'

'Have you done it?'

'Sort of.'

'What's top of the good list?'

'Unthreatening,' said Alice, adding after a moment, 'in the sense of not very sexually forward.'

My God, thought Martha, and she thinks that's good? 'And the bad list?'

'Beard,' said Alice without hesitation.

'Then forget him,' said Martha, thinking of Tom and the glowing sexuality which would light rooms and fire turbines, 'unless he shaves. There's no point going out with anyone who doesn't drive you mad with lust.'

Alice stared at the phone. 'Mad with lust? You've never struck me as being mad with lust for any of the men you've been out with.'

Martha stared at the phone. I *am* mad with lust, she thought in alarm. 'I just meant you've got to desire them. Otherwise you might as well join a sewing circle and spend your evenings chatting to old ladies about support tights and the terrible price of tinned salmon.'

Alice smiled. 'Actually, mad with lust wouldn't be at all bad, don't you think? I don't know what it would do to my surgeries, though.' She imagined herself frothing at the mouth as she tried valiantly to fasten Tabitha Tinkler back into her whalebone strapping. 'I think GPs and lust are probably mutually exclusive.'

You're wrong, thought Martha, staring at the phone. God, but you're wrong.

It wasn't till after Alice had gone that she remembered she had intended to mention Roland and the knickers.

It was when Alice was leaving that evening, carrying two strong black bin bags, in which every frog in her possession

264

was to be taken home from the surgery for Herman to inspect, that she ran into Tom again. He was smiling that salesman smile of his at Roland, who looked as though someone had just put a red-hot poker into his bottom. As she approached, Roland turned on his heel and disappeared across the waiting room into the Axminster.

'I was just explaining something to Roland,' said Tom cheerfully, beaming at Alice as she emerged somewhat the worse for wear from seeing the last few emergency extras whilst suppressing recurrent and disturbing thoughts of herself dressed like a cream cake, supporting a pale and weeping Lisa down the aisle of St Winifred's church.

She frowned uncomprehendingly at Tom. 'Sorry?'

'I was just telling Roland that as a landlord myself I have often wished that businesses could be evicted from open-ended leases. The trouble with an open-ended contract is that you really can't get people out when you want to. I think he was rather upset. I hadn't realised till then, you see, that you had an open-ended lease.'

Alice stared. 'What do you mean?'

'Oh, nothing.' Tom was airy. 'But he seemed to think I might mean that the Lammas Practice might not agree to move out of the building. I was telling him that in similar circumstances as a landlord I had to pay a considerable sum to my tenant – to cover all of her removal costs and to persuade her to waive her rights.'

Alice frowned and fiddled with her plait. 'Do you mean that Roland actually can't evict us?'

'Oh, he can get us out in the end – but it isn't easy, not if we don't want to go, and it can be expensive. You either pay your lawyers or your tenants. So I just pointed out gently how very difficult you could make it for him if you wished to do so. Strangely enough, I think he rather hoped I wouldn't mention it to you.'

Alice felt herself starting to smile involuntarily. Suddenly Tom Lovejoy looked like quite a nice bloke. I shouldn't have given him all that stuff about pus to wade through, she thought. And I've fed him to Martha . . . like Albert to the lion. He doesn't stand a chance. 'What did he say?'

'Not very much,' said Tom, 'but he was quite an interesting colour. Anyway, I must be off. Plans to make for tomorrow.'

'Oh?' said Alice, then could have kicked herself. Why did I ask?

'I'm hoping Martha will come to the coast with me for the day.'

'Oh, that's nice,' said Alice, hiding her slight dismay – born of concern that he clearly had a long way to fall when Martha chucked him – with a bonhomie completely out of proportion to his statement, 'have a great time.'

She glanced at her pigeonhole. There was a single package there, beautifully wrapped. Blue tissue paper, blue ribbon – it looked like something from Martha's shop. There was no card, but it was in her pigeonhole and a silver 'A' was inscribed on the package. It had to be for her. How very odd . . .

Alice looked around for Norma, but Norma was talking to a patient on the phone and Lisa had gone early. Well, everyone likes a present . . . She opened the package.

Oh my God! Who on earth would buy me red knickers? They can't be for me. Could they be from Tom? Were they meant for someone else? Oh my, I've unwrapped someone else's knickers. There wasn't a card. What on earth should I –

'Alice, my dear, I see you have found my small gift – just a token of my *great* esteem.'

Roland! Roland has bought me knickers. What on earth was he thinking of?

'I thought it might help us mend a few fences.'

'I . . .' Alice tried to say you couldn't mend a fence with knickers, but nothing came out of her voice box except the kind of noise mice make whilst cats are eating them.

266

'I wonder, whilst I – er – *have* you here . . .'

Not if you were the last man on earth.

'. . . if I could ask you to sign something for me? I felt that as you will be leaving so soon we really should get something *formally* written down – and I wanted to offer particularly generous terms to ease the blow. We do, after all, have a relationship that goes back for many years.'

He put an arm across her shoulders and Alice felt her trapezius muscle tense. If I were an Olympic shot-putter, she thought, you'd be flying over the Eastern Ukraine by now – always assuming you didn't exhale as you passed over Iraq, and thus get mistaken for a biological weapon and shot down.

'Roland,' she said tersely, trying to recover the necessary personal space to retrieve her dignity, 'I couldn't possibly sign anything without speaking to Ian and James.'

Roland sniffed, inadvertently creating a brief but welcome reprieve from garlic and red wine. 'I was merely offering to allow you to walk away from the building without any financial liability for the expensive repairs I shall have to make once you have gone.'

'Repairs?' I might have known it wouldn't take him long to counterattack, Alice thought with sudden clarity. He's not making a pass, he just wants me to think he is so that I'll sign and rush off in embarrassed confusion.

'Where can I start? We will need a complete replumbing, and the marks that you have made on the walls by the attachment of consulting-room desk units and slatted blinds. I can probably stretch to taking responsibility for converting the car park back to the pleasant lawned area it once was, but I'm afraid you must fund the rest. I have been speaking to my solicitor, Rodney Brascombe, and he agrees that this is most generous of me, as the building should really be returned in the state in which it was first loaned. I have to say, actually, he thinks me excessively generous.'

Oh God, thought Alice, and I'll never be able to look at

Rodney Brascombe again without remembering his hairy bottom. I bet he showed it to me on purpose so he could later undermine me in court. 'Roland, you're really not giving us very long –'

'My dear Alice,' the arm tightened again on her shoulder, 'if you were to ask me personally, as a favour,' there was a certain unmistakable emphasis on the word, 'then I might see my way to a little . . . compromising . . . on both our parts?'

Alice held herself rigidly still, wanting to be quite sure of what he was saying. 'Do you mean what I think you mean, Roland?'

'Alice, we understand one another so well. It cannot have been easy for you. I understand the needs of a woman alone and you can rely on me for absolute discretion. I have always admired your strength, and your very womanly presence is –'

Alice drew herself up to her full height, which not only helped her not to vomit but which also put her in a position to spit in Roland's eye, had she been certain that her aim was true and sure and would not result in saliva dribbling ignominiously down her chin.

'Roland,' she said as clearly and nastily as she could manage, 'I think I despise you more than any man I have ever met. I wouldn't sign your papers if you were the last thing between me and the abyss, and the abyss was full of insane and slavering gynaecologists dripping with pus, and if you don't take your hands off me right now I'm going to vomit all over your Oxford brogues.'

As she drove out of the surgery car park Alice could see him obliterating her name on the car-parking space with a tin of black paint. There would be no concessions from Roland now. Realistically, there never would have been. Still, she forcefully told the frog dangling from her rear-view mirror, I wouldn't want to stay in his building a moment longer than I had to anyway. And I must find a way to keep the practice going, if just to spite him.

268

The dangling frog looked balefully back, reminding her that Herman was, still, frogless, and likely to remain so unless she got her act together. Bugger Roland then; she had more important things to think about. Frogs, for one.

She got home to find that she was still clutching the knickers tightly, and slipped them hastily into her handbag as she opened the door. She should have thrown them at him. Still, the fact that she still had them would really annoy him. Nothing made Roland crosser than wasting his money.

The hall looked, she thought as she stepped inside, rather pointlessly white. In the kitchen Anemone was explaining the finer points of feng shui to Herman ('So people actually pay you to tell them that all of their energy will fall down the toilet unless they buy a goldfish, yes?'), whilst Fergus sat at the window with his Young Ornithologist binoculars.

'I hope you're not being lascivious, Fergus,' said Alice, as she put her bags of frogs down.

Anemone looked up from her feng shui wheel. 'If he is, by now Mrs Fingelstein from number twenty will be imprinted on his psyche and he'll spend his adult life helplessly searching for twenty-three-stone Austrian women with more facial hair than Rasputin without ever really understanding why.'

'Anemone, don't say things like that,' said Alice, whilst the thought crossed her mind that Fergus' sexual development and its monitoring was something she had always assumed she could leave to Rob. It had seemed only fair, given that she had had to go over the periods and penises ('Ugh, Mum, you're not serious!') thing twice with the girls. What if Fergus did grow up with some sort of unhealthy complex through being surrounded by women? 'Look, what are you doing, Fergus?'

Fergus looked wounded. 'Counting the weeds. Fred said I should count the weeds so he knew how much compost we needed.'

Alice sighed. 'I don't think Alan Titchmarsh will be

offering you a job quite yet. Put the binoculars away and make me a nice cup of tea. I have something to show Herman.'

It took about an hour to go through all the rest of the frogs. It would have been easier if Herman had expressed some doubt – but even though he seemed unable to describe the missing frog adequately, other than to remark upon its being green and amphibian, he was quite sure that none of those Alice had brought home was the one in question. Wherever the lost frog was, Alice was now sure she didn't have it. There were at least a dozen people who had borrowed frogs since Herman arrived – she would have to work out who they all were and get in touch.

Martha sat on the white bed for what seemed like an age with her hand on the telephone. This was not the bedroom in which she ever slept alone. It was her entertaining room, for the rare occasions when one of Laura's men came back to her house instead of sharing a suitably anonymous room at one of Cambridge's many inns of hospitality. This was her room of passion, her white silk room, the room where she and Tom had lain together in what had felt like biblical splendour. She was not a particularly religious woman, but his murmuring of the Song of Solomon had sent a thrill to her very inner being. 'Show me your face, let me hear your voice; for your voice is sweet and your face is lovely . . .' Her hand stroked the cool sheets tremblingly; her nerves were shot to pieces. She longed desperately to see him again – yet she felt as if she were being drawn into the eye of a storm, a place from which escape was uncertain and fraught with danger.

This was all too unfamiliar. This wasn't her. She was Martha – cool, controlled, the woman that walks alone. She didn't need a man. Didn't need to be rattled. Tom was beautiful, it was true – and they had been fantastic together, but it was over with now. To repeat the experience would be to risk the whole in-love-out-of-love thing that had so destroyed her mother.

But she had never wanted anyone this much. She ached for him. The feeling of him, the scent of him . . . It was purely physical, of course – purely physical, and so no emotional threat to her. It was just a physical lust – and, that being so, it would do no real harm to satiate it. At least, until it wore off. Hadn't that been her plan all along, to get him out of her system? Obviously it would just take more than once. Another night or two and he would seem like any other beautiful young man. That was all.

And then he rang. She knew it was him, even before she went over on her ankle reaching for the phone.

'Martha? Can I see you tonight?'

'Tom – I can't tonight. I have an evening with Alice. She . . . needs me this evening. I –'

'Tomorrow?'

God, she thought, I can't resist. 'Tomorrow's Saturday. The shop –'

'Forget the shop. I'll pick you up at eight thirty. I want to spend the day with you.'

Martha's heart lurched. A day with him. That should be sufficient, of course, to take the lustre off things, she told herself. Any man you spend a whole day with must surely lose his shine. But her excitement as she said, 'I'll be ready,' was not what you would expect when looking forward to the end of an affair. Watch yourself, Martha, she thought, and you'll stay in control. Determinedly she began to strip the bed. It didn't do to keep a man's scent like this. Even if this wasn't her real bedroom. Even if this bedroom was just one more of the many layers with which she kept herself securely cloaked.

Chapter Thirteen

Alice awoke the following day feeling rather bleary. It had been something of a late night with Martha, who had turned up in a strange mood, and spent most of the evening lying across her sofa with a large glass of Chardonnay and a plastic cigarette, asking searching questions about Rob and becoming progressively more dissatisfied with the answers. As the evening went by she had also become steadily less sober, without truly degenerating into being drunk.

'How did you know,' she had asked Alice at one point, lifting the silver-framed photograph of Rob which Alice felt obliged to keep on the dresser for the children's sake – albeit hidden behind a small fern, 'how did you know that he was the one? When did you realise?'

Alice had assumed this was really about Tom, but couldn't help feeling you simply couldn't compare. Only one of them had been an unfaithful bastard. 'I don't really know,' she said absently, 'it just sort of happened. It's a long time ago now.'

It wasn't enough for Martha. 'Come on, Alice, you can't wimp out like that – think about it. When exactly did you two meet? I mean, I know you met at medical school, but did your eyes meet across a crowded room? Did he throw his cloak over a puddle?'

Alice sighed. 'We met on my first day at Addenbrooke's – and yes, our eyes met across a crowded room. It was the post-mortem room, actually. I thought he looked nice, felt quite – well – a little tingle. He said it was love at first sight. Love amidst the body parts.'

'Yeugh. What were the first words he said?'

Alice smiled wryly. 'He said, "It's a liver".'

'What?'

'It was a post-mortem demonstration. They're used for teaching medical students. You all stand around in a ring whilst a demonstrator shows you parts of the deceased and explains what was wrong with them, what killed them. It's part and parcel of all medical schools. Anyway, the demonstrator strode up to Rob and waved this thing at him and said, "What do you think of this?" and Rob was staring at me, and said, "It's a liver," and we all fell about laughing.'

'Why?'

'It was a spleen,' said Alice, adding, when she saw Martha's part-mystified, part-revolted face, 'Medical humour, Martha, and you had to be there. It was, you see, obviously a spleen. He was supposed to say what was wrong with it – you know, infarcted, enlarged, diseased – but he couldn't take his eyes off me . . . Actually it hardly matters what sort of organ it was. The point was, he always said it was love at first sight.'

Martha sniffed. 'It sounds pretty juvenile to me. But you haven't answered me. You know what I meant.'

'I know. Well, I can't really remember the first intimate thing he said. He said it was love at first sight, but to be honest I think it was more that we swam towards one another, then got caught up in the same current of life.'

'How many real lovers had you had before him?'

'None.' Alice put her nose into her wineglass for a moment, drawing strength. 'He was the first, really. Just the odd fumble before that.'

Martha was shocked. 'God, are you serious?'

Alice sniffed. 'You're American. It wasn't so easy here, not twenty years ago. Mind you, Oliver was my second. That is weird.' She started to giggle rather helplessly. 'Rob called it the penis embargo. I'd saved myself, you see. Like left-over beans kept in the fridge.'

'And had he? Saved himself?'

'I thought so,' said Alice shortly. 'Perhaps he regretted it. Perhaps that was his problem.' It had occurred to her that this might be so, but it was hardly an excuse, was it? You sowed your wild oats before you got married, and if you happened to fall in love before you'd had a chance to chuck them about, well, that was just your bad luck, wasn't it?

'My first was before I was fifteen,' said Martha, letting the comment pass. 'In a haystack. I told him he was number three, though.'

'You were probably already rolling in the hay barns when I still thought the whole thing about the penis was some ridiculous story our teacher made up to conceal the ghastly truth,' said Alice, 'so I don't know why you're asking my advice about Tom. I did tell Rob he was the first, but only afterwards.'

'I wasn't asking advice about Tom. I just wondered about you and Rob, that's all. I'd never asked you.' Martha was genuinely surprised Alice should make such a connection.

'Sure,' said Alice drily. 'Have you slept with him?'

Martha took another large gulp of her wine, and drummed up a degree of bravado she wasn't certain she felt. 'I certainly have. It was splendid. Splendid.'

'Martha – you're not going to dump him and break his heart, are you?'

'Oh, I'm sure he hasn't got a heart,' said Martha, trying to suppress the feeling that she was betraying him by her words. How ridiculous – they had only had sex, that was all. Very, very good sex . . . but still just sex. She swallowed more wine. 'Wonderful penis, actually.' She giggled, coy with an overlay of Chardonnay.

'Martha!'

'Sorry darling,' said Martha, 'but I don't expect anything but a fling. I'm an independent woman and I mean to stay that way. That's the difference between you and me.'

'What do you mean?'

'First loves and first lovers. If your first love is your first lover you're in big trouble. Big risk of slipping up the aisle. I, on the other hand, have kept love and lovers very separate. You married Rob almost without thinking about it, and that's why you can't believe it could have gone wrong.'

Alice smiled grimly. 'I suppose you could say that. But then he was the one who changed his mind. I was happy. Some people stay happy for ever. I look after an old lady who fell in love with an Armenian over forty years ago, said goodbye to him for ever and has loved him ever since.'

'What an awful waste.' Martha poured more wine. 'Do you ever wonder about her? Marcie Crombie, I mean?'

'No,' said Alice, too quickly, 'never. I never do.'

'You do. You wouldn't be human.'

'If I'd wanted to ask her anything,' said Alice, 'I'd have gone to the inquest. Rob's inquest.'

Martha frowned. 'Don't you think you're suppressing everything too much, after all this time?'

'This is very soul-searching,' said Alice uncomfortably, peering at Martha closely. 'Are you expecting some sort of enlightenment from me about the nature of life and love? Because you won't get it, you know. I mean, I got it all wrong.'

'No, you didn't,' said Martha. 'It's all a lottery, I know that. I just don't know how people have the courage to make these decisions.'

'They made themselves,' said Alice. 'At twenty-one you assume you'll get married, so if you're with someone for more than two years, you marry them. You haven't had time to realise it's a lottery. You think love is for ever.'

'It seems to have been for ever for your old lady,' said Martha wistfully, 'the one with the Armenian lover.'

'Maybe. Or maybe if she'd stayed with her Armenian he'd have got fat and flatulent and all the romance would

275

have gone before they were thirty, drowned in a vat of cabbage soup.'

'You sound cynical,' said Martha sadly, 'almost as bad as me.'

Alice shrugged. 'Maybe I'd have been safer if I'd been cynical long ago,' she said.

'Safe is boring,' said Martha, surprising herself. 'At least you followed your heart.'

'That's what Herman Banescu said, oddly enough,' said Alice, 'when I asked him if he thought we should move back to Pipe Tree Cottage.'

'You're not going to?'

'I'm not sure.'

'You've got some issues,' said Martha, 'that's your problem. Moving house won't change that. You just need to stop dithering and get on with living your life.'

Alice sighed. 'I wish it were so easy. And by the way, you never warned me about those bloody red knickers Roland bought me.'

'Bloody red knickers? He gave those to you? They were fifty pounds.'

'They weren't!'

'They were too. Why? What have you done with them?'

Alice sighed. 'Well I could hardly keep them. I gave them to Daisy. She likes red.'

Martha sighed. 'God, you're a sad woman, Alice Vane.'

Those words had echoed in Alice's head all night, a night of dreams in which she bought Pipe Tree Cottage and moved into it to find it overrun by frogs – frogs in handcuffs shackled to the bedposts, to the doorknobs, to each other . . .

Her first waking thought was of Herman Banescu, and his lost frog. Her second thought was that Saturday morning meant morning surgery, as it was her turn to cover the weekend, but first she had to call in at the undertaker's office in Fox Colne, to sign a form of authority to cremate a patient of the Ridgeon Road practice who had died the previous day.

Parking near the hearses she rang the bell. Arthur Healey had not been her patient – she was to make the second medical examination that allowed his cremation to proceed. He had been ninety-six, a fragile man with Alzheimer's disease whose death had been a gradual and dignified process but who had had no memory at all of who or what he was by the time he died. Perhaps Rob found the best way to go.

An undertaker's office can be an interesting place, and Wellands of Fox Colne was no exception. Downstairs, all was a mixture of tasteful black and polished mahogany, with elegant baize-green walls. The receptionist who sat behind the shiny desk greeting the recently bereaved with one of a range of natural platitudes (she liked to vary them day by day) was almost as dour a woman as Jean – but she was happy, for she had found her vocation in a place where her grim countenance and extreme gloom were positive attributes.

Upstairs, though, sat Frank Welland, the undertaker, a man whose lugubrious expression and odd genetic problem with skin elasticity gave him the look of a man who had spent too much time doing impressions of a bloodhound. He suffered, Alice knew, from Ehlers-Danlos syndrome, a condition in which the skin really has no spring, and as a result appeared to have aged prematurely.

On his desk in the upstairs office lay a large and glossy catalogue of coffins, a pile of paperwork, and a punchball. Alice knew from previous experience that if you hit the punchball hard enough it said 'Come again then', with a wildly overdone Geordie accent and cackled hysterically.

Frank was on the telephone when she arrived, and handed her the form of authority to cremate with a nod. Beside him his son and sidekick, Jasper, was filling out paperwork. Jasper was one of those unfortunate young men who look as though they have been embalmed already. It was the make-up, of course. Sexual equality may be the modern fanfare, but somehow men still look awfully odd when they wear blusher. Undertakers look particularly odd, as the manner of applying it is learned in a somewhat different school to that of the rest of us.

Frank was grumbling. 'So you're telling me you've still got them? Well, what sort of a hospital are you, for goodness' sake, when you can send a man off to meet his maker with important bits missing? . . . Of course he would have wanted to be buried with them . . . The funeral's tomorrow . . . Registered post would be fine. I wouldn't put "dead man's dentures" on the label if I were you though . . .' He put the telephone down. 'Tragic case, Dr Vane. The late gentleman died unexpectedly in Yorkshire and came home without his teeth.'

'Yorkshire is a long way to go for teeth,' Jasper sighed mournfully, 'but then the late gentleman has rather further to go now. Further that is, even, than Huddersfield, which is where he became disunited from his dentures.'

They sounded, Alice thought, like a pair of gentlemen's outfitters escaped from a seventies farce. She was unsure as to whether she was expected to laugh or weep at the tragedy of it.

'I don't know how you do your job,' she said, in an effort not to ask the inappropriate questions which had come to mind (how far would not be too far for teeth, and would one travel further for, say, a false leg or a prosthetic nose?). 'It must be hard, dealing with grieving relatives and – well – dead people for the whole of your working life.'

'Ah,' said Jasper with a soulful nod, 'you should see us at the Undertakers' Ball, though.' Alice, he thought, actually seemed to understand his lot. A rare thing, that, in a woman. The girls he dated always got so hung up on what he did. 'That's when we really let our hair down. I'll tell you what, Doctor, how would you like to come along as my guest this year?' Suddenly, alarmingly, he was exposing the entirety of his upper gums to her. 'A woman such as yourself should get out more.'

'I, er, it's very kind of you, Jasper.' Alice struggled desperately for the right thing to say. 'But I'm . . . not ready for involvement at the moment.'

Jasper's face fell slightly, then brightened again. 'Oh – well, if things change before the end of the month, do let me know.' He looked suddenly sorrowful. 'I don't suppose I'll find another partner.'

So Alice said a silent goodbye to Mr Healey, confirming for the sake of law that his death did not arouse her suspicions in any way. Jasper insisted, as always, on turning the deceased over to confirm the absence of knives in the back, and she tried not to listen to his attempts at witty conversation, which hinged, sadly, on the transience of life, the cost of coffins, and the tragedy of Arsenal's defeat at Scunthorpe.

It was a relief to Alice to get back out into the fresh air and drive back to Cambridge. I seem to spend an awful lot of my time driving to Fox Colne, she thought, glancing at Pipe Tree Cottage as she passed it. And it was then that she remembered where she had seen a ceramic frog on the day that Herman Banescu had turned up at the surgery. She knew exactly which frog it was now, and precisely who had it . . .

Phoebe Hamilton had chosen a frog to take with her to Addenbrooke's, and it had been a frog Alice had not recognised . . . a china frog with staring eyes that hadn't had a name. That was it! Phoebe Hamilton had Herman Banescu's frog! She would go up to Addenbrooke's after surgery to retrieve it.

She was so relieved to have made the deduction that she didn't even notice Tom Lovejoy driving into the village as she drove out.

*

279

As Alice postponed her excitement and headed for the surgery, Martha was setting out with Tom. It wasn't shaping up to be the sort of date she had expected. She had assumed that he planned to turn up and take her to bed for twelve hours, satiating her and his appetites so conclusively that no further contact would be necessary for a day or two. She had made up the white bedroom with fresh silk sheets and put champagne to chill in the fridge – but no. He had breezed in, wearing jeans and a leather jacket, looking as though he had stepped out of a Diet Coke ad leaving a trail of panting women just out of view – and now he had announced that they were off on a day trip to Aldeburgh. Completely taken aback, she had agreed, rushing breathlessly upstairs to change into a silk dress and light coat. Well, he'd said Aldeburgh after all – she might be American but she was also English enough to know that there are some towns you just don't ever visit in jeans.

Now, as Tom drove along the final stretch of road into Aldeburgh, his firm, slightly bronzed hands resting gently on the wheel in a way that called to mind the care with which way he had caressed her thigh only a night ago, Martha faced her deep-seated unease that today would ruin everything she had built with such care, her protective shell, her invulnerable safety, her perfect, untouchable life. He looked even better in sunglasses. The urge to press her lips against that evenly shaven cheek, to inhale the scent of his beautiful skin and – well, and just *purr* – it was almost too great to resist.

But not quite too great. This had all the makings of a great sexual relationship that could last a few days – why ruin it by trying to be affectionate? Almost as bad as trying to be friends. He would be gone from Cambridge soon enough. She was safe. True, he had slept in her bed, which didn't happen often – but then, it hadn't been her personal bed. It had been the show bed, the white and sensuous bed, the bed in which she entertained, if she ever felt sure enough to do so. The bed in which she never slept alone.

Tom, of course, was making it easy by being charming. He could certainly talk, and the number of things they seemed to have in common made her feel quite relaxed. Now, as the radio played Rachmaninov's Second Piano Concerto she closed her eyes and smiled without unease. If today was going to be a bit of a fantasy then she might as well enjoy it. Alice was right, once Tom started leaving the lavatory seat up and flatulating (Martha hated the word 'fart', which made her think of pigs) in the bedroom, that would be it. It was perfectly safe to enjoy this whilst it lasted. All that rubbish schoolgirls believe about people being made for each other, people knowing each other's thoughts and feelings – it was complete nonsense and should be left in *Brief Encounter* where it belonged.

'Wonderful film, wasn't it?'

'What?' Martha was startled, oddly convinced he had read her thoughts.

'*Brief Encounter*. I always thought it captured the most perfect moment in a love affair – yet it didn't really, did it?'

'How do you mean?'

'Well,' Tom glanced sideways at her, his beautiful mouth curved in a wry smile, his eyes invisible behind the mirror lenses, 'if you watch *Brief Encounter* you could believe that the greatest passion is always at the beginning.'

Martha frowned. 'Don't you think it is?'

'It is in the film,' said Tom, 'because you don't ever get to see how it could have been. That day, it was the best, the most intense it ever could have been – but it was only half the story. I mean that's not how love is at all. My parents had a wonderful marriage, and they always said it got better day by day. You never saw a couple adore each other more.'

Martha bit her lip, wishing she could see his expression. 'My parents were divorced when I was ten.'

'I'm sorry.'

'Don't be.' She felt he was being trite.

'Martha, I'm not being trite. I mean, it's hard to imagine you can ever find the same as my parents had. That sort of thing is a rarity. I'm fortunate to have seen it.'

Martha wondered what his parents had been like. 'Are they still alive?'

He smiled again, fondly, and Martha felt herself tingle. 'No. They were quite old when they had me. I've a sister, though, Mariel – named after the actress.'

'Oh? Who were you named after?'

He grinned. 'Tom Jones. And before you ask, my mother did not throw her knickers at him. She wore half-moon spectacles and liked to crochet.'

Martha laughed, in spite of not being at all sure that she wanted the intimacy of knowing about his family. 'Was she a fan?'

'The first LP we ever owned was of his greatest hits. The next few were all the rest of his hits, together with several of him singing other people's hits. She really wanted me to be a singer.'

'What did your father do?'

'He was a vicar,' said Tom, 'amongst other things. What about yours?'

Martha didn't really want to say. 'Oh, you know. My father was in the air force – got stationed here with his squadron. My mother was English, so I was brought up over here till they split up. Then I stayed with her, spent my summers in Pennsylvania.' Her face was closed: don't ask any more about my mother. Don't spoil it.

He didn't. 'That must have been quite an upheaval, at ten.'

'Horrible,' said Martha, turning her head to look towards the coastal marshes. 'Can you sing?'

'A little – I'm baritone, but medicine sucked me in, I'm afraid.'

'Sing something,' said Martha on impulse, an impulse which she regretted immediately. Please don't make

282

yourself ridiculous, she thought, and please don't sing 'The Most Beautiful Girl in the World' unless you want me to vomit.

But Tom shook his head. 'And ruin Rachmaninov? I couldn't do it. I promise I'll sing to you one day.'

Martha felt a strange little fizz in the pit of her stomach. *One day . . . I promise . . .* She'd liked hearing those words, there was no getting away from it. Hence the fizz.

No. The fizz was nerves. I don't like what I'm getting into here. Assumptions, that's what. Men always do this. Make assumptions.

'Where shall we park?' She changed the subject abruptly, practical, thinking, there's never a parking space in Aldeburgh. Trying to pop into a parking space in Aldeburgh is like trying to cruise steadily around the M25 at sixty miles an hour. That should spoil the day – twenty minutes of creeping round the high street waiting for someone to leave a parking space, then watching whilst some Hitler-inspired old biddy drives her tank into it as if no one else counts and acts as if she's just conquered Poland.

But a space was waiting in Aldeburgh high street for Tom to swing perfectly into, as though he was James Bond, who never has to worry about parking in any of his films.

It's so easy with him, thought Martha. He makes it so easy to go with the flow.

When Alice reached the surgery she found a letter from an extremely eminent professor in London waiting on her desk. Frances had been accepted into a new trial of treatment for stage four melanoma, but had rung to turn down the place. It was experimental treatment and very new, said the letter, but 'your patient has disease so advanced that one can perhaps grasp her perspective'.

Can you, thought Alice, can you ever truly grasp another person's perspective? Perhaps a professor who spends his life trying to offer a crumb of hope to the desperate gets nearer than most. Life just isn't fair. Still, Frances should be on her way to the Caribbean now. She's made a decision when the chips are down. That's what I need to be doing – making a few decisions.

Morning surgery consisted of an unnecessary number of the worried well. It is widely believed in general practice that one-quarter of the people account for three-quarters of the consultations, but Alice thought this an optimistic view. She saw one person with tonsillitis and five more who thought they might get tonsillitis before the week was out, were she not to prescribe antibiotics. Three of them, moreover, declared themselves to be unresponsive to all but the most expensive varieties of antibiotic and one of them wanted to be signed off work for a fortnight on the basis that a sore throat upset his concentration. Last of all came someone she had not expected to see again so soon.

'Hello, Heather. What can I do for you?'

Heather Bunberry pushed her hair back from her face, revealing her habitually anxious expression, and stuttered slightly. 'I . . . er . . . I'm . . . just ab-bout out of contraceptives.'

'Are you sure?' Alice frowned, glancing at the computer screen. 'You had six packets only three months ago. Of course I can prescribe some more – I don't want you to run out – but could you have left them somewhere?'

'I . . . er, oh, p-probably. They might be in the b-back of the b-bathroom cabinet. I . . . could you check my b-blood pressure anyway?'

'Of course.'

Thoughtfully pumping up the sphygmomanometer cuff, Alice tried a little exploration of the hidden agenda. Might as well use all that training she'd had in unearthing it. 'Heather, is there something else you want to ask me?'

'I – no. No, that is, yes. Yes. I just – I need to . . . there's something I need to . . . I don't know where to start . . .' She glanced rather wildly around the room. On the window

284

ledge the framed photograph of Robert Vane and his three children glanced calmly back.

Alice saw it catch Heather's eye. It was Alice's favourite photo of Rob, taken in Southwold, just before they got thrown out of a tea shop because the four-year-old Fergus was too jolly and made crumbs on the carpet. Eight years ago. When they were happy and Rob had never heard of Marcie Crombie . . .

'Take your time, Heather. It's fine.'

But Heather's gaze had frozen, the tear running down stopped and faded, as if called back to base. Alice reached for her box of tissues in the hope of provoking another and getting at the true reason for Heather's being there. As a woman GP she got through at least two boxes of two-ply a week. Male GPs seem not to need as many tissues. On the other hand, perhaps because they don't have them on the desk the patients are less inclined to break down and require them. Perhaps she should try a no-tissue experiment – or do as Roland did and use that nasty waxed lavatory paper chosen by those who feel no responsibility for the state of their guests' cheeks (either cheeks).

She felt this could be her chance with Heather. She took a deep breath. 'Heather, you've obviously got something on your –'

The telephone rang, breaking the connection. 'Hello?'

'Hello, Dr Vane – it's Alana Hamilton.'

'Oh, er, can you hang on a moment, Alana?'

But Heather had recovered her composure and the moment was lost.

'It's OK, Dr Vane, really. I think I know where my pills are, now that you mention it. I must rush – I've got a hairdressing appointment.'

That could be true, thought Alice, bearing in mind the awfulness of that wig.

Even before Alice could mention the frog, Alana had started to speak, and it took Alice a moment to switch to her wavelength, get her brain into the right gear. Brains seem to function less well on Saturdays – or so Fergus always insisted. It was his reasoning behind abandoning all homework at seven o'clock on a Friday night when, he said, the mind-numbing effects of Saturday were already becoming imminent.

'Dr Vane? I'm calling from the hospital. I just wanted to tell you that Duncan and I are so pleased that you're buying the cottage back. I think you're so brave. And thank you so much for all you've done for Phoebe. She should be home next week. Oh, my goodness, the money seems to have ru—' The wittering was cut off, as if British Telecom had simply had enough. Perhaps there is an exchange somewhere with a row of terse-faced operators whose job is purely to cut off wittering. Now that would be some service, thought Alice – a million times better than flipping call waiting and last number recall.

She stared at the phone. Those children have been talking. I have not decided to move back to Fox Colne. I haven't decided not to either. I simply haven't decided.

The feeling that she was being swept away on a tide of what others thought best was at the same time overwhelmingly annoying and faintly delicious. Oh, just to sit back and let it all ride over. Rather like with Oliver, now she thought of it – although much less sticky . . .

There were no more patients to see for now, so she left Jean manning reception and went home, guns blazing. Should she adopt the calm but dry approach – 'Ah – Fergus, Daisy, Anemone, I gather I'm buying a house' – or the sarcastic – 'Thanks so much all of you'? Or maybe the harassed – 'What on earth were you thinking of?' Or how about Japanese drama – 'Oh my God, this is the final straw . . .'

'It was Fergus,' said Anemone, before she could speak. 'She – Mrs Hamilton – rang here looking for you and he told her we'd been thinking about it. About buying it. That was all. I promise. I heard him say it. She just jumped to conclusions.'

286

'And where is Fergus now? Putting Herne Road on the market, perhaps? Or making an offer on a larger property for the Hamiltons to buy when they're back from Dubai? Just wait till I get my hands on him.'

'He went to the Fir Trees,' said Anemone. 'Fred Ramsden rang about something and he went tearing off over there.'

'Tearing off? Are we talking about the same Fergus? I ask because on most Saturday mornings the Fergus that popped so delightfully out of my womb a dozen years ago has all the oomph of a sloth with an underactive thyroid.'

'I do wish you wouldn't make medical jokes,' said Anemone, 'they're lost on me. Anyway, it was some plot to do with gardening, I expect. And if you're going to beat him up, make sure he isn't wearing my Walkman before you start, won't you?'

Alice sighed. 'Is Herman up?'

'Fergus wanted to get him up but I wouldn't let him. He only just woke – he's in the shower. He won't be long.'

'How do you know?'

'There's no hot water left.'

At least, thought Alice, making coffee, we wouldn't have to do much to Pipe Tree Cottage as it's been repainted already. Although I'd never live with that duck-egg blue. Even worse than all this white (do I really think that?). And at least Alana's call confirmed that Phoebe was still in Addenbrooke's – and if Phoebe was there, then so was Mr Jeremy Fisher.

Should she tell Herman, shout the good news at him through the shower door?

No, best not to count your frogs till you catch them.

And then the telephone went before she could drink the coffee, and just as Herman appeared for his breakfast.

'Mum,' it was Fergus on the phone, sounding panicky, 'I need you to come, quick.'

'Fergus. What's wrong? Where are you?'

'I'm at the Fir Trees. I think you'd better come straight

here. And bring Herman, Mum – we need him.'

Alice hauled Herman out of the house, still clutching the Ricicles he had not yet eaten (he was hoping to sample the entire breakfast cereal range prior to returning to Yerevan). Before he had chance to argue she was in the car and on her way, alarmed by the tone of Fergus' voice.

'What's wrong?' asked Herman, but she had no idea.

'Something with Fergus,' she told him, 'and by the way, I think I've worked out where your frog is, but we'll have to do that second now.'

They were in the middle of the tourist traffic next to Queens' College when the second call came through to her mobile.

'Is that Dr Alice Vane?'

'It is, yes.'

'Cambridgeshire CID here,' said the voice rather importantly.

'Oh, hello,' said Alice, for lack of anything better to say, gripping the phone between her ear and her shoulder as she negotiated Silver Street where it crossed the river next to Queens' College, a famous spot at which, annually, students dress themselves up as aeroplanes and leap into the water. It was, as ever, awash with tourists gazing at the Mathematical Bridge and trying to remember who on earth Erasmus was, and, indeed, what on earth he had been doing at Queens' College in the first place – and fifteen assorted coaches all simultaneously attempting to park in one small parking space. You'd think the police would know better than to phone her on the mobile – it would be their fault if she knocked a dozen cyclists into the river.

'We need your assistance at the Fir Trees,' the important voice was saying, 'ma'am.'

'I'm just on my way there,' said Alice. 'What's wrong? My son, Fergus, is –'

But the voice belonged to Bernard Broad, holder of the Cambridge Policemen's Mess annual award for the

288

Absolutely Most Officious Copper Ever, and Alice was not likely to get much out of him.

'I'm not at liberty to say, ma'am,' said Bernard, 'over the airways.'

'Why on earth not?' Alice honked her horn and gesticulated at a particularly insensate Japanese woman who seemed to be trying to photograph traffic from underneath. The woman beamed and waved.

'Not a secure line, ma'am,' said Bernard. 'You never know who might be listening.'

'Well, I was on my way anyway,' said Alice. 'Five minutes.'

'Ah, thank you very much, ma'am. Good day,' said Bernard, and Alice swung onto Queens' Road and hurtled towards the Fir Trees. Herman patted her arm.

'I'm sure all will be well,' he told her reassuringly. 'Where are we going?'

'To see Tabitha,' said Alice crossly. 'I've a feeling this is going to turn out to be because of you.'

'But I cannot see her until I have found the frog. It would be too shameful.'

'You'll jolly well see her right now,' said Alice darkly. 'I can't be doing with this sort of drama in my life. I want a quiet life. I want a nice surgery with lavatories that no one fights over and partners who stay in the same country as me. I want to work with nice doctors who don't make me worry they're losing it, and who don't want to have affairs with my friends, and I want . . .'

'What do you want?'

Alice stared at the road ahead. The lights changed and she let the clutch up very carefully, as the clutches on Morris Minors can be dangerous when roused. 'I want my husband back.' A tear rolled down her cheek.

Herman gazed at her sorrowfully. 'You don't ask for much, you English women. Your Miss Tinkler was another. Thought my Uncle Tamas could forget her. He, with the soul of an Armenian pheasant. Ha!'

Alice cocked an eyebrow. 'Soul of a peasant, you mean, I think. Didn't he forget her, then?'

Herman shrugged. 'Of course not. How could he, a man like him?'

'She thinks he did,' said Alice, 'she said he went and married a – Oh dear, I haven't told Jean where I am!' She dialled the surgery where Jean was rostered for this week's Saturday reception duty. 'Jean? Could you call James and ask him to cover me if there are any more calls? I'm tied up.'

'I dinna know,' said Jean dubiously. 'Dr Ferguson is here but he's ootside digging lupins from the flowerbed. He says Dr Liversill will no get his lupins. Ye ken hoo he is aboot them. And Dr Liversill is there guarding his peonies frae Dr Ferguson. They're squared up like Japanese wrestlers. I'd no like tae interrupt them but I suppose I'll have tae in an emergency.'

Alice sighed, her mood not improved by the mental image of Roland Liversill clad in a Japanese nappy and little else. 'You could try Dr Lovejoy.' Even as she said it she remembered he was going to the coast with Martha. She seemed to keep needing Tom. Was it foolishly risky to depend on him, when he was clearly in pursuit of Martha and would soon, therefore, be one of her cast-offs, flung aside like a pair of Calvin Klein underpants mistakenly bought a size too small?

'Nae, Dr Vane, he called in earlier tae get his mail but he's gone oot for the day. Dr Ferguson will come if he's needed.'

How can one woman, thought Alice absently, sound so like a Kenneth McKellar record whenever she speaks?

As she turned into West Road a policeman waved her down. 'I'm afraid the road is closed ahead, ma'am. We have an incident.'

'I'm Dr Vane,' said Alice. 'You're expecting me. And this is Mr Banescu. You're expecting him too. What sort of an incident?'

'PC Bernard Broad at your service, and it's an armed

incident,' said the policeman, in his best Major Disaster voice. It was a voice most policemen rarely get to employ, although he had discovered that his wife was particularly susceptible to it late at night in a dimly lit room . . . so it was well-practised. 'Please go through, pull up just over there and wait outside the gate. The inspector is on his way.'

As Alice parked she spotted Fergus squatting behind a tree, and hurried over to him. 'Fergus!' she cried in relief. 'What on earth is wrong?'

'It's Tabitha, Mum,' said Fergus, 'sitting in her bedroom window with a gun.'

'What?'

'She is – that policeman was going past on his bike when I got here, and he heard her and called for reinforcements. But he's right – I heard it too. Shooting. It sounded just like a pop gun – they always say real shooting sounds just like a pop gun.'

Alice shook her head. 'Why on earth would Tabitha want to shoot anything?'

'She's had an argument with Fred,' said Fergus. 'He says she's just being bloody unreasonable, but . . .'

As Alice stared at his excited face in alarm, three police cars pulled up and disgorged a group of eager policemen wearing what looked like corsets. They milled around briefly, then disappeared into the garden of the Fir Trees. Alice felt her heart sink.

'This is crazy,' she said to Fergus. 'What are they thinking of? Tabitha couldn't possibly have a gun. She's never been further than –'

Oh my goodness, she thought. Tabitha was once a spy in Armenia. What if she does have a gun? Lord.

'Dr Vane? Thank you for coming.' It was the charmless Inspector Hammond again, veteran of the branch surgery break-in. 'I think you know the lady.'

'I do – but whatever are you doing?'

'Ma'am, a gun has been fired and we have a procedure for

armed incidents. I have to consider public safety.' He started to fiddle with his loudspeaker.

'Let me go and talk to her,' said Alice. 'You must have wanted me here for something, and I'm sure there's a rational explanation for all this.'

'I'm sorry, Doctor, we must follow procedure,' said the inspector. 'I hoped you'd be able to tell me about her state of mind and tell me who else is in the building.'

'There's nothing wrong with her state of mind,' said Alice, praying it were true, 'she's a harmless charming woman, and this building is home to forty elderly residents who are probably all in there right now wondering what on earth is wrong. Look, why don't you just ask Miss Tinkler what's going on?'

'Of course, ma'am, I'm not a fool,' said the inspector indignantly, and Alice realised she had hurt his feelings. He was the one who'd asked her out too. Well, blow *his* feelings, what about Tabitha's?

'Miss Tinkler,' Inspector Hammond boomed down the speaker, 'no one wants to upset you. Put down the gun, then we can have a nice cup of tea and talk about what's worrying you.'

There was a long, astonished silence, then Tabitha's voice came back clearly: 'Don't you blooming well patronise me – I'm not some daft old bird in disposable knickers with nothing but knitting between her ears!'

Oh dear, thought Alice, this isn't going well. There's no one more stubborn than an old lady who decides to be stubborn.

'Look, Inspector Hammond,' she said, 'I'm sure I can sort this out. Let me go in and talk to her. I do know her very well, and I think I know what all this is about. This scenario is very threatening and, in any case, Tabitha won't want her private problems aired over a loudspeaker.'

The inspector looked uneasy. He'd spent years dreaming of handling an armed incident and becoming a hero, but now it had happened he really wasn't enjoying it. If it went badly his career would be ruined, and it wouldn't do to get the doctor shot. It would be an awful shame too, given that he did so admire this particular doctor . . .

Most of his mind said no, you didn't send the doctor in to talk to the armed nutter, there were rules. But a tiny corner of his mind said, I bet she's right. And if she's right and I send the boys in I'll look a fool.

What the hell, someone clearly had to go in and talk to the old woman. You couldn't just shoot her, the Police Complaints Authority would have a field day.

'You can't go in alone,' he said, 'I'll have to send an officer in with you.'

Bernard Broad had been listening to the exchange rather resentfully. Whose crisis was this, anyway? He was here first. He'd called for backup and before he knew it all the armed lot had arrived from out of county and it was out of his hands. It would be the SAS in a minute, he knew the drill. So now he jumped forward, in his mind already seeing himself saving the day whilst a dozen SAS men filibustered amongst themselves in the road, trying to black their faces and put tree branches on their heads without anyone noticing. 'Sir, I would like to volunteer.'

Inspector Hammond sighed. 'Certainly not. I shall accompany the doctor myself. Bernard, I'm leaving you in charge. This way, Doctor.'

They went in through the front door, and inside the Fir Trees it was very quiet. Inspector Hammond stopped in the middle of the hall.

'What are you two doing?'

Alice realised that Herman and Fergus had followed her.

'We're coming,' said Fergus defiantly.

'Now look, young man,' said the inspector, realising this was the son of the woman he admired and could not therefore be cuffed round the ear even if policemen were allowed to do that sort of thing these days, 'this is a serious situation.'

Fergus folded his arms. 'I know Tabitha and Fred better than anyone,' he said firmly. Inspector Hammond looked at Alice.

'He's right,' she said. The inspector sighed and nodded. Either this was all about to be such a disaster that a few more people shot wouldn't make any difference to his career, or this was all a fuss about nothing. He just wanted it sorted out before the SAS came throbbing in by helicopter and made him look a fool by taking it out of his hands.

As Alice led the way along the main corridor and up the stairs Fred appeared from the direction of the residents' lounge.

'Ah,' he said, without surprise, 'good. She won't talk to me, you know.'

'She's up here.' Alice reached Tabitha's door, and knocked. 'Tabitha? It's Dr Vane. You must put the gun down, it's causing a lot of fuss.'

There was a brief silence, then Tabitha's voice came in sulky tones, 'They've been outside my window all bloody morning.'

'What have?'

'It's Fred's peacocks,' said Fergus at her shoulder. 'They keep flying onto the roof right by her window. She told me Fred would get no privileges again till he got rid of them.' He grinned.

'Fergus! You mustn't say things like that about Tabitha.'

'Why not? D'you think she can't have hanky-panky just because she's old?'

'No, of course not.' But that's what I did assume, thought Alice.

Tabitha opened her door. 'Is that really you, Alice dear?'

'Tabitha, you've caused an awful lot of trouble,' Alice sighed.

Tabitha frowned. 'It's all jolly stupid, if you ask me – all this fuss over scaring a few stupid birds. What is that policeman doing in here?'

'It's the gun,' said Alice rather desperately, wondering what questions the responsible doctor ought to ask during an armed siege. 'He's worried about the gun. Tabitha, is it real?'

'Don't be ridiculous.' Tabitha waved it disdainfully. 'This is my nephew's cap pistol, but it doesn't half scare the devil out of those blooming peacocks, stupid trumpeting creatures.'

Inspector Hammond felt weak with relief (apart from that mild regret which came from the knowledge that he was now unlikely to become a hero in Alice's eyes on this occasion).

'Madam, I don't think armed threat is the way to deal with your grievance,' he began pompously, but Tabitha dismissed him with a glare.

'Don't be so stupid, young man. If you can't tell the difference between a cap pistol and a deadly weapon then you should be on traffic duty. It's time someone sorted out this silly old man's bloody birds.' She nodded at Fred.

Fred glared at her. 'You know my delphiniums only grow because of those birds.'

Tabitha sniffed. 'Sod your delphiniums.'

Fred continued to glare. 'You could have *asked* me.'

'I've complained enough about them.'

'Yes, but you never *asked* me to get rid of them,' said Fred stubbornly.

'Are you saying you'd have got rid of them if I'd asked you to?'

'Maybe. Yes. You know I'd do anything if you *asked* me. Why didn't you?'

Tabitha blushed but looked sulky. 'I was cross.'

Fred folded his arms. 'So you caused all this trouble because you felt *cross*? Don't you think that's a bit excessive?'

Tabitha was unrepentant. 'No, I don't, I was angry. You get angry when you lose someone, even at my age. I certainly didn't think the Bow Street Runners out there would react the way they have, but I just wanted everyone to see how . . . how bloody furious I was. And I don't regret it for a minute, Fred Ramsden, so don't get all pompous with me just because you've lost your frontal lobes and think you're seven hundred years old!'

But Fred was suddenly sombre. 'When you lose someone? This isn't about peacocks at all, is it?'

Tabitha avoided his eyes. 'I don't know what you mean. If those birds didn't make so much bloody mess I'd be able to get some – Well, all right, it's not really about peacocks. They were just the final straw, hooting and honking on my window ledge when I was feeling so bloody sad. I just couldn't stand it a moment longer. No one would tell me where he was . . . and I just got . . . got cross.' Her face crumpled like wet tissue paper as tears began to course down it. 'I'm sorry – I'm being a silly old woman.' And then, as Alice hurried up to her side, Tabitha noticed Herman and alertness sharpened her face. 'Are you Herman Banescu? *Are* you?' And, as he nodded: 'Well, it's about time.'

Once the police had been stood down – a complicated process that seemed to necessitate a large number of telephone calls to people standing not two hundred yards away, and a great deal of heroic language about successful siege outcomes being used to impress people who had not had the benefit of a view of the proceedings – Alice found herself alone with Fred, Fergus, Herman and Tabitha. Outside a peacock passed mournful comment on its recent apparent brush with death, but Tabitha did not react. As she had said, Fred's peacocks were not really the problem.

Instead she turned her light blue eyes on Herman and held his hand in an iron grip. 'I am an old woman, Mr Banescu, and I've been rather a cross one recently. I have waited a long time to hear from Tamas, knowing that the only news I could expect to receive would be bad. The least I expect now is to hear what he had to say to me.'

Herman Banescu sighed. 'You're right. I am so sorry. I have been too ashamed to come and speak to you. I brought his ring for you, you see. I had it hidden safely in a money box. He was insistent that I should bring it to you, hand it to you in person. But you see I . . . I have lost the frog.'

'Sounds to me like you've lost the plot,' said Tabitha witheringly. 'What the devil is he talking about, Alice dear?'

'The money box,' said Alice, 'was a china frog. Herman brought the ring through customs hidden in a china frog, and he gave it to me for safe-keeping when he was ill and I . . . I temporarily mislaid it. This is all my fault.'

Tabitha sighed. 'Nonsense, dear. But Mr Banescu, nothing could be more important than seeing you.' She gazed piercingly at Herman. 'I thought you might look more like your father.'

'I do look just like my father,' said Herman, mystified. 'How do you know what my father looked like?'

Tabitha frowned, not comprehending. 'Because Tamas was your father.'

'Uncle Tamas had no children,' said Herman. 'He never married. He lived with my family in Yerevan. My father was his brother.'

A stillness came over Tabitha. She looked at Herman, then at Alice, then at Fergus, then back at Herman again. Herman and Fergus just looked puzzled, but Alice looked as if something huge was just starting to dawn on her. Then when Tabitha spoke her voice sounded tight and careful. 'He never married? He never blooming married?'

Herman shook his head, still not understanding, as Alice felt tears start to her eyes at the tension of it. Fergus shuffled his feet awkwardly, but Tabitha's intense gaze did not waver from Herman for a second. Alice wasn't sure if she was going to laugh or cry. 'No fat Russian woman with bosoms like watermelons?' For a moment Alice thought the tears were coming again, but then Tabitha let her breath out slowly, sat back in her chair and smiled. 'Well,' she said, 'the silly old fool. Never married. I suppose that makes us a pair of silly old fools. Wouldn't you say so, Mr Banescu?'

Herman frowned. 'I don't understand.'

'He told me he had married,' said Tabitha, suddenly, animatedly angry. 'Forget me, he said, the silly old codger. As if I could, as if I ever would want to. But I believed him, believed him about his fat wife and his potato field. I swallowed the whole thing, and I told him exactly the same load of rubbish myself. Forget one another. Ha! It's not so easy to forget when you have found the love of your life . . .' Her voice drifted into silence and she stared into the past. Fred put a hand on her other arm, and she did not shake him off.

Herman cleared his throat. 'You were the love of his life. I am so sorry I have lost the ring. It was his ring – a very precious and special ring. His mother gave it to him, and I don't know where she got it. He always kept it for you. He always said it should have been yours.'

Tabitha shook her head. 'How could it matter now? Besides, Mr Herman Banescu, I think the message he had to send to me was you, not a ring. What a pair of silly old fools. Never to marry. Never to fall in love again. What a stupid waste . . .' Her voice trailed away and she stared for a moment at Herman, then at Alice. 'I told you,' she said, 'moonshine in the mustard pot.'

Fred leaned towards her and took her hand, and then slowly and carefully sank on to one knee. It took a moment, as he picked the bad knee first and had to swap, but he made it eventually.

'I know this might seem an odd moment to ask,' he said, 'but if a ring is really all that important to you . . .'

Alice grabbed Herman and Fergus by an arm each and pulled them from the room.

'I think,' she said to them softly, 'that you and I need to leave these two to talk a little whilst we go and find that frog.'

Chapter Fourteen

When Alice and Fergus got to ward C3 at Addenbrooke's, leaving Herman in the concourse drinking cappuccino ('A hospital that sells Danish pastries in the foyer? This is proof of what was wrong with communism') she found Phoebe Hamilton in the middle of a major grump.

'Hello, Phoebe. How are you?'

Phoebe looked mutinous. 'Mum says I've got to give the watch back.'

Alice raised a brow at Alana, who was looking flustered and hot. She also now had Zachary with her, to Phoebe's disgust.

'Phoebe borrowed a watch off the boy who was in the bed opposite,' Alana explained, embarrassed, 'and now she wants to keep it.'

Fergus stuck his tongue out at Phoebe and Phoebe pulled a face back.

Alice ignored him. 'Phoebe, speaking of borrowing,' she said, 'I wonder if I could borrow Mr Jeremy Fisher for a minute? I need him for something . . .'

Phoebe's face crumpled and she began to cry. 'Oh dear,' Alana flapped around her anxiously, 'oh, Phoebe, don't cry – you'll pull on your stitches.'

'But you'll be cross with me,' wailed Phoebe in tones of clear manipulation. Over Alana's shoulder tear-filled blue eyes stared accusingly at Fergus, who shrugged and wandered off to play on a ward computer game with a boy with both legs in plaster.

'I won't be cross, darling, I promise.' Alana looked to Alice for support.

'The doctor will be cross then.'

Alice got a sinking feeling in the pit of her stomach, as if ten large frogs had just plopped in there simultaneously, then vanished.

'No, she won't, will you Dr Vane? Doctors are never cross, Phoebe.'

Don't you bet on it, thought Alice, steeling herself to smile. 'Have you still got Mr Jeremy, Phoebe?'

'I gave him to Finn,' said Phoebe, between crocodile tears, 'and he was going to be my boyfriend. But then stupid Jennifer that used to be his girlfriend came to see him and he wouldn't talk to me any more, so I said I'd keep his stupid watch and then he said in that case he'd take Mr Jeremy home and bite his silly head off.'

'Phoebe!' Alana was plainly shocked. 'What a wicked boy! Why didn't you tell Mummy?'

Phoebe sniffed. 'I told him he could stick Mr Jeremy right up his stupid arse,' she said haughtily, 'and then he could piss off.'

Alana gasped as though she might have the vapours (she was the kind of woman who might well have the vapours) and squeaked as if Phoebe's head had just revolved three hundred and sixty degrees followed by her spitting gobs of mucus at the wall. 'Phoebe, whoever taught you to say those terrible things?'

Alice was impressed. It didn't sound as though Phoebe needed much defending.

'The doctor,' said Phoebe proudly, 'the nice mental doctor who came to see Finn before he went home.'

'Oh my God!' Alana had to sit down. 'They say all psychiatrists are mad. I thought she'd be safe on a children's ward. I knew we should have put her in the private hospital. Dr Vane, you said she would be better off here but I don't think . . . Oh, Phoebe, where did you learn to say "arse"? Your father would never forgive me if he heard you say "arse".'

'Alana, calm down. She's just repeating words that she knows will wind you up – aren't you, Phoebe? You should read a child psychology book, Alana.'

Alana stared. 'Really?'

'Well, you might find it interesting. Phoebe, does this boy Finn still have Mr Jeremy?'

Phoebe frowned. 'I think so. You could go to his house and ask him. He might tell you – if he's stopped snivelling . . .'

But the nurse in charge was not prepared to tell Alice Finn's full name, nor his address, nor who was his usual doctor, nor who was his psychiatrist. 'I'm sure you understand,' she kept saying with less sympathy than you get from a drinks machine that's out of hot chocolate, until Alice, who did not want to understand at all anyway, left in a huff. She would have swept out of the hospital on a blaze of ill feeling, but it took ten minutes to get Fergus off the computer game and half an hour to extract Herman from the hospital concourse. She would find this Finn who had the frog, even if she had to ring every paediatric consultant in the hospital and beg for information on his whereabouts.

In Aldeburgh Martha and Tom sat on the beach together sharing fish and chips from an excellent place that even served battered trout and turbot – although somehow the spirit of the day had demanded your basic cod. Sitting close together on the pebble beach it seemed natural to Martha to lean against him, more natural still to feel his arm around her. It was *fun* to be with him like this. Well, of course, it would be fun to be with anyone, thought Martha, correcting any hint of wayward thought immediately; it was just that sort of a day. Behind them, only feet from the beach, elegant but chronically salt-damaged and surely unmortgageable houses gazed defiantly at the sea, challenging erosion to dare change the coastline when this was *Aldeburgh*. Ahead of them the sea was that same blue-grey of Tom's eyes – they were such clear eyes too. Imagine,

Martha thought, if we could just sail away. This very same sea goes round the whole world – we could just get in a boat and sail away.

She could still hear Rachmaninov's Second, sending its romantic tendrils to wrap around her, warm her . . . and yet the radio wasn't on.

'Penny for them.' Tom ruffled her hair, then kissed her gently on the lips.

Oh dear, she thought, I wish you'd just hurl me down on the shingle and snog me within an inch of my life . . . What can I say? She gazed resolutely at the horizon. 'I used to come here as a child. I made a fortune one summer selling pebbles to tourists.'

Tom chuckled. 'Selling pebbles? Couldn't they just help themselves to pebbles?'

She could feel his eyes on her face. 'These were special – I'd painted them first. Just little patterns. Red and blue blobs, actually, but I told them it was American folk art. I was earning pocket money.'

'Early sign of an entrepreneur. Martha?'

'Yes?' She had to turn to face him, and her stomach fluttered like a struggling rabbit. Heavens, this was something chemical.

'Martha, I have this prevailing urge to pin you to the beach and kiss you properly. Would you mind terribly if I did?'

'I . . . well actually, no . . . that would be very nice, actually . . .'

The afternoon lengthened into bliss, the sound of the sea lapping on shingle and the soft cry of warring gulls adding an unearthly atmosphere to the best kiss Martha could remember. She didn't really kiss much, as a rule, in fact she generally made it a bit of a rule not to. This kiss was like slipping into a seething, churning torrent of bliss – disorientating, stimulating, addictive. Should this be worrying her?

'It's disgusting, making an exhibition of yourselves like that. Someone ought to tell your parents. We don't have that sort of thing in Aldeburgh, you know.'

Martha started to float up from the pool of bliss to hear the shrill East coast tones of what seemed to be a character from a Monty Python sketch haranguing them, as Tom pulled her up to sitting. She tried to catch her breath but it was taking all her concentration not to flop onto the shingle in a jellied heap.

'Ma'am, I'm so sorry to have offended you . . .'

'Ooh-er,' said the woman. Martha dared not look at her lest she become hysterical with mirth. Tom was eloquent, though. 'You see, ma'am, I'm a British agent working undercover in Aldeburgh – a matter of national security – and I find snogging locals on the beach is excellent cover.'

'Well, I don't know . . .' Martha had a vague impression of something in a headscarf waddling off.

'Was that for real?' She started to laugh at last.

'I think it was. Come on – we need an ice cream,' he pulled her to her feet, 'even though I could stay here for ever.'

The trouble is, thought Martha, so could I.

Whilst Herman brewed tea and the children debriefed her on the day's excitement, Alice tried not to think about the practice. She had called in to lock up on the way back from Addenbrooke's, to find two frustrated patients in the waiting room and James practising his golf swing in the car park.

'I think it's stress, Doctor,' Jean told Alice anxiously after she had sorted out an ear infection and a self-esteem crisis. 'We had that Heather Bunberry back here again – said she really needed to see you and I'm sure she upset James. No idea why. He won't say, but Marjorie is coming to collect him.'

Resolving that she was going to have to tackle Heather

Bunberry once and for all if she was going to come in upsetting James, Alice had switched the telephones through to the medical answering service and driven home with a sigh of relief.

Now, with Herman and the children playing Scrabble in a corner (Herman kept winning due to his use of Armenian words without vowels whose existence no one could disprove) Alice went through her address book looking for telephone numbers of hospital paediatricians – a hardy and dedicated breed who, if they leave the hospital building at all, are almost always at home sleeping off their severe exhaustion. Well, apart from the one who kept vicuna, but then he did specialise in children's bowels so he needed some relief.

The first she rang had never heard of a boy called Finn, but she struck lucky with the second. Nick Carter had been at medical school with her – and Rob – and he was pleased to be able to help.

'Finn Selby,' he told her, 'nice boy, fell off a roof for love. I'll ring him for you myself. A toy frog, was it?'

But when he called her back two minutes later it was not so simple.

'He apparently gave your money box to a psychiatrist who admired it,' he told her. 'He thinks the psychiatrist was planning to give it to his girlfriend. I'm sorry, Alice, I'd like to have been able to help more. I may be able to work out who these people are on Monday. Actually Tuesday now, as Monday is the bank holiday. How are things with you?'

'Fine,' said Alice automatically, 'and you have helped. Really.'

'How's James?'

'Tired, actually. We've had a locum in – Tom Lovejoy . . .'

'Ah, Tom. He's quite a whizz, isn't he? I'd snap him up before another practice steals him. Say, you and he aren't.'

'Oh no, of course not,' said Alice.

'Why "of course not"? You've not switched sexuality on us, have you?'

Alice sighed inwardly. 'There are one or two women who can resist Tom Lovejoy, you know, and I'm not seeing anyone. Not yet. Look, Nick, thanks for your help.'

'Don't mention it. But take it from me, Alice, life's like driving a dogsled. When Ann left me I spent a year on my own. Gets you nothing in the end. Pick up the future and rattle its reins, that's my advice. Only look back when you're moving . . . Oh, I've just remembered, the psychiatrist is called Simon Frobisher. Bye.'

But when Alice rang Addenbrooke's all they would tell her was that Simon Frobisher would not be on duty for a week because he was on leave, so that was that for now. She sighed and looked up from the phone to find her children ranged before her, solemn-faced.

'What now? And if you're about to tell me that one of my patients is running amok in Sainsbury's with a rocket launcher and a small army of mercenaries then I really don't want to know. The call service can deal with it.'

'It's more serious than that,' said Daisy. 'We want to talk about moving house.'

Martha was heady with excitement and exhaustion by the time she and Tom got back to Cambridge. She felt as if she had been living on her nerves all day. The sea, the breeze, his kisses – it was as if she were on another energy level, as if she was walking weightlessly along a girder forty floors above New York, energised and unafraid. She had to remind herself of the potential drop. As they walked to her door her heart was pounding, the desire welling in her . . . This was getting scary. This was how people got carried away and started saying the 'L'-word and exchanging rings. This was the road to misery and pain and the whisky bottle – but it was paved with gold and scented with rose petals and so no wonder it was crowded with fools and littered with broken lives. She needed to be alone, safe in her own bed. Her private bed, not the big white one. Tom was overwhelming her.

Yet if he wanted to stay – how could she resist? Didn't that just show precisely why she should resist? Get a grip, Martha, you're acting like someone straight out of a Barbara Cartland novel. In a minute you'll be changing your name to Camelia and swooning on the carpet.

On her doorstep he kissed her. 'Martha, much as I want to – desperately want to stay . . .'

Martha felt herself vibrate in the middle, a sudden exquisitely intense vibration – like a metal music stand when an oboe hits 'B'.

'. . . I don't think I should. Today has been wonderful – so perfect that I don't want to push our luck too fast. I need to get my breath. Do you understand what I mean?' And she swallowed and nodded firmly, squashing the surge of disappointment into a small corner of her colon and hoping it wouldn't gurgle there until after he'd gone. 'Of course, Tom, I feel the same. I'm tired, I need an early night,' and she waved goodbye to him smilingly, trying not to mind.

Her own home. Solitude. Music, a warm soak, something out of the fridge, a glass of Chablis. Her own bed, alone. Her own bedroom – not the white one, where she had been with Tom, but her own room with the brass bed and the patchwork quilt and the twenty-two teddy bears who had helped her through the unhappy moments of her teenage years. Privacy. Silence. All of those things she so prized about independence. They were waiting for her – blissful, safe, sanctuary. Even so, a fit of pique made her wrench the fresh white sheets from the big bed and fling them into a crumpled heap in the corner.

An hour after he had left her, when she was sipping Chablis and pretending to herself that she was watching an old black-and-white film on TV, a film which just happened to be on the first channel the set had fallen upon, the telephone rang and she seized the receiver eagerly, hoping yet fearing it might be Tom.

'Hello?'

'Martha, hi.'

'Oh. Hello, Alice.'

'No need to sound so pleased,' said Alice drily. 'Martha, I've some news. I wanted to tell you . . . Martha, is that *Brief Encounter* you're watching? We've got it on here. Herman is addicted. I guess there's hope for you yet then – I thought you thought it was romantic nonsense.'

'It is.' Martha pressed 'off' guiltily, and lied, 'And I'm not watching it – I've Ashkenazy playing Rachmaninov on CD, that's what you could hear. What news?'

'I'm thinking about buying back Pipe Tree Cottage. We might be moving back to Fox Colne.'

'Oh, that's . . . Alice, are you sure?' asked Martha, momentarily forgetting the feel of Tom's lips. (But only momentarily – they came back to her as she spoke and nuzzled her subconscious neck.) 'I mean, it would be lovely to have you back in the village but – don't you think you're looking for something you won't find?'

'Of course not.' Alice was defensive, wondering exactly the same thing herself. 'But now is the opportunity to buy it. We were happy there. The hebes grew in the garden . . . I've got the money, thanks to Rob and his insurance. I might as well use it.'

Martha pulled her brain into gear. 'And not because you're expecting to find Rob there?'

Alice shook her head with more conviction that she felt. 'I can't find Rob anywhere now, not even in the churchyard.' Actually, she thought, I wish I could find him. He seems to have taken a bit of me with him and I need it back. Perhaps it's the part of me, she thought, that could grow hebes.

Martha stared at the phone for a long time after Alice hung up, thoughts of Tom Lovejoy revolving in her head. Perhaps she had always dismissed love too lightly all these years. It struck her now how very much she had used Alice and Rob to prove to herself that true love was a trap and a precipice, and marriage nothing more than a lottery. So Rob had betrayed Alice, and Alice had lost him, lost him twice over – but there was still something there, wasn't there, something that mattered? Something that was enough to make Alice want to be back there, want to remember rather than to forget, to take up the reins of being Rob's Alice again.

But, God, you had to be brave to contemplate that sort of commitment in the first place. Alice was brave – that was why she had married in the first place. You had to be either brave or foolish. I've never been foolish – and I've never been that brave either, thought Martha, sipping her Chablis and looking thoughtfully at the photograph of her father in uniform that her mother had given her before she died. Before she killed herself.

When Alice got off the phone to Martha her children seemed to expect her to adjudicate in a bedroom allocation war, all on the basis of a house purchase she hadn't really agreed to. So she switched off *Brief Encounter* which was, she felt, only worth watching for the music since the romance of it, however poignant, surely missed the whole point about permanence, and waded in.

Anemone, in particular, was apparently feeling aggrieved at Fergus' suggestion that she shouldn't have the biggest room in Pipe Tree Cottage on the basis that she was bound to be shacked up with some bloke in a couple of years' time and he, Fergus, would only have to redecorate.

'My room won't need redecorating,' she was saying, 'it will have great feng shui.'

'What, goldfish in the middle of the floor? Mum, tell her.'

Alice sighed. 'In the last few days,' she said icily, 'I've dealt with an armed incident involving Tabitha Tinkler and a pop gun, I've been on a fruitless search for a frog in a hospital ward whose ward sister learned her manners from a robot, met a man with the charisma of a rat dropping who thought he could seduce me by talking about gynaecology, had my patients refused lavatory facilities and my surgery turned over, had my former partner proposition me with knickers and have fallen over a bowl of goldfish on my bathroom floor – oh, and I have apparently informed the Hamiltons we plan to buy Pipe Tree Cottage. Do you really think it's likely that I've got the energy for anything else?' She sat at the table and glared at them.

'Well,' said Fergus cheerily, 'we can help decorate if you can do the deciding. Fred's promised to mulch the garden here before we go . . .'

'Mulch the garden? This garden? What for?'

'Your hebes,' said Fergus, patiently but practically. 'I said maybe they didn't grow because you'd been so sad, but Fred says they just need a good mulch, and when it comes to mulching, he's your man. He's a scientist, you know. He got me to count the weeds so he could calculate the right mixture. It's bound to work.'

Alice stared at Fergus, hearing an echo of Rob. 'Your father used to say that,' she said, looking at her son's red hair and realising how much more terrible it would be to lose him than to lose Rob, because Rob was already lost, he was gone, and Fergus was . . . so much of the best of Rob. I've said goodbye to my lover, she thought suddenly, but, look, I still have my friend.

Fergus looked uncomfortable, glanced at Anemone and Daisy, found them looking puzzled too. 'What, Dad used to say all that about weeds?'

'No, he used to say "It's bound to work". Don't you remember?' It's not just what he said, she thought, it's the way he said it.

Fergus blinked and then moved over to her, not sure whether he had said the wrong thing. You never really knew with Mum when she got upset. He gave her an awkward hug. 'I mostly remember him gardening.'

Alice smiled. 'He did do a lot of gardening,' she said, struck suddenly by the thought of how wrong she had been to blame her failure with the hebes on Rob. After all, had she ever, honestly, been any good in the garden on her own? Oh, she'd done a bit, it was true, but Rob had always helped. Had always done the mulching and, whilst bringing her cups of tea, told her how deep to put things, what ought to go where, and when it ought to go there. It was Rob who had surreptitiously dug up the things that died and put them on the inside of the compost heap so he thought she'd never find out. Fergus was right, the sorry hebes were nothing to do with her emotional state, they were all about mulch. 'So, you reckon you can sort this garden out then, do you?' She ruffled his hair.

'Definitely,' said Fergus firmly, hugging her and sensing that something had made her happy without being quite sure what. Maybe, he thought, if I make the garden nice enough she won't want to move and Daisy and Anemone will have to give up on their horrid plan to drag me away from here.

Daisy and Anemone exchanged glances. 'He's still not having the best room,' said Anemone *sotto voce*. Then, aloud: 'Shall I make everyone a nice cup of tea?'

'That would be nice,' said Alice absently, 'and biscuits.'

Fergus wriggled out of Alice's arms, for at twelve a boy can only be hugged for so long however much he secretly likes it. 'I'll get the biscuits.'

'You're not. You'll steal the digestives and leave the Jammie Dodgers and I don't like them, so *I'll* get the biscuits.' Daisy pursued Anemone and Fergus out towards the kitchen, any hint of approaching adulthood suddenly submerged in biscuit-competition.

Alice watched them go, then looked out of the window at the garden.

310

'Is this your husband?' Herman had a photograph. 'He looks very like your son.'

Alice nodded, not needing to look round for there were no other men's photos on the dresser. Actually, there were too many photos of Rob scattered about the house. It wasn't as if she needed photos to remind her of what he looked like, after all. The children had their own pictures and, well, filling your house with pictures of your dead husband looked rather retrospective. Old photos belong in the houses of people who don't have any new ones to look at.

'He actually is very like him,' she said, smiling out of the window at the hebes.

Herman couldn't see her face. 'Is that hard for you?' he asked.

'No, not at all,' said Alice, realising it was true. 'I always thought I'd lost Rob for ever, that he'd taken part of me with him and I could never be whole again – but I know now I was wrong. Part of him – the best of him – is still here with me.'

Herman came to stand behind her. 'The garden seems very important in all this?'

'Kind of,' said Alice. 'I moved the hebes, you see, from our old house – but after they came here they never did awfully well, whereas the ones on Rob's grave are enormous. I think I've put far too much symbolism into that.'

'You should never move hebes,' said Herman solemnly. 'Even in Armenia we know this . . . Ah, wonderful, tea and Jammie Dodgems.'

If I were to move the hebes again, Alice thought, watching Anemone pour out mugs whilst Daisy tried to hold a plate of biscuits out of reach of Fergus' hand and Fergus proved he was growing rapidly by reaching them, they might die. So if we go the hebes should stay here and be mulched. If we go.

It was late by the time she went to bed, after starting on the list of the pros and cons of moving, and by that time she had packed away all of the photos of Rob except one. One stayed on her dressing table, under the lamp where you could see it clearly. The one in which he was looking at her properly.

Chapter Fifteen

Sunday, thought Alice as the telephone woke her, ought surely to be a day of rest. So should I bother to answer it? It's bound to be for Anemone. But Anemone won't answer it. I've conditioned her to stay in bed when it rings by always answering it myself . . . I'll have to answer it or I'll have to live with the uncertainty of not knowing who it was.

She opened one eye. Bright sunlight was flooding into the room (whose idea were white muslin curtains?) and she felt for the phone with her eyelids screwed down.

'Hello?'

'Alice, it's Marjorie.' She sounded strained, Alice thought, as if she were about to burst into tears. 'I'm so sorry to telephone at such an odd time, but I couldn't sleep for worrying about telling you so I just thought I'd get up and do it.'

'Marjorie, are you all right?' Alice was bolt upright in bed, her heart pounding.

'Alice, I've been better. Listen, dear, there's no easy way to tell you this, so I'm just going to have to come straight out with it. James won't be in tomorrow. He's really not himself. You must have noticed how odd he's been recently – I found him yesterday waltzing around the post office with an old lady from the pension queue. She had a zimmer frame, he really shouldn't have . . . He said the loop video had made him mad with boredom – you know his sense of humour, dear – but his doctor says it's stress and he needs a rest.'

'Oh dear, Marjorie, is he all right now?'

'No, Alice dear, he's not. This business with Roland has

313

really upset him too. They had something of a set-to yesterday over the lupins.'

'So is this all because of Roland, Marjorie?'

'Oh dear, don't ask, Alice, or I'll start off again. Suffice to say, you know how James is about those lupins. He planted them himself, you know – and Roland stamped on the whole lot. It was a bitter blow. It's different for you, dear. I know you have to work with the ghastly man but you're not responsible for him.'

'Neither is James. Does he really think he is?'

'He can't help it, Alice dear. James *chose* Roland as a partner all those years ago. He agreed to let Roland buy the practice building when there was just the two of them. It seemed a reasonable plan when Roland was so keen and, well, James was never very business-minded, you know – always so trusting. But now he feels this mess is all his fault.'

'Oh, Marjorie, he mustn't feel that. Look, we'll think of something, tell James I know we will. Tell him to take it easy, have a rest, don't worry about anything, and I'll think of something.'

Watch what you're promising, Alice, she told herself, in case you can't think of anything. It's what Rob used to say, and he never did think of something. It was always me that thought of something. Me who sorted out the tax bill that year when it was twice what we expected. Me who dealt with the insurers when Daisy poured ink on the carpet and they didn't believe us. Me who sent the begging letters to the traffic police when Rob got tickets for parking outside the homes of sick old ladies. Me who arranged a hire car when Rob drove ours into a ditch the day before we went on holiday. . .

I always have thought of something before . . .

'Alice, I think James needs more of a break than that. It's very kind of you, dear, but it wouldn't be fair to any of you. You've all been marvellously supportive and marvellously kind, but James feels he's no longer safe, that the stress has affected his work. You know, he's been awfully forgetful recently, and we were afraid it might be Alzheimer's or something, but the doctor says no, it's stress and depression. At our age, my dear, it pulls you up short I can tell you. So I'm afraid we've decided that the time has come for James to look seriously at his life. He's going to retire. I'm sorry, Alice, but he won't be back at work at all. He'll be on sick leave until his retirement comes through – he can opt to draw his pension next month.'

'Oh, Marjorie, I'm sorry.'

'I know, dear, but you must have worried about him recently. It's not dignified for a man of his age to get into a playground scrap over the ownership of a few lupins – even if they were clearly our lupins. Especially the pink ones – I was particularly proud of the pink ones, you know. They were exactly the colour of our bridesmaids' frocks all those years ago. They were – Oh, listen to me, Alice, this is no good for his blood pressure, nor for mine. God knows I never could stand Roland, not since he felt for my bosom at the Cambridge Young Doctors' Ball in 1972 – but James was his partner for too many years for us to start fighting him now. He's simply ready to hang up his hat, dear. Don't be sorry for us – we're going to enjoy the rest. Perhaps Roland has done us a favour, stopped James going on in practice till he drops as so many others do. He needs a break and he's tired of general practice. It's all changed since his day, and he can't keep up any more. He can't get to grips with the computer at all. He says it's a disaster when he turns it on – all of his battleships got wiped out again yesterday and he keeps prescribing suppositories by mistake. You're young, it's all ahead of you – and James thinks very highly of young Tom, as you know – but it's our time to bow out. We want to start enjoying life and, well, you know how James always was about those lupins.'

When Marjorie had gone, after wittering about lupins and the climate of complaints against GPs and the fact that

GPs didn't get an afternoon playing golf these days and hadn't for some years, Alice stared disconsolately at the telephone.

So. Roland had groped Marjorie's bosom years ago and she had let him get away with it. Until now. Until James got stressed and Marjorie decided that that was it. And now James had thrown in the towel and there was just her. Well, her and Ian, strictly speaking, but Ian wasn't here, was he? The partnership at Lammas Surgery, as Rob had known it – the partnership of Roland Liversill, James Ferguson, Ian Stewart and Robert Vane – was finished. One in grotesquely private practice, one retiring with stress, one ten thousand miles away, and one dead. All that remained to show that there had once been a group of four male GPs working together for the good of their patients was the Widow Alice and a man who was probably currently sitting under a coconut palm wearing nothing but a thong. What would Rob have done now?

Rob would have dithered about what to do. Rob was never very good at making choices, was he? What to have in restaurants ('you choose, Alice'), what colour to paint the dining room ('I don't know about this red now I've seen it on the wall . . . what do you think about dark green?'), who to share body and bed with (Marcie or Alice?) – it was all the same. And who actually painted the living room? She'd had to paint it three bloody times. First red, then green, then red again. White had been such a relief after all that. She felt angry afresh with Rob for having been so earth-destroyingly undecided in life that now, in death, he was not able to pop into her psyche and help her make a clear smooth decision.

Actually, it was quite refreshing to have found this new angle on anger with Rob. Something new to shout at him about. But she, Alice, was no ditherer. She was a strong woman in control of her life. She made her own decisions and steered her own way.

She glanced at the clock on her bedside table, and her gaze alighted on Lisa's sketch of the proposed bridesmaid's dress, the dress in which she was to trip lightly and gaily down the aisle of St Winifred's church, a symphony of peaches and froth. Lisa, her employee and friend, whose livelihood was in her hands. Lisa would never hold down another job, not in a million years. And then there was Jean, Norma, Fred, Tabitha . . .

What was it she had thought yesterday? That they were *her* people, in a way. Oh, she wasn't indispensable – who is? – but she was theirs. She couldn't just give up on them. And look – now she had told Marjorie she would sort it all out. Could she really live with herself if she caved in and wound down the practice for ever?

No, she couldn't. Giving up was not her style. Even if we sink, she thought now, we'll sink fighting to the last. I said I wanted to show Roland, and I do. How *could* I have sent that hopeless, negative postcard to Ian? It's time I sent him an update. Poor chap, he's probably sitting in a mud hut somewhere eating bean soup, hoping for good news from home, and instead he gets reams of sad ramblings. He's supposed to be having six months away from it all, and it's going to follow him into the jungle. How unlucky that Roland chose his moment to pounce so very carefully, like a snake in the long grass, poisonous and accurate.

So she would have to try to make some decisions alone. Ian would understand that. And there was only one way to go on. She must take on Tom Lovejoy as a partner. Tom had proved to be excellent, and her own ridiculous prejudice about handsome doctors unfounded and unfair. Whatever her worries about his possible passion for Martha and the likelihood that one day soon he would find himself discarded into an abyss of rejection, he was surely the partnership's only chance. And Ian liked Tom – he had praised him to the skies. Indeed, he had treated Alice and James to a long recital of Tom's accomplishments and

317

exploits before he left for the Far East. Yes, she would speak to Tom.

'Hello, Dr Tom Lovejoy speaking. Please leave a message . . .'

God, thought Alice, not leaving one, he even sounds like a hero on his answering machine. Still, it would be no bad thing having a partner who was a hero. No bad thing at all.

Downstairs her children sat around the breakfast table rather sullenly, as the argument about bedrooms had not yet been resolved, and the intention was clearly that it never would be in the whole history of the planet if Fergus had his way. It was enough that he'd had to pretend he wanted to move – he couldn't be expected to make it any easier. Herman, however, was deeply involved with a bowl of Choco-puffs. His love affair with English breakfast cereals was developing into an all-consuming passion, and it was difficult to get a word out of him in the morning before he had sampled at least three.

'Morning,' said Alice brightly, wondering what the chance was that they would leap to their feet like cornflakes children and kiss her cheek cheerily. Not high, she guessed. For a moment she imagined what today would have been like had Rob been here – at least he used to kiss her cheek in the morning – but it was rather a distant vision and didn't hurt as it might once have done.

She was not wrong. Apart from Herman half waving his non-eating hand in a gesture of recognition, no one responded. She tried again.

'Listen, all of you, I need to speak to you.'

Anemone sniffed. 'As long as it's not about bedrooms.'

Alice gave her a quelling look – which was about as successful as Napoleon in the Battle of Waterloo. 'It's not.'

'It's a good job,' said Anemone, 'because I'm unbudge-able. Fergus will just have to wait till I've moved out.'

Fergus sniffed. 'It'll only be five minutes before she's

shacked up with some bloke – it seems a waste to have to paint a whole room again after five minutes.'

Anemone glared. 'I'm not shacking up, as you so delicately put it, with anyone – and, anyhow, as far as you know I might be a lesbian.'

'Oh, for heaven's sake,' Alice was exasperated, 'can't you just drop this? Fergus, we're not going to waste time arguing about what may never happen. Listen –'

'Don't you mind?' Daisy looked up from picking the raisins out of her muesli. She was, Alice noted absently, wearing rather more make-up than usual.

'Mind what? And why are you made up like that?'

'Mind if she's a lesbian. And I just want to look nice,' said Daisy. 'I've got a bed race rehearsal today. Tomorrow's the big day.' She had butterflies in her stomach. Mark Blackwell was one of the team pushing the bed. Each entry had to field six teams of four to complete the circuit, and Mark Blackwell was going to be there at the start. She could hardly wait.

Alice sighed 'I know. You'd think a bank holiday would be a day of rest.'

'You look like a rutting panda to me,' said Fergus sullenly, and Daisy glared at him.

'Oh, and how would you know?'

'I watch David Attenborough. You get to see rutting all the time on David Attenborough,' said Fergus smugly.

Anemone raised an eyebrow. 'You get the same on *EastEnders*, she said to no one in particular, 'but with rather less bamboo.'

'Well, I may look like a panda but at least you can see my face through the freckles,' said Daisy, wondering if Mark Blackwell would think she looked like a panda too. Looking Goth was all the rage, surely?

'Will you all just stop squabbling!' Alice was suddenly fed up with them. 'I'm trying to tell you something. With only me running this household you sometimes just have to listen . . .' and to her horror her voice cracked and a tear ran down her cheek. *Now* what's setting me off?

The children were simultaneously dismayed and enthralled. Herman shook his head regretfully but did not stop eating his cereal. Daisy nudged Fergus and muttered, 'See what you've done.' Fergus, privately shocked but determined not to show it, put out his tongue.

It was left to Anemone to explore further. 'What is it? Did someone phone?'

'Yes, Marjorie phoned.' Alice mopped her eyes with a tea towel and blew her nose resoundingly. 'I wanted to tell you that James has decided to retire early, so I'm completely alone now. Which makes it even more difficult to keep the practice going than it was before.'

'Ah,' said Herman, pausing at last (he had, as it happened, just tipped the plastic stegosaurus out of the Corn Pops into his bowl, so it was a good moment for taking stock) and folding his arms portentously, 'alone, you say. Now you are not alone, Alice, you know that.'

'That's right – you've got Ian,' said Daisy. 'You've still got Ian.'

'I know, it's just a shame he's prancing round the coral islands in a loincloth taking nail clippings from passing headhunters.'

'Is *that* what he's doing? Wow – perhaps I should be a doctor after all. Mr Blackwell says doctors are the greatest.' Fergus' attention was caught. 'But I thought he was doing really boring stuff.'

'Well, he's not on the phone,' said Alice, registering Mr Blackwell's opinion with an odd sense of warmth, 'so he's no help at this minute. He can't help with the ongoing nightmare of sharing a building with Roland when he's being so utterly impossible.'

'Why?' asked Anemone. 'What's he done now?'

'I can hardly bear to tell you,' said Alice, 'but I will. He bought me a pair of knickers from Martha's shop.'

'Oh, gross,' said Anemone.

'I know. Gift-wrapped.'

Fergus shrugged. 'I don't see what's wrong with that? When you buy me socks, I don't have a funny turn.'

'Fergus, you may not understand the finer points of knickers but you have to accept that when a man gives a woman red silk ones he's not behaving appropriately for a business relationship,' said Alice, and Herman sighed.

'There was a time when the only knickers in the stores in Yerevan were red . . .'

Daisy, though, was staring open-mouthed. 'Red knickers? Red? You don't mean the ones you gave me?'

'Oh – er, well, yes, Daisy, I did – but they were from me to you so that was OK – and they were very expensive . . .'

'You're wearing them, aren't you?' said Fergus, with a smug gloat. 'Imagine that. Wearing smarmy Roland's knickers . . .'

Daisy threw a biro at him. 'Shut up.'

Alice waved her arm vaguely. 'Look, the knickers are a side issue.'

'It's easy for you to say that,' muttered Daisy, 'since right now you'll be wearing black cotton ones you bought yourself in a five-pack from Marks and –'

Alice ignored her. 'This is about the practice surviving. I don't think there's much chance of it surviving, but I want you all to know that I'm not giving up yet, even though things look pretty bleak. I'm going to offer Tom Lovejoy a partnership to replace James. I know Ian likes him and I think we can try to give things a go. It may all be a complete disaster – we've got to move out of the Lammas building and I've no idea where we'll go – we'll probably end up holding surgeries on street corners and examining patients in the phone boxes in the marketplace, but I wouldn't want you to think I'd give up. It was your dad's practice, after all.'

'It's not Dad's practice now,' Anemone said, surprised, 'it's yours and Ian's. And, anyway, what would the patients do if you went?'

'And the staff?' Daisy joined in to put the boot in further, 'What about Loopy Lisa and Graveyard Jean? No one would ever employ them if you didn't.'

'Well, they could be extras in *Little Shop of Horrors*,' said Anemone. 'Jean could be the man-eating plant.'

Daisy giggled. 'All my friends think yours is easily the weirdest surgery in Cambridge. Everyone wants to register with you.'

'I'm delighted,' said Alice, 'and the staff are not weird, they're wonderful people. Remember I'm Lisa's matron of honour in less than three weeks.'

Anemone frowned doubtfully, 'I know – it's a bit quick for organising a wedding. Is she . . . ?'

'Yes, and it took her eight months to get him to agree to it,' said Fergus, adding when Alice glared at him, 'I heard it at the Fir Trees. Lisa's granny's best friend lives there.'

Alice frowned. Eight months? Either Lisa was begging for Dean's hand in marriage before she was even pregnant – possible, of course – or she was actually more than seven months gone. No, she would have said.

She took the children and Herman in with a gesture. 'So you think Tom Lovejoy would make a good partner? I mean, if he accepted? It all looks a lost cause – but then, he's not really got anything to lose either.'

Fergus shrugged. 'I wouldn't know what he was like – since I didn't have chance to stay down to dinner when he came.' Fergus adopted a wounded expression.

'Oh, dry up,' said Daisy. 'You're like a mucky CD.'

Anemone disagreed. 'I think he'll be great,' she said, 'as long as Martha doesn't dump him and break his heart.'

'If he's got a heart,' said Alice, 'that is.'

Anemone frowned. 'Of course he has. He couldn't take

322

his eyes off her at dinner that time. Shall I ask the tarot cards?'

Alice smiled, thinking: how nice it is that they don't separate lust from love, don't yet see that they can occur independently. Life is so much easier if you don't. You've a fighting chance that your husband's heart attack will be in Marks and Spencer, for example.

Fergus sniffed. 'I'm surprised you can't see into the future with the aid of a fish tank and an angled mirror,'

Anemone sent him a dark look. 'You just don't understand feng shui – that's your trouble. Your mind is closed.'

Herman finished his Corn Pops. 'I always used to think,' he said solemnly, 'that it's better not to see too far ahead. But frankly, any glimpse you can offer into what is to come would be most welcome. Do you think your cards could locate a china frog?'

Alice left them trying to decide what the lovers' card (that one again) said about the location of the frog. She needed a walk – to think things through. Perhaps she should go and have that shout at Rob's grave. God only knows he deserved it.

'I can't believe it,' Daisy was saying as she left, 'I'm wearing Roland's knickers,' but she was actually in no hurry to give them back. With fifty-pound knickers under her jeans surely she would have the confidence to win Mark Blackwell's attention? How could she not be impressive?

In Fox Colne Martha awoke, alone and bleary-eyed after a disturbed night. Dreams of Tom – at least, it was probably Tom. They were the kind of dreams that are more about what you feel than what you see. And what she had felt was ... urgent. She stared at the walls, a little disorientated. Her own private bedroom, into which no man had ever been invited. The room of her inner self. Undeniably New England twee, of course, from its Shaker furniture to its pink patchwork quilt, but no one ever saw it but her ...

The telephone rang.

'Tom?'

'Martha. Can I see you? I must see you . . .'

She trembled for the whole time it took him to get there, which was less than five minutes because he had been sitting in his car two hundred yards along the road, and didn't even think for a second about there being no sheets on the bed in the white bedroom because she had thrown them on the floor.

As Martha's door closed behind Tom, Alice drove past Pipe Tree Cottage and gave it a little smile. It looked good in the sunshine, even though the garden looked horribly neat, as if someone mowed it obsessively every Sunday morning, then trimmed the edges of the flowerbeds with one of those strimmer things that everybody owns but only real obsessives ever use more than twice. It was hard to imagine them all back there, back in their old bedrooms. Could they really go back?

She shook the thought away, and pulled up at Martha's house, intending to call in – but no. That was Tom Lovejoy's car. I might have known. Well, she thought, this will be interesting. It's not like Martha to admit a man to her bed twice. She pulled away again and parked at the church instead, walking up the path amongst the smell of cut grass and buttercups that reminded her so headily of times past. At least she could think of a few things to say to Rob this time.

He was only just off the path, on the slope, and someone had put fresh flowers there again. Who? A patient, perhaps? One of the children again? And so she stared at Rob's grave and asked him, 'What *would* you do now? Would you fight Roland and try to take the practice somewhere else, assuming it were possible? Couldn't you inspire me with some sort of feelings, from wherever it is you're meant to be? Couldn't you just be some bloody help?'

Rob's hebes sighed gently in the light breeze, and Alice

was aware vaguely of the Sunday churchgoers on the path behind her giving a wide berth to the mad muttering woman so clearly about to fling herself shrieking onto her husband's grave. The six Fox Colne bells were clanging discordantly (it still sounds like the theme music to *The Magic Roundabout*, she thought wistfully, but there's no Rob sitting in the garden of Pipe Tree Cottage and saying so any more. So many things left us when he did), birds were singing, and Alice suddenly felt a touch on her shoulder.

'Dr Vane, are you feeling OK?'

'Oh, hello, Lisa. Hello, Dean. I didn't know you came to church.' Dean, Alice noticed, was wearing jeans and an Ipswich Town top, whilst Lisa wore the sort of suit the Queen Mother might favour for Ascot, with the sort of hat crows might favour for living in. Dean looked rather pale and wan (as well he might, up against that suit).

'We don't usually,' Lisa beamed from beneath this monstrosity (they can probably see that at the early warning radar station at Fylingdale, Alice thought), 'but the vicar said we'd got to come and hear the banns if he was going to marry us. We've been once already. It's quite nice really, especially now they've got the new cool vicar with the tambourines and the guitar.'

'*Have* they?' Alice glanced surreptitiously at the church roof – surely bits of it would have fallen off spontaneously at the sound of a happy-clappy service?

Dean grinned, 'Course not. Just winding you up. Is this where your husband is, then?' Lisa nudged him viciously. 'Sorry – I didn't mean –'

'That's all right. Yes, that's Rob there. And yes, I'm fine. I might come into church with you, if you don't mind.'

'Ooh, you could pop back to ours after. I've got the bridesmaids' dress material there and Mum's started on yours. She wanted to check your hips.'

Dean blushed furiously and Alice suppressed a smile. Interesting that despite imminent fatherhood, Dean still

325

dissolved upon hearing the word 'hips'. She wondered what he was going to be like in the labour ward. Best not to get into that too soon, perhaps.

'How are the preparations going?'

Lisa looked proud. 'Really well. Dean had his stag night last night, Dr Vane – we thought with nearly three weeks to go it was a safe time to have it – and look at him, he's not even thrown up once.'

No wonder he looks pale, poor boy, thought Alice. Rob's stag night had been a month before the wedding too – not long enough, in his case. His best man had painted gentian violet onto the bits only she would see, and it had taken weeks to come off. Still, as Rob always said, he was guaranteed to be free of athlete's foot there for the whole honeymoon. She smiled as she followed Lisa and Dean inside. They had had some moments, she and Rob.

The church was as churches always seem to be – rather pointlessly sombre. It was a little chilly, despite the sun, with an old, vaguely musty smell that owed a little to Mr Sheen and a lot to bat poo. The organist was playing one of those awful organ voluntaries which church organists believe will put the congregation in a suitably reflective mood for worship (whereas in fact they just make them want to gang up on the organist and douse him with the contents of the font). Many of the congregation wore hats, but very few of them were under seventy. Some, those Alice remembered, smiled at her nervously, as if, she thought, she had the fallen woman in the hotel bedroom somehow attached to her still, as she'd been attached by association when Rob died. Perhaps, Alice thought, Marcie Crombie comes here too. The thought unnerved her slightly.

The vicar, a small nervous man, was about as happy-clappy a celebrant as the Pope is Buddhist, and the hymns seemed to have been chosen for their challenging rather than their musical quality. I haven't actually been inside here since the funeral, Alice thought, listening to Dean and

Lisa singing something which bore absolutely no resemblance to what the organist was playing (it was difficult to be sure who was wrong. The organist had volume on her side, but Dean and Lisa's version was more penetrating). When Rob died the church didn't really seemed to offer anything other than a waiting, unchanging and, above all, *old* atmosphere, which hadn't been particularly what she wanted at the time. She had not wanted to be soothed – but perhaps there was a haven for her here now. A place for the old Alice.

But I don't want a haven. I don't want to be the old Alice, coming home to lick her wounds. I may have moved away to run away – but since I went I've changed, I've grown up without Rob. Rob's Alice belonged in Fox Colne – but I'm not sure that I do.

And after the service, when Lisa insisted on hauling her home beneath the clanging bells for coffee and angel cake, and providing her with an illustration of her planned maid of honour outfit (in which, it was clear, she was going to look not only slightly but exactly and absolutely like a toilet-roll holder), the decision still hovered before her. Fox Colne or Herne Road? she thought. Where do I belong.

Martha heard the church bells too and she frowned. They came as distant chimes disturbing a dream of bliss, for she lay in Tom's arms across the scattered pink pillows, breathing the beautiful sandalwood scent of his chest and wondering how on earth he managed to get things so right, move so gently, kiss with such perfect sensuality.

They had talked afterwards. She had told him about her parents, her mother's death, things that she rarely told anyone. Perhaps it was because, in the heat of the moment and with no sheets on the white bed, they had finished up in her private bedroom, her sanctuary, her pink patchwork room.

Now she felt uneasy. She could just have said her mother

327

was dead. That's all she ever said to anyone – even Alice didn't know it all. But she had felt close to Tom, she had answered the question intimately because they were intimate at the time. Very intimate. She stretched languorously. I've never actually had a conversation with someone whilst they lay inside me before. Never felt someone still there as we talked. It made me pour out truths. Did he do that on purpose? Does he do that with all his women? We all have techniques – God knows I certainly do . . . certainly did. But I have no techniques with him – it all feels totally honest.

He was asleep now, his chest gently rising and falling, his face relaxed and defenceless. He was so beautiful. She moved a little closer, sharing the same space, breathing the air he exhaled, watching his lips. What beautiful lips, she thought . . . And then, very, very gently, so gently that it was almost imperceptible – but then with a just slightly increasing force, Tom began to snore.

It was just a small sound – the catch of breath in the throat, the slight whistle – it was nothing like your full-blown beer drinkers' snore, the ones that sound like a rutting pig trying to catch his breath before another attempt at procreation with an unwilling sow. No, this one was an attractive snore. It was . . . his snore.

Martha sat bolt upright as though she were a cartoon rabbit and someone had just run an electric current from her toes to the top of her head. Her jaw was clenched in shock. What the hell am I thinking? No one digs into my secrets and snores in my personal bed and gets another chance. If I go with the snoring today, then I can surely expect the full range of bodily noises tomorrow. What can I have been thinking of, *nice snores*? There are no nice snores – only the gradual deterioration from an animal grunt through belching and toenail clipping to nose picking and eventually the full-blown flatulation in bed. Martha was conscious of a rising feeling of panic disturbing the smooth happiness of the morning. My bed.

I told him about my mother. He's much too close. Much much too close.

Tense as a bow, she slipped carefully away from him, wrapping herself in her white linen robe and walking to the window.

Out there she could see the knots of people coming away from the church. Couples, condemned to the endless tolerance of one another's inescapable bodily noises. Individuals trapped into pairs by the ghastly ephemera of marriage and the total loss of privacy and good taste it entails. Pair after pair, couple after couple . . . whatever keeps the old ones together, when they even take out their teeth?

And wasn't that Alice's car parked by the church gate? Mourning Rob again, no doubt. She won't call in on me – not if she sees Tom's car here. What on earth must she think? After all, I'm behaving right out of character.

Tom sighed and she turned to look at him – losing her balance in the process and falling onto the carpet. And there was that too. She was clumsy around him. There was no doubt – he had some definite effect on her co-ordination, and it wouldn't do. She couldn't face him. She couldn't *do* this. It was just not safe.

Hastily she penned a note: 'Had to go out. Will call you later – Martha.' That covered it. Now, Martha, get yourself out of here before he wakes and smiles at you with those eyes and – as it surely would be – it's your undoing.

Behind her as she left Tom continued to snore, still secure in a dreamy post-coital bliss.

When Alice pulled up outside Herne Road Fergus rushed out to greet her. 'Mum, quick . . .'

'What . . . ?'

'It's Ian. He's on the phone . . . hurry. It must be costing him a million pounds a minute to phone from there.'

'Ian,' said Alice down the phone.

'Alice. How are you?'

A huge sense of relief settled on her as gently as a moth. 'I'm fine. You sound extraordinarily clear.'

'Sorry – should I be drowned out by chanting tribesmen roasting unfortunate strangers over jungle fires? It is quite civilised here, you know. They gave me an anaesthetic for my initiation ceremony – well before the scrotal bone-piercing.'

'Honestly, Ian, you don't change, you're still revolting.'

'Neither do you. You were always easy to wind up – Rob always said if you were a clock you'd run for ever. Fondly, of course.'

'Did he? Oh,' somehow Alice had not really thought of Rob having fondly humorous conversations about her with his partners. 'Ian – there are some problems here . . .'

'I know. I've telephoned James this morning too – I had a letter from him telling me that he was planning to retire and didn't know how to tell you, but I gather you know. And I was delivered your postcard a few days ago. I thought I'd better call you . . .'

'Ian, I thought you were deep in the dense dark jungle.'

She heard Ian chuckle. 'Alice this is the twentieth century, you know. The radio transmitter works perfectly well if we walk up the hill.'

'I suppose you've got a television too.'

'No – but we do get the world service and I sometimes pick up the cricket, Australian, you know, so not only do we always lose but the commentator's always delighted. Alice, are you OK?'

'I'm – well, you know, Ian. I'm muddling through, really. I suppose I'm letting myself get carried along by the flow, as I always do. Ian, I've decided to try and carry things on. I've just sent you another letter – why didn't you tell us we could call you?'

'You can't – but if I climb a hill again I can radio out to you again.'

'Why haven't you called before now?' She felt suddenly cross with him.

'Big hill, Alice, three days up, three days down, trekking party, leeches . . .'

'Oh, Ian, I'm touched. No one ever climbed a mountain with leeches just to speak to me before. Look, I've been pathetic – but I've come to my senses now, and I haven't given up. I want Tom to join us, join the partnership, and then at least if we go down we can go down fighting.'

'That's great news, Alice. I was worried when I read your letter. What changed your mind?'

'I've done too much running away and bowing out,' said Alice. 'That's why I moved house. That's why I wouldn't go to Rob's inquest. That's why I nearly let the practice go. Now I've decided to make my stand, even though I'm probably still a coward at heart.'

'No you're not, Alice, you always fight your way out. You always have. I've always admired that. Look at you. How many other women would have the courage to move house after their husband's death, to leave it all behind and start on a fresh canvas? Don't knock yourself, you're the strongest person I know. Listen, I'm coming back. Flight's booked already. I'll be back in two weeks at worst. We can do this together.'

'Oh, but your research . . .'

'The research will carry on without me. I'm only a small part of a team here, and I think the practice needs me more. We need to find a new place and stop the grass from growing under our feet. And, Alice – you have my full backing to tell Roland to go and boil his head.'

'You are picking up the lingo,' said Alice, too relieved at his normal, down-to-earth voice to argue. 'Do they boil many heads out there then?'

'Haven't seen a single head boiled since I got here. And, Alice – about Tom – you'd not find a better bloke. I've known him for years. Snap him up before someone else does.'

Someone else already has, snapped him up, thought Alice, although not in the way you mean – but Martha will spit him out when she's finished with him. Even so . . . 'Ian – it may not be enough. Roland is being truly impossible about the Lammas building. I don't know if we can even last until –'

'We'll sort it out,' said Ian, 'when I get back. Ask Tom's advice – he has all sorts of connections. Look, I must go, Alice, it's pouring here and I'm standing on the top of a mountain soaked to the bone talking to you whilst all the leeches in the eastern jungle head towards me, desperate for a snack, and this scrotal bone of mine is starting to throb again.'

'Oh, Ian, you are completely horrible.'

'I know, it's all part of my charm. See you in a couple of weeks.'

Alice felt as though a huge burden had lifted. She wasn't in this alone. Ian was coming back, and she had heard his voice. He was real again. For a while he'd felt as far off as Rob, someone you sent messages to from time to time without any real expectation of getting anything back. Now at least if she ended up trying to practise medicine from a tent on Midsummer Common, she wouldn't be alone. Ian would be with her. And maybe Tom.

She wondered how Martha would feel about her offering Tom a partnership. It would mean he'd stay around, and permanence certainly wasn't Martha's style, and it surely wasn't for lack of opportunity. She would probably never have slept with Tom in the first place if she'd thought he was staying. Mind you, she was obviously in way over her head already. Why else would he have been at her home on a Sunday morning?

'Mum?' Fergus, who was doing something in the garden, called, 'Martha's here.'

Perhaps, thought Alice, I'd better sound her out, fire a warning shot across her bows.

'Ask again,' said Martha, narrowing her eyes.

Alice sighed. 'OK. If I offered Tom Lovejoy a partnership, would he take it, do you think?'

'I really don't know. I've been sleeping with him, not reading his mind.' But he snored. I can never sleep with him again, surely? 'Why are you asking me, anyway? You should be asking him.'

God, she was thinking, with a terrible, heavy, cold feeling in the pit of her stomach, like ice cream with cement, he could be staying around. I've got to get myself out of this quickly.

'I know, but – I suppose I just wanted to know if . . . I just felt I should let you know. I mean, if it's serious with you and him . . .'

'Of course it's not serious – how could it be? This is me. I don't get involved.' Absolutely not, said her mind frantically, I've got to finish this.

'This . . . seemed different,' said Alice. 'You. Seemed different, this time. I thought perhaps you'd fallen –'

'Don't even think about it. I never do.' Martha was quick, almost quick enough to suggest Alice had only said what she was already thinking herself. She took out her plastic cigarette, which she seemed to be needing rather a lot recently. She'd have had a real one, but you couldn't smoke those in Alice's house. 'How different, anyway?' The question was casual on the surface but, like supermarket trifle, unnerving underneath.

'Caught up,' said Alice. 'Transported, I suppose. I was worried that –'

'I see what you're getting at,' said Martha. 'You thought if I was going to dump him he might walk out on you after you'd made him a partner. You know – devastated by blighted love.' When I say it aloud, she told herself, it sounds ridiculous.

333

'No, of course I didn't mean that. I just meant – I mean I wondered if . . . OK, are you? Dumping him, I mean?'

'Absolutely,' said Martha, determined to be determined (oh, but one more night, she thought, would have been . . . no, it could only have been disappointing). 'It was just sex. You can't have a relationship based on sex. It's got no depth.'

Alice shrugged. 'Sounds like as good a beginning as any to me.'

'Now you're being cynical.'

'No I'm not – just realistic. It's all a guessing game. Sixteen years I was with Rob, a relationship based on love, marriage, children, mortgage, history, memories, a shared interest in too much red wine and fondue on Saturday nights – the whole kindred souls job, with never an inkling that he fancied his women handcuffed. Look where that got me.'

'You're too caught up with the salaciousness of it, Alice. You're like a tabloid paper. You know, we all do stupid things sexually – use rude words or wear football strip or put ourselves in positions we wouldn't want to be photographed in.'

'You're not telling me Tom Lovejoy likes to do it dressed in Chelsea strip?'

'No, don't be silly. All I mean is that from time to time we all get ourselves into positions we wouldn't want to die in.'

'I don't,' said Alice.

'I bet you do. What about your Evening With Oliver?'

'Oh. Well, I suppose so.' Alice thought of the body chocolate. Imagine if Oliver had expired in the act. Imagine trying to explain to the coroner what exactly had been smeared with chocolate and why . . .

'Maybe you ought to find out how Rob ended up there with Marcie Crombie,' said Martha. 'Then at least you might understand. I don't see how you can move back to Pipe Tree Cottage if you're not prepared to confront that.'

Alice frowned uncomfortably as she watched Martha leave, feeling the echo of thoughts she had so far suppressed. How did this turn into a conversation about me anyway? she wondered. It was supposed to be about Martha.

Resolutely she picked up the telephone again and dialled. 'Tom?'

'Oh, Alice.'

'Tom, I'm glad I've caught you. I need to talk to you about something really important. Can you come over?'

'I – er – OK. I just got in and I was planning to – no, it's OK. I'll come right now.'

When she got back to Fox Colne Martha paced for almost an hour before she finally made the call to finish it. Tom had left. Just her note remained, his note added at the bottom. She stroked it briefly between her fingers, thinking of him frowning over it, of his hands holding and touching it . . . Of his *snoring* . . .

'Darling Martha, I'll call you soon,' it said in his strong, slanted hand. If you were to analyse that hand you'd get sexy, powerful, honest.

Did he know the rules of the game? Did he realise it was over? He must do, surely. It needed to stop now. Or could she risk letting things run a little longer, taking the pleasure, postponing the tiny bit of pain that, OK, she *might* feel today if she finished things?

But look at Alice. Look what happened if you slipped and threw in your lot with someone. Look what happened when they got close, got into your real bedroom. It always ended, and it left you damaged and raw, a wound too wide and deep to heal without scarring. It was unrecoverable. It left you lying awake at night listening to *snoring*.

Look at her mother – all those years of crying into her pillow over her bastard husband. He might have been a good father – but he had been a bastard husband. She had cried quietly after he had gone, had left her for good for a younger model with higher breasts who had never pushed a child down her birth canal – but Martha had still heard her. Later she had said, 'Never let a man right into your bedroom, Martha. Never do.' And Martha hadn't. Literally hadn't, until now. She would have to redecorate the pink bedroom. It was the only way.

Simple sex was so much healthier, so much easier to pick up and put down at leisure. Designated sex with designated sex-men in a designated sex-bedroom. Safe. What had caused this trouble was that she had tried to make Tom into the wrong kind of man. There are two distinct kinds of men – the ones you sleep with (which means you don't risk a re-match, which can only either tempt or disappoint) or the sort you let into your life (no sex). All the messy problems she had seen so often in friends and acquaintances began with mixing the two. She had broken her own rule and had begun to mix the two herself. So, no more sex with Tom.

God, he'd been good. If she stopped it now she'd never feel that touch again – those lips . . .

On the other hand, she had the memory. She could fantasise. Wasn't that what good sex was for? For fantasising about later, the ultimate in control? Come on, Martha, stop prevaricating – you know what you have to do. If you let this man into your life you'll be standing on the edge of the precipice for ever. Either he'll betray you, which would be unbearable, or he'll pall, which would be a tragedy. Just do it, then you can relax, feel the relief, feel the safety . . .

Her hand shook slightly, all the same, as she dialled, and a nervous desire clogged her vocal cords and tried to make them say, *Tom, come to me now and ravish me within an inch of my being, and keep doing it, keep on, keep on until I* . . . 'Tom?'

'Hello, this is Tom Lovejoy. I'm sorry I'm not here to take your call – but please leave a message after the tone.'

'I . . . Martha here. Tom, I'm sorry, but I think we should

336

cool things. It's been – wonderful – but – I wasn't looking for someone in my life right now. Commitment isn't really my thing. I'd like just to say it's been lovely but I really can't make it into anything more. Look, I'll . . . I'll call you some time. Really.'

God, you coward, Martha. Leaving that on an answering machine.

Well, that's what they're for. At least it gives him a chance to take it in before he sees me again. Which he will if he's going to be Alice's partner. Dammit.

That's better, that's safer.

Martha paced the room, agitated and upset, thinking, I can't have a man around me who unnerves me like this. Would he be upset? Or just politely crestfallen?

Why not call the agency? She would get Laura to send someone over tonight . . . The problem she had had with Bart had been a one-off. She was a performance-tuned creature. She could get marvellous sex out of any heterosexual man . . .

Well, maybe later. She didn't feel like ringing right now.

It was finished. Her fling with Tom Lovejoy had been fantastic sex, just that and nothing more. Fantastic sex is easily confused with something more. And if Alice was seriously going to offer him a partnership – well, he could be around for decades. She had done the right thing. She was sure of it. The fact that just now she needed to play Wagner extremely loudly and pour herself a large glass of bourbon was of no significance at all.

Chapter Sixteen

Oblivious to the ticking bomb that was his telephone answering machine, Tom Lovejoy arrived at Herne Road and strode up the garden path with a gleaming smile.

'Tom – come in.'

'Thanks, Alice. Here – I found this letter stuck in your box . . . I came as quickly as I could. Is everything OK?'

'Well, yes and no.' She took the letter, a handwritten envelope, put it in her pocket. 'Tom, come in, sit down.'

The children and Herman, sitting in the kitchen, watched with interest as Tom sat down at the table. Mordecai sidled over to the edge of his cage and spat a cherry stone at Tom's feet. Tom smiled, reached up and stroked the parrot's throat. 'He's very tame.'

Alice smiled. 'Rob used to tickle him. He never let anyone else near. He was a one-man parrot.' A bit like Tabitha. And me. Imagine, she thought fancifully, if you were actually Rob reincarnated and I didn't know it, like in *Carousel*. I've often imagined Rob coming back to see how we all turned out. Yet I don't fancy you. Actually I fancy almost anyone more than you. I fancy Mr Blackwell more than you. Even with his beard.

'Nonsense,' said Tom, 'I know about parrots. This one's a lady and she only likes men. It's not just Rob, she prefers men. Parrots are often like that.'

'Typical,' said Anemone, 'a sexist parrot. It's supposed to be a male. It's supposed to be called Mordecai.'

'You could always rename it Maureen,' said Tom cheerily, 'although I admit it lacks a certain biblical quality.'

Fergus glared. 'Mordecai doesn't know she's got a boy's name. You can't change it now.'

'I don't know,' Daisy grinned teasingly. 'Maureen the parrot has a certain ring to it . . .'

Alice sighed. 'You know, you lot can feel free to go and do the other things at which you so excel,' she said pointedly, 'like squabbling, eavesdropping, making a mess . . .'

'That's OK,' said Fergus cheerfully, 'we'll stay and listen.'

'I too,' said Herman, beaming, 'if you don't mind.'

I suppose, thought Alice, in some ways it's easier to do this with them here.

When she offered him the partnership Tom seemed completely delighted.

'That's absolutely marvellous,' he said to Alice, shaking her hand, then standing and pacing as if consumed by an energy he had to release. 'I'd love to stay on with you. I'd hoped – I'd really hoped and planned to settle in Cambridge anyway. I'd made my mind up – I was going to stay here even if it meant trying to start up alone. Alice, I can't tell you how much I appreciate this. I'm sorry about James, of course – he had seemed a little tired lately, as you say. But I'm truly delighted to be offered the partnership. I won't let you down – and I've even got some ideas for where we could go with –'

'Tom – I'm glad you're pleased,' said Alice, interrupting awkwardly, feeling like the one who had to spoil the party when he was just so pleased, 'but there is still the problem that there may not be a practice for you to join. We may have nowhere to go.'

'Well,' said Tom, 'it would, as you know, be very difficult for Roland to evict us.'

'I couldn't bear to stay,' said Alice. 'The man makes Sidney the Evil Mollusc look like Mother Teresa.'

Anemone stifled a laugh. 'Sidney the what?'

'Evil Mollusc,' said Alice. 'Fergus invented him in a comic strip he wrote a couple of years ago. Don't you remember?'

'He was a giant land snail,' said Fergus crossly, 'and I didn't invent him, I brought him home from school.'

Alice shrugged. 'Well, it's the way I think of Roland. He bought me knickers, you know.'

'Oh dear,' said Anemone, 'I can see that would be a problem from a land snail.'

'It's certainly a problem from Roland,' said Tom. 'Unsolicited knickers are pretty heavy, I'd say.' She glanced at him suspiciously, but he was not smiling. 'You know, Alice, that could be considered sexual harassment. A well-worded solicitor's letter might give him a scare.'

But Alice shook her head. 'No. Much as I detest him I couldn't do that, it's too . . . sordid.'

'He's not worth the hassle anyway,' said Anemone, adjusting her beads delicately. 'It would be letting him know he's got to you.'

'I know,' Alice sighed, 'although I just can't bear to let him beat me either.'

'Listen, Alice, I have an idea about this.' Tom spoke carefully. 'It's an idea I've had for a while. I've been trying to talk to you about it, actually, but the time was never right.'

'An idea? Go on then.'

'Well, it's . . . In fact, instead of telling you, why don't I show you?' He was suddenly full of energy and cheer. 'We can go in my car.'

'I don't really think I've got the –'

'Come on, before you shout me down I'd like you to see this. Actually, I'd like you all to come with me and see it –'

'Even me?' asked Herman, surprised.

'Of course,' said Tom. 'Partnership is like marriage, you know. You take on the relatives.'

'But I'm not a . . .' began Herman, then followed them out anyway. It had to be more interesting than driving round and round the same circuit of his brain worrying about the whereabouts of his frog.

*

Central Cambridge was moderately busy, even though it was Sunday. Teenagers strolled in the sunshine, eating burgers and eyeing up teenagers of the opposite sex, ignoring anyone over twenty and wondering how they could possibly cram all the living they needed to do into the next few years before they passed twenty themselves and became unutterably sad and past it. A variety of bells tolled for one or other of the two reasons that Cambridge bells toll – some in an attempt to remind people either of precisely why it was that one or two shops were closed and there was less traffic, but most to remind people which college was about to serve lunch.

'Great,' said Anemone when they got to Parker's Piece and headed along the path to the Pavilion with its giant posters outside.

'"Exhibition",' read Herman on one of them. '"Commerce as art in the twentieth century, from ice-cream kiosk to candy-floss stall." Have we come here for lunch?'

'It's an art exhibition,' said Anemone, excited. 'I went with my art class. It's caused a bit of a fuss – but I think it's great.'

Alice was puzzled. 'Why have you brought us here?'

But Tom smiled mysteriously and annoyingly, and Alice bit her lip to stop herself from kicking his shins.

Parker's Piece was looking lovely in the summer sunshine. The grass was green and had just been mown, and all over it people lay, stood, sat, played, threw balls, cycled . . . Near to Alice a small Chinese child, dressed in what appeared to be half a duvet, ran to her father and was swung joyously into the air. A few yards away an elderly couple held hands and strolled towards the big Victorian lamp at the centre where the footpaths crossed. On a park bench a young couple kissed frantically and closely, apparently in the mistaken belief that this would disguise the fact that his hand was inside her shirt. Over to one side

341

the beautiful façade of the University Arms Hotel gazed across the grass proudly . . . and in front of it a group of students played five-a-side beach ball. Straight ahead of them stood the Pavilion, one-time cricket pavilion that the great Hobbs went out from to bat, now art gallery and host to the controversial ice-cream kiosk exhibition.

'Is this where we're going? The Pavilion?'

'Absolutely,' said Tom, smiling that mysterious smile. 'I think you need to see inside.'

Anemone was enthusiastic. 'I've been trying to get Mum to come to this. It's brilliant – it says so much about the way commercial art has replaced actual art in the collective consciousness without us even being aware of it. It's the ultimate in the use of the mundane to express the sublime. It's supposed to be about – What are you staring at?'

'You. You do talk cobblers in A level art,' said Fergus, 'doesn't she, Mum?'

'That is an interesting expression,' said Herman before Anemone could rise to it, 'talking cobblers. Where I come from the cobbler is a –'

Alice frowned. 'Look, Tom, if you are trying to deliver some really deep message – something to do with the idea that if you can have an ice-cream kiosk in the Pavilion then you can have a surgery anywhere, even under the broccoli counter in Sainsbury's, then you can just say it. We don't have to pay to go in.'

'I thought that's what they were doing now,' said Daisy, 'having doctors in Sainsbury's next to the broccoli. I'm sure it was on the news.'

Alice shrugged. 'I'm not about to take up my stethoscope next to any pile of vegetables, thank you very much. Tom, why don't you just tell me what the point is?'

But Tom looked annoyingly mysterious. 'Just come and look around the exhibition. Then I promise I'll explain.'

The Pavilion looked from the outside like just what it was, a place where men in white trousers once came to eat Victoria sponge in the middle of long tests of English endurance involving the crack of leather on willow, whilst their wives battled grimly and furiously for the right to butter the sandwiches. It had not been a cricket pavilion for many years, however, despite the testaments to Hobbs' best innings which lined the walls, and for the last year or so it had been a rather peculiar art gallery, the sort that everyone knows about but no one much goes into.

Tom spoke quietly to the semi-comatose girl at the door, who seemed oddly happy that they shouldn't pay, and they tripped in through the vestibule into a large airy frontal space, with a number of doors leading off. The feel of the whole building was faintly Swedish and yet faintly traditional Tudor. It boasted a glass roof, which gave it a feeling of freshness, and some rather Habitatish leather sofas elegantly arranged around the edge. In the centre, defiant in its incongruity, stood an ice-cream kiosk, the sort that would once have been towed around by a small Italian man on a bicycle but is now more often attached to the back of a Daewoo and used to annoy commuters. Beside it stood a fully fledged ice-cream van, the sort that play 'Greensleeves' so loudly that they sound as one would imagine Evelyn Glennie would sound if playing whilst under the influence of a banned substance. The ice-cream machine was whirring appetisingly. It was, said its entire demeanour, not an ice-cream kiosk but art.

Fergus was the first to approach the kiosk, which stood alone and unaccompanied, like something left behind when everything else had gone.

'I'll have a Ninety-nine, please,' he said to the van, cheerily and with flamboyant cleverness. 'With two flakes.' This, he felt, completed the tableau. But to all of their astonishment, a gloomy Italian man arose from his hiding place down inside the kiosk and handed Fergus an orange lolly.

Fergus stared. 'This isn't what I asked for.'

'This is art, mate,' said the Italian who, despite possessing a black and very continental moustache, sounded as though he had grown up on the Isle of Dogs. 'Think yourself lucky it ain't plastic,' and he disappeared again into the bowels of his machine.

'Well,' said Tom, 'what do you think?'

Anemone sighed. 'I keep telling you all – I think it's fabulous.'

Alice raised one eyebrow. 'You're doing A level art – you don't count.'

'It's very nice, if you ask me,' said Fergus, 'for an ice-cream kiosk.'

Daisy frowned, not wanting to admit ignorance about art but quite unable to see where art came into it. 'No one is asking you. Anyhow, what's the point? I mean, where is it art?'

'You'll start her off,' said Fergus warningly, but too late.

Anemone waved her arms expressively. 'Don't you see, it's working art, it's functional. It's supposed to be about the small pleasures that slip into the greyness of ordinary lives and transport us momentarily, purely through func-tionality, into the realms of kings and giants. About useful art, art in what's around us, in utility . . .'

'You've been reading the programme,' said Fergus.

Herman smiled. 'In Armenia if something is in a gold frame and hanging on a wall we call it art, if it comes in an ice-cream kiosk and hands out ice pops we call it an ice-cream van.'

Fergus shrugged. 'You can't expect sanity from a girl who's turned her hair into a weapon for braining flies.'

Anemone turned her back on him pointedly and rattled her plaits.

Alice turned to Tom. 'It's very . . . interesting . . . but I still don't see why we're here. I mean, are you suggesting we should try and buy somewhere like this, or are you trying to say that all sorts of odd things fit into all sorts of odd buildings?'

'Interesting? Is that really what you think?' He flashed his teeth and she wondered absently if they were really that white or if it was an optical illusion caused by his tan. She sighed.

'Look, to be truly honest, Tom, I think it's daft.'

'Exactly,' said Tom, 'it's daft. Absolutely potty – and not making any money. Not even enough money to pay the rent for the last three months, so the exhibition is finally closing. Which is why we don't need to buy somewhere like this. You see, the whole point is that this is all mine already.'

'What?' Alice was mystified. 'You mean you've bought the ice-cream kiosk?'

'No,' said Tom, 'I mean I own the Pavilion. This building. It's mine. I own it.'

'You own it?' Alice wasn't sure where he was leading. 'Are you saying you own other properties in Cambridge?'

'No,' Tom spread his hands, 'just this one – which is why I think it would make a marvellous surgery.'

Alice stared. What a crazy idea – turning an art gallery into a surgery. 'I . . .' He was serious. He was waiting for her to say something. 'It would cost a fortune to convert it. It would never . . .' She stared at the domed roof, suddenly taken aback by a vision of this as the central reception area, complete with Tabitha Tinkler being forklifted out of one of those sofas and Mr Sykes and his blue suede shoes doing the full concert Elvis in the far corner. She shook her head. 'It would need planning permission, a lot of converting, new equipment . . .'

'We'd get a grant towards it from the Health Authority, get a loan for the rest – just as if we were building a new surgery. The meeting I went to the other week – they're desperate for someone else to set up in the centre of town. I sounded them out. I've wanted to tell you for a while but the time was never right and I was afraid you'd think I was

345

trying to push you into a corner over partnership. Alice, they promise me that planning permission could be rushed through. We could be in here in under a month. Come on.' He took her hands and, just for a moment, she could almost see the attraction. Heaven help Martha . . . 'We can do this, make a go of it here. I know we can.'

The children were buzzing.

'Wow. This is really cool. You must say yes, Mum, it's a brilliant idea.'

'I think it's a real shame that most people are too ill-educated to appreciate modern art – but if the exhibition is finished anyway . . .'

'He's right, it's a brilliant idea. You know you could do it.' That was Daisy in her right ear. 'Just think, Mum, you'd be right in the middle of town.'

Alice smiled drily. 'So if I had a sudden urge to rush out and buy Doc Martens, or needed to remedy an acute shortage of cash for pocket money I could easily relieve them between patients.'

Daisy shrugged. 'I just meant it would be convenient.'

'It's got great feng shui,' pronounced Anemone, pacing the floor wisely, 'even without fish.'

'Gosh – no fish? Still, I expect we have to replace the lavatories with holes in the ground. I'm sure the patients would dig their own when they understood it would prevent their energy seeping away via their bottoms.' Alice looked around the building again, playing for time, trying to picture it emptied of ice-cream vans and filled instead with smiling NHS staff dispensing sympathy, wisdom and penicillin . . . Well, no, actually with Jean gazing dolefully out of the window and Lisa sending patients round the bend through sheer dippiness. It was a mad idea.

'Ah, Alice, you are such a doubter,' said Herman, gazing dreamily at the walls. 'This is a wonderful building. You could exhibit art around the walls. Perhaps this is the boost you need.'

'That's it. You need a boost, Mum.' Daisy was enthusiastic. 'It would make a change.'

Alice tried to glare at all of them, not wanting her glowing spark of enthusiasm to be visible until she was sure it was not about to be extinguished. 'How do you know what boost I need? You know, if I could have two minutes' peace in order to link my ears to my brain, I could discuss this with Tom and come to a meaningful conclusion,' she frowned. 'So in the meantime can I suggest you all buy an orange lolly from Luigi Desperado here and take it outside onto the grass?'

Tom watched them as they grumbled out. 'It's what the practice needs, Alice – it's a site, a central site – and it would be the cheapest option by far.'

'It's quite a leap of faith to see this place as a surgery. And to find out it's yours . . .' she was aware of a rising excitement, 'golly, I'd been thinking about renting somewhere. I never imagined we could own our own premises. But it could be perfect. Are you sure you'd want to let us convert it? I mean, the commercial rent on a property like this just as it is must be astronomical. You could turn it into almost anything that would make more money than a doctor's surgery. Alternative therapies, for instance. People could come here to have their cellulite massaged away with extract of Uruguayan sloth milk and have giant Japanese women walking up and down their spines for pleasure. You'd be giving that up for – well, you know the financial restraints on the NHS. After expenses you'd be lucky to see tuppence and all the free scratchy toilet roll you can carry.'

Tom shrugged. 'No matter. This would be for my benefit. Alice, I'm not just being an altruist – I want to stay here. Cambridge has – everything I'm looking for.'

Oh God, thought Alice, with dawning trepidation, you're in love. It's happened already – and I know it's all bound to go wrong for you.

'Tom, what if –'

347

But he interrupted: 'Alice, this would be my investment in our shared future. And besides,' he gestured towards the ice-cream kiosk where the sullen Italian now lolled with a Cornetto, 'my venture into the world of art hasn't exactly been a huge success.'

'Oh, I don't know . . .' Alice eyed the Italian with amusement. 'It certainly beats the exhibition of chastity belts they had last year in the museum of local life hands down. Used chastity belts, they were, and all rusty on the crotch.'

Tom sighed. 'It may be different. But it's still gone bust. They haven't paid their rent for months. We tried to come to some sort of agreement – I've had my lawyer on the case for weeks – but the backers have now disappeared, taking various people's money with them so there's no hope there. The artist will have to find somewhere else to put his work.'

Alice eyed the kiosk wistfully. 'If all else fails he could always set it up on Hunstanton beach. It would probably do rather better.'

'So – what do you say?'

They found the children and Herman outside eating lollies and watching the world go by.

'Well?' demanded Daisy as soon as Alice and Tom emerged. 'Are you going to do it?'

'Yes! I mean there are things to sort out . . . and I'll have to ask Ian when he gets back . . . but, well, YES!'

I hardly dare hope this will work out, she thought. And what if Tom changes his mind? After Martha's inevitable rejection will he still want to stay?

But caught up in the cheering and general delight of her children and an elderly man from Armenia to whom it all seemed actually to matter, how could she say no? It was a way out. It was an answer!

If only things could work out for Tom and Martha too. Alice was sure that when she next saw him Martha would have done it, would have cut off the buds of their relationship before they could flower. How defeatist, and how sad. At least she and Rob had tried. Well, she had tried. Perhaps he had too.

And right now she needed to think herself, and she needed to talk. To Ian. And to Rob. The urge to talk to Rob grabbed her suddenly.

'Look, I've got a couple of things to do before I get back. I'll see you all at home. Anemone, could you put some potatoes on for supper?'

None of them noticed Colin Blackwell cycling across Parker's Piece, but he noticed them. How could he not notice Alice? The most beautiful woman in Cambridge? She doesn't even see me, he thought, ignoring the fact that he had shot past at fifteen miles an hour and she had been looking the other way. He was inclined to think meta-phorically. If she doesn't see me, he thought with sudden resolution, then I must take drastic action and change myself to make certain that she does.

Despite being included in so much family banter, despite being dragged across Cambridge to look at ice-cream kiosks and being involved in police raids on elderly ladies with peacock-phobia, Herman Banescu was quite glum. He had lost the ring. He had callously and carelessly stuffed it into a china money box. He sat at Alice's kitchen table and hung his head into a mug of tea.

Anemone watched him with anxious eyes. 'Mr Banescu, is there anything we can do to help?'

Herman sighed. 'I don't think so. I have messed up. I'm completely useless.'

'Oh, I wouldn't say that,' said Anemone, determined to cheer him up. 'You can peel potatoes, and you're quite good at standing in the background chuckling. Come on – I need some help.'

But Herman would not be consoled. 'I should never have come . . .'

349

Anemone sighed. 'You were keeping a promise. If you hadn't then Tabitha would never have known that your uncle had always loved her.'

Herman shrugged. 'I could have written to her. It wouldn't have made any difference.'

'But it would. You made a promise.'

Herman sighed. 'I have let him down . . .'

'Guess what.' Fergus burst into the kitchen, full of excitement. 'You'll never guess.'

Anemone looked unimpressed. 'So why don't you tell us, then?'

Fergus was not deflated. 'Fred Ramsden and Tabitha Tinkler are going to get married. Don't you think that's brilliant?'

Anemone frowned. 'I suppose so. Don't you think they're a bit old?'

'That's ageist,' said Fergus, 'and anyway, Mr Blackwell says in this millennium people will live to be a hundred and twenty.'

'If I hear once more that Fred is nine hundred and ninety-nine and pays his nursing home fees by turning compost into gold then I think I'll vomit,' said Anemone darkly.

Fergus shrugged. 'Please yourself. Where's Mum?'

'Gone for a drive,' said Anemone, using the family metaphor for Mum having gone to the churchyard, and Fergus nodded sagely.

'Well,' said Herman, who now had tears in his eyes, 'it certainly alters my perspective. After all, what is a lost metal ring compared to human love?'

Anemone peered at him curiously. 'Why are you sad?'

'I am not sad, I am an Armenian.'

'And that makes you cry?'

'No,' said Herman indignantly, 'it makes me emotional. It makes me passionate. It's a wonderful thing when two people are in love.'

'I suppose it is,' said Anemone, who had always thought

that romantic life ended at the age of twenty-nine. Wow, she thought suddenly, think of all the extra years I've got to play with. Come to think of it, even Mum is actually barely out of nappies when it comes to love. She'd never bring a new bloke back to Fox Colne, though. Imagine bringing a new date to Dad's old house . . .

'Well, I think it's soppy,' said Fergus, unable to contemplate the thought of his friend Fred betraying their brotherhood by marrying some floozie.

'Just wait, Fergus Vane. In a year from now you'll be sighing around the kitchen because some spotty girl has snogged you behind the bike sheds.'

'I will not.'

Herman stood up. 'Well, you know, I think it's time for me to go home.'

'Oh no, don't.' Daisy came into the kitchen just in time to catch the end of the conversation. 'At least stay till tomorrow. It's the bed race tomorrow. You wouldn't want to miss that.'

'The bed race? You English are very strange. Why do you race in beds?'

'It's for charity,' said Anemone, 'one of Cambridge's annual peculiarities – but this year Daisy has a starring role.'

Herman shrugged lightly. 'Ah well, I suppose it won't hurt. And it may be for the best – I have just read my horoscope in this medical magazine. I do not usually read horoscopes, but I was led into the magazine by a very interesting piece on prostate glands. The stars say that if I travel too quickly on Monday I will damage my nose irretrievably. Do you read your horoscope?'

'Generally,' said Daisy, 'I make a point of not.'

Alice, a few miles away in the churchyard at Fox Colne, listened to her own voice echoing round and round in her head. The Pavilion. Her and Tom and Ian, carrying on together. A new start. Until now she had wandered along an easy path without Rob. He had not been with her, but he had been only just over a hill, just out of sight. Now she was going to step away and leave him behind for ever. It would all be completely different, and she needed to tell him.

But I still can't believe any of it has happened, she thought. 'It was so unlike you, Rob,' she told the grave disconsolately. 'I thought I knew you so very well.'

Beside her Rob's hebes rustled, thick and comfortable, passing no comment she could discern, and she plucked a white flower idly and counted its tiny petals.

Love you, love you not, love you, love you not . . . She dropped it before she could finish, but not before she could see that the hebe would conclude that she loved Rob. Which Rob? The one she thought she knew, or the one he really was?

'Why do I feel like this?' she asked Rob's grave. 'Why can't I forgive you? Even now, when I came to say a sort of goodbye?' She sat wearily on the grass beside his grave, and something crinkled in her back pocket. It was the letter Tom had found in the letterbox. She eased it out. Rob wasn't going anywhere for a minute – so she might just as well read it. Doubtless it was some note from a patient wittering on about the lack of interest the entire medical profession was showing in their bunions . . .

She opened it, did not recognise the handwriting, read it – and reread it – with dawning shock, a twist of the gut . . . *Oh my God, it's from Marcie Crombie!*

'Dear Dr Vane,

I have wanted to speak to you for a long time but, as you know, I have made many visits to you about trivia without plucking up the courage to speak. So after so long I've decided to write a letter, the coward's way. You see, I'm not the person you believe me to be. For a regrettable and ultimately tragic part of my working life I was known as Marcie Crombie, and I was with your husband, Rob, when he died. I thought I could put it behind me – but my past is a recurring dream. I realise you may not wish to talk to me, but I do think it could help us both. If you would agree to meet me please leave a message on my answerphone and we could perhaps have a coffee together at the Angel Hotel.

Yours sincerely, Heather Bunberry.

Alice stared as around her the world stopped rotating completely and much of what she had believed flew off it and was lost, hurtling into deep space. Heather Bunberry, Marcie Crombie. How did you get from one to the other? It wasn't an anagram. They didn't rhyme. What on earth does she want to see me for? Alice asked herself. Do I want to see her? Oh God, I did her smear for her. How could she deceive me into thinking . . .?

This was a message from Rob, wasn't it? This was a sign. She had been sitting here, wondering again how he could have done it, who he really was – and in her pocket, all along, was a letter from a woman who might be able to answer the question.

Should she go and meet her? It would be madness for the old Alice to go, madness for the new Alice not to.

'What do you think?' she asked Rob. 'Do you think knowledge is power? I have to find out what the hell you were doing, Rob, because I'd have bet my life you weren't that sort of man.'

There was no answer from Rob, so Alice called in on Martha, but Martha was lost in crises of her own.

'You've really done it?' Alice was surprised when she saw her, even though she had half-expected it. 'You've finished it over something that trivial? You're mad.'

Martha drained her wine and poured more. 'Snoring is never trivial. It's when you start thinking it is that you're in trouble.' It was seven hours since she had left the answering machine message for Tom, and he had still not replied. She

353

didn't know what she wanted him to do. To come striding in and make love to her one more time? To leave the country? To sleep with someone else and prove himself a callous bastard? This would be much easier if he were a callous bastard, because she wouldn't be hurt, she would be relieved. She wouldn't have to feel responsible for the way he was feeling, to worry about causing him pain. Did she feel his pain as if it were her own? Of course not. What rot. 'I can't bear snoring. They never snore the first time. It's if you let them back into your bed that it starts.'

Alice sighed and stared out of Martha's window, towards Fox Colne church. 'Are you saying you've never been in a relationship where you've tolerated anything? Toilet seats left up, *Match of the Day* – any of it?'

Martha shrugged. 'There's nothing in that sort of relationship that I need. I choose to be selfish, and that's my choice so it's fine. I've never misled anyone.'

'But you do,' said Alice, looking at her tearful cheeks. Only Martha could cry like a china doll, of course, with perfect round tears falling evenly and gloriously, leaving her eyes unreddened and her skin unflushed – but they were, nevertheless, real tears. 'You do mislead, you misled Tom by so obviously falling in love with him when you'd already decided it wasn't to be allowed. People think you're playing by the rules. Look at you. You're obviously in love with this man. Head over heels – and literally. You virtually can't stay upright in his presence. You're a graceful woman with more poise than the entire Royal Ballet but when he's in the room you turn into Coco the Clown. It just goes to show,' an edge of sadness crept into her voice, 'love makes clowns out of all of us.'

Martha leaped to her feet and started to pace, agitated. 'Oh, now you've done it, now you've said it. That word. You're putting it into my head. Of course I'm not in love with him. How could I possibly be in love with him?'

'Chemistry?' Alice sipped her wine and watched Martha

354

through narrowed eyes. 'Emotion? You fell into it, Martha, I watched it happen. It was completely outside your control and that's what you can't handle.'

'That's rubbish.' Martha was vehement. 'I knew exactly what I was doing. I'll admit I did feel a . . . a particularly compelling attraction . . . but I –'

'Lust,' said Alice, 'that was obvious.'

'Lust, then – but that's not nearly the same as love. I've felt masses of lust. If lust was ageing I'd be a hundred and six by now. But it was never love – you have to be willing to fall in love for it to happen to you. That's why so many people fall in love between the ages of sixteen and twenty-two – that's the age when you're open to it. If you haven't by then, you realise how unsafe it is and you become cautious – you don't let it happen. It can't happen if you don't let it.'

'Rot,' said Alice. 'You fell in love. I can see it, everyone else can see it.'

'What do you know?' Martha was frightened now, needing to convince Alice in order to convince herself. 'You've only been in love once and it must have been because you wanted to be, because you still love him now, even when he's destroyed you, don't you?'

Alice frowned. 'I . . .' tears started to her eyes, 'I don't love him in the same way as before. I don't know if you can still love someone the same way when they turn out to be not the person you thought they were, but I know you can't love them in the same way when they're dead. And he hasn't destroyed me. I'm not destroyed.'

Martha bit her lip. 'I'm sorry – I didn't mean that. I just – This was nothing like you and Rob. We hardly spoke, Tom and I. We were just like a couple of teenagers, couldn't keep our hands off each other.'

'Rob and I really were a couple of teenagers,' said Alice, 'when we met. You know, I don't really know what happened to that.'

Martha lit a cigarette. 'My mother loved my father long

after he was dead. Even though he'd left her years and years earlier. She never stopped loving him. It was the biggest, most complete waste of emotional energy I've ever seen, will ever see. All her capacity for anything else left her when he did, and she never picked it up again, not even after he had moved to Kansas with a bimbo named Lola. It finished her.'

Alice stared at her friend, trying to imagine what it must have been like growing up with that. Eventually she said, 'Love is something interactive. I can love Rob the way he was, but I don't think it can go on and on. Not in the way you mean. You can't properly love someone who's gone – you can only love the way they were, the way it was with them.'

'Well,' Martha stubbed the cigarette out decisively, 'it's done now. It's over. Finished. Done. Look, I'm glad Tom's accepted your partnership. I'll just have to hope he's going to be civilised about things, that's all.'

'It's your life,' Alice sighed. She had wanted to ask Martha what she thought about the Marcie Crombie thing, but she could hardly do that in the middle of this sort of crisis. 'I hope Tom will still stay,' she mused aloud.

'Well, thank you very much.' Martha tried to turn her distress into resentment. 'Not that I expect loyalty . . .'

'Oh, don't be ridiculous,' said Alice crossly. 'You know full well why I hope he stays. He can save the practice. With the Pavilion we've got a real chance of making a go of it.'

Martha sniffed. 'Well, don't expect me to stay a patient.' She was aloof now. Alice had seen it before when men came into her shop to buy négligés for their wives, then made inappropriate jokes about the probable colour of Martha's smalls. She left, exasperated.

But as she drove home she wondered about her own life, about the twenty-year-old Rob and Alice who had seemed to be growing together so very convincingly and yet had finished up so very far apart. Did Marcie Crombie hold the answer to the question that had burned her for so long? It was time she confronted the side of Rob which must have existed but which she had clearly always refused to see. Time she found out exactly what had gone wrong with her own marriage. If only, she thought, I could be sure I can deal with the answer.

As Alice made her decision Colin Blackwell acted upon his. He had turned up his recording of Jacqueline du Pré playing the Elgar in honour of the moment, for he was a passionate man. He faced himself in the mirror and took a deep breath, and he said a mental goodbye to the man reflected before him. Not a bad-looking fellow . . . not Chippendale material, it was true, but then, he was a history teacher not a stripper. Well, apart from that one time when he was a student and desperate for the cash, but he had kept a firm grip on the policeman's hat, which had done an admirable job in covering his embarrassment. He raised his hand, razor drawn, and bit by bit, stroke by stroke, hair by hair, his beard dropped into the bathroom sink and was sent hurtling by the force of the cold mains into the dark and ancient sewers of Cambridge. Women never trust men with beards, isn't that true? Except Santa Claus, of course. But then, he thought sorrowfully, some things in life will always be inexplicable.

Well, this was a big move – but, by crikey, the woman was a goddess. His Cleopatra, his Helen of Troy, the face that had surely launched a thousand hearts if his was anything to go by . . . and somewhere under this lot he was sure there was a reasonably prepossessing face.

Slowly, in front of him a brand-new Colin Blackwell emerged, phoenix-like, from the growth which had for so long overshadowed him. On CD Jacqueline's Stradivarius wept, but he smiled. Today was the beginning of the new him. Just wait till she saw him.

Chapter Seventeen

Alice let herself in for the bank holiday surgery on the morning of the bed race. Bank holiday surgeries are, thankfully, usually brief, and it was nice to be in the building secure in the knowledge that Roland would not be there.

Someone was there, though. She found Tom Lovejoy in reception, staring with glazed eyes at a full double page of illustrated skin diseases which he had clearly pulled out of one of the weekly journals, and looking like a man who has had an overnight acquaintance with a whisky bottle and has come off rather worse. Oh dear, she thought. Poor Tom.

'Tom? Are you OK?'

'Alice.' He started, attempted to sound light-hearted, but was far too obvious about it. 'I'm fine, really. Just catching up on some bullous diseases of the skin. As you do when you've been dumped by your dream woman, really.'

'Tom, I'm so sorry. For what it's worth, Martha divides her men very strictly into lovers and friends. She's never been one to settle in a relationship.'

He smiled bitterly. 'Not for more than a few hours, it seems. Don't worry about me, Alice, I'm a grown-up. I'll get over it.'

Will you? she thought. I never did – at least, not till now. What does that make me?

'What are you doing here? It's my duty day.'

'I knew Daisy was in the bed race, so I thought I'd come and help you with surgery, get you away on time.'

'That's really kind, but you should go home, Tom,' she

358

said, 'you really don't look well. I'll be fine.'

He shook his head. 'Got some work to do. I'll be in my room. This changes nothing, Alice. I'm with you and Ian, forging ahead. Don't worry.'

'Oh, Tom, that's wonderful to hear, but I . . .'

'Hm?'

'For what it's worth – about Martha. I think she's a fool. I only hope she realises it herself.'

Predictably, since it was an emergency surgery and therefore intended for dealing with only the direst of physical ailments, Alice saw a string of the worried well followed by the Pembertons, who could be better categorised as the outraged well.

There are, Alice felt, a variety of diseases unique to bank holiday surgeries. These include non-specific unwellness, a condition of those who don't like the thought of their jobs very much, and tickle of the throat, a condition which causes no suffering at all but huge anxiety on the grounds that it might turn into a cold before Tuesday. More annoying even, though, than either of these two, are emergency nits. Believed by parents to be bigger and more voracious that normal nits, these require emergency niticide lest the entire brain be leeched through the skull before routine surgery hours. Parents of children with emergency nits cannot wait till Tuesday – indeed they often cannot even wait until morning. This morning's infested family were the Pembertons from Madingley who were, Alice felt, the sort of people who would have been in the first lifeboats off *Titanic*. They took half an hour of her time, during which they demanded an overview of the entire life-cycle of the head louse and its place in Darwinian evolution.

When she finished surgery shortly afterwards, having pretended to believe a man who claimed to have given up smoking ten months ago and yet still contrived to smell like a packet of Rothmans because it was easier than disagreeing with him, Tom had gone, leaving a note saying, 'Gone to meet MP re planning permission. See you at the bed race.'

On a bank holiday? He must have won Sarah over at that meeting he went to. He was actually a jolly useful person to have about. The fact that he was so very like Rob couldn't count against him. You can't give up on everything just because one thing doesn't work out.

She had one other thing to do – had decided to do it from here and not from home. Alice dialled a Bury St Edmunds number using the telephone in reception. It was an answering machine – she waited for the beep.

'Alice Vane here. I'll meet you for coffee at the Angel at ten o'clock tomorrow.'

She'd done it now – and she'd better get her skates on and go back into town. It was nearly time for the bed race.

The central Cambridge streets are for the most part closed to traffic. Only Kings Parade usually admits cars, for reasons known only to the town planners (and since they spend most of their time twinning themselves with a selection of European cities known as much for the quality of their beer as for the merits of their civic administration they are rarely around to explain themselves). Kings Parade is therefore a place of lost Frenchmen trying to turn their Citroëns round, and of huge swathes of Japanese tourists staring upwards at the dreaming spires of King's College chapel whilst simultaneously contriving to be photographed in front of a college porter. But today it was instead the scene of the bed race.

The bed race circuit was scheduled to begin at ten on the cobbles beside Great St Mary's, the University church, which charges tourists several pounds in order to give them vertigo and angina by coaxing them up its tower. From college gateways all over the city the beds entering the contest were beginning their progression to the starting line. Beside the Senate House a large gang of first-aiders were officiously practising their head-bandaging techniques on one another so that the end result resembled a South Korean field hospital after a deranged surgical nurse has gone crazy with a roll of crepe bandage.

Outside Great St Mary's a crowd was gathering, and by the time Alice had managed to make her way to the first-aid post the beds were beginning to arrive to an enthusiastic reception. Most were more go-karts than beds, in truth, but with such an array of handsome and burly young men pushing them no one was about to complain.

Alice made herself known to the first-aiders just as the St Alupent's School bed arrived at the start post. There, on the mattress, at the helm, sat Daisy, clear-eyed and proud, crash helmet riveted to her head, but otherwise dressed from head to toe as a belly-dancer. She was a vision of excited prettiness in her red helmet, her long blonde hair artfully arranged to cascade out beneath it and across her shoulders for the benefit (she had written in her diary) of everyone who was observing and who should happen to like hair, and not particularly for that of Mark Blackwell.

Alice felt a lump in her chest. What would Rob say now? Would he be proud? Or would he want to thump that tall handsome teenager pushing the bed and devouring Daisy with his eyes?

And blow me down, if that wasn't Mr Blackwell waving at her from one of the back bedposts. Mr Blackwell *sans* beard. Extraordinarily, from what she could see from here he had proved rather handsome beneath the fuzz; a manly chin. Enough, woman. Just think body chocolate – that should do it. You've got quite enough on your plate already.

The crowds were four abreast along Kings Parade as more beds arrived. There were a few interested tourists even though it was out of season (as far as it ever is out of season for tourists in Cambridge, which is not very far). On the other side of the cobbles, next to the Senate House, Alice saw Tabitha Tinkler, holding hands with Fred. Now wasn't that nice . . .

It was a bright, warm day. A silver sun half peered out from behind a scudding white cirrus, as the Great St Mary's clock struck three-quarters. The crowd stirred restively and Alice spotted Fergus over by Ryder & Amies with a St Alupent's School scarf and a crowd of dangerous-looking schoolboys much like himself. He looked immersed, belonging, and she was suddenly filled with pride in him, in all of them, struck by how well they were all doing, really, without Rob. How well they would still be doing just as long as Daisy managed to remain whole today. Thank goodness she was wearing knee-pads – actually, together with the Doc Martens, they added a certain *je ne sais quoi* to the belly-dancer's outfit – kind of Turkish harem maid with attitude.

'We've done well in the start draw. We go off fifth this year. Far less potential for trouble, I'm sure,' said a voice at Alice's shoulder, and she turned to see the new, clean-shaven Colin Blackwell there.

'Oh goodness,' she said, to cover her sudden fluster at the proximity of the hitherto unseen chin, 'you've left your post.'

He beamed ruefully. 'A moment's reprieve. I came to see if you were happy with your doctor's walkie-talkie. And look, don't worry – I'll look after her.'

'I know you will.' Alice was really not sure what else to say to Mr Blackwell, for friends are one thing, teachers another, and she was not sure in which context he was presenting himself. She cleared her throat awkwardly as he took a deep breath. 'You've shaved . . .'

'Er – Alice – I wondered . . .' They had spoken together, and he flushed. 'You go first, please.'

'Oh,' said Alice, 'well, I was just saying that you've shaved.' She was conscious that Daisy was scanning the crowd for her. 'Was it – er – planned?' What a stupid question. It's not as if you can accidentally shave off your beard. Mind you, you could singe it in a school chemistry

362

lesson, or get it caught in an electric car window and thus render it tatty.

'Charity job,' said Colin Blackwell cheerfully, 'easier than leg waxing. Actually I'd forgotten I had a chin. Do you like it?'

Alice smiled. 'Er – well, yes. Yes, it's a very nice chin.' Actually, she thought, it *is* very nice; he looks a different man. Was it OK to say so without him thinking . . . ? I mean, it's not as if I'm flirting with him . . .

'I – look, er – Alice, I wondered if you'd like to –'

'Dr Vane!'

Alice swivelled to find Lisa at her side, Dean uneasily in tow like a Corfiote donkey under the midday sun. Lisa looked huge and Alice wondered again if she had lied about her due date.

'Lisa, Dean. Have you come to watch the highlight of the Cambridge calendar?'

Lisa grinned broadly. 'Ooh no, Dr Vane, we're looking for pompoms for the bridesmaids' shoes. There are so many shops open today, it's brilliant. Dean thinks I'm barmy, you know, but I told him we girls have to have pompoms. I expect it's our hormones, don't you?'

These last words were directed rather archly at Colin Blackwell, who so completely did not know how to reply that Alice could actually *see* him trying to will himself into a hole in the ground. She heard him choke slightly into where his beard used to be and mutter slightly desperately that indeed he did.

'Well, we must get on Dr Vane . . .' Lisa and Dean trailed off into the crowd, leaving the silence between Alice and Colin Blackwell somewhat warmer and more amused than before.

'I was just wondering –' he began again, but the five-minute race bell sounded, shrill and urgent, summoning him back to his post, and Alice watched him go with slight relief, glad not to have to decide how to reply to what must surely be another invitation. She wasn't sure that she wanted to say no – but then, she wasn't sure that she wanted to say yes either. Really, it was so much easier not to be asked. Just think body chocolate . . .

Just then Daisy caught sight of her and waved frantically. Alice waved back as the Great St Mary's church bed trundled up in the nick of time. Constructed out of a pair of old pews, it looked, Alice thought, as if it had needed a certain amount of heavenly intervention even to reach the start of the course, and could be expected to move at the pace of the church's modernisation.

'Hi there,' said Martha.

'Hello, how are you?' Alice peered at her.

Martha wore Ray-Bans behind which her eyes gave nothing away. She was, as always, impeccably dressed in Ralph Lauren's latest, a pale camel cashmere cardigan flung casually about her shoulders. Alice could detect no sign of sleeplessness, of regret, guilt, or enormous self-doubt. 'Fine. Are you nervous?'

She did seem tense, thought Alice. You couldn't see it behind the shades, but you sensed her eyes darting, checking, like Daisy's pet rabbit when it escaped under a car and pretended not to notice all the family trying to crawl like US marines under the exhaust pipe to catch it.

'No,' she said, 'terrified out of my mind. And I saw Tom this morning, by the way. He wasn't looking his best.'

'Oh,' said Martha. 'Look, don't start. It's done with. You know my rules.'

'I wasn't starting,' said Alice. 'Did you think I should?'

'Oh, don't start your tricky psychotherapy stuff with me. I had enough of it when you tried to stop me being scared of spiders.'

'It worked, didn't it?' asked Alice – perfectly reasonably, she thought.

Martha sighed and pushed her glasses back into her hair. Her eyes were tired. 'Only for little ones. I've absolutely no need to get accustomed to big ones – I absolutely don't want to want them near me.'

Alice smiled. 'Great oaks,' she said, 'from little acorns. Do you want to pop over this evening? You look as if you need a chat.'

'I – I might. Look.'

The police were waving an ambulance through to deliver the Addenbrooke's bed, a hospital model with four hearty-looking doctors in surgical gear ready to push it. They were almost certainly orthopaedic surgeons, Alice thought – all that pulling people's hips around gives them biceps to die for.

On the bed, glowing with smugness, sat Sister Annette Goodenough. Her boyfriend, Simon the psychiatrist, had nominated her as driver, and her name had been drawn second out of the nominees' ballot in the doctors' mess. (The gynaecology registrar's blow-up doll had been drawn first but declared marginally less able to steer than a woman and had therefore been disqualified.)

Annette was delighted at the decision, and delighted with Simon, to boot. Whoever had given her the idea that psychiatrists weren't sexy? Some of them were a little odd, it's true, but they did get to retire a few years early and there was bound to be lots of prestige in private work, counselling nutty pop stars and alcoholic socialites. Yes, a psychiatrist was quite a catch.

Annette wore a nurse's uniform and elbow pads – she planned to play to win. Triumph in the bed race, triumph in life, that was her motto. Her mascot was tightly taped to the bedhead. She was ready to compete. Simon Frobisher had interrupted his week's leave to come and watch, so she was determined to shine.

They were counting down to the start when Alice saw him. There he was, as plain as the nose on her face, fastened to the hospital bed with a roll of surgical tape: Mr Jeremy Fisher. Phoebe's frog. Her frog. Herman Banescu's frog.

There was no mistaking those peculiar bulging eyes – this was the frog which she had lent to Phoebe Hamilton in Addenbrooke's children's ward. She had found the lost frog!

She gripped Martha's arm tightly. 'Look, Martha.' But it was too late.

'GO!'

The beds surged forwards along Kings Parade with more heaving than you get when England play at Twickenham, and the crowd surged in behind them. Alice was left, impotently clutching her walkie-talkie, reflecting on a brief but disturbing impression of Colin Blackwell, his face clenched with determination, propelling the St Alupent's School bed forward towards victory. It was really rather stirring, in an odd sort of way.

Well, she thought, the race would take at least forty minutes. Mr Jeremy wasn't going anywhere unexpected. She would just have to make sure she got him back at the end.

The bed race was always a fast and furious event, and soon the beds were strung out with the Fawkes College bed in the lead and the Addenbrooke's bed close behind. Daisy, steering valiantly, was more or less in the middle of the fray. Mr Blackwell had long since dropped off his pushing post as the pushing teams worked in relay. The pushers now included his son, Mark, and Daisy was in her element.

'Come on, you girlie lot, give it some welly,' she roared indelicately, and Mark Blackwell – who knew a chat-up line when he heard one – decided he might just dare ask her for a date at the end of the line. Ahead, the leading beds fought with gloves off for supremacy.

For Alice it felt like for ever, even though the bed race is a fairly short event, as the wheels tend to fly off if anyone is expected to keep going for too long. There was, once Daisy disappeared beyond the crowd of onlookers hotly pursued by Mr Jeremy Fisher, a long, silent wait before the gradually mounting cheering told her that the circuit was nearly complete and the leading (and surviving) beds were on their way back.

For Daisy the excitement was almost unbearable. The intense competition between many of the colleges led them to attempt to nobble one another's beds in droves, but no one was mean or unchivalrous enough to try to nobble the school bed so Daisy was running in third place by default. She was going for a place! A series of clashes had left few others in the running. Even the sight of Fergus and his gang of form four thugs pulling faces at her outside the back entrance to Sidney Sussex could not take the wind out of her sails. Close behind her was Annette on the Addenbrooke's bed. She had thrown off the bounds of decency and was letting all the repressed feelings of years out at the junior doctors currently pushing her along. 'Call yourselves ortho-paedic surgeons?' she was shouting. 'I've seen better biceps on psychiatrists! I've seen more muscles on prawns. D'you want us to be beaten by a team of schoolboys?'

Behind them the Great St Mary's church bed, by dint of not having been involved in any foul play, was the next in line. The vicar had got off to mediate in an argument further back, and without having to sing psalms as they went they moved an awful lot quicker. It just went to show, they felt, that there are very good reasons for there being so few vicars driving in Formula One.

The race was drawing inexorably towards its climax when ahead of Daisy the Fawkes College driver leaned down and flung a metal pole into the wheel of the St Alupent's College bed, causing the wheel to fly off and sending it careering off line. Sadly for the villains, however, the runaway wheel tangled with their own and dispatched them ignominiously into a bollard next to the Round Church leaving Daisy and the St Alupent's School bed completely in the lead.

Daisy couldn't believe it. True, the hospital team were close behind and she could tell her pushers were flagging –

and even the strongest encouragement she could come up with would be nothing compared to the mouthful of abuse she could hear from that nurse behind them – but they were nevertheless in the lead. The roar of the crowd was about her ears, the taste of victory on her lips.

Mark Blackwell had rejoined the bed for the final lap, with his father on the other back post. They were sailing up Trinity Street now. She could hear Addenbrooke's behind.

'Faster!' Annette was shrieking. 'You brainless wimps!' The crowd were cheering, Daisy's heart was pounding . . . any minute now they would see the finishing post . . .

And then the wheels fell off the school bed.

It ground to a halt in the middle of Trinity Street, and Colin Blackwell barely had time to haul her off it before the Addenbrooke's bed, unable to slow in time, crashed heavily into the back of them and fell immediately to pieces. The china frog on the front smashed unnoticed to the ground as Annette Goodenough was flung by her makeshift seatbelt back against the bed frame, still shouting, 'Get out of the bloody way!'

Daisy began to cry.

Alice, twenty yards away, could not see what had happened through the surging crowd, but she knew something had happened from the way the cheering turned to 'Aah's. And no one appeared when they should. She pressed 'transmit' on her walkie-talkie.

'What's happening?'

'Crash . . . Trinity Street,' said the first-aider, the line crackling terribly, '. . . hurt.'

Oh God, thought Alice. Oh no. How many? Who? She picked up her medical bag and started to push through the mass of people – and then the crowd parted miraculously, and she saw them. Like something out of *Chariots of Fire* – which had been filmed on this very spot – there was Colin Blackwell running towards her, and he was carrying a helmeted belly dancer in boots. Daisy.

'Daisy!' Alice's heart was in her mouth. It must be serious. Was she breathing? Could she have . . . ? 'Is she OK? What happened?'

'Get out of the way, Mum!' shouted Daisy, and then Alice saw the other three, Mark Blackwell and the two sports teachers, carrying what remained of the bed between them, staggering towards the finish. Behind them the remains of the Addenbrooke's bed were being similarly gathered up, but as none of the orthopaedic surgeons had initially been prepared to carry Sister Annette Goodenough they had had to wait for her psychiatrist to rush up and load her onto his back. The Great St Mary's bed, trundling along behind, was closing fast . . .

But the end was very near and there was no passing anyone now. And so it was Daisy who won the bed race, Colin Blackwell carrying her triumphantly over the line and then dropping her back onto the mattress deposited by the rest of the team – upon which they all collapsed in a laughing heap. For the first time in the history of the bed race the St Alupent's School team had triumphed over the rest. It was all rather heroic.

And Alice, watching them all, watching Mr Blackwell in particular, thought: you actually are a maybe, without your beard. I could really consider . . . her heart fluttered oddly, a nervous fear which was not entirely pleasant, but not unpleasant either. Perhaps.

'Isn't that . . . ?' whispered Martha beside her, and Alice nodded.

'Oh,' said Martha, 'Alice. I do think you should say yes to him. He's rather yummy.'

Alice glared at her, suddenly irritated by the casual flirtatiousness, even though this was Martha being the way she always was. 'You,' Alice said suddenly, 'shouldn't even be looking. You've only just discarded Tom. You're not allowed to start on another one. Not even vicariously.'

Martha stared. 'I . . .' she began, then turned suddenly

369

and fled into the crowd. Alice stared after her guiltily, then thought, what am I feeling guilty about? My daughter's just won the Cambridge bed race and I've got to go and hug her.

She was about to go over to the winners when Herman appeared anxiously at her elbow. 'Did she win?' he asked cheerfully.

Alice clapped a hand over her mouth. 'Oh, Herman, I'm sorry. I forgot for a minute. I saw the frog – it's this way. Come on . . .'

And so, appropriately, it was Herman who found it, scrabbling amongst the bits of china in Kings Parade. It was wrapped in tissue, and he did not want to unwrap it. That task, he now felt, belonged to someone else . . .

Tabitha smiled when Herman gave her the ring. By then they were sitting on the low wall that runs along the front of King's College. Around them the remains of college beds were limping home. Daisy had been borne away victorious by Mark Blackwell and a crowd of his cricket chums, looking, as Anemone put it, slightly more smug than a very good actor playing an extremely smug person might look on a night when she happened to feel pretty smug anyway. Fergus and Anemone were still there, though, as were Fred and Herman, forming a small circle around Tabitha. Tourists bustled by, a pair of seagulls circled the spires of King's College chapel and cried about waves and the shortage of herrings. Alice wondered if they oughtn't to leave Tabitha alone, but she wouldn't have it.

'This is it,' said Herman. 'This is what my Uncle Tamas wanted me to bring to show you.'

'Go on, then,' said Fergus impatiently. 'Open it. It's come such a long way to see you.'

Tabitha opened the wrapping and they heard her sigh. It was a broad band of reddish gold, thick, and quite plain except for an engraving on the inside. She held it very gently, as if it might break.

'I remember it, of course. His mother's ring. Her name is inside it.' A tear welled up and ran down her cheek like dew on parchment. Fred produced a large hankie from his pocket and passed it to her silently. She squeezed his hand, dabbed and looked at Herman. 'He saved it for me.'

Herman nodded. 'He wanted me to bring it to you.'

A tear ran down her cheek. 'He offered it to me when we said goodbye, but I said he should save it for his wife and his daughters.'

'He kept it for you,' said Herman, and she smiled.

'Silly fools, we both were.' She fingered the ring. 'Keeping ourselves like toys never taken out of the box,' she pressed it back into Herman's hand, 'like those people on antique programmes who are so, so proud that the train set which they never unpacked is worth more than if they had taken it out of the package and loved it to bits. I am going to wear Fred's ring, Herman Banescu. I am indescribably grateful that you have brought me this gift, given me back my Tamas who I had thought for so long belonged to someone else – but now I give it back to you. Take it home now, and give it to your children. It should be theirs.'

Later, Tabitha and Fred ducked out of the mêlée and wandered away and down towards the river, where they decided to take a chauffeured punt along the Backs. Here the day was tranquil, the cry of a moorhen and the splash of water running down off the punt pole overriding more distant sounds of traffic and people, so that those became something you had to focus on in order to hear them at all. Here was the Cambridge of long ago, of Harold Abrahams and *Chariots of Fire*, of scented ladies sipping tea on the lawns and idle young men arguing the minutiae of the sonnets whilst stretched out long on the grass sipping Pimm's. Today's Cambridge was the very same, in part through mimicry and affectation, but most by genuinely not having changed very much at all. A smear of the new

371

millennium can do little to spoil the gleaming of the layered jewels of centuries.

The chauffeur, a tireless medical student named Max, steered the punt deftly between the unmanoeuvred tubs of tourists and students heading for the Bridge of Sighs. It was nice, he thought, to see an old couple who could still be as romantic with one another as if they were twenty.

'That was my college, you know,' said Fred, pointing at St Alupent's mellow façade as they drifted by. 'I was gardener there for years. I actually helped fix the gargoyle on that bridge.'

Tabitha smiled. 'I know. You're as old as the hills. Well, I can handle the age gap, even though my mother would have said you're far too old for me.'

'Quite,' said Fred, 'but you needn't worry. My pension will last me out, buy us a little house.'

'I know it will, you made pure gold out of peacock dung – you've told me.'

'Exactly.'

'As long as you're otherwise sane,' she said, 'I'm not complaining.'

He kissed her cheek. 'You're the nicest woman I've known, and I've known a few. Can't think why some fellow didn't snap you up.'

'Oh,' said Tabitha, 'well, I never allowed it, I suppose. Oh look. It's your friend Fergus . . . I think he wants us.'

Fergus was on the bridge waving. 'Fred, Miss Tinkler. Mum says do you want to come back for some tea?'

Fred put his arm around Tabitha and settled back on their cushion. 'One advantage,' he said, 'of great age, is that sometimes, when pursued, one can pretend to be completely deaf.'

Tabitha giggled complicitly. 'I quite agree. Tell me, can you hear me when I tell you I expect my ring from you very soon? At our age you never know how much time you've got left and I'm not wasting any more of it.'

'Do you know,' said Fergus to Alice a moment later, 'I know they could see me – and I'm sure they could hear me – but they just pretended not to be listening.'

A short distance away Martha's shop, unlike most in Cambridge, was closed. Sloaney-but-dim Philomena had been sent off in tears, after an uncompromisingly ratty Martha told her she looked like something out of a Jilly Cooper novel and was lowering the tone. Poor Philomena's protests that Martha had never before objected when she came dressed in her hunting gear had fallen on deaf ears and Martha told her not to come back until she had been to Marks and Spencer to buy herself some suitable cardigans.

Now, out of sight of the window Martha stared at herself in the full-length mirror, tinted with a hint of bronze to flatter the customers. Her reflection stared back at her curiously. Was this guilt? Was she suffering the pangs of one who has hurt the feelings of a man she had rather come to like? Surely it was kinder to get out now rather than risk him thinking she might be ready for some sort of commitment. It just went to show what a disaster it was when you tried to make friends out of your lovers.

What must it be like, though, asked a little voice somewhere round about her heart (probably my pancreas then, she thought, because I haven't got a heart, not when it comes to men), what must it be like if your lover really *was* your friend? What must it be like if he didn't abandon you to a long-drawn-out death of tears and regret, if he stayed around and loved you and laughed with you till – well, till the end? Till you were old and grey and one of you went off to the great bingo club in the sky?

How awful would *that* be, to lose someone after all those years? The risks just got bigger, that was for sure. Like living life on a knife-edge, dependent. Surely nothing was worth it. Surely nothing was worth that risk?

Nothing was. People just got sucked in, that was all,

because they couldn't resist it when they felt like this. When they felt this kind of awful yearning that she had for him, this feeling that every crowd is empty unless he is there, that every day is pointless unless he is in it, that every waking moment needs his presence just to touch it with sunlight . . .

God, she sounded like a Barbara Cartland novel, like the bit when the heroine suddenly realises she is in love.

Daisy was in love – her cup of happiness was complete. She was queen of the day, and Mark Blackwell had asked her out. Even the fact that Colin Blackwell was in her mother's kitchen drinking tea and eating that sultana cake that Alice only ever defrosted when she felt like showing off to visitors couldn't dampen Daisy's happiness. Alice and Colin Blackwell watched her disappear upstairs to get changed, and Alice smiled.

'It's been a wonderful day for them.'

He smiled in return. 'For me too.' And Alice blushed. 'I – er, wondered if you . . .'

She panicked quickly. He's going to ask me out. I can't cope with this right now. Stop him. 'I – er – I hope you didn't hurt yourself, carrying Daisy.'

His face fell. Misjudged it again, and now he'd got rid of his beard too. Still, the world did seem to be a different place, seen from a beardless point of view. People seemed much less suspicious. He stood up to go. 'Of course not, I'm so glad we had a good race. Splendid result.'

'Yes, it was . . .' Golly, he's shy. This is painful.

'I – er, well, thanks for the tea.' God, he thought, it's like trying to buy condoms from the chemist's at sixteen – I just can't ask her.

'That's OK, you're welcome.' He was actually very nice, she thought, but she really couldn't handle being asked out. Not when she had to do what she had to do the next day.

Chapter Eighteen

Alice set off for Bury St Edmunds the following morning before she could even think about not going, deliberately putting herself onto that automatic plane she normally reserved for waiting in supermarket queues as she whirred round the house. She deliberately drove in the fast lane, in an attempt to give herself something more to concentrate on than the fact that she was on her way to see Heather Bunberry, woman of negotiable virtue, bondage expert (apparently) and the last person to see Rob alive. Ever.

West Suffolk is one of the prettiest parts of the country, a land of rolling greenery, of cow-parsley lanes and rose-thick hedgerows, of thatch and flax and smug fat cows in cosy organic huddles. Sadly, though, none of this rural Utopia is visible from the A14, which is embanked within an inch of its life between Cambridge and Bury St Edmunds, and where the peak of entertainment for the bored driver is the passing glimpse of a Little Chef afforded for a brief second on a bend just after the second exit for Newmarket. Even this was lost on Alice, as her mind wandered back across the years, remembering yet again the moment when she knew. When she knew not just that Rob was dead, but that there was some awkwardness in the imparting of the news that was more than just the natural reticence of those dreading the inevitable reaction. She had to *excavate* it out of them.

'What do you mean, he was not at the hospital? Where was he then?'

'He – er, was in Cambridge. I understand it was his heart, ma'am, just happened very suddenly. They've taken him to

Addenbrooke's now. Is there someone you'd like to have with you?'

'No. What do you mean? He *was* at Addenbrooke's this morning – he was there on a course.'

'I can't comment on that, ma'am. Is there anyone you'd like to have called?'

How often had she gone over and over that day in her mind, trying to reconstruct it with a new ending? I must be, she thought, the only woman in the world to wish her husband had died when he was in bed with me. It's ghastly.

Trying to shake off thoughts which could only rattle her composure at a time when she really needed it, she turned on the car radio for company. Sadly this was, as always, akin to listening to Radio Oslo in a blizzard, as what the Morris Minor lacked in horsepower it made up for in engine noise. (Normally she took comfort from Fergus' insistence that Radio Oslo is probably always in a blizzard anyway.)

The usual chain of rambling 'if's were still chasing one another through her brain like hounds after a fox. The sequence was inevitable, running non-stop until it had completed its painful tumble. Even if you had to accept that Rob would have a heart attack, then if he had had it with her, she could have saved him. She could have resuscitated him until the ambulance crew raced in and did their macho bit. And did he have to have had a heart attack? Had what they had been doing, he and Marcie Crombie, alias Heather Bunberry, been too vigorous for him? Might he otherwise, during ordinary, unexciting sex with her, Alice, have had a bit of warning angina, have gone off to the hospital and got it checked out, had a nice neat angioplasty, been put on lipid-lowering drugs for ever, and finally checked out at ninety-three of old age. And even if he finally had to die, even if it really was written on a stone in the giant rockery of the fates that that was always intended to be the day Rob died, couldn't he have been doing something else, somewhere else, with someone else? Almost anything else would have done.

She reached Bury St Edmunds in a state of compounded tension, which was then made worse by the fact that the Angel car park was full. The nice doorman offered to valet park her car somewhere else, but from the nervous look on his face he was more accustomed to cars with a proper first gear and a handbrake that wasn't older than he was, and, in any case, her little Moggie might end up trapped next to Marcie Crombie's car, whichever that was. No, she corrected herself, next to Heather Bunberry's car. There is no Marcie Crombie. So instead she drove around the corner to the nice GP surgery where she herself had done part of her training some years earlier and parked in one of their slots. The walk would calm her down.

It was only a short distance on foot to Angel Hill. There people milled around the entrance to the Abbey Gardens. An ice-cream van sold cider lollies to people old enough to remember them whilst children demanded giant chocolate things on sticks and their mothers winced and fumbled for ten-pound notes. Expensive ladies tripped out of clothes shops laden with carrier bags, busy explaining to their husbands on the mobile phone that that was what you had to pay if you wanted quality classics, and a suit like that would last for decades. A traffic warden stalked the parking area like a particularly territorial heron, remaining ever hopeful despite being condemned to work in a particularly law-abiding town in which everyone's car was positively encrusted with car park tickets and parking permits. Three small underoccupied boys who ought to have been in school sat on the pavement in front of the Angel comparing the size of their gobstoppers whilst elderly ladies sucked Parma violets and joked that Lord Shaftesbury really had a lot to answer for and you couldn't get good chimney sweeps for love nor money these days. There was something reassuringly local about Bury, especially for Alice, who spent so much of her time in Cambridge where every second person was both visiting and lost.

The Angel Hotel rumbled gently today with very unclandestine people, Tuesday morning not being a time for clandestinity in Bury St Edmunds. Even so, Alice could not quite suppress a shudder at the memory of her night with Oliver. Entering through the front door she had a sudden urge to turn and flee, to join the boys on the pavement or the women in the clothes shops and forget all about her appointment with fate – her appointment, in a way, with Rob.

But her feet knew what she had to do, even if she didn't, and so moved themselves sequentially and unrelentingly until she found herself in the coffee lounge being shown to a seat.

Heather was there, sitting behind a tray of coffee and an inappropriate mountain of chocolate éclairs. Alice didn't recognise her at first – without the blonde wig she had neat brown hair, cut to her shoulders, pinned back from her face. She looked like an ordinary pretty girl – but nervous – and for the first time Alice wondered not what she had to say, but why exactly she needed to say it.

She sat down cautiously, wondering how you opened the conversation with the woman who had been in bed with your husband when he died. She might have opened many conversations with Heather before – usually along the lines of, 'What can I do for you?' – but then it's easy for GPs with patients, that stethoscope giving them permission to move smoothly and effortlessly from 'Good morning, Mrs Simpson' to 'Are you having problems with your bowels' without even a change of inflexion or an effort at social nicety. But as soon as I remove my metaphorical white coat, Alice thought, I'm bereft. I have no idea what to say to this woman at all. I've spoken to her so often, yet now she's a complete stranger and I have the social confidence of a zebra at the lions' annual dinner dance.

Mind you, why should I be the one to start? This wasn't my idea.

Heather cleared her throat.

In the end it was not what Alice had been expecting to hear. After all this time, after all the things she had thought about Rob, all the things she had told the hebes on his grave, to find that Heather had not after all been a moment's unreined lust and curiosity, that Heather had had a different claim on Rob . . . Like the news of sudden death it was easy enough to hear but impossible to take in all at one go.

'I had always loved him,' said Heather, 'from the first time I saw him, when I was fourteen and he was sixteen. He said it was love at first sight. For both of us.'

Alice smiled tightly to cover the pain in her left ear (what a stupid place to get a pain at a moment like this. Why not in my chest or my stomach? Must be a trapped nerve). 'He was very good at love at first sight.'

Heather gave her a direct look. 'I was the first. When I lost him to you it ruined my life . . .'

It was a challenge, but Alice shrugged bitterly. What glory in being the first love at first sight, if there were several after you? 'He never mentioned you. Not ever.'

Heather bit her lip, took a swig of her coffee. 'No. Well. If you don't let go of the past you're not free to talk about it. We were inseparable, Robert and I. Then he went away to medical school – and he never came back. There was nothing wrong between us. One minute he loved me, the next he . . . loved you. I was nothing. It was over.'

'Love at first sight,' said Alice woodenly. 'As you said.'

Heather sighed. 'He wrote and said it was all over for us, that he'd changed, that I would change too. But I never did. The years went by and I still wanted him, still dreamed of him. I tried to go on without him – but when I messed up my life in a big way he was still in my mind, like a thread of hope holding me together. I couldn't believe, feeling like that, that wherever he was he didn't still love me too. And so when it was the right time, when I'd stopped being in a mess, I came looking for him. I came after him and I found him. I didn't think about you. Why should I? He was mine first. I just wanted him back.'

Alice stared into her sad intense face. How unhealthy, she thought, to love the wrong person for so long. But then, isn't that what I've been doing? She frowned awkwardly. 'I always thought – I mean, the papers said you were a prostitute.'

'I was. I always wanted to be a dancer, but I ended up as a stripper. I met a useless bloke, ended up working in a club in London. There I discovered I had a talent,' she smiled humourlessly, 'for making rich men feel good.'

Alice couldn't see it at all. Heather as a waitress or a secretary, definitely. Heather as a teacher, or managing the food department in Marks and Spencer and getting stressed when the blueberry cheesecakes didn't arrive or someone was sold an out-of-date shepherd's pie. But Heather as vice queen of the West End? Surely not.

Heather was reading her expression. 'I know what you're thinking. But men don't always want the obvious types,' she said defiantly. 'I was very good. I made a lot of money and I'm not ashamed of it, so you needn't look at me with your middle-class prudery.'

'So why did you stop then?' Alice was angry, not feeling understanding or even curious, sensing that they hadn't reached the point of all this yet and not at all sure that she wanted to get there. 'If you were so good at pleasing rich men, and so proud of doing it, why give it all up?'

Heather shrugged as if it was obvious. 'One day I'd had enough. It happens. You get older. I'd saved enough to start somewhere else, so I got out. I was independent, I had money, I'd even started writing romantic novels. I had everything I wanted except one thing. So I looked for Robert. I looked him up in the *Medical Directory*. It gave him to me in black and white – it even gave me his phone number. I moved to Cambridge, and I called him up to win him back.'

'As deliberately as that?'

Heather nodded.

'And he came running?' Alice tried to stifle the hurt by keeping her voice level. Robert, indeed. He was never Robert. Well, to his mother – but then she does it to be proprietorial too.

Heather frowned. 'He came. He was quite nervous, quite curious too, I suppose. I think he'd felt guilty for years.' She looked up. 'I mean, it was an awful thing he did to me. But he came in the end – how could he not? I told him I needed to see him. I begged him to come. I told him I'd wanted him and waited for him all my life, that I couldn't breathe another breath without him – so he came.'

Alice swallowed hard, but her words still came out as a bit of a squeak. 'You make it sound as if he didn't have a choice.'

'He didn't, really. He owed me that much.'

Alice felt her anger rising, at Rob as well as Heather. 'That's ridiculous. He was a husband and a father – how could he owe you anything?'

Heather shrugged, and a cold silence settled between them. A waiter wandered into it to ask if they wanted more coffee in the pot, then withdrew rather nervously when he found himself engulfed in a wave of silence and ill feeling.

Unanswered questions nagged at Alice's stomach. She did her best to ignore them, nervous of more answers. Had Heather really mattered? Had the seduction succeeded? Perhaps Rob had been nostalgic? Perhaps curious? Perhaps just greedy?

'How long had he been seeing you?'

Heather sighed. 'A couple of weeks. But you see, I should have told you. I didn't want to believe it at first, but it was guilt really, not love, that's why he was there. He felt he must owe me that if I loved him so much. I think he just wanted to make me happy, to have it both ways. I made him sleep with me. I made him. When I told him what I'd become, what my life had been . . .' her eyes filled suddenly with tears, 'I think he was dreadfully shocked. I . . .' she began to cry, 'I wanted to hurt him. I wanted him to feel so guilty that he'd come back to me. And I think I convinced him he must surely still love me. But he didn't. It just took him a couple of weeks to realise it.'

Alice swallowed, pain lancing her unexpectedly in places where it had lanced before, places long since healed. A couple of weeks is bloody *long*. How many times did he and I make love in those two weeks? Did he go from me to her? From her to me? Did we mingle for him, did our smells mix in his nostrils like herbs in the rain? Did he ever think of her when we were . . . ?

I really don't want to know that. She swallowed. 'So why did you want to talk to me? Why now?'

Heather stared at the carpet. For the first time her composure seemed less than certain, her eyes less bold and unassailable. 'I needed to tell you how it was. I owed him that. Owed you that.'

Alice felt tears prick like sherbet lemons. 'I already know how it happened.' It came out as a squeak, a feeble attempt at imperiousness, which flapped nervously on the carpet like a sparrow with a broken wing. She cleared her throat. 'Rob had a heart attack on your bloody bed, that's what happened.' Her voice rose slightly, and a couple at the next table glanced over in surprise. 'He was having an affair and he died in bed. I can't see any other way of looking at it.' She seized a sugar cube and ground it between her fingers. 'He wasn't having tea with the vicar, was he?'

Heather looked at her directly. Tears hung in her eyes but did not fall. She has probably, thought Alice suddenly, grown at least as good as I at holding tears in there, reflective but unshed. It was an unwelcome thought, crediting Heather, as it did, with some humanity.

'He didn't want to hurt you, you see,' Heather said, 'but

382

he couldn't bear to hurt me again either. I thought he still loved me, I so wanted it to be true, and I almost believed it. But that day . . . Look, he'd want you to know about that day, about what he said to me. All this time I've carried it but I can't let go of it till I tell you how it was.'

Alice felt her throat tighten with nerves. She tried to take a deep breath, but couldn't. An absurd desire to laugh seized her urgently, and she giggled – once, quickly, awkwardly. 'For three years I've been trying to talk to him. I haven't even been able to start to say what I feel. And now he's dead he's going to talk to me. That's bloody ironic, don't you think?'

Heather maintained her watered gaze. 'I suppose so. He'd never talked about you till then, that day, and I didn't ask. I was afraid I'd break the spell. But that day, after we . . . he was different – he said we had to talk. He said that it had all been a foolish mistake, that he loved you, not me. He was saying goodbye, it was over.

'I wouldn't listen – I suppose I didn't want to hear it. I was crying, I said he couldn't leave me like that, not again, that I couldn't bear it. He said he was sorry – then he sat down suddenly. I wanted to believe he was just having a twinge of guilt. But he got the pain in his chest. I could see that it was serious – he was so pale, and clammy. He asked me to ring you. "Get Alice," he said, "please get Alice." I panicked. I didn't want to call you. I called the ambulance instead but by the time they got there . . .'

Alice watched her with a divorced fascination. Could Rob have realised he was actually dying? Why would he? A man of his age?

What if, like those near-death-experience people on afternoon chat shows, he had really seen St Peter standing beckoning him towards the pearly gates, and had known that he was finished, and had said, 'Just a minute, your saintliness, got to leave a message for Alice'? Would it help? She felt confused, her clarity of view muddied as she was sucked back three years, back into the mire of his duplicity.

'Did he say anything else?'

Heather was pale. 'No, that was it – he just said, "Alice, please get Alice." That was it. I hated you so much for that, for being the one he wanted after all. But it ate holes in me. I knew I had to tell you. He'd have wanted me to tell you. And now I have.'

Chapter Nineteen

Alice negotiated the route home in a daze, weeping silently, emotion trickling relentlessly out of her tear ducts. It had washed her lenses right out – she had had to revert to the specs under the dashboard. There was an ache of disbelief in her stomach, a vice of misery round her head. Rob having an affair? It terrified her how easily she believed it, how little she thought of him now. A love affair with an old flame, with someone who actually *meant something* to him and not, as she had imagined these three years, an erotic impulse he could not resist, born of some deficiency in herself. It had been something of significance. His old sweetheart. Had he found that the spark was still there, found her better than the woman he had replaced her with?

How could he have done that to us? Alice asked herself. What on earth was he thinking?

Probably nothing. She hiccuped as the tears caught her, keeping her eyes firmly fixed on the road whilst her seeing mind saw only Rob and Heather. Probably just thinking with his penis.

It took her an hour to get home – forty-five minutes to drive back to Cambridge and another fifteen parked around the corner to try to hide the state of her face, since it was half term and the children might be in.

It was not only the children: when she finally got back to the house she found Martha waiting for her, looking slightly whiter, as Anemone put it when she opened the front door, than a cricketer's smalls. She was sitting on the sofa in the living room clutching a cup of very strong tea, whilst beside her Daisy made inappropriate small talk about her own taste in boys, shoes, clothes, make-up, music and religion, the absolute self-centredness of teenageness rendering her certain that such enlightenment would relieve Martha's distress or at least, as she said defensively afterwards, take her mind off it.

Alice couldn't help feeling that her own emotional churning made Martha's agonies over Tom seem trivial.

'You know, I don't know why you're feeing so sorry for yourself,' she said darkly. 'It's a simple enough choice and you've made it.' Rob betrayed me. Rob didn't love me. Or even if he did – he actually believed he might still love her more . . .

Martha sighed. 'I know. I didn't expect to feel this shitty, though. He's only a man.'

'That's probably what they said about Romeo,' said Daisy helpfully, 'but Juliet still killed herself.'

Alice was impatient with the whole thing. 'I'm making coffee,' she said shortly, 'and then I might go for a walk,' and Martha had no choice but to follow her to the kitchen.

'Have you seen him?' she asked, as she trailed behind, 'I know he's been trying to call me. Has he spoken to you?' Alice could see now that she had been crying. It made her no less attractive – this was Martha after all – but it was a sign of a crack in that steel mask she wore so well where men were concerned. Perhaps it went to show you couldn't preserve yourself, that whatever you did you got pain, so you might as well have the fun first. Maybe that's what Rob had thought too. If he'd thought at all.

'No,' she said to Martha, 'assuming that you mean Tom, he hasn't spoken to me about you, and yes I've spoken to him briefly. I've been busy.'

'I've never felt so unearthed by anyone,' said Martha. 'I don't like to think he might be feeling like this. I mean, it's not as though we – I mean, it had been such a short time. Barely a fling.'

'Look, Martha, he's upset. He was obviously going to be upset. What did you expect him to do, throw a party?'

Martha sniffed, offended. 'I can see you're in a bad mood. Perhaps I should go away and –'

Alice cracked suddenly, as completely as if she were a mirror dropped onto rocky ground from a thousand feet in the air. Her face paled, showing the few freckles which hung over from childhood, normally invisible within the rosy blush of good health. 'I'm in a bad mood? Yes, I'm in a bad mood. You're not the only one whose life hasn't gone the way you planned it, you know. For God's sake, Martha, stop being so bloody self-indulgent. You're . . . you don't know how lucky you are that you've got someone like Tom hanging around you to make decisions about. Here you are, going on and on about not wanting to make him unhappy, not wanting to see him, wishing you hadn't had such fantastic sex, wishing you'd never met him – doesn't it ever occur to you that maybe you're better off than most people? Doesn't it actually occur to you that if I could have Rob back alive again the *last* thing I'd be doing is refusing to see him?' Tears were streaming down her cheeks again and she stopped, suddenly, shocked at the sudden rush of anger which had seized her and shaken her like a rag doll until she was limp.

Martha was impressed. Alice was well overdue for an explosion. Martha belonged to the Californian school of psychotherapy, which taught that it all had to come out somehow, somewhere, and a good primeval scream was the best way of ensuring that it did. Stuff English reserve – it was the price they paid over here for being so anally retentive.

'Alice, I'm sorry, I've been grossly insensitive.' She sat Alice down at the kitchen table where a large number of cereal packets vied for attention as no one had cleared away the breakfast things, put an arm around her shoulder, handed her a cushion to cry into and shut the kitchen door

387

against eavesdroppers. 'But you needed a good shout. What brought it on? Has something happened? Has someone said something?'

Alice stared with unseeing eyes at a special offer on the muesli. Save ten tokens and get the chance to buy a tea tray for slightly more than the usual price. 'Yes – no. Nothing. Nothing's changed. I just . . . I just met Marcie Crombie. In Bury St Edmunds. We had coffee and chocolate éclairs – that's where I've just been.'

Martha was astounded. 'Chocolate éclairs? How did this happen?'

Alice screwed the cushion up into a mere semblance of its former self, tried to drill up some bitter humour. 'Someone made choux pastry into little sausage shapes and filled them with cream.'

'Alice, I marvel at your ability to introduce bad jokes into the moments of grimmest emotional turmoil. I mean, for God's sake, how did you come to meet her?'

'It doesn't matter how – it's turned everything upside down. I don't know what to think any more. All the rules have changed. None of it was what I thought, what I've been imagining. But then the truth is never what you imagine it to be, is it?'

'What truth? You're making no sense, Alice.'

'She wasn't just some trollop he took a fancy to,' Alice sighed. 'She was an old girlfriend of his, Martha. He had been seeing her for two weeks.'

Martha was shocked. This was not what she would ever have expected. 'Alice, I don't know what to say. I – It doesn't seem like Rob. My God, how do you feel?'

'I don't know. I don't know how I feel. Shell-shocked, I suppose. As though the ground has been pulled from under my feet. I mean it *doesn't* seem like Rob, you're right – but it didn't seem like Rob the way I thought things were either. That's always been the problem for me: not knowing who he was. I think I need time to think about it.'

388

'You're not the only one,' said Martha, with a touch of bitterness. 'You know, I'm going to take myself off to Camberdown Manor for a couple of days. I need to escape and recharge. Actually I think I'll catch a train this evening. Why don't you come with me?'

Alice smiled a watery smile. 'Because I'm me and you're you. I'm not health farm woman. I'm middle-class Cambridge professional woman. I become deeply cynical when someone wants me to pay to spend an hour lying on a leather couch having my eyebrows electrocuted and Dead Sea slurry pasted all over my private parts. My remedy for stress is to put Puccini on the CD player – very loudly – and sip in a highly restrained fashion at a glass of white wine.'

Martha frowned. 'You sound like Inspector Morse.' Mine used to be to take some fine young man and use him until he gasped, she thought, but the fight's all gone out of me at the minute. I'll have to go for the Dead Sea slurry. At least it always works.

'Maybe so,' said Alice mournfully. 'Inspector Morse was destined to be alone too, wasn't he?'

'That's rubbish,' said Martha. 'No one's destined to be anything. You can change your mind any time, Alice. You don't have to play the lonely widow for ever.'

Alice glared. 'How would you know what I have to play? If ever anyone lived by a daft set of rules it's you. Anyway, maybe I don't know how to form relationships either. I've only ever really been in one, and it ended in disaster.'

'You have to start somewhere,' said Martha, exasperated, not liking that 'either' (but then Alice was very stressed). 'Maybe you should start by saying goodbye to Rob.'

'I have done.' Alice was indignant. 'What do you think this is, Hollywood? D'you think I'm sitting chatting with his ghostly presence every evening whilst a phantom quartet play Vivaldi? In any case, I couldn't possibly come with you, I've got things to do here. And I've got guests.'

'Oh, your old Armenian friend.'

'Herman's not old. Fred, on the other hand, is really very old. Fergus is going to be his best man, you know.'

'Fred? Getting married? *Old* Fred?'

'Yes, they're having trouble over getting the marriage certificate. They couldn't find him on record at all, and he hasn't got a birth certificate. I had to give him a certificate of existence in the end. Fergus says it's because he's seven hundred years old.'

Martha laughed. 'It would explain how he got to the top of the Fir Trees waiting list, wouldn't it? After all, this *is* Cambridge.'

Alice smiled slightly, surprised that she still could. Now that she had finished crying and finished shouting she felt oddly normal, oddly OK. 'I suppose it would. Makes you think, doesn't it?'

'What?'

'Getting married at their age. I mean, if Fred and Tabitha think there's a future for them together, with him all of seven hundred and her at least eighty-two, what business have any of the rest of us got, giving up on life?'

Martha frowned, immediately indignant again. 'What do you mean, giving up on life? I'm not giving up on life. Just because I want to end a relationship doesn't mean I'm giving up. I just don't want all that . . . that chaining to a man, to domesticity, to watching his toenails grow and get cut over and over again. To never quite knowing if he'll . . .' She trailed off, aware that Alice was staring at her with an I-told-you-so face. 'You didn't mean me.'

Alice shook her head. 'No. I meant me, actually, but you must admit you're pretty touchy. He's really got you running scared, hasn't he?'

'Certainly not. I'm just protecting my assets.'

Alice sighed. 'Martha, I love you dearly and I'm telling you, maybe you should stop running so fast and just have a look at what it is you're running from.'

Martha got angry, and then even angrier because she

knew it looked defensive and she had nothing to defend. 'I know exactly what I'm running from – and I'm not running. Oh, bloody stop it, Alice, you're doing your tricky psycho thing. I don't need that from you. I can pay people for that.'

Alice shrugged, wounded. 'I wasn't doing anything except stating the obvious. You're running from life.'

Martha felt tears behind her eyes. 'That's rubbish. What would you know about life?'

'A darn sight more than you, from the sound of it. At least I've taken risks.'

'Well, you're no advert for taking risks, let me tell you. Look at you, you're even hiding behind your specs like you used to.'

Alice let that pass. 'You're head over heels in love with him, Martha. What's the point in trying to pretend you're not?'

Martha panicked then, lost her cool, said the unforgivable. 'Because I'm bloody not – and, in any case, if anyone runs from life it's you! Look at you – white walls, soulless house, garden full of dead plants. It's . . . it's passionless. Don't talk to me about self-denial. You're leading a . . . a *frigid* life, Alice. You've squashed all the colour out of it and turned yourself into a human ice cube in a grey existence and now you can't stand it, all because you just can't forgive Rob. Well, don't try to live vicariously through me instead. I've done things my own way for three decades, I can do them my own way for three more!' She slammed the door behind her as she left, and before Alice could utter another word.

Alice stared after her. A final tear coursed down her cheek, and hesitated, as if slightly shocked to find itself there, hovering at the corner of her mouth, waiting to see if there were any more. But surprise had dried them as they began, or perhaps she had exhausted her lachrymal glands – so she felt just the needle-tip pricking of pain instead. She and Martha hadn't had a row since . . . well, they simply hadn't had a row. Not ever.

How could she say those things to me?

Are they true?

But Martha had gone, with the swift freedom of the unfettered, and Alice had to stay behind and just get on with dealing with things. It was, she thought resentfully, easy to be self-indulgent when you were single – and then regretted thinking it at once. After all, you can't measure one person's pain against another's. Rob being lost to her for ever didn't detract from the way Martha felt at breaking up with Tom. And when you thought what had happened to Martha's mother, it was no wonder Martha had problems with relationships. What sort of a friend was she, Alice, to let her go off like that? But there was, as she said to herself, no time for dwelling on it. She had too much to do at home.

And as Alice tried all afternoon not to dwell on it (and failed despite conducting the practice's monthly menopause clinic and ending her day feeling completely overwhelmed by wombs), Martha sat in a carriage on the London-bound Network South East train and watched as the details of people's lives drifted past her. Rapid glimpses into by-the-railway gardens, impertinent peeks into privacy – here a climbing frame, there a neatly polished car, a flash of green, children walking from school, someone's Flymo left outside unplugged . . .

Don't they have crime in Ponders End, then? Whoever leaves their Flymo outside unplugged? Neighbourhood Watch, that's what it is. Neighbours and coffee mornings and sharing recipes for trifle . . .

She felt as though she was in something of a daze. Someone seemed to have turned down the colour saturation of the world.

'Do you think,' she had asked her startled but gormless assistant that afternoon before she left, 'that the grass at the back of King's College is as green this year as it usually is?'

But Philomena never noticed grass because she spent almost her whole life sitting on Liberty sofas wearing cashmere cardigans and drinking tea with lemon whilst making small talk with men named Toffo and Binky. Grass did not figure heavily in her agenda and she felt lamely for a response. 'Gosh,' she had said eventually, wondering if Martha was on something, 'I really couldn't say, actually.'

Perhaps, thought Martha now, there's no problem with the way I'm seeing things, perhaps it simply is grey, the world from out of a train window. Perhaps being next to the train track stains it grey. A grey man standing gazing at his grey allotment . . . blocks of flats reaching skywards, a dog, a child, a washing line . . . so many people living in ordinary domesticity, settling down in pairs like fur seals and putting their geraniums on the patio together . . . How can people live so greyly?

Look at me, she thought sadly. Just because some part of me – for argument's sake you could call it the heart but it could just as easily be the sex drive – felt attached to one man, the whole world has palled. It has palled because I cut off all of its endless other possibilities in their prime.

It's all so grey now. It was always grey. Mom was always crying, in grey houses in grey towns. Whilst Dad – Dad was always smiling. He always had beautiful women on his arm, women with red lipstick and shiny shoes, and he charmed and cajoled his way into business, succeeded at everything he did. He was always carefree and happy. She, Mom, was the one who loved, the one who was eventually destroyed. Dad was the one who had it all.

Was that because life was better for him, or was it because he was a shallow bastard that didn't give a shit about anyone, even me?

As the train carried Martha further and further from him, Tom Lovejoy stood outside the Pavilion. He was watching the last remnants of the art exhibition being loaded onto a removal truck whilst his lawyer, David, a man so hard that you could have used him to mine bauxite, expressed his opinion on the whole thing via the mobile phone airwaves.

'I don't know why you didn't just leave the stuff for the backers to collect, Tom. They're the ones who owe you money, remember.'

'Don't worry,' said Tom good-naturedly, 'you'll get paid.' As he smiled two women walking past him quite incidentally stopped and gasped, even though (as one said afterwards) they were seventy-six and ought to know better.

'Look, David,' Tom was saying, 'they made me an offer in kind, and I have accepted it.'

'I really don't know,' David said, exasperated, 'what's the point in having a lawyer if you won't take my advice? They owe you thousands, Tom, them and their harebrained art scheme, and you plan to accept just one picture instead? You could have kept the entire blasted exhibition and sent them packing.'

Tom, though, smiled his mellow smile. 'Life's too short,' he said, 'and anyway, it's not a picture they offered me. You'll have to come and see it in the surgery when it's all done.'

'So you really are staying here then? Has the man with wings on his feet finally been weighted with concrete?'

Tom's smile wavered slightly. 'I really am. It's time I had some roots.'

'I don't believe it. Unless . . . Ah. Who is she?'

Tom smile disappeared. 'She isn't – but you're almost right. She nearly was.'

'You're not telling me a failed romance has got you hanging around? Take it from me, Tom, I've had three wives and none of them was worth it.'

'Which only proves you don't know how to choose 'em,' said Tom, 'scientifically speaking.'

'Now, Thomas, you're not sitting and pining, are you?'

'Don't be silly,' said Tom. 'This is me you're talking to.'

He heard David sniff. 'Well, if you want my advice – which you clearly don't, of course – it would be to say don't waste your time waiting around for the one that got away. There are plenty more fish in the sea.'

'The trouble is,' said Tom ruefully, to nothing, when David had rung off, 'I'm attached to this one fish by a very strong line.'

Everything was oddly quiet at the surgery the next day. Tom and Alice entered an unspoken pact not to mention Martha, and got on quietly with planning the move, whilst Roland avoided them completely by being off with a bad cold. Alice suspected that Tom had said something to him about the knickers, but did not want to ask.

She felt numb, altered, as if everything she had ever thought about anything had turned out to be wrong. She didn't know how to begin to dissect her reaction to what Heather had told her – so she was not even going to try. She had shut it into a corner of her mind and planned to leave it there, alone, to ripen, whilst she ran on autopilot and let things happen; whilst the staff at the surgery buzzed and whispered about their new premises; whilst Tom used all sorts of contacts to persuade the planners that the need for a surgery was so great that they must consider the planning application today with a view to passing it at once, which they obligingly promised to do.

Morning ran into afternoon, leaving Alice no chance of getting home for lunch. With James off now and no locums to be found for half term they were swamped with patients, and she felt lucky to snatch a sandwich. It wasn't as if the children needed her – they were probably all doing exciting half-term stuff elsewhere, so she might just as well get on.

She was wrong: the children were at home executing Fergus' plan for the garden. He had fetched Fred and his truckload of compost from the Fir Trees – although he had

395

to bang on the shed door for quite a while before Fred would emerge.

'What were you doing?'

'Surfing the Net,' said Fred inscrutably, 'checking out my investments.'

'Wow,' said Fergus, 'do you have many?'

Fred shrugged. 'I bought a few shares over the years. Between you and me I own this place, for a start.'

'You don't! But I thought you turned peacock dung into gold.'

'I do,' said Fred. 'Why do you think I'm the only man in it? And I made my money out of compost years ago. I invested it and it saw me secure.'

Fergus and Fred were able to spend a couple of hours spreading mulch over the flowerbeds in a rich sweet layer.

Herman was forbidden to help with the spreading because of his heart, so he made them endless cups of tea whilst Anemone leaned idly by drinking it. She might not be able to add much physically, she told them, as she could not risk straining her artist's hands, but spiritually she could bring a whole extra dimension.

The mulch smelled as though five thousand peacocks had been ill in a pit for a week, but if it made the garden look better and therefore made Alice want to stay in Herne Road it would be worth it. What else could Fergus do? He was sworn to pretend to go along with Anemone's daft idea. He had already given Finn Selby his entire collection of *Star Wars* coins to get him to ring up Phoebe Hamilton and ask her how she was, for all's fair in love and war, and if Phoebe decided she wanted to stay in England because she thought Finn might be interested in her then her parents wouldn't move. But it had backfired. Phoebe had told Finn Selby to piss off for having stolen her doctor's frog. You couldn't ever get it right with girls.

Fergus sighed. Fred said you never cured anything by trying to turn back the clock, whatever that meant. And he must know if he was seven hundred years old. He certainly knew a darn sight more than two stupid teenaged girls, that was for sure (Fergus' unquestioning acceptance that wisdom increases with age was one that the residents of the Fir Trees found particularly endearing).

It was a bright day, a good day for gardens, at least till the dreadful girl with the Barbies in the house opposite, who was apparently confined to bed with a rash, took it upon herself to open her bedroom window wide and shout, 'Yuck! Pooey!' endlessly from on high.

'No wonder things haven't grown very well,' said Fergus, 'but they haven't ever grown since we moved in. Mind you, Anemone says they don't grow because of the feng shui and Mum thinks it's her being sad.'

'Rubbish,' said Fred. 'They don't grow because the crook that built these houses took off the topsoil. Probably sold it to some landscape gardener. Nothing could grow properly in what they left you.'

'Really?' Fergus was relieved that there was, after all, no innate deficiency in his mother that was outwardly manifest in the failure to grow hebes. Perhaps she wasn't as sad as Anemone and Daisy always said. So perhaps they were wrong about everything else too. Perhaps they wouldn't have to move at all.

That evening, when Alice got home, the house was welcoming and warm. Daisy had cleaned the kitchen from top to bottom in the hope of being allowed to stay out late with Mark Blackwell, and the garden was looking surprisingly well-loved, despite smelling quite ghastly. Alice felt a new, surprising affection for it. This is our home, she thought. We should be grateful for it. I don't really think we should think about leaving it now. But what about the children and what they want? What about Fergus, who has spent a whole day spreading manure as his farewell gift to Herne Road?

And then Alice got a postcard from Frances. It arrived on

397

the Saturday morning and it made her mind up, quite suddenly but entirely irrevocably, about absolutely everything. She must have been, she told herself afterwards, right on the edge of making her mind up anyway – one thing surely cannot otherwise push you into such certainty. Nevertheless when she read it, it seemed to shift her angle of view to one of such clarity that she felt it really had been the one thing that changed everything; that it had been decisive, in the end.

It was the usual sort of postcard, once one of many stacked on some faraway postcard stand, where the air smells of sea shells and the distant sound of a steel band mellows the warm moist air. A Caribbean beach, a palm tree, a brown body mostly exposed to the sun. It landed face up on the mat, a breath of another life, and Alice's first thought was who would send her a card from somewhere so exotic? Surely Martha hadn't suddenly done a bunk and gone abroad?

But no, it was from Frances. Frances casting off the traces with either astonishing denial or astonishing bravery. Knowing her, Alice was certain it was the latter.

Dear Dr Vane, this is called burning your boats. We're here in the Bahamas, Gareth and I, the sun is glorious and I've a beautiful tan. Ironic for me, I know, but what's to lose? I'm not feeling too bad, and it's so wonderful here that we've decided we're not actually coming back. We're starting a new life. Gareth has got a job DJ-ing here, and I'm going to just . . . bum about and look at the stars. It was what I was doing in Cambridge anyway, but maybe not from quite the same angle. We'll see how long it lasts – but then you can find a whole lifetime in a minute if you make it stretch. Good luck and think of me. I'll stay in touch.

All my love, Frances

There are different sorts of courage, thought Alice. There's ignoring your troubles, there's looking them square in the eye and being determined to fight them – and then there's deciding that if you can't overcome them then you might as well be doing some more living and win that way. Frances is living. She can't fight her disease, but she can accept it and grab on to life, and let life do the fighting for her. I wonder if I could be as reckless in her position; as committed to my choice.

And that's what I need to do. I need to stop making my way carefully through life, shouldering my regrets like a rucksack full of old bricks and bits of sharp things. I need to stop feeling gently for the least painful route and hiding old photos in moments of particular pain. I need to make the decision I know is right and stick to it.

She picked up the phone and rang the Hamiltons before she could worry about it any more.

'Alana? It's Alice Vane. Alana, look – I'm ringing about the house. I'm sorry if this is bad news – I mean, if I've held you up at all by letting you think . . . You see, I've decided not to move at all. We're going to stay here in Herne Road. I'm sure you'll find a buyer but it won't be me.'

Now I just have to tell the children we're not going, she thought when she'd rung off. I'll have to choose my moment. I hope they're not too disappointed. And I have to do something about these white walls.

Whilst Alice declared her decision, Martha was doing her best to disengage her brain and prevent it from making any decisions at all. Certainly not any rash ones, like ringing Tom Lovejoy. It was important not to show any weakness in that respect – particularly not to herself.

And she was failing. Martha had always enjoyed Camberdown Manor before. A few days of self-indulgence whilst a succession of slim but strong Swedes attended to her vitamin E and algae levels usually brought about a real

399

recharging. Doubtless, she had always felt, if she had emotional needs – which she didn't as she lived her life on an even keel, emotionally speaking – then they would be solved there too. But she was not an emotional woman. True, she cried when she listened to Puccini, but that was art, not emotion. That was why this hitch over sleeping with Tom – and actually kissing him – seemed so major, of course – because compared to her calm emotional state it was. True, there were a few bits of stuff locked away in a private box somewhere, but she had lifted the lid once in therapy and had very quickly realised that self-flagellation is a particularly pointless activity for the thoroughly well-adjusted independent woman. There's no point looking at old pain.

She lay on a white towel in a warm room, her face in a camomile cushion whilst her back muscles were stroked steadily by someone who had trained in Tokyo, he claimed, on sumo wrestlers, her mind in a whirl of attempted rationalisation.

Sexually, of course, she was a highly charged and demanding creature. Probably that was the real problem – good sex was bound to have a bit of an emotional impact. It was just a matter of recognising it for what it was, and avoiding imagining it was something else. Because imagining something else was like stepping out onto quicksand – a couple of steps and suddenly you were sinking and there was no safe way to go in any direction.

As she closed her eyes and breathed deeply at the thought of all the toxins leaking out of her body right now, including those toxins which represented silly, schoolgirlish thoughts, the piped music CD ran out. Martha let her mind drift. Away from Tom, away from her father and mother . . . She was a strong woman, she was regenerating her mind. She had never needed a man to define her. She didn't now.

In the manager's office they put the Rachmaninov CD on the player. It was the next one on the pile – on such odd moments of chance are fortunes and fates built and lost. And as Ashkenazy eased into the first few chords of the Second Piano Concerto Martha was transported. It was a day in Aldeburgh and a kiss on the beach. It was being held close on crisp white sheets and feeling so completely cherished that nothing, absolutely nothing would ever be the same again. It was realising that sometimes you could go too far without intending to, and then maybe there's no safe way back to where you were before, to where you were safe and strong. It was knowing that you were totally different for ever. She began to cry.

Daisy was accustomed to life at home being predictable, if odd, and it was something of a surprise to come home after a perfectly pleasant Saturday loafing around town, wearing her Doc Martens and snogging Mark Blackwell on every available street corner, to find that the hall was turning burgundy under Alice's roller, and Herman, astonishingly, was on a stepladder applying gold stars to the bits that were dry. ('This is a very Armenian design, you know. It reminds me of St Gregory's cathedral in Yerevan . . .') It was such a surprise, actually, that she quite forgot to complain again about the pong of bird poo on the garden.

'Er . . .' she said teenagely, standing at the foot of the stairs and trying to look amused but impressed.

'D'you like it? We've been painting all day.'

'It's great,' said Daisy, 'really smart. I thought you only liked white walls.'

'Not any more,' said Alice. 'It was time for a change.'

Hormones, thought Daisy. Perhaps it's the menopause. Is this when you get it, then? 'Is it OK if I go out with Mark tonight?'

'Again? That's fine. Back by nine o'clock, though, please. I'd like to feel that I at least manage a glimpse of you from day to day.'

Daisy arched an eyebrow. 'That's very early. Can't I –?'

'Nine. I need to talk to you all, and I obviously have to make an appointment. Do you promise to be back?'

'OK. Mum, you're not still doing those horoscopes, are you?'

'No, Anemone is. Why?'

'Just checking.' She ambled up the stairs to reload her eyelashes with mascara, and was only slightly startled to discover that the bathroom door was now lilac.

When she was out of sight Alice tiptoed down the stairs and looked up Daisy's horoscope in her copy of *GP* which lay on the kitchen table.

'Venus moves into your sign, so if you have never snogged a cricket captain in full view of his team, today might be a day to try it.'

Upstairs Daisy slipped into Anemone's room and found Fergus and Anemone there already.

'What's going on?'

'I dunno,' said Fergus. 'She only bought the stuff today. Two pots of that gloopy red. She was asking me if I really wanted to move.'

'What did you tell her? You didn't start whingeing about being able to see the bloody rugby field again? You did promise.'

'No I did not, and for that matter Mark Blackwell plays rugby so I'm not the only one who might want to be close to the ground this winter.'

'I'm not some bimbo who has to hang around the touchline.'

'You look like a bimbo with those eyelashes.'

'For goodness' sake,' Anemone interrupted them, 'Fergus, what did she say? About moving, I mean.'

Fergus shrugged. 'I don't think she's all that keen to move. She's only doing it for us. And don't glare at me. I truly honestly did not whinge.'

'That's why she's painting the house purple then,' said Anemone, sitting on her bed. 'It's because she wants to stay here. That'll be what she wants to talk to us about this evening, I bet you. We'll have to act surprised.'

'Well, I'm really glad,' said Daisy, sitting beside her. 'It'd be such a pain having to get buses in from the village.'

'You mean you don't want to move back to Pipe Tree Cottage either?' Anemone was exasperated. 'I thought we all did. Well, all of us except Fergus and he doesn't count.'

'Oh, thanks very much.' Fergus tried to grab her pillow and throw it but she hung on, pulled him down and sat on him.

Daisy peered at her through Fergus' flailing legs. 'You mean you do want to move back?'

Anemone shrugged. 'It doesn't really matter to me. Like you say, in a couple of years I'll probably be shacked up with some bloke.' She crossed her eyes and they all rolled around giggling.

By quarter to nine the hall was impressively burgundy down two sides, Fergus and Anemone having been roped in to roll, and the bathroom ceiling was turning blue.

'It is,' Herman said, as he completed the first coat of gloss to the hall skirting boards, 'as though God has suddenly taken a rainbow and flung it at the house, leaving the colours to liquefy and run all down the walls.'

Alice sat back on her heels and watched him. 'You and I need a rest. Anemone can finish the bathroom door.'

'No I can't,' called Anemone. 'I'm designing a goldfish.'

Alice pulled a face at Herman. 'Come on, I'm supposed to be looking after you, not using you as a decorator.'

Herman wouldn't have it. 'Nonsense – I am honoured to be given a task. You have made me part of your household, accepted me as if I were more to you than a foolish old historian from another land.' He finished his skirting board and eyed it in satisfaction. 'I think I may do my library in Yerevan this colour.'

'Is it a big library?'

'It is the most important museum in Yerevan,' said Herman, 'but unimportant compared to being a doctor.'

Alice shrugged. 'I look after people's bodies, you look after their souls.'

'Ah,' said Herman, 'not their souls, their minds, perhaps. In Yerevan they go to St Gregory's cathedral to soothe their souls.'

'Are you a religious man?' Alice asked.

'Of course. Did I not tell you that Armenia is the oldest Christian country? Yes, I can see that I did. I am the museum curator, you have to allow me my little quirks – but you don't have to be religious to have your soul soothed in the cathedral. It is a very calm and quiet place, very old.'

'Perhaps I should have come long ago,' said Alice with a wry smile. 'Cup of tea?'

'I never refuse tea.' Herman followed her into the kitchen. 'You have problems with your soul?'

Alice filled the kettle. 'I've had problems getting over losing my husband.'

'Of course,' said Herman, 'but I think there's nothing wrong with your soul. If there was, you could never welcome a stranger, could never spend your days giving so much to so many people.'

'Looking after people medically is my job,' said Alice. 'There are plenty of doctors without much soul, believe me.'

Herman shook his head. 'No doctor without a soul could give an aspirin to a dying man with the charm and faith you showed me.' There was a twinkle in his eye and Alice grinned.

'You know very well it's the right treatment. OK, if that's having a soul I can accept that I have one. I suppose the problem is that I haven't really got on with my life since he died.'

Herman fetched the tea bags and looked thoughtfully at the breakfast cereal, which lived in the same cupboard. 'Would you mind if I . . . ?'

'Of course not, help yourself.'

Herman tipped cornflakes and milk into a bowl whilst Alice made the tea. Then he said thoughtfully, 'Perhaps you are measuring progress in the wrong units.'

Alice raised an eyebrow. 'What do you mean?'

'You smile, you laugh, you shout, you love your friends and extend your love to strangers. You make yourself responsible for an old man and his lost frog and agree to dress – in your own words – like a toilet roll in order to act as bridesmaid. And you paint your house like a rainbow with stars on the ceiling and goldfish on the walls. This is what we would call living in Armenia.'

Alice stared at him for a minute, then she started to laugh. 'Do you know,' she told him, 'you make me sound entirely mad.'

Herman smiled and finished his cereal. 'You are entirely charming,' he said. 'And I shall return to Yerevan much enriched.'

By nine o'clock everyone was back painting. Daisy had returned glowing from her date and even Fergus had tarted up the bathroom woodwork. The children had passed no comment at all on this profound change in decorating style – other than to remark on one colour being a particularly good one to apply, and another refusing to stick to the ceiling but having an affinity for hair. Alice wondered what they actually thought she was up to – there seemed to be an active conspiracy to say nothing. Perhaps they thought she was painting to make the house more saleable. Goodness knows what sort of buyer would go for these colours. One high on something, probably.

Or maybe they thought it was art therapy. It was certainly taking her mind off the various little nastinesses Roland brought into her daily working life. The previous day she had found a note in her pigeonhole wondering whether she might acknowledge his small gift in writing, as he was anxious to know if it was to her taste. She would have liked to strangle Roland with the knickers, should at least have returned them, but unfortunately Daisy had proved completely unwilling to part with them on the basis that fifty-pound knickers wouldn't come her way very often, leaving Alice feeling that she had slipped very slightly off the moral high ground as far as Roland and the knickers were concerned.

It was not, though, until she had put the brushes away and drunk a glass of white wine that she tackled the children.

'Listen, everyone. We need to have a serious talk.'

'Yee . . . s?' They sat, like the three wise monkeys, lined up on the sofa whilst Herman sidled off to make tea. So like Rob, all of them. It hadn't been so easy to see it when he was alive.

'It's about moving house. I know this should have been more democratic, I know that's how we do things – but I'm afraid I've taken a unilateral decision.'

Fergus nudged Daisy. 'Is this something about the arms race?'

Daisy nudged him back. 'Don't talk rot.'

'I wasn't. Mr Blackwell told us about it. Unilateral disarmament . . .'

'Fergus,' said Alice, 'I admire you for proving you have listened to nice Mr Blackwell for at least ten seconds of one of his lessons, but this is nothing to do with the arms race. It means I decided something by myself, even though it affects us all – and I'm sorry if you're all really disappointed or if you think I've been heavy-handed, but I think in the end it was something I needed to decide for all of us. You see, I've decided I want us to stay here. Not to move back to Fox Colne.'

There was a brief silence, noteworthy for its lack of a sense of shock or outrage, then: 'Well, of course you have,' said Fergus matter-of-factly, 'otherwise you wouldn't have

406

spent the evening painting this house to look like the set of *Star Trek IV*.'

'I thought you'd think I was doing it because I was putting it on the market.'

'Are you crazy?' Anemone grinned. 'No one would buy a house with a purple bathroom and a red hall. It's like walking into the womb.'

Alice frowned. 'You all seem amazingly . . . unsurprised. I thought you'd be really disappointed. I thought you were all really keen to go back to Fox Colne?'

Daisy and Anemone looked at one another, but it was Fergus who spoke again. 'We thought it was what you wanted. Well, they did. I thought maybe it was a bad idea. Fred says it's going backwards, and Mr Blackwell says that if you run looking backwards you fall over your feet, and –'

'He means in cricket,' said Daisy drily. 'He only ever talks about cricket.'

Alice was conscious of an odd feeling of disappointment that Mr Blackwell's conversational repertoire was so limited. 'Much of the law of cricket,' she observed lightly, 'can also be applied to life.'

'Well, I'm really glad we've got a gloopy red hall,' said Fergus firmly. 'I never wanted to move even in the first place. It was Anemone's potty idea.'

'Don't you blame me. As I remember it, you're the one that told the Hamiltons we'd buy their house. In any case, the feng shui is better here,' said Anemone crossly.

'Well then, that's settled. You can come and help me choose a colour for the kitchen.' Alice had been expecting an argument and couldn't believe she'd got off so lightly.

'Can I do some painting?' Fergus was always eager where there was potential mess involved.

'As long as it's not gloss,' said Alice. 'After all, you can't be Fred's best man with paint in your hair.'

They spent the whole weekend painting. Tom, the mournful

Tom who had turned up for a late supper on Saturday night and not really left since, spending the whole evening playing Scrabble with Fergus and trying not to get the letters 'M-A-R-T-H-A' arranged on his stand, actually proved his worth as a tall man on the Sunday by consenting to do the inaccessible bits, and Alice began to feel a real sense of achievement.

There was only one problem. She still wasn't thinking about Rob. It was all there in her mind, churning around – the knowledge that her conversation with Heather Bunberry was having a huge subterranean impact that she really needed to expose and think about – but she just wasn't ready to examine it yet. She just couldn't. And on the Sunday evening, when Fergus and Anemone announced out of the blue that they'd like to go to Fox Colne church and tidy Rob's grave Alice didn't want to go with them. She needed to be quite sure what she thought about all this before she told Rob.

Chapter Twenty

It was a few days later that a new crisis arose, when Alice found Dean Grabber on the emergency list to see her.

She sighed when she saw him there. Pre-wedding nerves again? Please don't let this be about sex. It had been bad enough last Tuesday when he had confided his worries about Lisa's ravenous sexual appetite and whether or not he could cope for an entire honeymoon. Alice had taken this to be a roundabout request for Viagra and had forborne to offer any, delivering instead a small homily on the difference between the sexual performance the average male can produce and that which magazines and laddish talk lead him to believe that everyone else is managing. Still, hearing the nitty-gritty from Dean she had needed to remind herself sternly several times that all GPs are by definition immune to embarrassment.

Looking in his notes now she saw that he had been back to see Tom at the last Saturday emergency surgery feeling fluey and itchy – pre-wedding nerves again, no doubt, such is the variety of presentation of problems of the psyche – although Tom had sent off a blood test to be on the safe side . . . Now where was it? She rooted around on her desk, and pressed the intercom to call Dean in.

Dean looked a rather sorry figure when he opened the door. There was a droop to his shoulders, a lack of gleam in his eye. Even so, it took her a moment to spot what was wrong.

Many doctors have a blind spot when it comes to jaundice. You'd think, Alice had often said to herself, that a yellow person would be so very obviously different from a pink one that there was no way you could miss it – yet she knew she was not alone in finding it hard to spot. Jaundice is like a dinosaur under the bed – easy to miss if you don't look for it but ridiculously obvious once you know it's there.

It was there today. Dean, Alice realised, was the colour of a ripe banana.

Dean told her he had been feeling under the weather more or less since his stag night just over a week ago. It had been a sane and sensible stag night – with only a few high jinks on the riverbank to erase the embarrassing experience of the strippogram turning to be his best friend, Joe's, little sister, Melanie, earning a bit on the side. Well, they *had* all finished up thigh-deep and naked in Fox Colne duck pond, and he had not been allowed out of the water until he had performed several forfeits including drinking the best part of a pint of it – but it had been a warm enough evening, he couldn't possibly have caught a chill, whatever his mother said – I mean, his thing hadn't even shrunk, he'd checked afterwards. Diameter and length.

He hacked hollowly – he felt really pretty sick and shaky, and he'd gone right off his beer – and the funny yellow colour his eyes had suddenly gone this morning had worried him into making another appointment with Dr Vane, even though there was always the inherent risk with women doctors that they might want to examine his testicles. Of course, there was nothing wrong with his testicles, but women doctors were all the same, all his mates said so (in those rather wistful tones which he took to mean that no one had actually found out for himself). That was the real story behind all those Well Man posters they put up all over the place, they'd told him. 'Get your blood pressure checked,' the posters said. 'Are you looking after your heart? What's your cholesterol? Do you smoke? Oh, and by the way, if you've never felt your own nuts, your doctor will be delighted to grope them for you.' Everyone said that's what was on them. And it was obvious women doctors would be the worst for it. They'd need the practice.

'I had a blood test,' he said now, keeping one hand vaguely in the area of his tackle lest Alice should make a sudden lunge in that direction. 'Dr Lovejoy did it – but I feel a bit worse now, and I've gone a funny colour.'

Alice smiled. 'You needn't look so nervous, Dean. I won't bite, although I would like to feel your liver.'

Sometimes we are so keyed up to hear one particular word that we hear it even when another is actually spoken. Dean leaped up as if stung. 'What d'you need to feel them for?'

Alice smiled. 'You look as though you might have yellow jaundice – I need to see if your liver is swollen or sore.'

'Oh, I get you. My *liver*.'

'Indeed.' Alice could guess what he thought she had said. Testicles probably. Most young men seemed to come into her room convinced that she would want to feel them. Even when Fred Ramsden had come for a medical – extraordinarily fit for however old he was (he had no medical records) – he had said, 'Just as long as you're not checking my tackle. I know that lot's fit as a fiddle.'

Now she told Dean, 'Your test isn't up on the screen. Let me go and see if it's arrived in today's post.'

She found Dean's test results on the morning pile and told him the terrible truth, promising, as he departed for hospital, that she would tell Lisa.

Lisa was not in reception, having started her maternity leave the week before, so Alice called in to see her after surgery.

'Lepto what?'

'Leptospirosis, Lisa. It's a viral infection. He'll be –'

'How'd he get it?'

'Well – you get it from rats. From rats' urine, to be exact. I should think in this case the village pond is to blame. There are rats around there, and when poor Dean fell in it and drank –'

411

'Poor Dean? I'll give him poor bloody Dean. Where is he?'

'He's going into the infectious diseases ward, Lisa. Don't worry – he'll be OK.'

'Not if I get my hands on him he won't,' said Lisa. 'He's tried every flipping trick in the book to get out of marrying me, but swimming in rat wee, that really takes the biscuit. If he really didn't want to marry me why didn't he just . . . just dump me and . . . and buy a bloody rat?' She dissolved into tears and hiccups. 'Will he be better in time for the wedding?'

Alice handed her a handy box of tissues, one sheet of tissue being never enough for Lisa, who approached boxed tissues with the same flamboyance she applied to the rest of her life. 'You're going to have to postpone, Lisa. He won't be better in a week, but he should be in for four weeks. Look, he was devastated when I sent him in to Addenbrooke's.'

Lisa snivelled into a fistful of Kleenex. 'Everything's ruined now. The stupid sod, why couldn't he have got drunk and managed to be left on a train to Glasgow like my brother?'

Alice sighed. 'He didn't mean it, Lisa. It just means you'll have to put things off for a month.'

'Put things off? If they get put off any more they'll be conducting the whole bloody ceremony round my bed on the delivery ward.'

'Lisa, when is your baby due, honestly?'

'Four or five weeks,' said Lisa miserably. 'Everyone thinks I'm nearly seven months pregnant but I'm really eight.'

'Oh, Lisa, why did you pretend?'

'I was afraid if I said then no one would have let me plan the wedding till afterwards. Dr Vane, don't you dare tell anyone. I'm going to get married before this baby comes out if I have to tie my ankles together.'

As if it hadn't been a difficult enough day, Roland cornered Alice at the end of it, looking truculent.

'Alice, a word?'

'Can it be quick, Roland? I'm busy – there's so much to sort out before we move. Did you have a chance to read our letter? We hope to move out in a month.'

'Yes – I did read it. I will of course expect a full three months' rent in lieu of notice. I'm rather disappointed in you, Alice. I had thought you might have been more loyal, yet I now discover that moving out early seems rather high on your agenda. I'm so sorry that you're choosing to leave me before the lease is up.'

Alice abandoned her good manners, which were rather tattered and torn when it came to Roland anyway, and removed her imaginary sword from her metaphorical scabbard. 'I would have thought you'd be delighted to be rid of us, Roland. You can get on with your money-making schemes now and forget you were ever a doctor.'

Roland sniffed. 'I think you'll find that attitude won't get you very far. I have many friends amongst the Cambridge medical fraternity.'

Alice decided not to rise to that. 'I'm sure you have.' No one I know. 'But we're going as soon as we can. Our professional relationship is untenable, Roland, you must be able to see that.'

He moved closer. 'I would have thought your relationship with me had rather more potential than that. Tell me, Alice, my dear, are you by any chance wearing those rather pricey red knickers, right now?'

'I'm bloody glad I kicked his shins,' said Alice to Tom afterwards, when he called round to Herne Road for coffee and to hear all about it, 'although stamping on his foot that hard might have been going a bit far. He's gone for an X-ray.'

'Serves him right, if you ask me,' said Anemone, from the corner of the kitchen. 'He's such a slime. What do you suppose his birth sign is?'

'Oh, Roland couldn't possibly have been born,' said Alice,

pouring coffee for Tom. 'Roland just oozed out of someone's darkest nightmare. Like ectoplasm. Tom, when is the soonest that we could possibly move? I mean, I know we said a month or two, but I can't stand another minute of him. I can't bear it when he comes and paws at me mentally – it's like sharing a building with Swamp Thing – and anyway, it wouldn't surprise me if he locks us out after what I did. And after what I said.'

Anemone grinned. 'I don't see why. You were probably only speaking the truth. He probably *is* impotent and it probably *is* only three inches long, and I know it's true you wouldn't go near him if he was the last man on –'

'All right, you don't need to remind me. Tom, is there any way we could bring things forward and move earlier? Much, much earlier? It wouldn't matter if we had to camp out and things were a bit chaotic. I mean, given that it might help prevent murder being committed . . .'

Tom considered it levelly (oh, you are a nice man. Martha is just so crazy to have dumped you). 'Well, if I get builders in round the clock we could probably have the bare bones of the surgery ready in the Pavilion next week. I don't know how it would look. It might all feel a bit Heath Robinson for a while, but if you don't mind roughing it . . .'

'I don't care,' said Alice, 'let's start packing.' She kissed him suddenly on the cheek. 'Thank goodness you came here. Much as I adore Martha she really is a prize idiot.' She clapped her hand to her mouth. 'Oh God. I'm sorry – I –'

'My mother,' said Anemone airily to no one, 'could put her foot in it for England. If putting your foot in it was an Olympic sport she'd have captained the England team.'

'I'm so sorry, Tom. I didn't mean to make you feel – I mean, it's none of my business, I'm just . . . well, she's my best friend and you're my partner. I can't help worrying . . .'

'It's OK.' He shrugged, drained his cup. 'There's really no secret. I'm madly in love with the woman and she's taken off to have herself pummelled and starved until she's sure she's not in love with me. It happens. No one ever promised life would be perfect and there's no law that says things always work out.'

'Well, she's a fool,' said Anemone, 'and if you ask me . . .'

'Which nobody was,' said Alice, over the top of her daughter.

Anemone ignored her, '. . . if you ask me your stars are perfectly matched. She's obviously bound to come back to you.'

'Thank you, Anemone.' Tom nodded seriously. 'I shall treasure that thought.' He smiled his handsome-devil smile.

Hm, thought Alice, broken heart but still devastating. Ladies, lock up your daughters.

Anemone felt her heart flutter. Wow. Far too old for her, though. Almost as bad as her mum's thing about Sean Connery. I mean, what? Still, she waved to him from the front door as he drove off in his sports car, wow. You had to have something to set your standards by.

Alice was surprised to find a postcard from Norfolk on the mat the following morning saying that Martha was staying there for a while and Alice wasn't to worry. There had been a couple of phone calls from the health farm – I'm-all-right-but-ask-me-nothing sort of calls – but she had never mentioned Norfolk. Indeed, Martha had always shuddered at any suggestion she accompany Alice and her children to the North Norfolk coast over the years. Perhaps it was an exercise in self-flagellation – or perhaps Norfolk held a deeper significance for her. Still, there wasn't much Alice could do; Martha hadn't given an address. Alice wondered if Tom knew where Martha was. Perhaps he could go and sweep her off her feet. Still, you never knew with Martha, that could backfire badly. She held on to her independence like a drowning woman.

It was another bright day, a happy sun sitting bright in a blue sky, reminding Alice uncannily of poor Dean and his jaundice. It was rendered brighter by the knowledge that she didn't have to see Roland and his foot, as it was the day of Fred and Tabitha's wedding and she and Tom had persuaded a locum GP to cover the surgery in exchange for lots of pleading and a large sum of money.

Fred and Tabitha were to be married by special licence in St Alupent's College chapel, an ancient building in whose wall the bones of the founding saint reputedly rested. Virtually all the residents of the Fir Trees had been wheeled over for the occasion, the resulting crocodile of wheelchairs and zimmer frames managing, by the peculiar laws which govern traffic congestion, to hold up central Cambridge traffic for some hours after the wedding had actually taken place.

Herman was to give Tabitha away, and he was quite overcome with emotion. 'I feel so honoured,' he kept whispering to Alice, 'that I, a stranger, should be asked.' But Tabitha said she could see no one more appropriate, given the circumstances. She wore a white meringue – also as promised. She didn't see why she shouldn't, she said – white was her best colour and if you couldn't look ridiculous at eighty-two, when could you? She didn't look ridiculous, though; she looked like an ancient and rather magical fairy godmother.

Surely Tamas would have been delighted, thought Alice. A full circle has come round and life has begun again for Tabitha and Fred. Will it ever really begin again for me?

She was chatting to Matron ('I don't know, Dr Vane, honeymooning in Armenia at their age, and going off to stay with that odd little man . . .'), when Tom appeared and interrupted her.

'Alice. I've been speaking to the builders and I've called in a few favours. We're definitely on for next week for moving into the Pavilion. I've just got a removal firm organised for Sunday, and I'm off now to speak to the staff, ask for volunteers to help.'

Alice could have hugged him. 'Oh, that's marvellous. That is fantastic!' To be out of Roland's clutches at last! 'Ian isn't going to believe it when he gets back. I can barely believe it myself. Did you hear about Roland's toe? Apparently I actually broke it. Do you suppose he'll sue me?'

'I doubt it,' said Tom. 'He wouldn't want the scandal. Can you imagine the fun the press would have? We could give them the whole story – loo rolls, lavatory doors, arguments about parking . . .'

'No one would ever believe it,' said Alice admiringly.

Tom smiled. 'People believe anything about doctors these days.' Alice thought that his smile did not quite reach his eyes.

'Have you heard from Martha?'

'No, I haven't. I think I have to accept she's the one that got away.'

'I don't know, Tom,' Alice sighed. 'Anything could still happen, you know. Nothing like you has ever happened to her before.'

He brightened slightly. 'So I have made an impression, then? I thought perhaps I was just one of a trail of breast-beating men scattered weeping across Southern England.'

Alice shook her head. 'Not really. She's a very careful person, Tom. She keeps her heart to herself. She's gone to Norfolk, and that's something I've not known her do before either.' I've said too much, she thought, I shouldn't interfere. I spend my entire working life interfering, I shouldn't do it in my spare time.

Tom was looking rather pale suddenly. 'Do you know where in Norfolk?'

'On the coast. She sent us a postcard of Holkham Beach.'

'Holkham Beach. But that's where her . . . Are you sure?'

Alice frowned. 'What's wrong? You look as if you've seen a ghost. Tom? What's so awful about Holkham?'

But all Tom would say was, 'I have to go and find her,

Alice. I have to go now. Will you cover for me?'

'Alice, come and be in a photograph.' Tabitha took her arm. 'Now tell me, have you finally decided to stay in that nice little house of yours that Fergus is so fond of?'

Alice allowed herself to be swept along, glancing back at Tom, who had disengaged from Tabitha and was heading out of college. 'Yes, we have. We thought perhaps it was better to stay there. We've been –'

'Absolutely. No point taking a step back to try and go forwards. Confront the past by all means, but there's no need to wallow in it. Otherwise, my dear, you end up like me. Is handsome young Tom all right?'

'More or less,' said Alice, 'although I think he's suddenly had to go to Norfolk.'

Martha had once loved Norfolk, long ago, before her mother spoiled it for her by dying there. The impulse which had led her north rather than back home was still worrying her, but now she was here, in the place where her parents had spent their honeymoon, the place her mother had come back to repeatedly to drown her loss in bottles of whatever she could buy, the place where she had finally managed to drown herself in the literal sense using one bottle of whisky and one good-sized ocean. It was as if she expected to find an answer. An answer to what, she had no idea.

Now she sat on the beach, which was as bare and bleached as anything in New England. That was why her father had loved it – until her mother made it haunted for him. He never came back here again. How could he, after all?

The sea was far out, a mile of ridged and rutted sand exposed, and the *café au lait* of the sand and pale grey-blue sky reminded her of the home of her childhood. There were few people about. A hundred yards away a couple strolled hand in hand, whilst a large dog rushed around them in ecstatic excitement. The beach was beautiful in its way.

There was no sign, no plaque that said this was the place where Martha's mother had died. Martha didn't even know for sure that this was the place exactly, just that it was near here, just like here. That was all she had ever known, ever wanted to know.

The tide had turned in the distance and was heading in slowly – Martha could hear the muted roar of the waves. The sea and sand were the same coffee grey, the water distinguishable only by the movement of the waves and flecks of foam. Beautiful colours, she thought absently. Soothing and calm.

Three boats lay on their sides in the sand, waiting for water to buoy them, helpless and forlorn. This was a watercolour scene, serene and empty. She had been so happy here as a child, but she had never been back in all these years, not since her dad left and took all the fun with him. And now all the fun's gone out of me, she thought. I've already lost what I feared losing. My safety.

There was a shriek over to her left, and two small vivid boys in scarlet jumpers cycled frantically across between Martha and the sea, bumping over the ridges in the sand like small tanks fleeing from battle. They looked about seven or eight to Martha, who was not good at judging the ages of children, one pursuing the other, and neither particularly steady. Both were laughing fit to burst – and as she watched one fell from his bicycle, collapsing beneath it onto the sand. The other stopped, reminding her of that wonderful Rolf Harris song about two little boys each having a wooden horse, and helped him up. It was all over too quickly even for her to rush over and help, and then they were up and off.

After they had gone the scene did not seem the same. It was as if, Martha realised, the two bright boys with their noise and exhilaration, had taken the colour away with them, leaving it a drained and lesser thing.

And it seemed to her that she was like the beach. She

might be serene and beautiful, co-ordinated and elegant – but ultimately she was colourless. She lacked some quality, some essential ingredient without which you cannot vibrate with life. When had she lost it? Where? Or had she never had it in the first place – never, that is, until he came into her life? When she fell in love?

Because she *had* fallen in love with Tom, of course she had. What was the point in pretending otherwise? Pretend it to other people, fine, but you can't pretend to yourself, she thought. Not when you're basically honest. You can't help inner honesty when you're American. It's only the English who conceal their feelings best of all from themselves.

This had to be love. The only alternative was that she was in the grip of some strange psychiatric condition – yet Alice, who should surely know if that were the case, seemed convinced that it was love. It was just like it is in all those awful pop songs, a mixture of indigestion, palpitations and obsession. Everything the Beatles wrote suddenly fitted perfectly into context. How pathetic she was.

The couple with the dog reached the closest point that their path would take them to Martha and glanced at one another. Everyone knew there had been suicides on this beach before. Something about the melancholia of the colours, local people said.

'D'you think we should see if she's OK?' asked the woman, as the huge dog turned in the sand and flung grains of it all over her. 'The tide's coming in.'

The man shook his head. 'You can't just walk up to a stranger and ask them if they're planning to end it all. Anyway, she's probably just having a rest on her walk.'

The woman frowned. 'She does look a bit sad. Perhaps if we walk back slowly . . .'

Martha stared at the sand and contemplated the truth. That this empty sadness she felt was loss, but that Tom had not taken anything from her that he had not himself given her in the first place; that she was no more incomplete now than she had been before she met him. She felt she now saw herself for what she truly was. A barren island. A woman whose life would always be empty because she valued invulnerability more than love. Tom was my chance to be something else, to be truly vulnerable yet truly alive, she told herself – and I was so afraid of it that I threw him away.

Is it too late? If I went to him and said, 'Tom, I love you' – if I dared to go to him and say what my mother said so pathetically and endlessly to my father, said, 'Please stay with me because I can't bear to live without you', what could happen to me? The worst that could happen is that he'd say, 'Well, you'll just have to, so piss off' and I'd lose him. I'd be no worse off than I am now.

In the distance a figure walked out onto the sand past the two with the leaping dog, who seemed to be walking ever more slowly. Perhaps they think I'm contemplating suicide, she thought. Maybe I should give them a little wave. But no, they were speaking to the lone figure. She frowned. Perhaps it was the father of those two little boys. Perhaps he was afraid they had been swept out to sea. Where were they? The Norfolk tides could be funny – but no, two small specks far over the other way, that was them, wobbling and bumping over the sand.

Martha got to her feet and wandered towards the edge of the sea, watching her toes sink slightly into the ribbed sand. The tide was coming in fast now, the colours blending so that the sand and the sea and the sky were all one. She conjured up the image of her mother standing here that night, full of introversion, and regret, ready to die of depression and alcoholism (and maybe actually accidentally, when all was said and done) – but really dying of not being able to live without him.

Can I really risk all that? Can I risk finding myself here like her?

Well, I'm here now, aren't I? Am I made of the same stuff as my mother, the sort of stuff that could just give up and let

421

the seas engulf me and swallow me up? Could I honestly just walk out there now and not stop, just because he told me to piss off and never bother him again? Am I enough like her?

Of course I'm not. I know I'm not. This is stupid, truly stupid. Did I really need a look at the seashore in Norfolk to tell me that I'm not like my mother, that I don't have a self-destructive impulse, that I'm strong? I've always known I wasn't like her. So what am I doing here, morbidly staring at the sea she drowned her sorrows in? Why the devil aren't I back in Cambridge making at least some effort to get and keep what I really want? To hell with it. Nothing's *ever* stopped me getting what I wanted before. Where is that bloody man? I've got a few things I need to say to him . . .

A sound drifted to her on the wind, piercing her thoughts with something familiar. Singing. Who would be singing on the beach?

She glanced back at the collection of figures in the distance. One had detached itself from the other two and was coming towards her slowly. She caught snatches of something on the sea breeze, of a baritone, quite strong, 'Be my love, for no one else . . . this yearning.' Oh my God. It was Harry Secombe. No – no it wasn't. Much too tall. Much too . . . He was singing beautifully. He seemed to be singing to her. How bizarre, some madman on a Norfolk beach was singing to her. She'd better run . . . And yet, he *was* singing to her. There was something very familiar about that silhouette. It could only be . . . Could it really be?

I'll sing for you one day.

And Martha began to run, to run back across the sand towards him. And as she ran she saw that he was running too, running fast towards her.

'Tom!' The wind whipped her words away from her and carried them to him. 'Tom!' Her heart was thudding, her breath coming in gasps. The air roared past her ears, wet sand splashed all up her legs and her hair plastered dankly across her forehead. She tripped twice on invisible ridges in the sand, kept her balance by the skin of her teeth, then, when she had almost reached him, tripped and flew inelegantly through the air, landing face down in the wet sand in front of him.

'Martha!'

'Tom!' She struggled to her feet and fell into his arms at speed, laughing hysterically, gasping for breath. 'Tom! Tom, it's you! I can't believe it's you!'

He swung her into the air, triumphant, laughing. 'Martha – thank God I found you! I was afraid for you. I thought you'd come here to –'

'Don't even think such a thing. Oh Tom, I'm so glad you're here.'

'Why didn't you tell me where you were? How could you run off like that?'

'Tom, oh Tom, I've been so stupid, such a bloody fool.'

'You certainly have – but I'm no better. I should never have let you out of my sight. Martha, I –'

'Tom, I have to tell you that I can't live without you.'

'Well, thank God you've realised it. Come here!'

She couldn't kiss him for laughing, in the end, and laughter is infectious and then he couldn't kiss her either, and so they walked, holding hands, in some vague direction that wouldn't get them anywhere for a while.

'Do we know what we're laughing at?'

'This is all just so Jane Austen,' said Martha. 'I can't believe I've just been an integral part of so impossibly corny a scene.'

'It's not corny yet.'

'I don't see how it could get much cornier.'

'Then let me show you,' he said.

Across the sands the couple with the dog looked at one another and the woman sighed. 'I wish we had the video camera with us. It's like something out of *From Here to Eternity*.'

423

The man shrugged. 'They're barmy. I wouldn't lie in wet sand just for a snog.'

'You've got no romantic soul, you.'

He grinned. 'I'll tell you what, if they have a shag I'll run home and get the Sony.'

She shoved him playfully. 'You are awful.'

'I know. Come on, judging from the way they're snogging the only risk now is that they'll both suffocate. Let's go for some chips.'

Chapter Twenty-one

Whilst Tom pursued Martha across Norfolk beaches, Fred and Tabitha were departing for their honeymoon in Armenia – and they were taking someone with them. Herman Banescu was going home.

Alice drove them to the airport for their flight to Yerevan, accompanied by Fergus, who felt that, as best man, his duties extended to seeing them through to passport control. He was a little worried, he told Alice in the car as they waited for their passengers, that he ought to have given Fred some wedding night advice but Alice said she was sure Fred would manage.

'D'you think they'll manage in Armenia?' asked Fergus anxiously. 'I mean, they live in a rest home.'

'They'll be fine,' said Alice, watching Fred wrestling with Herman for the right to carry his suitcases. 'They live in a rest home, not a nursing home. It's a glorified hotel really – they're fitter than a lot of people half their age.'

'So why don't they just live in a house like us?' asked Fergus, puzzled.

Alice shrugged. 'Well, Fred owns the Fir Trees, so you could take the view that he does live in his own house and just takes in lodgers. But really I think they live there for the company. It's like going to university – you get to have a wild time with people of your own age and no one else can interfere.'

'So now they're married they might move out, get a place of their own?' Fergus was thoughtful.

Alice smiled. 'It's a nice thought.'

Fergus looked important. 'Well, I'll talk to them about it,' he said rather officiously. 'It's my job to advise and I've got a few suggestions.'

Heavens, thought Alice. He may have the best of Rob but he's a heck of a lot more decisive.

It was a jolly drive to the airport, even though Alice hated goodbyes, with Herman wearing his uncle's ring this time as he said he wasn't going to take any more chance on frogs. It was a valuable ring, he explained, and very old, and it had been very likely that someone might not like him taking it out of Armenia, but no one would mind him taking it back in. He was extremely excited about going home, and waxed lyrical to Fred and Tabitha about the wonders of Armenia, the great Cathedral of St Gregory and the beautiful churches and museums, the fantastic cathedral museum, the most important in the whole country, of which he himself was curator, and Alice realised she was going to miss him, his quiet presence, his rather profound statements of wisdom.

'Who on earth is going to finish the Corn Pops?' she asked him.

'Aha,' said Herman, 'fear not, I have them packed. No need to worry.' He would not, he told her, even consider leaving England till she promised that she and the children would come and visit him in Yerevan, and so a deal was made that they would meet again in a year.

They had to spend an inordinately long time at Heathrow. Check-in had been two hours before the flight, an interval Alice felt sure was designed to relieve incarcerated travellers of everything they had in their wallets prior to their actually getting on the plane. 'I mean, why is there always a shop selling shoes?' she asked Fergus. 'I can understand arriving at the airport and discovering you've forgotten your tie, or your book, or even your camera film – but how many people arrive and realise they've forgotten their shoes?'

Fergus shrugged. 'People will buy anything if it's there,'

426

he said wisely. 'I bet if there was a shop here selling empty boxes people would buy them.'

And indeed it seemed there was one, for Herman found it and insisted on buying small but empty boxes for each of his nieces and nephews. There seemed to be an awful lot of them.

'What on earth have you bought all those for?' Alice asked him as he collected his change.

'Ah,' said Herman, 'because an empty box is the most interesting gift of all. It is like life. It exercises the imagination.'

'I don't think it's interesting,' said Fergus. 'I mean, there's nothing in it. You have to find stuff to put in it yourself.'

'Exactly,' said Herman. 'It is full of possibilities.'

The call for the flight seemed to come upon them quite suddenly and it was time for the three passengers to clear customs. Alice hugged them all, whilst Fergus kissed Tabitha and shook hands manfully with Fred and Herman.

'I'll look after the peacocks,' he told Fred, 'and I'll tell you about my ideas for your future when you get back.'

'When I get back? Whatever happened to e-mail? They have e-mail in Yerevan, don't they, Herman?'

'Of course we do,' said Herman indignantly. 'Did I tell you that Armenia is the oldest Christian country in the world? In AD 301 after St Gregory –'

'You make sure his family knows he needs to see a doctor,' said Alice to Tabitha. 'He needs an exercise test at the very least, and he needs to stay on the medicines they put him on at Addenbrooke's.'

'Stop worrying, for heaven's sake,' said Tabitha. 'You may be our doctor but we can take care of ourselves.'

Then they were gone, out of sight, and Fergus insisted on taking Alice right to the top of the tower to watch the plane departing so they could wave until it disappeared. And when the Armenian flight took off and was swallowed by the clouds Alice found to her surprise that she was smiling, she who wept when Fergus got on the bus to go to a rugby match, and that it didn't seem like a goodbye at all – they were all far too happy for that. Perhaps she was getting better at goodbyes. She had felt for a long time as if every goodbye was a reflection of the last time she saw Rob, that every goodbye should be imbued with the kind of things you say the very last time you ever see someone – but the feeling seemed to have receded now, very recently, and she was not sure why.

Fergus put his arm round her. 'Are you OK, Mum?'

'Yes,' she said, and smiled at him. 'Yes I am. Fergus, did you know Herman was curator of the cathedral museum? I hadn't realised.'

'Course I did,' said Fergus. 'That's why he was so worried about that ring.'

'What do you mean?' Alice was puzzled.

'It's the ring of St Gregory,' said Fergus, 'the founder of Christianity in Armenia. Herman's Uncle Tamas had it for all these years without knowing what it was, but Herman knew the minute he saw it. It had been lost since a big earthquake nearly a hundred years ago, and if they'd caught him taking it out of the country he'd have lost his job and maybe even been put in jail. He said it was worth a fortune.'

'And he still brought it for Tabitha?'

'He was honour bound,' said Fergus seriously, 'so he had to – but he was jolly pleased to get the chance to take it home again. It belongs in his museum.'

Alice stared after the invisible plane with admiration. There had been more to Herman than met the eye. 'Why didn't he tell me?'

'He didn't want to worry you,' said Fergus, 'and he knew if he told Tabitha she wouldn't be able to keep the ring, and that wouldn't have been fair. It's important to be fair, don't you think, Mum?'

'Of course I do.'

Fergus watched her thoughtfully for a minute, then said something which had worried him for a long time. 'Dad wasn't fair to you, though, was he?'

Alice frowned, trying to find something that would help. 'People can't always be fair to everyone, Fergus. Your father always did his best, and he loved us all. You just have to forgive him the rest.'

Which is what I've been trying to do all this time, she thought. If I could just forgive him it would help me most of all.

Three days later, after a superhuman effort on the not-murdering-Roland-with-a-blunt-and-grubby-instrument front by Alice, the practice moved, and the Pavilion Surgery was born.

Everyone Alice could think of asking had been roped in to help, and all had come, even though it was a Sunday. Most of the staff were there – even Lisa, who although too heavy with child to actually lift anything, had come to supply a constant level of faintly irritating postponed-wedding chat. Probably, reflected Alice, fighting the urge to strangle her, people work best when they are ever so faintly irritated. It keeps them on their toes.

There was also a sprinkling of journalists. There was a certain amount of interest in the story of a practice moving into the old cricket pavilion. Not only were the Cambridge papers snapping photos, but the infamous *Yes* magazine had decided they would make a good human-interest story for the half-page between the society beauties and the society parties. Alice guessed that Lisa, who rather incongruously hoped to feature in the society weddings section of the magazine, had had something to do with getting them along.

Martha and Tom arrived a little late, with a faintly suspicious glow about them which, Alice felt, did not need exploring. Martha, although dressed in the most ordinary of jeans and a sweatshirt, managed to spend the day looking as though she was a *Vogue* model posing at her editor's whim with a group of removal people and a rather scruffy lady doctor. Tom looked like the matching Disney cartoon hero. Obviously they were made for each other – no one else could ever have measured up to either of them.

It had taken them less time than Alice had expected to get everything loaded onto the van. The district nurses turned up halfway through to make sure no one was stealing their dressings or their scissors, and to Alice's surprise and secret pleasure Colin Blackwell arrived with his son, Mark, and took over the loading of the waiting-room chairs. Mark's presence spurred Daisy to a positively mammoth effort, and by three o'clock in the afternoon they had completely finished shifting their possessions and Fergus had volunteered to make the tea.

Alice wandered quietly into her new consulting room, as they all sat on boxes congratulating one another, to sit alone for a moment and look at her walls. Yellow walls.

It was basic. She had a chair, a desk, a filing cabinet, a large box of personal effects and a working sink. But everything else could wait. This was going to work. On top of her box was a large sign, hastily painted by Anemone on a piece of plasterboard but managing, nevertheless, to convey the essence of things for now: 'The Pavilion Surgery. Dr Ian Stewart, Dr Alice Vane and Dr Thomas Lovejoy', said the sign importantly. The Pavilion Surgery. Rob would have been impressed.

Alice stood it on one side and rooted in her box. Lots of frogs, of course – and mixed in with them, pens, a box of paracetamol, spectacle case, a photo of Rob and the children. She got the photo out too. It was the one she had always had in her room, the nice photograph she had taken in Southwold. The one, she suddenly remembered, that had made Heather Bunberry cry. Rob smiled out of it, every inch the family man, transparent as clear water, uncomplicated, trustworthy . . .

Alice stared into his eyes, trying to remember what he had really been like, before all her memories were tainted by his death. What was Rob? Likeable. Full of bonhomie. A kind man. Affectionate. Fatherly. Hopeless with anything mechanical. Liked clothes but could never make up his mind what to wear. She smiled slightly – the bedroom used to be littered with his try-ons every morning. Indecisive to the last.

She caught her breath in sudden surprise. Indecisive. That was Rob through and through. Sweet and kind and indecisive. The Rob that Heather Bunberry talked about is far nearer to my Rob than the one I was left with before. My Rob was persuadable, gentle, affectionate, endearingly lovable, always, always indecisive . . . and kind. Maybe that was his undoing.

'Alice!' She looked up, startled out of her thoughts, as a familiar figure burst into the room and enveloped her in a bear hug.

'Ian!' Alice leaped to her feet, allowed herself to be whisked off them. 'Oh my God, Ian, it's so wonderful to see you! I wasn't expecting you till next week. When did you get back? How come you're early?' She propped the photograph on her desk.

'I got into Heathrow this morning. I got a standby seat – came via Australia . . . My God, woman, how fast have you moved? I went looking for you at the old place and there was only a rather sad sign saying that the surgery was now closed and all enquiries should be made to Parker's Piece. When I got here and saw you all setting up I could hardly believe my eyes. It's amazing! '

'I know. I know it is – it's all thanks to Tom. It's been a bit chaotic – I mean, we hadn't planned to move till the end of the month, but I couldn't bear Roland any longer, I'm afraid, so we did it in a hurry. What do you think of the place?'

'I think it's great, it's absolutely fantastic. I think you've done amazingly well. How are you, Alice, how *are* you?'

'I'm good, really. I'm just so relieved we've got out now.'

'I'm relieved you've got out too. Roland must be spitting fury.'

'He is. I broke his toe last week. We're going to be talking through solicitors from now on. How was your trip? I'm so sorry you had to curtail it.'

'It's fine, really. It's good to be back, good to be needed. How have you really been, Alice?'

He looked at her searchingly but Alice ducked it. 'We've all been great. Fergus is doing grade seven on the clarinet, and Daisy's been working on the Elgar and won the Cambridge bed race. Anemone's writing horoscopes for medical magazines and I've painted the house purple.'

'And James?'

'Better – much better now that he's not working. The last couple of weeks were worse for him. Roland stamped on his lupins, you know. Still, when I broke Roland's toe in two places it cheered James up no end. Apparently he laughed from the first to the fifteenth hole and started again in the clubhouse.'

Ian grinned. 'I heard. You leave Roland to me. But you shouldn't be moping alone in your room on a day like this. Come on. Let's have our first new partners' meeting.'

'So what do you think?' asked Lisa, as she and Jean leaned on the new reception desk watching the array of friends and helpers eating Jean's rock cakes (more rock than cake).

Jean frowned. 'I dinna think much of yon ice-cream van. Hoo mony surgeries hae' you ever seen wi' an ice-cream man in the reception area?'

'I think Dr Lovejoy thought it would be something different.' Lisa fiddled smugly with her engagement ring, and Jean's frozen countenance melted slightly.

'Och, Dr Lovejoy. It's such sad news aboot he and that woman.' She nodded at Martha as though she were Snow

432

White's step-mother and had just instructed the huntsman as to whose heart he was to bring her.

Lisa stared. 'Why? I think it's really sweet.'

Jean sniffed. 'He'd have been perfect for our Dr Alice. It's not right, her being all aloon like that.'

Lisa grinned. She was in sparkling mood now that Dean's colour was more of a magnolia and the wedding had been successfully rearranged, two weeks late but still a good week before her baby was due, and her dress let out yet again. 'I don't think she'll be alone for long.'

'Why? What do you mean?'

'That Mr Blackwell,' said Lisa confidingly, 'he's got his eye on her. Look at him watching her.' She gesticulated at Colin Blackwell, who was deep in conversation with Fergus. (They were comparing bad jokes and Fergus was being forced to concede that Mr Blackwell knew at least as many bad jokes as he did.)

'How do you know?'

'I'm to be a married woman, Jean,' said Lisa smugly, for when a girl has persuaded *Yes* magazine to cover her wedding her views on relationships are unquestionably correct, 'I can tell.'

Later that evening, tired but faintly exhilarated, Alice sat on Rob's grave as a melancholy evening sun fought to cast a few last golden rays onto the hebes before sinking exhausted beneath the Cambridge spires which formed the horizon. She ran her hand through the soft branches, atoms of Rob, and watched the shadows creep over Rob's soil as if a blanket were being slowly drawn up to warm him. She hadn't been here for a fortnight – but today it felt like the right place to be. Somewhere between talking to Heather Bunberry and sitting in the new surgery with Rob's photo an answer had come for the questions she had had for Rob. She felt better than she had for years.

'All this time,' she told Rob now, 'people tried to tell me

433

you died having meaningless sex. They thought that made it better, but they were wrong. Believing that would have meant accepting that I'd never really known you, and I couldn't bear that. My Rob wouldn't have had meaningless sex. I couldn't understand it so I couldn't forgive it.

'But Heather Bunberry has given you back to me. You weren't a man with hidden vices at all, you were soft and indecisive and a fool, a man who spent too much time looking backwards. You were always telling me how wonderful it was when we were first together, as if instead of getting better and better you always felt the best had already been. Maybe that's what happened with her. I ought to hate you for it, I ought to be so angry with you for being so stupid – but I don't, I'm not, not any more. I know you so well – you would have felt so desperately sorry. It's all over with, it's all forgiven.'

She wondered what it meant for her now, to forgive Rob. A fresh start? The chance simply to sigh less? What endless possibilities must surely be created purely by sighing less, since you would not be wasting nearly so much breath. She could probably climb Everest with all that saved breath.

Of course, you only really know you've made a new start when you're six months down the line. Where does a new start begin? With a cancelled house move? When you paint the bathroom purple and put silver stars on the lavatory seat?

Perhaps all of these things. 'I do miss you,' she told Rob and his hebes. 'I tried to wipe you out of my life by painting it all white, but all I was doing was erasing myself along with you.' It was, she felt, the most coherent thing she had ever said to Rob's grave, in all this time.

I should put some of Fred's mulch on these hebes. Rob would like that, even if it did make a pong.

Beside her Paddy nosed about with suppressed excitement. Alice smiled. We're all OK now, really, she thought. Rob's widow, Rob's children, Rob's parrot, Rob's dog. We're all OK with Rob now.

A short distance away Colin Blackwell had called in on the Hamiltons (whom he knew well) in Fox Colne to see how Phoebe was getting on since her operation. And so it was that he saw Alice's unmistakable Morris Minor parked beside the church and forgot Phoebe Hamilton entirely. Instead he found himself at the church gate, just as Alice was leaving. Oh God, he thought, here I am lying in wait for her and she's weeping on her husband's grave. I should have realised that's what she'd be doing. I can't let her see me. Spying on a grieving widow – how would that look?

There was a suitable tree right by the gate. Everyone knows that people never look up when they walk along – and if she did see him, well, he would just have to think of something intelligent and believable.

If it hadn't been for the Hamiltons' cat he would have got away with it. The Hamiltons' cat, however, was a particularly whining creature, and it had been feeling rather rattled recently. With Phoebe ill and Alana's inability to cope with anything at all whilst this was the case, the neighbours had been feeding it, and they had expected it to live off an expensive but inferior cat food like some ordinary neighbourhood cat. It had therefore begun to hunt mice in the churchyard in protest, but was not above begging passing strangers to adopt it and open a can of something better. Now, spotting Mr Blackwell stuffed into a laburnum tree three feet off the ground, it decided to make a major play for sympathy. It leaped onto the lower branches of the tree and attempted to display the kind of whining affection it hoped would be endearing. When Alice came down the church path Paddy barked excitedly into the air after it, and she looked up and spotted Mr Blackwell in the branches over the lich-gate. He was forced to come up with a fast explanation.

'Bats,' he said to Alice as she frowned up at him. 'I

435

thought if I sat up here the bats wouldn't notice me. I'm very interested in bats, you know.'

'Ah,' said Alice, reflecting again that beardlessness had rendered him rather handsome. 'I see. Pipistrelles, I suppose. Do you often watch bats?'

'Oh, now and again,' he said, trying to dismount and getting his jacket caught inelegantly on a branch, 'when I'm passing. I was just calling in to see Phoebe.'

Alice smiled. 'Here, let me help you.' She unhooked his jacket and noticed, in the process, that he smelled rather nice.

'It's a nice evening,' she said, dimpling slightly, 'for bats. Maybe a bit early in the day for them, though.'

Colin Blackwell looked embarrassed and decided to come clean. 'Actually when I saw you I didn't want to disturb you. It seemed better to hide.'

Alice smiled, finding him much easier to relax with without the beard. 'I was just visiting Rob's grave. It's not a problem – you shouldn't have worried.'

'Oh,' said Colin, wondering how to respond to that one. 'That's nice' might offend, and 'Do you come here often?' would be just awful. 'I feel a fool,' he said. 'I was actually hoping to catch you – to see if you'd like to come to a concert with me? They're doing Vivaldi at West Road music hall two weeks on Saturday, and I've got two tickets – but I've been stood up.'

'Oh?' Alice was mildly offended. What sort of an invitation was this?

He smiled. 'Yes – since Mark discovered your daughter he's cancelled all prior engagements with me.'

Well, I do love Vivaldi, thought Alice after she had accepted. I need something to look forward to on the other side of Lisa's wedding. He might not obviously be my type, insofar as it seems reasonable to suppose that Rob was my type (and he was nothing like Rob) – but I really do like Vivaldi, and in any case, it has to be better than body chocolate at the Angel Hotel.

436

The next two weeks shot by in a whirl of settling in to the new surgery. Anemone and her A level art friends had offered to supply art work to decorate it, and the foyer was now hung with an astonishing and striking set of pictures which provoked comment from patients every day. Alice had put Anemone's nude self-portrait upside down in one of the spare rooms in the hope that no one would notice but sadly her daughter had found it there and it now hung proudly behind the reception desk. Fortunately, art being what it now is at A level, there was very little chance of anyone recognising that it was Anemone, or even that it was a nude, but Alice felt that wasn't the point. The point was, could you really have a picture of your naked daughter in your surgery?

In the middle of it all Alice found time to entertain the Martha and Tom unit for supper together with a surprised but delighted Colin Blackwell, and found the new couple refreshingly happy and Colin both charming and good company. The fact that Daisy was completely mortified to find him there when she was dating his son was by the by. Indeed, as Alice said, if you looked at things the other way she could have been the one to be mortified that Daisy was dating Colin's son. Even Daisy's comment that she saw her Blackwell first did not sway her.

By the time the postcard arrived from Fred and Tabitha – the front of which showed St Gregory's cathedral with the heading, 'Armenia, the world's first Christian country' and the back of which said, 'Dear All, fantastic time, huge excitement caused by Herman finding long-lost ring for museum, see you soon' – the house in Herne Road had been completely repainted and Alice was adjusting to sleeping in a turquoise bedroom with gold and silver stars on the wall and a huge orange goldfish painted above the bed. She really wasn't sure if it was right for her. It might well, as she told Daisy and Anemone who had designed it, have been

437

right for the little mermaid, but she could get used to it.

It must surely explain why all of her dreams recently had been of floating, including the one about Lisa's wedding, the one in which her peach bridesmaid dress had been so bouffant and full that a breeze had caught her as she walked up the church path and she had floated right away.

The Saturday that was Lisa's wedding day dawned at last. Alice awoke early to the sound of birdsong, a warm sense of expectancy, and the sight of That Dress hanging on her wardrobe door. As she stretched she thought of her own wedding day, and to her complete astonishment found herself laughing. On that occasion she had awoken – so early that it had still been dark, had crept downstairs for milk and found Rob wedged in the kitchen window, where he had become stuck half an hour earlier when trying to deliver a single red rose onto her pillow. You couldn't say he hadn't loved her.

She sat in the garden of Herne Road drinking coffee and reading the latest postcard from Frances, who was continuing to defy fate and have a wonderful time in the Bahamas. It was gloriously sunny, with a cloudless sky and the kind of gentle breeze Cleopatra had to pay men with palm leaves to imitate. The garden looked lusher than usual – the hebes were definitely perking up. Like me, she thought. I'm perking up too. Perhaps, she had said to Fergus whimsically, I am linked to those hebes at some deep and mysterious level, so that when they blossom I do. But Fergus had laughed scornfully and said he'd already got two mad sisters, he could do without a mad mother, thanks very much. And anyway, that theory was old hat – Fred had said the problems with their garden were all down to topsoil, and nothing to do with being sad at all.

In Fox Colne Martha also woke in her pink New England bedroom. The six bells were chiming some extraordinary attempt at a tune and she sighed luxuriously. Beside her Tom sighed gently and she nudged him.

'Don't you dare snore at me, Thomas Lovejoy.'

'You snore,' he said, opening one eye.

Martha's jaw dropped. 'I do not.'

'You do too, I'm just too much of a gentleman to complain. Anyway, I love it when you snore. You're like a little gerbil.'

'I . . .' Martha didn't know what to say to that. 'I? Snore? Oh my God – a gerbil? I don't know what to say . . .' It didn't matter – he didn't give her chance to say much anyway. Which was fine.

In Bury St Edmunds Heather Bunberry was also awakened by the sound of bells, although there were rather more of them since she lived only feet from the cathedral. She lay and luxuriated in the linen pillows and listened to the tropical birds in the Abbey Gardens squeaking for their freedom. She wondered whether it had been the right thing to do in the end, telling Alice like that. She had looked so shocked, so pale that Heather had worried she might have done her some harm. Some greater harm, that is, than she had done her already.

But surely the truth was always better than wondering. And now that she was making a fresh start it was important to close that last door on the past. Why had she spent so long looking back when there were so many other wonderful doctors about? She was going to enjoy being the wife of a GP in Bury St Edmunds. She would become a pillar of local society. And she had so nearly become nothing but a pillar of something else, like Lot's wife, unable to turn properly away from the past. Well, the past was done with now.

At the foot of her bed her wedding dress hung, pristine and sparkling. And why shouldn't she wear white? She was starting with a clean slate. She smiled.

*

It was, Alice felt as she fastened Lisa into her bridal gown (a Lucrezia Borgia-style affair which concealed her advanced pregnancy remarkably well) going to be interesting. The further two week's gestation that had passed with Dean's illness had seen a burgeoning of Lisa's bosom of Rubensesque proportions. The valiant dressmaker had been concentrating so hard on expanding the skirt that she had failed to notice Lisa's bosoms becoming the kind of things that start balloonists fantasising about circumnavigating the globe. Now they heaved upwards like giant peaches. Alice was rather worried about the effect that it would all have on the vicar, who was a rather nervous fellow at the best of times – but it was Lisa's day, and its very dissimilarity from her own actually made it all the more fun. And Lisa looked beautiful, draped in a cloud of white lace like a giant mosquito net.

Outside Alice heard Fox Colne church chime an unmelodic twelve o'clock. So often she and Rob had awoken to those chimes – now he slept endlessly beneath them, even today when the Fox Colne bell ringers had clearly got together on Lisa and Dean's behalf and tried to make the six bells play the theme to *EastEnders*. She knew it was meant to be the theme to *EastEnders* because they had been practising it for weeks, but Rob would still have said it sounded like something out of *The Magic Roundabout*. He would have enjoyed this. She smiled broadly.

'Oh, Dr Vane, you do look lovely. Doesn't she look lovely, George?' Lisa's mother was hurtling around the house being unconditionally thrilled with everything and every-one she saw. She was an exceptionally large woman so this was slightly hazardous behaviour – but this was a momentous event in her life, and she had the poppy-red suit to prove it (indeed it was so poppy red that had this been Oxford Street rather than Fox Colne she might easily have been hailed from a bus stop). It would be the first time in generations of her family that there had been a wedding before childbirth – and a white wedding at that. The neighbours would be so jealous, especially that snooty woman Martha Coleman along the way. What was the point of selling fifty-pound knickers when it had taken her till she was thirty-four to keep a man. All those handsome young things she was forever taking home – you never saw one of them come back twice, did you? She had checked. Through proper ornithologists' binoculars.

By the time the photographer from *Yes* magazine, who was called Venetia and was clearly rather grand, had taken dozens of shots with accompanying jotted-down copy – of Lisa ('preparing for her big day in her small but stylish family home'), and of the bridesmaids ('a vision in loveliness dressed in Lisa's favourite peach'), and spent some time regaling them with tales of celebrity weddings she had been totally unimpressed by ('I mean, choosing a Snow White theme, I ask you, the bride hated her step-mother. I mean honestly, darling . . .') – they were running late. Lisa's two small nieces, dressed like the obligatory cream puffs, were picking the petals out of their bouquets, and the church bell was chiming twelve. Lisa, though, was looking pale and nervous, and had become unusually quiet. Alice held her hand whilst her mother fussed off after aspirin.

'Alice – do I look OK?'

'You look lovely. All you have to do now is relax. You're pale, though. Shall I find your blusher?'

'No,' Lisa caught her breath, 'I'm fine. I've just got butterflies in my tummy. I'm so afraid something will go wrong.'

'Nothing will go wrong,' said Alice firmly, 'it's all very easy. Believe me – I've done it. You'll love it.'

'I hope so.' Lisa looked up with sudden sharpness. 'I'm sorry, Alice, I shouldn't have asked you, should I?'

'What do you mean?'

'This must be really hard, when you and . . . the other Dr

Vane got married in the same church.'

Alice smiled. 'It's not hard, it's lovely. I'm pleased you asked me, and in any case, it brings back good memories. Rob and I were very happy that day. We were always very happy, actually.' She was surprised to hear herself say it but it was, she realised, absolutely true. She had lots of good memories of Rob and they were what mattered. Lately the good memories seemed to be surging over the bad like waves across a beach. Recognising that she had not been fundamentally wrong about Rob meant that the memories were hers again.

The bridesmaids and Lisa's mother had left for the church with the photographer in a flurry of fuss and excitement ('Does anybody want a wee-wee? Bryony, stop picking your nose. Come on, everyone, we're going to be late . . .') and Venetia had clambered into her Mercedes soft-top and followed on behind shouting, 'See you at the church gate!' Now only Alice, Lisa and her father remained. He smiled at them.

'Are you ready?'

Lisa stood up, ramrod straight. 'Oh God.' She stared at Alice through panicked eyes.

'What? Lisa, are you OK?'

'I – yes, of course. I'm fine. I'm just . . . nervous. Butterflies with hobnailed boots on.'

'You're going to be fantastic.'

'I know,' said Lisa, smiling bravely. 'I know I am,' and as she stood up to leave the house Alice thought she looked radiant. She felt tears in the back of her own eyes, remembering that look, remembering the day she herself wore it. And she missed Rob – not angrily, not painfully, but just sadly, and with a huge and sweet sense of relief.

The church was only a hundred yards away, and so they had decided to walk in procession. A small village boy had been paid to persuade a large black cat to cross their path for luck. As they approached he heaved the poor creature in

442

front of them and then pursued it at great speed towards the church. It looked, Alice thought, suspiciously sooty for a black cat. Behind him raced Dean's brother, videoing this spontaneous moment for posterity. Lisa seemed silent with nerves. I hope to goodness Dean's there, thought Alice. I expect she's terrified that he won't have turned up. Where are Ipswich Town playing today, I wonder?

Fox Colne church looked beautiful in the sunlight. A small crowd of interested onlookers were gathered, obscuring Alice's view of Rob's grave (she was not to know that Lisa's mum, who had a heart of gold beneath her vast layers of adipose tissue, had organised them thus). The vicar and the choir were waiting outside as Venetia took a dozen shots of Lisa arriving ('radiantly'), Lisa walking through the gate ('with a glow of excitement'), Lisa adjusting her train ('. . . of Nottinghamshire lace which Lisa hopes will become a family heirloom') and then they headed up the path to where the vicar and the choir awaited them. As they reached the church porch they heard the organist play a single fanfare note and the congregation stood.

Dean was there. Alice could feel Lisa relax at last as they straightened her train and prepared for the short walk down the aisle into Lisa's family history and the pages of *Yes*. The organist burst grandly into 'The Arrival of the Queen of Sheba', and with Dean beaming with pride, they were on. Alice was vaguely aware of a sea of faces, of patients, of surgery staff, of the video whirring. Whatever I do in my life from now on, she thought, I'll be doing it with people who will forever remember seeing me dressed as a toilet-roll holder. And who cares?

They headed down the aisle very slowly indeed – Lisa clearly wanted to savour every moment – and the Queen of Sheba had a chance to arrive, wander round for a while and have a cup of tea in the time it took them to reach the vicar. He was looking nervous. He's probably terrified of Lisa giving birth on the altar steps, Alice thought. It's funny how

443

some men are unnerved by late pregnancy. It's as if they think the waters may break in a flood and wash them away. She gave him an encouraging smile. Dean looked at Lisa and squeezed her arm. She took a deep breath and handed her bouquet to Alice, who staggered slightly under its weight (nothing was done by halves in Lisa's family, you had to grant them that).

'Dearly beloved . . .' began the vicar, and Alice was suddenly quietly aware that Lisa had been holding her breath and was now letting it out very slowly. It was a familiar sound to anyone who has ever been to an antenatal class and listened to the breathing exercises. Alice frowned. Surely Lisa couldn't be . . . No. No, she looks fine. You've watched too many TV medical dramas, Alice. People have been joking for weeks that she'd go into labour at her own wedding. You've let them get to you. Relax.

Things were going beautifully. The congregation sang the hymns lustily and the vicar made a very nice speech about the parallels between supporting one another in marriage and supporting your local football team. The atmosphere when they came to the exchange of vows was hushed and moving.

'Dean, will you take Lisa to be your wife? Will you love her, comfort her, honour and protect her, and, forsaking all others, be faithful to her as long as you both shall live?'

'I will.' Dean gripped Lisa's hand and Alice heard that breathing again. It must be nerves, she thought.

'Lisa, will you take Dean to be your husband? Will you love him, comfort him, honour and protect him, and, forsaking all others, be faithful to him as long as you both shall live?'

'I will.' Lisa spoke on a gasp.

'Dean,' said the vicar, repeat after me. 'I, Dean, take you, Lisa . . .'

'I, Dean, take you, Lisa . . .'

Alice smiled and remembered, and heard Lisa's mother

444

starting to cry copiously in the front row.

It was shortly afterwards that the problem became apparent. Dean had repeated his vows with perfect diction but as Lisa began she gasped and seized Dean's arm, and finally Alice knew for sure.

The vicar faltered. It seemed at first, Alice thought, that as Lisa had leaned forwards he had been slightly stunned by the sheer extent of her cleavage.

'Is everything OK?' he asked.

Lisa turned and looked for Alice. 'Alice . . .'

Alice moved towards her, whispered beneath the rising sound of the congregation's sudden concern. 'What is it? What's wrong?'

Lisa grabbed her hand and pressed it against her own abdomen, an abdomen now almost the size of the Rock of Gibraltar and certainly as hard. 'The baby. I think it's coming, Dr Vane,' she whispered.

'Calm down, love, you'll be fine. Just tell me, are you having contractions?'

'Yes . . .'

'Oh my God,' said Dean at the top of his voice, 'you can't have the baby in here! Someone call an ambulance.'

After that it was all chaos, as Lisa's mum rushed forward. 'Oh, my little girl! Are you all right? Mum is here . . .' She turned to Dean. 'This is all your fault. Now look what you've done!'

'Now hang on a minute.' Dean's mother appeared out of the fray. 'I don't really think it's fair to blame my Dean. Everyone knows that it takes two to . . .'

In the background Alice could see Venetia making frantic notes. And I can just imagine, she thought resignedly, what she's writing.

No one found out what it took two to do, although they could easily guess, for Dean, kneeling beside Lisa, waved an arm angrily. 'Oh, shut up, Mother. Lisa? Speak to me.' But Lisa just puffed frantically and hung onto him for dear life.

He started to sound panicky. 'Dr Vane, is she really having the baby now? What should we do?'

Alice looked at Lisa, who was puffing tellingly. 'First labours aren't usually very fast. I don't think we need to panic. Lisa, has it only just started?'

Lisa shook her head. 'No – up till now I could stand it.'

'Er – are we in trouble here?' asked the vicar, feeling his worst nightmares starting to materialise as unavoidably as his twin daughters hitting puberty, something which already preyed constantly on his mind even though they were only four years old. 'Shall I fetch a chair?'

'That might help,' said Alice. 'Lisa, how often are the pains coming?'

'I don't know. Every couple of minutes.'

Alice swallowed. 'When did they start?'

'Early this morning. I think it's been about eight hours.'

'Eight bloody hours? Why the hell didn't you tell me?' Dean's voice was a squeak.

'Because it's taken me eight bloody months to get you in here – sorry, Vicar – and I wasn't about to let a little thing like this get you off the hook. Stop trying to be masterful, Dean Grabber, it doesn't suit you. Dr Vane . . . how long have I got?'

Alice put a hand on her stomach. Obviously good quality contractions, but this was hardly the place to assess the state of the cervix. 'Well, possibly not very long, Lisa. I think we'd better call an ambulance. Does anyone have a mobile phone?'

Everyone, it appeared, had a mobile phone. Whilst someone went outside to use theirs Lisa began to cry. The vicar, reappearing with a chair from the vestry, cleared his throat. 'Do you – er – want to carry on in the meantime?'

Lisa pulled herself up to her full height, which wasn't far. 'Of course I do. I'm not going in any ambulance till we're married. I haven't come this far for nothing.'

At the head of the aisle Venetia was impressed. What

446

fortitude. This would make a fantastic spread. All she really needed was for the bridesmaid to deliver the baby . . .

Lisa's mother rallied round. 'Look, love, all that can wait. The last thing you want to do is risk your health.'

Lisa was unimpressed. 'Shut up, Mum. Get on with it, Vicar.'

Dean stood uncertainly. 'Are you sure? You can't have it here, you know.'

'I bloody can,' said Lisa, on a gasp. 'Please, Vicar, can I do it crouching down?'

'No you can't.' Dean was in a panic. 'This is my baby too. Come on, we're going to hospital.'

'I am not. I never said I'd promise to obey and I'm not starting now. You say your vows and I'll say mine and then I'll go to hospital . . . I want to be married when I have my baby. Where were we?'

The vicar looked doubtfully at Alice. 'Dr Vane, what do you recommend?'

'Well,' said Alice reasonably, 'the ambulance will be a few minutes. You may as well go on.'

'Oh please, Dean,' said Lisa, 'I'll do whatever you say if we can just get married first. Alice, you tell him . . .'

The vicar was looking rather rattled. 'Oh, very well. Though this is most unorthodox, I must say.'

He stood again. Dean crouched next to Lisa, who hung onto the chair. She had adopted a squatting position which rather alarmed Alice – but then they did encourage all sorts of positions in the first stage of labour. Assuming this was still the first stage of labour . . .

'I, Lisa Marie, take you Dean Tarquin, to be my –'

'Lisa Marie?' Dean was taken aback. 'I never knew you were called Lisa Marie . . .'

Lisa was concentrating hard. 'It's better than Tarquin. Hurry up.'

The vicar was on a runner. '. . . my wedded husband, to have and to hold from this day forward; for better, for

447

worse, for richer, for poorer, in sickness and in health, to love and to cherish till death us do part, according to God's holy law; and this is my solemn vow.'

Lisa took a huge breath and got it all out at the speed of sound: 'and this is my solemn vow. Dr Vane, I think I've got to push. What should I do?'

'Try not to, Lisa. Try just to take shallow breaths through the pains.' Alice squatted beside her. 'Have you finished, Vicar?'

'I don't think –'

'Finish!' shouted Lisa, 'because any minute now I'm going to give birth on your carpet!' It was a threat not to be taken lightly, in the circumstances.

Dean leaped to his feet. 'Shall I run and get the Walkman?'

Lisa grimaced. 'What? What are you taking about?'

'You said you wanted to listen to "Bat out of Hell" in labour. You kept on about it enough.'

Lisa was shouting now: 'I didn't think I'd be in labour during our wedding, did I? Vicar, will you please get on with it . . .'

The vicar was looking very pale. 'In the presence of God, and before this congregation, Dean and Lisa have given their consent and made their marriage vows – oh goodness, you haven't exchanged rings.'

There was a quick fumbling and more muttering as the exchange of rings was accomplished in record time. 'I therefore proclaim that they are husband and wife. Those that God has joined together, let not man divide. You may, if you wish, kiss the bride.' Golly, the vicar thought, the PCC only just bought this carpet. I wonder if we're insured?

Lisa pulled a face. 'You are joking. That's what got me where I am right now.'

The vicar felt he needed to reassert control of proceedings. 'Do you know, whilst we're waiting, perhaps we should sing the next hymn. Muriel, the next hymn, if you please.' But when Muriel hit the keys for the opening chords of 'Jerusalem' he winced. 'I think perhaps something a little quieter might be more . . .'

Lisa's mother, until now rendered almost speechless by having no real role to perform, took over. 'If my daughter chose "Jerusalem" then we're jolly well singing "Jerusalem". How many weddings d'you think she's going to have?' She turned to the congregation with a challenge in her eye. 'And what are you all looking at? Sing.'

She was a formidable woman, and so they sang: '*And did those feet in ancient times . . . Walk upon England's mountains green?'*

'Dr Vane . . .'

Alice kneeled beside Lisa. 'You'll be fine,' she said, with rather more confidence than she felt. 'Shall we go outside?'

'No . . . I can't move.'

Sometimes, thought Alice, there's absolutely nothing a doctor can do other than look confident. 'Just do little puffs when the urge comes, just puff it away. Try not to push. You're doing very well.'

'*And was the holy Lamb of God.'*

They all heard the sound of an ambulance siren in the distance.

'*On England's pleasant pastures seen?'*

Alice delved beneath the layers of net which disguised Lisa's lower regions. and felt around to assess the proceedings with the kind of lack of tact that midwives are famous for. This was no longer the time for modesty, even in church. God would surely understand. After all, cervixes were presumably his idea. What she felt was unmistakable.

'Lisa, the baby's just sitting there, waiting to come out. Do you think you can hold on till the ambulance . . . ?'

But Lisa couldn't – the urge to push was overwhelming, and now that she had let herself go she simply couldn't stop. She shook her head and gripped Dean's hand. 'Get them out of here.'

Venetia could not believe her luck. What drama. What excitement. This beat celebrity weddings with hundreds of cauliflower-nosed guards and fifty frames wasted trying to get the bride's smile right. This was life! Perhaps she should forget celebrity photography altogether and go into news work. The first Fortescue-fforbes to have a serious job . . .

But the congregation was going nowhere until they had fully sung England's most popular hymn.

'And did the Countenance Divine . . . Shine forth upon our clouded hills'

Alice had virtually disappeared into Lisa's skirt in an effort to preserve some modicum of modesty as the paramedics rushed up the aisle.

'And was Jerusalem builded here . . . Among these dark Satanic mills?'

They were, by chance, the same paramedics who had arrived at the surgery to find Alice ministering to Herman Banescu. Now they were delighted to be able to take part in the unfolding melodrama and insisted on trying to put Lisa onto a wheeled stretcher as the assembled wedding guests, sharing in enthusiasm what they lacked in tonal quality, roared forth about chariots of fire and wondered how come the film of that name got a hymn written about it. They were concluding that they would indeed build Jerusalem in England's green and pleasant land as the paramedics wheeled Lisa, clutching Dean's hand furiously, out of the church, closely followed by the intrepid Venetia.

They were only part-way down through the churchyard, though, when Lisa uttered a great howl and they had to stop.

Inside it was left to the vicar to close the stunned proceedings with a prayer, and as he did so the sound of a baby's cry echoed through the stone porch and the congregation attempted to rush outside to a man to see and admire. Fortunately the resulting crush meant that most people were stuck in the door waving their arms ineffectively.

'It's a little girl,' said Alice to Dean, wrapping the baby in the paramedics' blanket and passing her to Lisa, 'a little girl. She's beautiful.'

'Wow,' said Dean, remaining at the moment of parenthood about as eloquent as ever. 'Wow, Lisa. This is like . . . wow.'

'Wow,' said the paramedic who had clamped the cord, wondering how many pints he'd get out of this one. It certainly beat being first on the scene to a naked woman with her toe caught in the bath tap, particularly when you bore in mind that she had been sixty-six and almost as big as the bath.

There was a risk that they would all be submerged in the wave of emerging guests, and it was only then, as Alice looked up from the drama that she had been a part of, that she realised that they were next to Rob, right next to his very spot. How he would have laughed. Only you, Al, he would have said, only you could go to a wedding as a bridesmaid and end up giving immediate and necessary treatment to the bride. Only you . . .

Dean was glowing. 'We're going to call her Alice,' he told everyone proudly, 'after the doctor.'

'Oh,' said Alice, warmed and delighted, 'oh, that's lovely. Thank you, Dean.'

'That's OK,' said Dean generously. 'Lisa wanted a name out of Disney and Alice is her favourite.'

Just think, Alice told Rob as the ambulance pulled away, if she'd liked Pocahontas best. Pocahontas Grabber. Now that would be something.

'So it was nothing like your wedding, then,' said Anemone, finding Alice sipping white wine later in reflective mood.

Alice grinned. 'I wouldn't say that,' she said, a little wistfully. 'It was – a bit more physical than my wedding to your dad, but I think all the best weddings have the odd farcical moment.'

451

'What was farcical about yours?'

'Oh, small things. My stocking fell down as I walked up the aisle. And during the signing of the register my Great-Uncle Arthur subjected the entire congregation to a spontaneous rendering of "For those in Peril on the Sea" to entertain them. Oh, and the vicar kept calling your father Rodney. There's always something.'

Anemone giggled. 'I think weddings should be fun. It's a shame when they're boring.'

'Well, Lisa's wasn't boring,' said Alice. 'Actually, it was rather splendid. It should keep Fox Colne talking for decades, and I dread to think what's going to appear in *Yes* magazine. Tell me, do you really not mind not moving back there? You were the one that seemed to want to go back most.'

Anemone shook her head. 'No, not really. I mean, it's a nice village, but I can't imagine being there without Dad. This is our home, you made it for us after he died. Anyhow, it's a much better colour now. Martha says it shows you've finally got rid of all your dammed-up angst.'

Alice smiled. 'That's the Californian approach.' She had not told Anemone about her meeting with Heather Bunberry. Maybe one day.

'I meant to ask you something,' said Anemone cautiously. 'Yes?'

'Whatever happened to those glasses you used to wear? In all the pictures of you and Dad you've always got these great big owl's-eyes specs on, but after he died you got little wire ones, and contacts. Where did the big ones go?'

Alice shrugged. 'Oh, I don't know. Long lost.'

'Oh,' Anemone laughed. 'Daisy said you'd buried them with Dad. I thought that was a daft idea.'

'Absolutely daft,' said Alice.

Epilogue

Martha surveyed the garden in Herne Road dreamily (she did everything dreamily at the moment). 'It's certainly come on, hasn't it? I mean, I'm no gardener, but the hebes look fantastic, considering how you used to moan about them.'

'It's quite something, isn't it?' said Alice, smiling. 'I'd never have believed a bit of peacock dung could do all that.'

'Neither would I,' said Martha. 'Maybe it wasn't the dung that did it; maybe it was you.'

'Oh, don't you start.' Alice shook her head at her. 'I can remember when you were the last person to give any credence to the idea that my emotional state could be tied in with the state of my hebes. Actually, I remember a time when you refused to admit emotion could have any physical effects at all, even when you started falling flat on your face every time you looked at a certain Dr Lovejoy.'

Martha grinned. 'OK, I was a fool, I can admit it. But you must admit, everything seems to have gone right over the last year.'

'I know, a lot of things sorted themselves out last year. But Pipe Tree Cottage scotches your theory about my emotional state. Since those two moved in and peacock-dunged the garden it's turned into far more of a jungle than it was when we lived there.'

'Yes, it's certainly recovered from the Hamiltons' strimmer, hasn't it?' Martha put a hand on her stomach absently. Pregnancy suited her, gave her a serene glow on top of the natural beauty. 'I'm surprised the postman can actually find the house at all these days without a machete.'

'I don't suppose the Hamiltons are troubled by excessive grass growth in Dubai,' Alice smiled. 'I haven't quite forgiven them for leaving their neurotic cat with us, though. The vet says its got post-traumatic stress disorder. And how do you argue with a vet? I should have been a vet. A vet's patients can't disagree with him.'

'That sounds heartfelt. Haven't your home deliveries started to tail off yet?'

'Not a bit of it. I wish *Yes* magazine hadn't identified me delivering Lisa's baby when they did their famous spread. That flipping reporter works for ITV now you know, she's like Kate Adie with pearls, and I've been left with a permanent reputation. Alice Vane, first choice doctor for earth mothers everywhere, no matter where they want to give birth, how and who with. In the last twelve months I've delivered babies in pine-scented pools, babies on cushions, babies on canal boats – last weekend I delivered a baby whose mother wanted to push her out to the sound of a live string quartet.'

'Wow,' said Martha, who had heard much of this before but was impressed by the last bit. 'Did she get what she wanted?'

'No she didn't, she got a trio. The viola player passed out.'

Martha laughed. 'You're having me on.'

'I wish I was,' said Alice. 'Come inside and sit down before your ankles swell up – and before you ask me, no I won't deliver your baby in Fox Colne pond.' I just know Martha's ankles would never swell, she thought.

'Ha ha,' said Martha. 'As if. I'm American, I want technology.' She eyed Alice thoughtfully. 'I do still miss having you in the village, though, especially now. You're not sorry you didn't move back?'

Alice shook her head. 'No. Not at all. I didn't really want to see Pipe Tree Cottage sold, of course – but when I heard who had bought it I was delighted. Almost keeps it in the family.'

Daisy, still working on the Elgar in the burgundy living room (she wouldn't give up whilst Fergus was still doing the Mozart), watched them coming back into the house. From her vantage point of youth they seemed extremely old to have started new lives.

She wondered if her mother would marry Mr Blackwell. They did seem quite happy together. True, he was only five inches taller than her, Daisy – so there seemed not much chance of him throwing her in the air and catching her, but he was OK. It hadn't lasted for her and Mark, of course, but they were still friends. Anyway, as Herman said in his last e-mail, she shouldn't think of it as getting dumped, she should think of it as being handed an opportunity to find someone better – and Mum must be relieved. Poor Mum – it must be difficult having your daughter dating your boyfriend's son, particularly on top of the hairy types Anemone had started bringing home from art college. Some of them looked as if they just got out of the swamp.

If they did marry she might get to be bridesmaid again – she had really enjoyed doing it for Martha and Tom. She planned to keep the dress for when she was in the finals of Young Musician of the Year. As she surely would be before Fergus ever was. If she could only manage this bow-work. She sighed and went back to the beginning.

Upstairs Fergus frowned as he heard it yet again. She was getting quite good. Where was his clarinet music?

A few miles away in Fox Colne churchyard the bells tolled discordantly as a bell-ringing group from Portsmouth tried to play 'A Life on the Ocean Wave' and the hebes on Robert Vane's grave rustled in gentle protest in the breeze. Pipe Tree Cottage sat snug and welcoming in the sunlight, the large privet blobs which had once been trimmed and strimmed into chickens now casting interesting shadows on the path. A peacock sauntered casually across the grass and Fred Ramsden, sitting on a deck chair, smiled as Tabitha made her way through the tangled greenery towards him with a tray of tea. 'Still glad we took young Fergus' advice and moved here then?'

She put the tray down between them. 'Of course I am, although I must say you don't normally expect to move back out of a rest home ten years after moving into it. But he was right – we couldn't live in an old folks' home now we're married.'

'You mean you don't want me surrounded by all those willing women with their vast corsets and heaving bosoms.'

'Don't flatter yourself, Fred Ramsden. I just thought it was time we made a proper home for your bloody birds.'

'Seems to have pleased everyone, then,' said Fred, 'although it's a shame about that din.'

Tabitha smiled as she stirred the pot. 'What do you think it's meant to be this time?'

He shook his head. 'Sounds like *The Magic Roundabout* to me.'

'Honestly, Fred,' she said, 'sometimes I wonder about you. Tea?'